IN BETA

Published by Inkshares, Inc., Oakland, California
www.inkshares.com

Edited by Adam Gomolin & Matt Harry
Cover Design by M.S. Corley
Interior Design by Kevin G. Summers

ISBN: 9781947848504
e-ISBN: 9781947848320
LCCN: 2017962691

First edition

Printed in the United States of America

THE GIRL IN
THE FALLS

BICKLETON WAS A town frozen in time. Always had been, always would be.

Years passed. Skinny trailer park babies aged into hunch-backed millworkers. People suffered pulmonary heart disease. Green algae dripped long on the sides of trailers. But nothing really *changed*. Nothing new ever came to Bickleton.

Except, Todd thought, *now something has.*

He moved briskly down the sidewalk, despite his slight limp, the result of a car accident freshman year. He was consumed with his thoughts. He was a high school junior now, seventeen years old, with fiery red hair that wrapped back around his head in a ponytail. "Party in front, party in back," he liked to joke, though truth be told there was never much of a party.

Todd was a jazz band kid, and he *looked* like a jazz band kid. He had that scraggly not-quite-through-puberty sort of vibe, and he wore sunglasses while he played his saxophone because he saw Bill Clinton do it on Arsenio Hall and he thought it looked cool. He was wearing those sunglasses now, and they blocked most of the light that flashed down through the over-head dogwoods. Today he wasn't carrying his saxophone. He was carrying something else: a pickax, over his left shoulder. He wondered if a pickax was cooler than a saxophone.

Somewhere behind him, tires squealed. He turned to see a rusty Dodge Ram barreling toward him. As it grew closer, bass shook the spring air, and he heard the rap group Kris Kross.

The truck slowed, windows rolling down, and a head poked out. It was a face Todd knew and did not care for. The face sneered at his pickax.

"Hey, Yosemite Sam! Mining for dick cheese?"

The face exploded in laughter. Todd lifted his ax and inspected it.

"Yes, mining for dick cheese," he said, trying to sound sarcastic. But not *too* sarcastic.

The engine roared, and the truck careened down the street. Todd watched its bumper sticker recede in the distance: *You might be a redneck if you have more guns than teeth.*

Todd shook his head. The Johns. One or two were rarely a problem. It was when they got together that you had to worry. Problem was, they almost always traveled as a pack. He looked over his shoulder at the parking lot. There was no sign of more trucks. Good. He didn't need any more interruptions. Today he was a boy with Somewhere to Be.

Todd absentmindedly began humming "Heigh-Ho," and moved off the sidewalk. He passed under the Bickleton High School marquee. "Congratulations, Class of '93!" the sign read. Todd shook his head. What was a Bickleton diploma worth, anyway? Everyone ended up down at the mill eventually.

"It will come out all right in the end," his great-grandmother used to say to console his worries. She was eighty-seven when she died, and she'd been prom queen senior year and married the Bickleton Vandals' first baseman. Todd's grandfather had been a manager at the mill, and they'd owned a house on the bluff.

"Easy for you to say, Eema," Todd grumbled to himself.

The road curved south. The dogwoods disappeared, and the land opened into pastures. A few Highland cattle watched him from beyond a fence, their dull eyes jerking mechanically with his gait. Todd turned off Main Street and passed Hunsaker Oil, where a logging truck rusted under a small wooden watchtower.

He hoped Eema was right—he hoped it all did turn out for the best. He knew that for the Johns, it likely would. They at least had good jobs waiting for them. But for kids like him—the band kids, the geeks—well, he always thought the logging truck was a good metaphor for the slow decay into oblivion. That was his fate.

At least, it'd been his fate until yesterday. But things may have changed. He didn't want to count any blessings just yet, but there was something interesting up Jewett Creek. And for the first time in his life, he felt a surge of hope that maybe Eema was right. Maybe his future held something bright.

A tan Honda Civic zipped by on the road, and he heard the shriek of girlish laughter through an open window. He waited for the car to disappear over a crest, then climbed the guardrail and down the bank of Jewett Creek.

He paused at the bottom, winded. It was shady down there by the stream. Quiet. In the sudden stillness, a moment of déjà vu washed over him. The sunlight seemed stuck in the same position as when he'd come the day before. He saw the same plastic grocery bag. Even the gurgle of the creek seemed repetitive, looping its wet notes again and again. He shook himself. It was a memory from yesterday, that's all. He pushed on, leaping over rocks, listening for the low roar of the waterfall.

He scrambled under an arch of blackberry vines, and then he saw it: a flat horizon of water falling over a short cliff. Rock Ridge. It wasn't tall, maybe twenty feet, but there was something majestic to it. The pool at its base shone clear and dark.

Todd stepped onto the dirt packed down by years of summer blankets. Sun-bleached Rainier cans and Otter Pops wrappers littered the ferns. He touched the slippery moss of the falls and inched toward the water. The cold mist sprayed his face. His heart beat faster.

Is she still here?

"Hello!" he shouted.

He heard rushing water and nothing else. He tightened his grip on the grain of his pickax and stepped back, regarding the rock face for a moment. It occurred to him, as it had the day before, that this could all be an elaborate prank. He looked around, waiting for a John to burst out laughing. His eyes darted around, looking for speakers, any evidence that could explain what he'd found.

He leaned on the rock, pressing his cheek against it. His thin red mustache bristled against the moss.

"Hello?" he repeated.

For a moment, nothing. Then: a girl's voice. Faint within the rock.

"You're back."

Todd grinned. Good. She was still here.

He leaned into the rock. "I've got one for you. Ready? Here it goes. So, they dug up Beethoven's body last week?"

He paused, letting the anticipation build. "They found him *decomposing*."

From deep behind the falls: "That's terrible."

"I know!" He felt giddy. "What's yours?"

Her voice was so thin he had to strain to hear her. "Why can't you hear a pterodactyl going to the bathroom?"

"I dunno, why?"

"Because the 'p' is silent."

Todd laughed genuinely. *Why is it so much easier to talk to a rock?*

"All right, stand back. I'll get you out."

He brought the pickax above his head and smashed it down into the cliff. There was a terrible clang as metal scraped rock, and small sparks glinted off the blade. Shivers ran down his arm, followed by pain, and he yelped and dropped his ax.

He stood there holding the pickax he'd borrowed from his dad, trying and failing to remember if he'd ever used it before. He'd assumed breaking through the rock would be easy, like it was in cartoons.

He swung again, but more slowly, driving the blade against the rock. It clanged, glancing off, and the smallest chip broke free. He swung six more times, until sweat beaded his brow. He'd guessed the rock was no more than a few inches thick, given how close the voice sounded. Now he worried he'd been wrong.

He put his cheek back to the rock.

"How's it going out there?" asked the faint voice.

"Fine. You okay?"

"Yeah. What are you doing?"

"G-getting you out. I've got an ax." Todd held up the ax as if she could see it.

"An ax? Todd . . . I thought you'd bring a jackhammer. And some other people."

"They're coming," he lied.

"I need you to go tell someone. No more jokes. I need to be out of here."

"Uh—yeah, I know."

Truth was, Todd hadn't told anyone. She was *his* secret. In a town like Bickleton, a secret was currency. It was something to be treasured. A secret made you special. "I promise tomorrow I'll—I'll get a bulldozer."

"I can't wait another day. I need you to get the police, or—"

"Can I be of assistance?"

Todd jumped and spun around. He had been so focused on the girl, he hadn't heard anyone else approach. His heart pounded in his chest. Not more than a dozen feet away stood a man.

He was a sawed-off little fart, wearing a Hawaiian shirt and a fanny pack tucked under a ballooning gut. He flexed stubby fingers and fixed Todd with beady black eyes. Todd noticed that the man was breathing easily, despite the fact that the only trail to Rock Ridge wound steeply down through a boulder field. The hair on the back of Todd's neck prickled, and he had the vague sense he *knew* the man. Where had Todd seen him before? Bickleton was too small a town not to recognize him.

The man took a small step forward and cleared his throat. "Is there anything I can do to help?"

"Yes." Todd gulped, unsure whether he should feel trepidation or relief. "There's someone trapped."

He waited for the man to scoff or panic, but he just stood, staring at Todd.

"Is that right?"

His piggy eyes peered out from behind thick glasses. The forest suddenly felt still. As if everything had been paused. Todd shifted, uneasy.

"Do I know you?"

The man grinned and nodded, as if he found the question funny. "To a degree, yes. You come here often?"

"To Rock Ridge?" Todd scoffed. "No."

The man glanced at Todd's pickax. "That won't work, you know."

"So, what should we do?"

"Oh, I wouldn't worry about it."

The forest was too quiet, as if the birds had disappeared. The only sound was the rush of water. Todd, who'd been in exactly one fight before—freshman year, with two of the

Johns—had the strange sense that he was about to fight the man, though he didn't know why. The man took another step forward.

"How many times have you been down here?"

"Saturday, then again today."

The man nodded eagerly. "Did you tell anyone else about this? What you found?"

Todd shook his head.

"And how did you find it? Something . . . bring you here?"

"No. I was just out on a hike and heard a voice."

The man fixed him with his gaze for a few more seconds, then seemed to relax. Todd wanted more than anything to get away. He took a step back, making to follow the creek.

"Well, I need to go get the sheriff. So, I'll be back."

He circled around where the little pool drained into the creek, his relief growing with every step he put between himself and the strange man. He stepped over a log and glanced backwards.

The man was fumbling in his fanny pack. Todd watched him produce a long metal cylinder. He seemed completely absorbed in the action, no longer paying attention to Todd. The man's brow furrowed as he punched small black buttons.

Todd turned and ran. He crashed through the underbrush, dropping any pretense of nonchalance, giving way to his terror. Branches stung his face, blinding him. He gasped for air. A poplar sprang up in the gloom of the undergrowth, and he tripped, sprawling. His palms flew out, and he fell into the creek. His head plunged through the freezing water, and he felt a shock of pain as his chin split on a rock.

He pulled himself up to sitting, and despite his throbbing chin, his first thought was of the man. He glanced back, blood flowing freely from his face, waiting for the man to step out of the forest. Seconds passed. The creek carved its way over his wrists, numbing his hands. His leg ached where he'd smacked it against the poplar tree. But at least the man was gone.

Todd's breath slowed. Why was he so scared? What was it about that man? Todd was nearly a foot taller than him, so why had he been so spooked?

He thought sheepishly to his dad's pickax. It was in the clearing, next to the pool. Well, he wasn't going back to get it. The girl was right about needing more help. As soon as he got out of the forest, he would tell Sheriff Jenkins everything that had happened over the last two days. The girl, whoever she was, couldn't be just his secret anymore. He would bring the adults, as she'd asked. He stood, touching his chin and pulling his hand away to examine the crimson blood that covered his finger.

There was a sudden white flash, so powerful that for a moment, it wiped out all sight and sound. Then it was gone, and Jewett Creek was empty. There was no trace of the man. No trace of Todd. Only the gurgling water, the cool spring breeze, and the flutter of grosbeaks hopping from branch to branch.

SECRET OF BICKLETON

"IT'S NOT FAIR!"

Jay Banksman hurled a Super Nintendo controller against the wall and fell back into his sleeping bag. He stared at the tiny TV screen from the corner of one eye. The Metal Mantis clacked its claws in a looping animation before the screen drifted to black, a small window fading up: "Sadly, no trace of them was ever found . . ."

"Why do we suck so bad?" Jay groaned.

"We need experience." Colin Ramirez sighed.

Jay looked skeptically at his friend. "Like in real life? Or experience points?"

"Uh, both."

Despite Colin's massive stature, he had managed to sit in the lotus position, cross-legged on his sleeping bag. Jay was aware—as he always was—how strange the two of them looked together. Colin was giant, curly black hair hanging over his forehead, covering his dark eyes, almost reaching the wisp of mustache that smeared his upper lip. Compared to Colin, Jay was whitish and smallish. Between freshman and sophomore years, while the other kids had all hit their growth spurts, Jay had lingered and perhaps even dwindled. A few weeks ago, digging through old photos for their graduation slide show, he'd stumbled upon a home video from Christmas four years prior. He was horrified by how short and slight he'd been, darting under the Christmas tree to grab presents like a strange bird.

At that moment, though, they were wrapped in the darkness of Colin's basement, and free from judgment. They'd built a little cave for themselves along the far wall, where the finish gave way to cold concrete and stained Persian rugs. Haphazardly strewn in front of them were a Sega Genesis, a Super Nintendo, and roughly two dozen games. The only "furniture" was a shelf full of Colin's old toys: a tub of Pogs, He-Man action figures, a Lite-Brite board, and a Teddy Ruxpin. Jay rubbed his eyes and sighed.

"We've got the sword and the boomerang forged to level five. Undine's level six. We just need . . ." But he trailed off, too tired to think of what it was they needed.

Above them, the basement ceiling creaked with footsteps as the rest of the Ramirez family woke up. With every step, Jay and Colin tensed, expecting to hear an exclamation and then feet trampling toward the basement stairs. The footsteps receded, and Jay relaxed. He lay on his back and watched dust motes float through the light that now filtered through the sliding glass doors leading to the outside porch. He shifted his legs to catch some of the warmth.

"God, it's just that stupid Mantis Boss."

"Did you get the game guide?"

Jay rolled his eyes. "No, *GamePro* keeps saying next issue, next issue, but—"

As he spoke, Colin fished out a small cupcake with pink frosting from his sleeping bag.

"Happy birthday to youuu, happy birthday to youuuu . . ."

"Eww. Don't sing so quietly. It's creepy."

Jay took the cupcake and sniffed. "How long's that cupcake been in there?"

"Just a few hours."

Jay scarfed it down. The sweetness hurt Jay's unbrushed teeth. His eyes were dry from a night of gaming; they'd been staring at that stupid screen for so long.

Colin produced another cupcake and mechanically chewed it.

"Happy birthday," he said between mouthfuls.

"Thanks, man." Jay yawned, stretching and grabbing his half-full can of Mountain Dew. "One more go?"

Someone upstairs stomped across the floor, heading toward them. Jay and Colin froze, eyes wide. The basement door swung open. Jay and Colin scrambled into action, switching off the Super Nintendo, turning off the TV, burrowing into their sleeping bags. Behind them, someone thundered down the stairs. Jay squeezed his eyes tight, but it was too late. There was a scream of indignation, and then Mrs. Ramirez—Colin's mom—was rushing over, yelling in Spanish:

"*¿Qué están haciendo aquí?!*"

She pointed at the rat's nest of sleeping bags and the food on the floor. Mrs. Ramirez was a small bullish woman who wore lots of makeup and terrified Jay. Jay noticed how the thick shoulder pads under her blouse turned her torso into a brick wall. She had one earring dangling in her left hand as she ripped their Super Nintendo from the wall. Jay and Colin bolted out of their sleeping bags in protest, but she rounded on them, now speaking in English.

"What do I have to do? Chain you to your beds? No games on a school night!"

"But, jeez," Jay pleaded, "it's my birthday."

She stuck a finger in his chest. "I'm calling your mom. No more sleepovers. No more games, period. Colin, I'm throwing your Nintendo away!"

"No! Mom! Please, anything but that."

"She's not *really* gonna do it," Jay whispered.

Mrs. Ramirez spun back to Jay. "*Cuidado con lo que dices.* Don't you try me, Banksman."

She pointed at the ceiling. "Upstairs. Now. March!"

MAIN DRAG

DESPITE MRS. RAMIREZ'S fury, there was, in fact, still plenty of time for Jay and Colin to get to school. After a leisurely stop at the Morning Market for coffee, they enjoyed the scenic route.

Jay never drove. He didn't have $14 for a driver's license, let alone money for a car. So, he sat in the passenger seat of Colin's Volkswagen Bug, which had been salvaged together from at least five other Volkswagen Bugs. Its body was mostly black, but its two front wheel wells were yellow, and its bumper was orange. To start it, Colin would stick a screwdriver in the hole where the ignition should have been, turn it, then ring a doorbell that was nailed to the dashboard. The car had only three gears and refused to go in reverse. When it ran, which was about 75 percent of the time, its backfire sounded like a shotgun blast, and its exhaust routinely caught fire, shooting large jets of flames through the tailpipe. The kids at school jokingly called it the "Batmobile." Someone had gone so far as to spray-paint crude Batman logos on its sides, with large penises hanging off the bats. Colin had blacked out the penises but left the Batman logos intact.

It was in the Batmobile they now rode. The rattle of its engine was so loud, Jay and Colin had to yell to be heard. Colin's enormous frame was smashed up against the steering wheel, so that his coffee sloshed and spilled in one hand while he gripped the bucking steering wheel with his other.

Jay shivered in the cold that seemed to blow in from every direction through invisible seams. He fiddled with the radio dial, a crude installation that stuck out jarringly from the front panel. By adjusting the knob a micrometer at a time, he slowly fiddled his way through static, past the Cinnaburst and Juicy Fruit jingles, until suddenly a clear signal popped in. They listened for a moment as a rhythmic guitar looped over and over, and a drum machine kicked out a beat.

"Oh, that's *good*," Colin noted.

"It always is." Jay popped open the glove box and grabbed a notebook, waiting.

When the music cut out, Jay reflexively pounded on the dashboard until it came back. Finally, it faded, and a man with a slow, low voice spoke.

"That was Beck, playing 'Loser.'"

Jay scribbled: "Beck. 'Loser.'"

". . . the first single from a career . . . we'll all be watching . . . with great anticipation. And this," added the radio voice, "is Marvelous Mark, the DJ with real underground hits . . . the world's not ready for this stuff."

Jay and Colin shook their heads in silent agreement. Despite his name, Marvelous Mark didn't sound that marvelous. His voice was softer than the DJs on the few FM stations that filtered into Bickleton. They had to crank the radio to hear him whenever he came on. And he accentuated his speech with pauses so long, Jay sometimes thought the radio had gone out. Despite all this, his music taste was esoteric and dangerous and nothing like the bland pop that blasted the halls of Bickleton

High. One of Jay's deepest thrills was that he'd discovered the hidden gem, 669 AM, all on his own.

"Up next . . . we have . . ." Jay leaned in as the radio died. Then he put the notepad back in the glove box and ruffled around. "You still got the Columbia House Music Club catalog in here? I could see if they have Beck."

Colin shook his head. "Nah, it fell out."

Jay stared down at his feet. There was a hole in the passenger floor, roughly the size of a backpack. The Columbia Music catalog wasn't the first thing to fall through it, and Jay kept his feet braced against the frame whenever he rode. The Batmobile didn't have seat belts, and it was one of Jay's biggest fears that Colin would slam on the brakes and send him tumbling down to meet his doom.

"Ah, well." Jay readjusted his feet. "I've got mine at home."

"Mmmm." Colin nodded, distracted. They were entering "the drag." It began with "the bluff," a small gravel turnout that served, in theory, as a vantage point. It did have a lovely view, overlooking the bony Skookullom River, and was perfectly poised to capture sunsets melting over the far bluff. But Bickleton residents had seen sunsets aplenty, and no one ever stopped there, aside from the Fourth of July and high school after-parties, when the next morning would find Rainier cans and condom wrappers littered amid the dusty gravel. Most of the time, though, the viewpoint was empty, as it was now.

There wasn't much to Bickleton. Nestled in the Cascade Range, surrounded by national forest, it was possibly the most isolated town in the state of Washington. Jay was always reminded of this driving through Bickleton's tiny "commercial district." There was the Drug Mart, the Bowl-o-Rama, Petey's Barbershop, C&C Distribution Services (whatever that was), followed by the Classy Chassis car repair shop, with its terrible sign that was always lit: "We want your body."

There was the Bickleton Theater, the town's single-screen movie theater where Colin worked as an usher. It only showed about seven movies a year and was currently stuck on *Indecent Proposal*, which neither Colin nor Jay had seen. Instead, they were salivating over the small "Coming Soon" sign under the marquee that listed *Cliffhanger* as coming in May. It was Jay's goal to catch *Cliffhanger* in Bickleton and then skip town by the time *Jurassic Park* rolled around.

After that came the Bickleton Insurance Company with the tagline "Make your insurance as good as a '57 Chevy," the Bickleton Creamery, and Golden Flour Bakery. As they passed slowly by, Jay craned his neck, looking for fellow students. He thought he saw a few kids inside the Golden Flour Bakery, but he couldn't make out who they were. And then the Batmobile began backfiring loud cannon blasts, and Jay pressed himself back in his seat, embarrassed. Once they passed, he leaned forward again to pull a shrink-wrapped magazine out of his backpack.

Colin leaned eagerly over, nearly plowing into a pack of freshmen hiking up the small hill. Jay seized the grab handle to keep from dropping his book bag through the floor.

"What's that?"

"The new *Serious Gamer*."

"How come it's wrapped in plastic?"

"Because . . ." Jay spun it around to show Colin a single black floppy disk lying loose in the back. ". . . it came with a free demo."

"What?! How come mine didn't come with that?"

Jay shrugged, ripping his finger through the plastic to pull out the magazine. "Dunno. I must be a *valued customer*. How long have you been subscribing?"

"Six months."

"Yeah, see, you got to stick with it at least a year, probably. Although, this is the first time they've sent me anything, to be honest."

Jay flipped the little black disk over in his hands. There was a single sticker over the front that read *The Build*. It looked as if someone had printed the label on a dot matrix printer. Colin peered over, reading.

"*The Build*. Never heard of it."

"Me neither. Let's see if they mention it in here." Jay thumbed through the magazine. "Oh my God!"

Colin swerved in alarm.

"What?! What is it?"

"Dude, *Wing Commander III* is coming next year with full-motion video and branching story arcs! It's gonna be on *CD-ROM* technology. 'Don't watch the game, play the movie.' Wow, what a tagline. And guess who plays Blair?"

"Who?"

"Mark Hamill!" Jay buried his head in the pages. "Oh, it's got Jonathan Rhys-Davies from *Indiana Jones*, Biff from *Back to the Future*."

"Wow, on CD-ROM technology . . ."

They passed blocks of mobile homes. Most of the aluminum siding was faded and chipped, yards were littered with rusted car parts, and satellite dishes rimmed the roofs. The front of half a Volkswagen Bug leered out from under an ancient tarp. Above it a tattered American Flag, purple from sun exposure, fluttered in the morning breeze. A yellow "Dead End" sign was pockmarked with bullet holes. They started to turn down the road to C-Court, but Jay shook his head.

"Let's go to A-Court."

"Seriously?"

"Yeah, I'm feeling lucky."

They continued down Main Street for another minute before turning into a sea of proud Fords, Chevys, and Dodge Rams. To their left, a metal cage topped with barbed wire held the school's five buses but was otherwise empty. Two of the buses were delivering a line of kids to school, which sat small and nestled in the gently sloping hill. Colin wound his way through the rows of trucks, and Jay shook his head while reading the bumper stickers: "Proud to Be a Redneck," "Vandal Nation," "Hometown Pride."

"What a joke." Jay snorted. "Might as well say 'Proud to Be Ignorant.'"

"Welfare Pride," Colin joined in.

"Incest Pride."

Colin turned off the Batmobile, and they both got out and stretched. A ride in the Batmobile was like riding a mechanical bull, and Jay woke up sore pretty much every day. He still felt disgruntled from their stinging defeat at the claws of the stupid Mantis Boss, but now he was starting to feel sick from a night of no sleep. They watched a stream of students shuffle off a bus and into A-Court, and Jay nodded.

"Y'all ready for this?"

Colin looked incredulous. "You want to go *through* A-Court?"

"Not *through*. We'll sneak in the side, stealth our way through Little Mexico, and pop back out before anyone notices."

"But what if someone does notice?"

"We're due for a change in luck." Jay cracked his knuckles. "I think today's the day."

TURTLES PIES

THE BICKLETON HIGH campus was broken into several main buildings. The biggest were A-Court and C-Court. A-Court was nearest to the main parking lot and thus more important. It held the principal's office, the largest classrooms, the cleanest blackboards, the prettiest kids, and the school's only vending machine.

Out its rear spewed a little grassy lawn and a small hill. Atop the hill sat the library, where the school's timid souls fretted away the periods until last bell. Next door was shop class, full of screaming saws and churning drills and a collection of squat brutes—largely disregarded by the rest of the school—looking for trouble.

Then there was the horticulture building, some portables, and C-Court, which was a poor man's A-Court. It was smaller, and shabbier, and the windows never let in enough light. The kids who went into C-Court were dumb, poor, or had a chip on their shoulder. They were smokers, skinny kids in big jeans, or big kids in skinny jeans. They threw rotten apples at the baseball field and even got beat up by the Johns, very occasionally giving a black eye that the Johns would solemnly carry back into A-Court.

C-Court was too raw for Jay's tastes, and A-Court was too vanilla (or so he told himself). He lived mostly in Tutorial, and the portable suited him mostly fine. However, last week, item number H5 in the school vending machine had been switched from cherry pie to Teenage Mutant Ninja Turtles Pie, and this change had not gone unnoticed. Stevie Melbrook and Todd Hammond had bragged about successfully entering A-Court, purchasing Turtles Pies, and living to tell. They were reported to taste slightly metallic and heavenly.

Today, Jay felt emboldened to follow in their footsteps. But penetrating A-Court in the morning, when the other Bickleton seniors were caffeinated and on alert, was madness. Jay—high from a combination of his birthday, a lack of sleep, and the strongest black coffee the Morning Market could make—had a plan. The interior of A-Court was a square. In each corner, a small corridor led to an entrance. On the south side, the main corridor led to the parking lot and was flooded with students. Going through that corridor would have led Jay and Colin into the massive herd of the baseball team (i.e., insta-death).

On the west side of A-Court, a second corridor led to the parking lot, but by way of the main office, where the administrators and Principal Oatman lived (i.e., torture and interrogation).

The north corridor led to a cement walkway that branched off to C-Court, the library, shop class, horticulture, and the portables. It was possible to safely penetrate A-Court through that route, but Jay and Colin would risk running into sur-prise jocks heading early to shop class (i.e., also insta-death). Plus there was always the chance that a stray John, Amber, or Gretchen would use their locker, and Jay didn't know where their lockers were.

The safest way was through the east corridor. It led south to the parking lot and north to C-Court, and was inconvenient to everyone. This corridor was unofficially called "Little Mexico." At some point over the last decade, the school's significant Latino population had taken camp there and claimed its lockers.

The Latinos were no friends of the jocks. Colin wasn't really "one of them," as he hung out with Jay and the other nerds. But he'd tottered around enough with them as babies, and gone to enough quinceañeras, that he was safe around them. And Jay, a fellow outcast and friend of Colin's, was safe as well.

Now, as Jay and Colin tiptoed past the lockers, a tall Latino teen sang his version of Tom Petty's "Free Fallin'": "And I'm freeeeee! Fri-joles!" A group of Latinas broke into giggles.

As they met the edge of Little Mexico, Latinos gave way to cowboys and jeans and sweatshirts with "The Gap" written over their fronts. Jay peered around the corner. The vending machine was nestled between a break in the lockers and the drinking fountains. It wasn't far, but it would leave them exposed.

"Hey, you two!"

Jay's head snapped up. Gretchen, Amber, and Liz Knight were staring at him. Every hair on Jay's body leapt up. The jig was up. Gretchen, Amber, and Liz were the paragons of A-Court. The prettiest, most popular girls in the school. Staring at him. They could call all manner of fury and hellfire down upon him. Jay stood, frozen, awaiting their judgment.

Liz stepped forward and Jay shrank back. Gretchen and Amber were beautiful, but it had always been clear that Liz was in a class of her own. Her skin was smooth and dark, a mix of white and Latina. She strode the two cultures effortlessly, to everyone's awe. Like everyone in Bickleton, Jay had known her for as long as he could remember. Back in first grade, back when the playing field was more level, they'd even held hands once. That was ages ago, of course, and he was certain Liz had forgotten. Now, Jay stared into those dark green eyes, trying not to panic.

She stood looking down at him. All A-Court jokes, rumors, and trends filtered through her. If she laughed at it, gossiped about it, or wore it, so did the rest of Bickleton. The current wave of baby doll dresses and knee-high stockings were Liz's latest doing. She was constantly voted most popular, best smile, best hair, most likely to—

"Um, hello?" Liz snapped her fingers in his face. "Yearbook boy? When do I get my yearbook?"

"Oh, uh. W-we're actually not on yearbook," Jay stuttered.

Liz sighed. "Then what good are you?"

Before Jay could respond, the three girls whipped around and headed toward the bathroom. Colin wiped his brow.

"Whew. I thought for sure we were goners."

Jay stared wistfully after Liz and shook his head. "I've never wanted to be in yearbook so bad."

They tiptoed toward the vending machine. En Vogue's "You're Never Gonna Get It" blasted from a boom box. The northern doors clanged open and Jay jumped. But it was only Wacky Zach hobbling in on crutches. A few freshmen pointed and shouted.

"Hey! Zach's back!"

Wacky Zach spun around and pretended to check his back, then he lifted a crutch and played it like an air guitar. The crowd clapped.

Feeling emboldened by the commotion, Jay squared off with the vending machine. Its sides were carved with decades of abuse: "Brandi loves Marc," "For a good time call 365-4492," and a slew of nasty words too terrible to repeat. Colin fished in his pocket for quarters while Jay shook his head.

"No, my friend. My treat."

He plunked his coins into the machine. Behind them, a group of girls was talking loudly:

"Oh God, how could Donna not have seen that coming?"

"It was so obvious Pierre wanted her for more than just her modeling career."

"I don't care how many times they play that episode; I love it."

"Jeez," Jay whispered to Colin. "How many times are they gonna air that episode?"

"You watch it?"

"Of course I watch it." Jay pushed the "H" and "5" on the vending machine. There was a whirring noise, and two Turtles Pies dropped into the metal bin. "It's on literally every day."

Colin scooped up the pies and handed one to Jay. "Speaking of which, you catch that last Simpsons? Bart and Lisa start writing for Itchy & Scratchy."

"No," Jay said, turning slightly pink. His mom had only just gotten a used TV.

"Then how are you watching *90210*?"

"I told you—"

Jay was about to take a bite of his Turtles Pie when a hand clamped on his shoulder, spinning him around. There, leering over him, were seven senior boys. Jay knew them well. They wore Big Dogs and Stüssy shirts under loose flannels, Blazers and Mariners hats spun backward. They were the Johns.

"Yeah. Tell us about *90210*."

In all, there were fourteen boys named John at Bickleton High. All of them were on the baseball team. In fact, they *were* the baseball team. It was an odd phenomenon in Bickleton that unless your name was John—or, with one exception, Jeremy—you didn't make the team. Jay used to curse his fate that he was born only three letters away from making the baseball team. Because if you didn't make the team, you didn't date the Ambers, Gretchens, or Lizzes, and you didn't land a mansion on the bluff.

The baseball team, called the Bickleton Vandals, was the biggest deal in Bickleton. Its fan base seemed to grow every year, filling the bleachers of even their practices. Millworkers flocked to their scrimmages, drinking and shouting as if they were at the World Series. Even though the team *never actually played any games.* They never got on a bus to play the rival towns of Klickitat, Cougar, and Battleground because someone was always sick, or injured, or it "just wasn't the right time." Yet this one seemingly critical fact was lost on the town's enthusiasm.

Jeremy McKraken took point in front of the Johns. He always took point. He was the Vandals' first basemen and team captain. He was not tall, but he was broad, with a broad face, a thick brow now crinkled in anger, and wide blue eyes. The girls called him Bickleton's Luke Perry, and he dated Liz Knight. Now, he nodded at Jay, doing his best Donnie Wahlberg impression.

"Also . . . give us those pies."

Jay's heart pounded. He forced himself to take a deep breath.

"Knock it off, Jeremy. You don't know the Ninja Turtles."

Jeremy grabbed Jay by the shirt.

"Who says?"

Behind him, Jay heard the Johns snickering. "Nice jeans, bugle boy."

Jeremy's face was inches from Jay's. "I love the Ninja Turtles."

Jay squirmed. "Oh yeah? What are their names?"

"Brian. Dennis. Mike. Carl."

"That sounds like the Beach Boys."

Jeremy pulled Jay off his feet and threw him across the floor. The surrounding students burst into laughter and formed a circle around them. Amid the sea of faces, Jay saw Liz, Amber, and Gretchen watching. His face burned crimson as a deep, familiar bubble of anger roiled in his stomach. He looked helplessly to Colin, silently pleading with him. Colin looked away, his face red with shame. Jeremy chuckled.

"If I say the Turtle's name is Brian, it's Brian."

He grabbed the Turtles Pie out of Jay's hand and took a bite. Jay hauled himself up, trying to muster his fury. He crossed his arms.

"Leave me alone, Jeremy. It's my birthday."

Jeremy's mouth stopped, mid-chew. His eyes went even wider. The Johns' heads swiveled over, grinning, eager with anticipation.

Jeremy burst into laughter. Pudding flew from his mouth, spattering Jay's face. Jeremy was doubled over now, hands on his knees. He was laughing so hard, tears formed under his eyes.

"Happy birthday."

The Johns roared.

"How old are you, twelve?"

"You look like Macaulay Culkin."

Jay stood frozen. Something in his brain switched. Without thinking, he charged Jeremy. The blow took Jeremy by surprise, knocking him over. Jay was dimly aware that the laughter had stopped around him. Wrapped in a sea of limbs, he hurled his fists as hard as he could into Jeremy's chest, not caring how they landed, just wanting to hurt him.

Then blows began to hit his own body. He had the vague thought that he was being punched, and then a fist slammed into his face, and his vision went white. The weight atop him shifted, and a thick arm grabbed his throat. He choked, eyes watering, gasping. The other background voices began to fade.

In what felt like the far distance, a droll man's voice spoke: "Gentlemen, let's save the wrestling for gym class, shall we?"

The arm around his throat relaxed. Jay fell to the floor, coughing, vision flooding back. He saw Principal Oatman looking down at him, his face as expressionless as the faded brown suit he wore every day. He was leaning over Jay, his stupid pocket square dangling out. He sighed.

"So . . . who wants to tell me the story?"

Before Jay could catch his breath, Jeremy blurted: "It was self-defense! We were just joking around and the dude went ballistic. He's a real head case. I think he might be thrashed on weed."

Principal Oatman turned his monotone gaze back to Jay. "That true, Mr. Banksman? You *thrashed*?"

Jay shook his head, standing and wiping pudding out of his eyes. "He stole our Turtles Pies!"

Mr. Oatman addressed the crowd. "Who threw the first punch?"

Everyone but Colin pointed at Jay. Mr. Oatman nodded.

"Right. Go see Miss Molouski."

"What!?" Jay stomped his foot. "What about him?"

Principal Oatman simply shrugged. "What about him?"

The first bell rang, and students slipped to class. Jeremy turned to go with the Johns, giving Jay one last nasty smile. Jay watched them leave, grumbling.

Mr. Oatman snorted. "Sorry, Banksman. That's life."

GUIDANCE

JAY RAPPED HIS knuckles on the thin wooden door.

"Come in," Ms. Molouski's voice croaked. Jay pushed at the door and the faint sound of music grew louder. George Michael's voice struggled out of a tiny desktop speaker.

Behind her desk, Ms. Molouski stood with a broom and dustpan. Jay saw she looked thinner and more tired than usual. As the school's sole guidance counselor, it was her job to filter out all the school's behavioral issues, making her essentially Bickleton's liver. And she was failing spectacularly.

Her eyebrows rose in surprise at Jay's face as he limped into her office.

"What happened to you?"

"Jeremy McKraken."

She nodded and strode over to a mini fridge, pulled out a pack of frozen peas, and handed them to Jay, who clamped them on his face.

"That's my last pack of peas, so please steer clear of Jeremy for a bit, huh?"

Jay pressed the frozen peas to his forehead, soothing the ache around his eye.

"I love how everyone keeps telling *me* to avoid *him*. Like it's my fault I got beat up."

Ms. Molouski returned her attention to the shards of glass that ringed a water stain and some scattered flowers on her floor. Jay watched the pieces work their way into the carpet as she tried to sweep them.

"Want me to get the vacuum?" Jay offered.

"Nah." She gave up on the glass shards. "Vacuum broke three weeks ago. No budget to order a new one."

Jay knew she was surprised to see him. He was a kid with no disciplinary history. When he came to visit her, which he had a few times the year before, it was for real advice. Not that he'd gotten anything that helpful. Now, she puffed her hollow cheeks as she straightened, dumping her half-full dustpan into the trash can.

The room reeked of stale cigarette smoke, though the window behind Ms. Molouski's desk was open, and a spinning fan flooded the room with unseasonably frigid air. There was a faint trail of smoke coming from the ashtray on her desk, which was full of cigarette butts. The only contrast to her drab gray walls were the small splashes of goldenrod file organizers.

"So what can I do for you?" she asked as she closed her office door to the lonely, empty hallway.

Jay took an uncomfortable folding chair across from her desk.

"Ask Principal Oatman. I think he's hoping you can give me guidance on how not to get beat up by Jeremy."

"Ha!" She cackled. "That's easy. What were you doing in A-Court?"

"Yeah," Jay muttered, "think I'd have learned that one by now. Also, since I'm here . . ."

Ms. Molouski braced herself.

"What am I going to do if I don't even get a waitlist?"

Ms. Molouski shook her head.

"Jay, we've been through this. You're not getting into college."

"Miss Rotchkey disagrees."

Ms. Molouski grimaced at the name.

"Yeah, well, forgive me, but I'm not holding my breath that her little experiment produces us a college grad."

"She says this is the year. She says if we had better than a 3.5 and ace our SATs, we oughta be able to crack a state school. And community colleges legally can't turn us—"

Ms. Molouski sighed. "Jay. Hon. We have a zero percent college admissions rate at this school. *Zero. Percent.* A diploma here is worth less than the paper it's printed on."

"That is insane!" Jay retorted.

"I know it. You know it. Doesn't change a thing. Look, I'll tell you the same thing I tell every kid who comes in here asking about college. You did all the right things, and you're still going nowhere. That's life in Bickleton. Some kids in the world may be born lucky, but they sure ain't born here."

Jay made to interrupt, but she held up a hand.

"Want my advice? Kiss McKraken's ass. Get a decent job down at the mill. You're smart. Capable. Work hard, do right by the Johns, you'll be able to buy your own house. Then, if you are lucky, and wind up at Kay's bar at just the right moment, you can knock up a pretty girl, and in eighteen years I'll be having this same conversation with your kid."

She gave Jay a thin smile.

"What if I just leave?"

She chuckled. "There's the door."

Jay rose and muttered through gritted teeth, "Thanks."

He stopped at the door and turned.

"You know, I don't think I'm asking too much. I'm waitlisted at six schools. Four state schools, two community colleges. And those community colleges have to accept me."

Ms. Molouski's chair squeaked, and now she, too, was standing, unsteadily, hands gripping her desk for support. For the first time, Jay saw a small sparkle of life peer out of her sad basset hound eyes.

"You probably won't believe this, but I was your age once. I've been in this town a long time, and I hate to see good kids get their hopes up."

"Isn't that your job? To help us achieve our dreams?"

"No, my job is to help you figure out your options."

"But you just told me I didn't have any options. That my only option is to kiss Jeremy's ass just to get a job at the mill!"

She shrugged. "Welcome to Bickleton."

TUTORIAL

JAY EASED THE Tutorial classroom door shut, trying to slip in unnoticed. Instead, the door clicked loudly, and a roomful of eyes turned to stare. Ms. Rotchkey paused her lesson, hovering over her desk, big owl eyes looking at Jay from behind thick glasses. The silence of the room was overwhelming.

"It's not my fault I'm late!" Jay protested. "I got jumped by Jeremy—tell her, Colin, I—"

Ms. Rotchkey's gnarled claws tapped out a beat on her wooden desk.

"And a-one, and a-two and—"

The classroom broke into a rendition of "Happy Birthday."

Jay blushed, bringing the frozen peas down from his swollen eye, lopsided grin beaming at the class.

"Aw. You guys—"

"I told them," Colin blurted.

Tutorial sat above the rest of Bickleton High, an island in the surrounding pines, technically one of the "portables," though it was secluded from the other math labs. If you were a student and seeker of enlightenment, this one small room held pretty much your only hope of a real education in Bickleton. Ms. Rotchkey had founded Tutorial as a school within a school, a place where kids who wanted to learn, could. Mr. Oatman had given her autonomy, and she had lured kids like Jay and Colin to her classroom with the promise of a single word. College. She had helped the lot of them through admissions guidelines and SAT prep to achieve a goal that had eluded Bickleton for as long as anyone could remember.

Now, the two dozen desks sat mostly empty, as students instead enjoyed beanbags and overstuffed armchairs against the side walls. Bohemian lamps bathed the interior in comfortable orange, and oak bookshelves filled the walls with thrilling titles like *Notes from Underground*, *A Confederacy of Dunces*, *Diary of a Drug Fiend*, and *Labyrinths*. The Johns or Liz never set foot in Tutorial, but if they had, Jay was certain even they would deign the room cool.

Shayna, a tall drama girl, eyed Jay's face as he moved toward his desk. "What happened to you?"

"Made a play for some pies."

A second girl gasped. "You went to A-Court?"

"Yeah." Jay glanced angrily at Colin. "Without backup."

Colin looked sheepish. "*All* the Johns were there."

Ms. Rotchkey tsked. "You guys make it sound like a war zone."

"It *is* a war zone, Miss Rotchkey. You don't know, you never leave this room."

"*You* never leave this room," Ms. Rotchkey retorted.

"Today I did and look what happened?!"

Marlene, a young Latina, leaned in. "What happened?"

"Well, I got jumped, didn't I? I had to fight 'em off all by myself because this guy"—Jay jerked his thumb at Colin—"is apparently to delicate to . . ." He glanced around, noticing something.

The desk behind his friend was empty. "Where's Todd? He was the one talking up those pies."

Ms. Rotchkey tapped an attendance list. "Didn't make it in."

"Huh." Jay frowned. "He was so proud of his attendance. Hate to see a man's dreams squashed."

But Jay's attention was already diverted to the class computer. An IBM PS/2, which was Bickleton's only computer, as far as Jay knew. Ms. Rotchkey had secured it by threatening to make public the $10,000 Mr. Oatman had recently paid for new baseball equipment. Mr. Oatman suspected the town would take his side in that battle, but gave in anyway.

The IBM PS/2 was Jay's everything. He loved browsing *Microsoft Encarta*, the six-CD encyclopedias that came with the purchase. He loved watching the tiny pixelated movie clips on Cinemania. And more than anything, he loved the games. *Duke Nukem. Wolfenstein 3D. Scorched Earth. King's Quest VI. Monkey Island 2.* And especially the world-building games: games like *SimCity 2000* and *Populous*. Jay could get lost in those worlds for hours, building small towns and civilizations, adjusting budgets, responding to natural disasters. He ordered by mail every world-building game that came out. Then he would tote them back and forth to Tutorial, squeezing in spare hours wherever he could.

Currently, Jay was building a pixel-perfect re-creation of Bickleton inside *SimCity 2000*. In fact, he'd pitched Ms. Rotchkey on letting him use first period for independent study to pursue his passion in city planning. *SimCity 2000* was not a game, he argued, but a stepping stone into college.

The reconstruction—which Jay nicknamed Poopville—was thorough. He'd even borrowed a topographic map from the library, landscaping the peaks around the Skookullom River into perfect mirrors of the original. He'd sculpted the main street of businesses, a high school, even a police department next to the city park. He'd landscaped out individual blocks (as best he could) to represent the houses of Bickleton.

Jay loved it. He loved imagining Colin and Stevie in their homes, loved watching their cars leave in the morning to go to work. He loved thinking of Jeremy's and the Johns' homes. Sometimes, after a particularly bad run-in with the Johns, he would release a fire on their virtual houses and imagine the Johns screaming inside. Then he would carefully rebuild their houses, his compulsion for order outweighing his desire for revenge. *SimCity 2000* gave him a sense of control he never found elsewhere in his life.

At the moment, Stevie Melbrook was at the keyboard, blocking his access.

Like Jay, Stevie was overly fond of the class computer. Like Jay, she had convinced Ms. Rotchkey to give her first period every other day to use it. Unlike Jay, her interest ran deeper than games. She was teaching herself to code in C++ and had long ago earned a reputation as the smartest person in Bickleton High—a label that mattered to no one except Jay, who thought it should be his. She was small and pixie-ish, with thin glasses and a gratingly upbeat voice. Jay's blood cooled to see her on the computer (during his time, no less), and he stalked over. The computer was hissing and clicking like an angry robotic cat, and Jay realized its modem was active.

"What are you doing?"

Stevie pulled a floppy disk out of the drive.

"I'm backing up everything."

Jay pointed to the screen. A grainy video of a half-empty coffeepot played in the upper right corner.

"Looks like you're streaming that coffee machine again."

Stevie had recently taken to monitoring the Trojan Room Coffee Pot at the University of Cambridge. It was, she had proudly told Jay, the world's first live video feed.

"I'm doing both." Stevie smiled. "Windows 3.1 glitches are already legendary. It gets 'out of memory' errors constantly, and I haven't backed up anything yet, have you? Though," she mused before he could answer, "the addition of real mode support and batch install are strides forward in—"

"Yeah, well, it's my day to use the computer."

"Okay, the next time someone pours a cup of coffee—hold that thought!" Stevie exclaimed. "I've got mail."

Jay leaned in, unable to help himself.

"Who'd be desperate enough to write you?"

"Dolos75. I met him in a Delphi message board. He lives in Sydney."

Jay squinted suspiciously at the screen. "How do you know? He could be in Czechoslovakia. He could live right here in Bickleton. How do you know it's not Colin sending love letters?"

Colin blushed a deep purple. "It wasn't me."

"I'm just saying—"

"And it's no longer Czechoslovakia, Jay; it's the Czech Republic and Slovakia," Ms. Rotchkey called over.

"I think it's likely he's from Australia," said Stevie, who hadn't moved from the computer. She read aloud: "'Hey, Stevie. Sorry for the typo in the previous letter. This keyboard I'm on is barely useable.'"

Jay looked at her blankly.

"The spelling. USE-ABLE." She pointed at the word. "That's Australian spelling!"

"Probably another typo."

"Jay brings up a good point, though," Ms. Rotchkey interrupted. "How do we know this person is from Australia? Or, more broadly, how do we know anyone is from anywhere?"

The class braced themselves. Ms. Rotchkey fancied herself a philosopher: there were thick tomes on the bookshelf with heavy titles like *Twilight of the Idols*, *Being and Nothingness*, and *The Passions of the Soul*. Nobody in Tutorial could master philosophy to Ms. Rotchkey's satisfaction, and anyone who tried to answer her questions usually only got a frown of disapproval.

"How do we know anything to be true?" she continued. "How do we know what I know, what you know, is true?"

Jay sighed and slumped into his seat. He hadn't meant for his bickering with Stevie to catapult them into a lesson on existentialism.

Ms. Rotchkey peered over her glasses at her reluctant class. "Epistemology will be covered on finals."

Colin raised a hand.

"'Postulates are based on assumption and adhered to by faith. Nothing in the Universe can shake them.'"

Ms. Rotchkey frowned, considering.

"Show-off," Jay hissed.

The loudspeaker crackled, startling the students. "All students please report to the gym for an all-school assembly."

The students instinctively stood, and Jay followed suit, mournfully staring at the computer he wouldn't get to use.

DARK HOUSE

IT WASN'T A stench, but a lingering smell: a deep-fried medley, hardened by years of abandon. If you lived in the smell, like the Recluse did, you didn't notice it. It was only when a window was opened, and the sweet Bickleton mountain air poured in, that the stagnation became obvious. But windows were rarely opened, and the front door was used as little as possible.

Besides the Recluse, the only person who ever smelled it was Jim Hanky, the grocer. By arrangement, Jim delivered five full plastic bags of groceries to the Recluse's house every Tuesday.

"Who's the guy in the blue house?" Jim's coworkers would ask. Those who knew the Recluse, who'd done the route before, shook their heads. The Recluse never came out. He never spoke. He only nodded, pulling the bags in through the door, one at a time. He never opened the door more than was necessary, and he never made eye contact.

On the rare occasion Jim got a glimpse inside the house, he saw rooms with boxes stacked to the ceiling and a small hallway clogged with boxes. The Recluse carefully labeled each box in neat handwriting: *Time Magazines '86,* stacked above *'92–'93*

Disney Movies, which sat on top of *'80s classics, Columbia House Music Catalog,* and so on.

The boxes continued into a small dining room and then into the kitchen, framing the fridge and stove. They squeezed the house's livable space into a single, tiny corridor that wove through the rooms. Amazingly, no matter how claustrophobic the house was, little clutter lay outside of the boxes. Everything else was clean, even the boxes themselves; the cardboard was straight, bright, and new, the stifled air acting as formaldehyde.

The Recluse liked to keep his house preserved. Others might call it a mess, but to him it wasn't messy. After years of compromise, he finally had everything just the way he wanted it.

ALL STUDENTS

THE TUTORIAL KIDS stood at the back of the line to enter the assembly. Jay instinctively looked for Jeremy, though he knew Jeremy would never be caught dead at the end of any line. Odds were Jeremy was up front, but Jay didn't want to take any chances. Even with all the teachers around, he didn't trust Jeremy would leave him alone. Especially not after he'd stood up to him. Jeremy would be looking to make an example.

Jay looked through the glass door leading to C-Court. C-Court was smaller than A-Court, and it housed less practical classes, like art, band, drama, and gym. And then the center was crowded with lunch tables, for all the students in patchwork flannel and baggy jeans who lived off the school's hot lunches. There was little room left for the meandering line of students pushing their way through the gym's single door.

Jay caught his reflection in the glass. The skin around his eye was still huge and puffy. The swelling had stopped, and he no longer kept peas pressed to his face, but it was still warm and sensitive to the touch.

"I look like the Elephant Man," he mumbled to Colin as they filed into C-Court.

"It'll be gone by prom."

Colin looked mournfully at the prom posters decorating the walls. Prom was Friday after next, less than two weeks away.

"Not that *that* matters," Colin muttered.

"If we beat the Mantis Boss, we have to ask someone."

Colin shook his shaggy hair. "How's that?"

"It's called rewarding milestones. Like that poster in the home-ec room. With the cat wearing sunglasses."

"'Cat-titude is Everything'?"

"Exactly. We just need the right cat-titude. Beat the boss, get the girl."

Colin scanned the crowd. "I'm not sure there are any girls left to get."

"Bad cat-titude."

The last of the students swept toward the red doors of the gym, and Jay and Colin crowded in behind them. As they entered, Jay caught a glimpse of the parking lot, where the sheriff had parked at an awkward angle before the doors. Jay nudged Colin and they stopped for a moment, dread filling them. Jay had assumed the assembly would just be another meeting about prom. Clearly, there was something else going on.

They filed into the gym, where the murmurs of four hundred students poured off the bleachers and echoed across the walls. Girls in bejeweled jean jackets and hyper-color scrunchies sat in rapt attention. The teachers were somberly aligned across the front row. The assembly had apparently already started, because Elmer Jenkins, the town sheriff, stood in the center of the gym, addressing the bleachers.

". . . spoken with several students who saw him walking. Two elementary school kids claim that Todd, or someone who looked like him, headed down into Jewett Creek. We have some evidence that he was hiking down there. We're still looking into it."

Jay and Colin climbed to an open space at the top of the bleachers. Jay's body felt stiff from his earlier beating, and he grunted as he sat next to a sophomore.

"What's going on?" he whispered.

"Todd Hammond didn't make it home last night."

Jay's blood froze. Todd, who sat next to him in Tutorial. Todd, who they teased because he was never absent. The entire gymnasium was quiet, absorbing Elmer's words.

Elmer's left eye twitched as he continued: "I'm not here to cause a stir or scare anyone. But we need your help. If anyone has more information about Todd, please see me following the assembly. I'm sure I don't need to tell you, but his parents are very upset. Until we know where he is, everyone, *please*, use the buddy system when walking to and from school, hiking, or going out at night. Mrs. Hammond would like to say a few words."

The room was dead quiet as Todd's mom clicked across the gym floor. Even from a distance, she looked much like her son. She shared Todd's red hair and freckles, his tall, gangly disposition. She took the microphone and turned to the student body.

"Some of you know Todd better than others. A lot of you have been in school plays with Todd. *A Midsummer's Night Dream. Some Like It Hot.* He loves to make people laugh. And he's thoughtful. He would go out of his way to help me, or his sister, or the neighbors. Or any of you. I know Todd didn't run away. So if any of you—"

Mrs. Hammond's voice broke. Jay felt a lurch of pain in his stomach and tears welling in his eyes. In middle school, Jay had been good friends with Todd. He used to spend the night at the Hammonds' house. He'd eaten meatloaf with Todd's family. He looked around the student body and saw that many faces were crying. His gaze landed on Todd's sister, sitting with her sophomore friends, her face in her hands, her body shaking.

"If you have any information about how or why he disappeared—"

And she broke off again. Principal Oatman, who was not known for compassion, placed a gentle hand on her back and led her away. Then he returned to the podium and spoke blandly about safety. Jay shook his head, not listening. Todd had been at school only yesterday. And now he was gone.

Mr. Oatman muttered something about prayers for Todd's family, and then the assembly was over. Despite four hundred students leaving the gym, the only sound was the squeak of sneakers on the waxed floors. Jay and Colin pushed their way through the students filing out, breaking away from the crowd and slipping out the small rear door. They stood on the balcony that overlooked the baseball field.

For several moments, they stared out over the sea of green grass. The sun was high over the strand of poplar trees that separated the school grounds from the surrounding pastures, eating away the frosty shadows. It was Colin who broke the silence.

"You think he's . . . ?"

"No." Jay shook his head emphatically. But he couldn't think of anything more to say.

AROUND THE BEND

IF JAY HAD hoped Ms. Rotchkey's second period would distract him from the awful dread in his stomach, he was wrong. The students took their seats in total silence. Nobody was in the mood for beanbag chairs. Minutes ticked by as the class waited for Ms. Rotchkey to return. Kids began to whisper. No one spoke. Everyone cast sidelong glances at Todd's empty seat. Shayna and Marlene imperceptibly scooted their desks away from it. The silence was unbearable, and Jay was about to pinch Colin just to break it, when the door flew open. Ms. Rotchkey stormed to the front of the class. Her fingers were trembling as she flipped through a lesson plan and adjusted and readjusted her glasses.

Jay had only seen Ms. Rotchkey furious once before, when Bill Winkler—a student she'd invited to attend Tutorial—turned out to have joined because of a dare from the Johns. Every time Bill came to class, he'd step in dog poop and intentionally grind it into the carpet. It was three days before Ms. Rotchkey caught on, and another week before she got rid of the smell. That day, she had carried Bill down to the principal's office by his ear.

Jay saw her anger welling up again as she mumbled to herself, face pink.

"Second period. Second period we're—"

She snapped her lesson plan shut and paced back and forth. She wheeled around to face them.

"Does this seem fair to you?"

The class blinked. She continued. "Does it seem fair that I find out Todd is missing at the assembly? With the rest of the school? The same moment the school janitor finds out? They don't have the courtesy to give me a call? I could be out there looking for him!"

She slammed her lesson plan down and strode to the back of the room. She gave the class a warning look.

"Stay put."

Then she burst out the door.

The class stared at one another, mouths agape. Ms. Rotchkey was usually the one talking the students down. Jay leapt up, rushing the computer.

Stevie slammed her palms on her desk. "You're gonna play video games?!"

"Hey, it's not like we can leave and go look for Todd *right now*."

Jay cleared the free trial disks for CompuServe and America Online out of the way, then powered up the screen and pulled *Serious Gamer* out of his bag. He stuck the blank disk into the drive and double-clicked the A: DRIVE icon. A small window popped open, and there was a beautiful pixelated background of serene mountains at sunset. A small sign in the foreground read *The Build*. Loud synth music played the song Jay had already heard twice that day.

"It's playing . . . 'Happy Birthday'?" Jay questioned. "Did you guys do this?"

From her desk, Stevie squinted at the screen, then shook her head. Colin shrugged.

Jay turned back to the load screen. The song was playing on a loop. Jay clicked and the music stopped. Another window popped up: ENTER THE NAME OF YOUR TOWN.

Jay reflexively typed in "Poopville," after the town he was building in SimCity.

The screen flashed again, and he was looking down on a pixelated swath of land. In the center of the screen was a brown patch of land filled with little roads and houses. Tiny cars puttered up and down the streets. Encircling the tiny community was emerald-green forest. Jay frowned.

"It's just a *SimCity* rip-off," Colin muttered.

"With worse graphics." Jay consulted his *Serious Gamer* magazine. "That's it? What a waste of a floppy disk."

Colin squinted. "It's greener than *SimCity.*"

Several heads swiveled at the sound of footsteps coming up the ramp outside. Jay leapt from the computer, expecting the wrath of Ms. Rotchkey. But it was Derek Deckford, the thin sophomore who always wore a bow tie when he worked the front office.

"You guys get to go home early. Ms. Rotchkey says. Extenuating circumstances. Come back tomorrow and call if anyone hears anything about Todd."

PROPOSITION

JAY AND COLIN decided not to go to the Ramirez house, considering Colin's mom would likely be home. Instead, they drove aimlessly around Bickleton. The sun was out, caressing chocolate lilies and miner's lettuce in golden warmth. After two disappointing laps, and talk of whether *Æon Flux* was better than *Ren & Stimpy*, they puttered up the gentle hill to Midtown Park, which held the library, community center, police station, and a small public pool that was closed indefinitely. What *was* open was the Bickleton Creamery.

Like A-Court, the ice cream store was the domain of the Bickleton popular crowd, and normally off-limits for geeks like Jay and Colin. But with the rest of the school still in class, Jay and Colin saw an opportunity.

They sprawled out on the grass, Jay fiddling with his *Frogger* watch while taking bites of his triple fudge. The park sloped down to look over the roofs of Bickleton, and the Skookullom River and Cascade Range lay just beyond. The Skookullom was blue with haze, and Jay saw small trees high up on its ridge, blowing in the wind.

Colin slurped a strawberry milkshake while rambling: ". . . and finally, Totoro shows up at a bus stop with a big leaf protecting him from the rain . . ."

He'd been talking for several minutes in deep, rumbling breaths, pausing every few sentences to laugh softly at his own jokes, his tree-trunk legs impossibly crossed in the lotus position.

Jay sighed, not really listening, urging his LCD Frogger up through traffic. He was familiar with most of Miyazaki's movies, not because he'd seen them, but because Colin was so fond of recounting them.

"Ya gotta see it," Colin chuckled, shaking his head.

"Ya know, when I eat ice cream"—Jay examined his cone—"I try to train all my senses on it. Really get the full experience. We're gonna be old someday. When we get old, we lose synaptic connections. We'll walk the same mental pathways, over and over. Ice cream will never taste as good as it does right now.

"To be young"—Jay raised a finger prophetically—"is to truly experience life."

They were silent a moment.

"You think we should go look for Todd?" Colin asked.

"Yeah." Jay nodded. "But you know, I've been thinking. He probably skipped town? Had the same idea we had, just beat us to the punch. In fact"—he gave Colin a sidelong glance—"we should go after him."

Colin shifted uncomfortably. "Leave Bickleton?"

"Yeah. Look, Todd probably hitched a ride to Portland. He's probably yucking it up with a bunch of coeds right now. Partying his pants off. Miss Molouski and everyone else acts like it's such a wild idea to leave, but we could do it. We don't even have to wait till graduation."

"You said you still needed to save up money . . ."

"With your savings, we could get an apartment in Portland. I could get a job. I don't care where. Working at McDonalds, is better than living here, and that's just till we start college. We could go this weekend, if we wanted. What do you say?"

"I say . . ." Colin shifted uncomfortably. "I say . . ."

Then Colin froze. His mouth worked in small little motions, but his eyes stared ahead. Jay followed his gaze. A red Land Cruiser pulled up on the curb below them. Liz, Amber, and Gretchen got out. They were laughing and gesturing, as if there had been no assembly about a missing kid. As if there was nothing that could bring three gorgeous high school seniors down.

They started up the lawn, toward Bickleton Creamery, and then Liz's gaze fell on Jay and Colin. She turned to her friends and whispered. Amber and Gretchen looked up at Jay, nodded, then hurried on into Bickleton Creamery.

Liz began to climb the hill. Jay and Colin simultaneously straightened, preparing to flee. Jay's heart was pounding, adrenaline flowing. Experience taught him that whatever was about to happen, it wasn't going to be good. He looked around wildly, half-expecting Jeremy to rush out and grab him. But there was no one there. Just them, and Liz.

Liz waved tentatively. She stopped when she saw Jay.

"Are you guys okay?"

Jay's heart skipped a beat. His hand went self-consciously to his face. "Yeah, the swelling's going down—"

"No, I mean, Todd. You guys knew Todd, right? *Know* him, I should say." She kept on brushing the hair from her eyes, as if she were nervous.

Jay nodded. "Yeah. He and I used to tub together. I mean our moms put us in tubs together. When we were little."

He could feel his face heating up. "We've known each other for a while."

Liz gave a small laugh.

"I hope he's okay."

"We think he left for Portland."

"Ah, dang. And right before prom, too." There was an awkward pause as her gaze lingered on Jay. She seemed to be working up to something. "Say . . . are you guys . . . going to prom?"

Jay shot Colin a look. "Maybe. If we don't follow Todd's lead and leave. But, uh, we'd have to find some dates—"

"Oh, I need a date, actually. My date canceled."

"Oh . . ." Jay's heart began to pound. "I'm sorry to hear . . ."

"Do–do you maybe want to go?"

Jay's heart was exploding. "With . . . you?"

Liz gave a brief nod.

Jay's brain went blank. His mouth moved, but the words came out all foreign and jumbled. "Y-yeah, s-sure. That makes a lot of . . . a lot of sense. Neither of us has a date. We go together, you and I. Sure, yeah, let's go. Together. To prom."

Liz hesitated, waiting for more, but Jay was frozen.

"Great. Well. I'm sure we'll talk more soon."

Then she turned and headed back down the hill, leaving Jay stunned, staring unseeing at the Cascade Range.

DEBRIEF

"THE HELL WAS that?" Jay shouted toward the Skookullom River.

They had pulled out onto the mudflats, the short spit of sand that stretched from lower Bickleton, where Rattlesnake Creek emptied into the greater waters of the Skookullom. In late spring, the water level had receded to uncover a patch of solid-brown sand that ran halfway across the river. It was compact enough for kids to walk on, and big enough that smaller, lighter cars, like the Batmobile, could drive across it.

Colin stared out at the water. The river was a thick chocolate brown, full of sediment. Come August, when the glaciers started melting, it would run milky white with silt. The lumber mill had cleared the trees on this side of the river so that the cool spring sun fell on the sand. Colin bent to pick up a stone and skipped it upstream, where the water pooled. Jay paced back and forth, hands combing his hair.

"How is this happening? In what universe does this happen?"

"Happy birthday, I guess?"

Jay stopped, staring at the large square warehouses upstream. The industry that was the backbone of Bickleton.

A mountain of bald logs obscured the McKraken Mill. Behind that, Jay could just barely make out two fruit-packing plants, Duckwall and United Fruit Co. A third lot, Bickleton Erector's Corp, was shut down, with a chain-link fence surrounding it and a sign that read: "No Trespassing, Dangerous Conditions." From where he stood, he could hear the hum of air conditioners, the beep of forklifts. Jay shook his head.

"It's too good to be true."

Colin skipped another stone. "You're not gonna go?"

"Oh, I have to! It's Liz Knight, for God's sake."

"I didn't know you liked her?"

"Everyone likes her, given the chance. You know, we held hands once?"

Colin nodded.

"Yep. Back in first grade," Jay reminisced. "We were swinging in tandem, our hands reached out. Just sort of happened. I bet she still remembers. Prolly why she asked me!"

Colin frowned. "I thought she was going with Jeremy?"

"Musta dumped him. Musta wised up. And she knows Jeremy hates me, and she wants to get back at him."

"Jeremy's gonna be mad at you."

Jay shrugged. "Jeremy's always mad at me." He spun around and grabbed his best friend. "I get to go to prom with Liz Knight! I don't know how we did it, Colin, but we are in the money. I need a car! I gotta get a driver's license! I need a suit. And friends, I need friends. Who am I going to hang out with at prom? Colin, you gotta come. Oh God: Colin, can I borrow some money?"

He caught a disapproving look on Colin's face.

"I'll pay you back!"

"I thought you were saving to leave town?"

"It's Liz. Knight."

Colin looked away wistfully. "I'll lend you the Batmobile."

Jay placed a hand on Colin's shoulder, touched, but also imagining what Liz would say if Jay rolled up in that piece of garbage.

"Thanks, buddy. Let me think on that."

THE LAST
BIRTHDAY

JAY CONTINUED HIS stream-of-conscious chatter to Colin until his throat went dry, and then he just stared into the river. Eventually, the sun drew near the eastern ridge of the Cascades and disappeared into dark shadow. Shivering, they went back to the Batmobile.

Colin dropped Jay off outside his house, wishing him a final happy birthday, and Jay headed up the short walk to his home, still lost in thought. His house was not much to look at. It wasn't the worst house in Bickleton, but it was far from the best. A three-bedroom bungalow built back in the early 1900s—when Bickleton was still being settled by the great western push—its front awning had been pushed slightly askew as the earth underneath had slowly settled. The paint on the siding was chipped and peeling, moss grew on the roof, and a permanent layer of funk stained the gutters black. It was small and drafty, but—unlike the neighbors'—it was at least clear of rusty farm equipment.

Jay flung open the front door. In the corner of the living room, a potbellied stove blazed, issuing wisps of pine smoke. On the couch, Kathy Banksman was leaning forward, in the middle of a conversation with their neighbor Tara. Kathy had beehive hair, glasses, a gap in her front teeth, and a half-smile that men had once found irresistible. The television was on, blaring *Thelma & Louise*, his mom's favorite movie. She turned as Jay walked in, and Jay saw she wasn't smiling.

"So you decided to come home, eh? Must be tired, are we?"

Jay stared at her blankly.

"You know who I saw at the bank today? Mrs. Ramirez!"

Jay's mind rewound back to the day's beginning, when he and Colin had gotten balled out for playing *Secret of Mana*. It seemed like a lifetime ago, and he realized he was exhausted. Kathy stood up from the couch.

"Jay Harold Banksman, it was supposed to be a birthday sleepover, not an all-night orgy of—" She froze. "Good God, what happened to your eye?!"

Tara, a short, strong woman, had also stood. Her eyes ablaze with indignation on Jay's behalf. He turned his face away from the two women, embarrassed.

"Did someone hit you?"

"Nah."

"Who did this? Are the Johns bothering you—"

"Mom—" Jay interrupted. "I'm going to prom."

His mom slid back. "With who?"

"Liz."

Kathy screamed. "Liz Knight?!"

"Liz *Knight*?!" Tara repeated.

"And *she* asked *me*. Just this afternoon."

"Liz Knight. Asked *my* son." Kathy could hardly register it. She shrieked again, hugging Jay so hard the pressure hurt him. "Oh my God. I have to call everyone." She pointed at Tara. "*You* have to call everyone."

Tara, who had no kids, nodded gamely. Any hint of Jay's trouble over morning video games evaporated as Kathy bustled gleefully through their tiny kitchen.

"Oh my God, this is a *huge* deal! Why is no one calling anyone?"

"It only happened two hours ago."

"Yeah, but the news must come from us. I need the envy. Oh, I need the envy. C'mon let's sing! Happy birthday to you . . ."

Kathy disappeared into the kitchen and then rounded the corner with a green cake and eighteen candles. On its face was a crudely drawn picture of three Ninja Turtles, and the words "radical dude." Jay blew out his candles, and then his mom handed Jay a magazine.

"I got you something."

It was a *Nintendo Power* magazine. On the cover was Michael Keaton as Batman, and the title "*Batman Returns:* The Bat, The Cat, The Penguin."

Jay grabbed it. "No way!"

"A yearlong subscription."

Jay looked up sharply.

"Mom . . . I'm leaving after graduation, remember? To college?"

Kathy crossed her arms in her most combative stance.

"You really want to set foot out there? After the bombing of the World Trade Center? And that poor Rodney King?"

"Those are two different states."

"What about the starving kids in Somalia, or the war in Bosnia?"

"It's not like I'm enlisting in the army."

"What about the New Kids on the Block? You want to end up dead in a plane crash like them?"

"I'm probably safer in a plane than the Batmobile."

"Pfft." But a smile was already returning to her face. She shrieked girlishly and grabbed the Garfield phone on the counter. "Oh my God, Liz Knight! Who should I call first?"

"Congratulations, again." Tara ducked out the door. "See you tomorrow, Kathy."

Jay's buried his nose in *Nintendo Power* and made his way to his bedroom. A lonely smattering of posters—*Cliffhanger*, *Terminator 2*, *Backdraft*—adorned peeling wallpaper. The only furnishings were two bookshelves built from salvaged lumber and cinder blocks, a few large Tupperware drawers, and a bed. Since Jay couldn't afford a computer or gaming system, he used what little space there was in his room to build a shrine to his favorite vocation. His bookshelves were devoted entirely to back issues of *PC Gamer*, *Serious Gamer*, and *GamePro*. Jay flung himself on the bed, gazing idly at the Heather Graham poster tacked to the ceiling above him. He looked into Heather Graham's eyes and thought back to the events of the day, smiling. What a birthday.

His thoughts wandered back to that game demo. *The Build*, it had been called. He let his *Nintendo Power* fall to the floor and picked up his *Serious Gamer*. He'd never seen any previews for a game called *The Build*. Who made it? There were no publisher logos on the load screen. He flipped through the magazine, looking over its glossy pages for a write-up that would explain the disk. But there was nothing. He lay back in bed, thinking. Even a third-rate *SimCity* might still have some mileage. He should really give it another shot. He smiled and closed his eyes. It had been a good birthday after all.

LIZ WIPED

THE NEXT MORNING, Jay and Colin stood huddled under the school library awning, lost in conversation. The library rounded like a large yurt, overlooking both A-Court and C-Court from a knobbed hill. They could watch the students bustling to and from class, keep tabs on the Johns, and, on this particular day, allow Jay to gauge the effect of his prom date on the student body. As Jay spoke, he kept one eye on the kids passing by, waiting for someone to glance in his direction and recognize him as the Guy Going With Liz. He was watching so intently, he jumped when a sudden, sharp voice barked over his shoulder.

"We're organizing a search party for Todd this weekend."

Jay spun around. Ms. Rotchkey stood before the library doors as they banged open and kids poured out. Ms. Rotchkey waited with her hands on her hips. Jay felt his cheeks color in embarrassment. With everything that had happened with Liz, he'd all but forgotten about Todd. Now Todd's absence came rushing back, and he felt sick to his stomach that nearly twenty-four hours had passed and he'd yet to do anything to help.

"Oh, that's great," he replied.

"Can I count on your help?"

"Yes."

"Anything you need," Colin said.

Ms. Rotchkey nodded, then turned to the next group of kids.

When the two of them were alone again, Jay lowered his voice and returned to their conversation.

"Please?"

Colin shook his head. "Have you seen your face?"

Jay had spent the morning staring into his mirror. Though the swelling had gone down, the ring around his eye had turned an ugly purple.

"She needs to know I'm not scared."

"You *should* be scared," Colin snorted.

"I need A-Court to see me." Jay grabbed Colin's sleeve and guided him down the steps.

Jay had an ulterior motive for heading back to A-Court. He hadn't received the reaction he'd been expecting that morning. He'd pictured handshakes of congratulations, a slow clap, maybe even an invitation to hang out in A-Court. But so far, none of the kids shuffling back and forth between buildings had even looked at him. He wanted a show.

Jay pushed open the doors and strutted past a corridor of lockers covered in pictures of Cindy Crawford and Marky Mark, continuing to pull a reluctant Colin toward A-Court. They passed the main office, and just as they were nearing the front entrance, the doors banged open. High-pitched yells filled the cavernous hall. A-Court quieted, and every head turned to look at the interruption.

"Get your hands off me!"

Sheriff Jenkins stood just inside the doorway, breathing heavily, his face purple. He wore aviator sunglasses, and his mouth was shrunk into a thin line. Tugging furiously to get away from him was Liz Knight. Sheriff Jenkins had her hands clasped behind her back, and she writhed, straining painfully, her arms bending at awkward angles. Her hair fell across her face, but Jay could still see her mouth twisted in a snarl. She was doing more than just protesting her treatment: she was struggling like an animal, as if she were fighting for her very life.

The A-Court boom box was blasting Aerosmith's "Livin' on the Edge," but somebody quickly shut it off. Now the entire hall was quiet, except for the squeak of Liz's sneakers, and her grunts and snarls as she tried to get away. A sophomore boy next to Jay muttered, "Must be that time of the month." Nobody laughed.

Ms. Shirell stared frozen, mouth open, before she turned and huffed off to fetch Principal Oatman. Liz suddenly stopped struggling. She seemed to realize she was no longer outside, and her eyes lifted to take in the lockers, the vaulted ceiling that merged into a skylight at the pinnacle of A-Court, and then finally to the wall of students silently studying her. Her gaze darted around the room, registering the details with mounting horror.

The door to the administrator's office opened and Principal Oatman stepped out. Liz's head whipped around.

"Principal . . . Oatman?"

Principal Oatman nodded acknowledgment. "Liz. What's this?"

Elmer relaxed a little, but looked suspiciously at Liz, as if he expected her to resume her fight at any moment. "I found her lying on the shoulder of Main Street."

Mr. Oatman stared at Liz. "Is she *hurt?*"

"Not that I can tell. She was . . ." He looked uncomfortable. "She was sobbing and sorta . . . screaming at the top of her lungs."

Jay elbowed his way through the students to hear better.

"I stopped to ask if she was okay, and she tried to run. I caught her, and she's been fighting me tooth and nail ever since."

"Well, maybe we take off those handcuffs."

Elmer shook his head. "If I do that, she'll run."

Liz gulped a sob and dropped to her knees. Mascara tears streaked her cheeks. Jay's mind flashed through the terrible possibilities: *Had somebody died? Or had she found Todd?*

Strange gurgling noises were starting to come from Liz's mouth. Oatman fidgeted, increasingly uncomfortable.

"Take her home to her parents!"

"I called her parents. They're meeting us here."

Before Mr. Oatman could object, a gray shape approached the glass doors. A tall, tired-looking man with gray hair rushed through the door. Jay recognized Terry Knight, Liz's dad. He rushed to Liz, his arms wide. But as Liz turned to him, she shrieked in terror, falling to the ground and scooting away, until her back was pressed against the locker. New tears flowed down her face.

"Oh my God. Sweetie, what's wrong?"

Liz screeched, flailing her limbs. "Don't touch me!"

Mr. Knight startled and stepped back. He looked between the students and Sheriff Jenkins, stricken.

"Help me get her home!"

Sheriff Jenkins took a step toward Liz. "Hey. Hey, Liz."

Liz cowered into the lockers. Principal Oatman turned to the rest of the students.

"Miss Shirell! Let's get everyone to class, please!"

Administrators and teachers poured into the hall, ushering fascinated students away from Liz. Jay leered over his shoulder as an office aide grabbed his elbow and pulled him toward the north doors, unable to tear his gaze from where Liz was fending off the three men trying to help her.

DR. SHREK

JAY WAS IN agony the rest of the day. Nobody in class paid any attention to Ms. Rotchkey, who showed none of her usual enthusiasm for calling the class to order.

Jay's stomach felt sick with worry for Liz. He'd never seen anyone so full of . . . what, exactly, had that been? They may not be close, but they were going to prom. He wanted to be by her side.

A second thought had also taken hold. Liz had seemed terrified of Elmer, and even more so of her own dad. What would she do when she saw him? Would she recognize him? Jay stared down at his notebook, the glory of the last sixteen hours slowly washing away. He waited as seconds dragged on, until finally the last bell rang. He grabbed *The Build* disk, stuffed it in his backpack, and yanked Colin back down to A-Court.

The cavernous space had cleared out quicker than usual, and there were only a few stragglers left, hastily slamming locker doors. Jay knew the rest of the school was probably processing Liz's breakdown the same way he was.

He peered through the sliding window into the front office. Miss Shirell was organizing a stack of tardy slips. He rapped on the glass, and she slid the window open.

"Yes?" She nodded tartly.

Jay took a deep breath. "I was wondering if you could tell me what happened to Liz Knight? I'm going to prom with her."

Ms. Shirell raised a skeptical eyebrow.

"She'll be back in a few days. You can talk to her then." Ms. Shirell slammed the window shut and returned to her tardy slips. Jay stood beside his friend, indignant.

"How does nobody know about Liz and me? Where are the school's gossip queens when you need them?"

There was a squeak of sneakers behind them, followed by a small cough. Jay turned to see Derek Deckford rolling back and forth on his heels, adjusting his bow tie. He glanced nervously around the empty hall.

"You guys looking for Liz?"

Jay nodded. "Yeah, she okay?"

"She's at Dr. Shrek's," Derek whispered.

Jay shot Colin a glance. All kids hated Dr. Shrek. Liz would never go to him willingly.

"Thanks, Derek."

Derek nodded and scurried into the front office. Jay and Colin strode off to the Batmobile.

"Frick," muttered Colin as he started the car. "Can you imagine? Losing your memory? I think there's *certain* memories I could never forget."

"Like what?"

"Well, like, freshman year, in woodshop. I remember Chris Hargrove went and got this big rock and dropped it into the band saw. It shot out and hit a propane tank, and the class actually caught fire. Remember, they had to evacuate the whole school?"

Jay nodded vaguely. "Jeezus. How was he not expelled?"

Colin shrugged. Jay adjusted the dial of Colin's radio.

"This is 669 AM," drawled a familiar voice. "You're listening to Marvelous Mark in the morning."

"It's not morning anymore, Mark," Colin muttered to the radio.

"I got a real special one for the cool kids out there. That's right, if you've had enough 'Achy Breaky Heart,' listen up. This is My Bloody Valentine, with the song "'Only Shallow.'"

They listened in silence as Colin drove, while grinding guitars gave way to a high milky voice. Jay nodded appreciatively and pulled their small notebook from the glove compartment.

"What'd he say? My Bloody—"

Suddenly, the radio cut to silence. Jay banged on the dashboard, then tried turning the dial to pick up another station. Nothing.

"Dang it," Colin moaned.

"Broken?"

But just as suddenly, the radio came back on. Jay recognized the Beach Boys, though it was a song he'd never heard before. He switched the dial, but the song persisted no matter what station he landed on.

"Stupid car," muttered Colin.

Dr. Robert Shrek's office was even higher up than the heights, past the main strip of town. A large wooden sign outside Highway 24 proclaimed: "Dr. Shrek. If you've got cancer, we've got the answer." After a short drive uphill, the single lane opened into a kidney-shaped parking lot that wrapped around two smaller buildings: Dr. Shrek's office and the waiting room. Dr. Shrek was a stern man who greatly disliked people; he kept his waiting patients as far from his work as possible.

As they rattled into the parking lot, Jay was amazed to see it filled with Chevy trucks and smaller hatchbacks. They got out and trudged to the waiting room. Jay saw Principal Oatman and Sheriff Jenkins.

"I advise you to keep that opinion to yourself," Jay over-heard Mr. Oatman say.

"But if Liz has whatever got Todd, it might be contagious. We could have an epidemic." Sheriff Jenkins noticed the boys passing, and quieted.

A string of dangling bells jingled their arrival to the rest of the waiting room. The space was packed, full of talking kids, and few noticed their arrival. It felt like A-Court all over again. The dozen chairs were full, and kids were leaning against walls, sitting on laps, or lying on the floor. Nearly half of A-Court was there. Jay wondered if Todd's search party would generate the same excitement.

Jay noticed Gretchen and Amber in the corner with two big bouquets of flowers. Jay stared, wondering whether they would acknowledge the conversation he'd had with Liz yesterday, but they didn't look his way.

Stepping over outstretched student legs, Jay and Colin made their way to the white-haired nurse behind the front desk. She peered over wire-rimmed glasses at a *People* magazine. On the cover was a photo of a fiery plane wreckage, and the caption *New Kids on the Block, No More: Tragedy at 35,000 Feet*. Before Jay could open his mouth, her eyes flicked up.

"She's with her family. They've requested privacy. You can wait"—she motioned to the room—"wherever there's space."

Jay was about to sit, when suddenly the door flew open. Mr. Knight stood in the entrance, face white, stress lines everywhere. He searched the kids until he found Amber and Gretchen.

"Girls, would you come with me?"

The front desk nurse stood up in protest, but Mr. Knight shook his head.

"I'd like her to see them."

Jay shot up and raised a hand.

"I'm going to prom with her!"

The entire room, which had gone silent, turned to look at Jay. Jay flushed, avoiding eye contact.

He heard Gretchen mutter, "God, give it a rest."

Mr. Knight sized Jay up, then turned to Gretchen, "That true?"

"Yeah . . ." Gretchen looked reproachfully at Jay but didn't say more.

Mr. Knight ushered Jay and Colin to follow, and the four teens trailed him out of the waiting room and over to Dr. Shrek's office. Inside was a short corridor with two doors branching left and right, and a glass-paned door at the far end, with the stenciled words "Dr. Robert Shrek." Mr. Knight turned into the first room on the right.

The room was small and clinical. Liz's mom, the spitting image of Liz with an extra thirty years on her, sat in the corner. She looked up as the four of them entered. She was dark-skinned, but had her daughter's piercing green eyes. She mustered a smile as they entered.

Aside from two chairs, the only other furniture was the bed where Liz was spread out, leather straps pinning down her arms and legs. Liz stared straight at the ceiling with cold, glazed eyes. Her head turned slowly to the newcomers, and her eyes fell on Gretchen and Amber. They waved.

"Hey, sweetie. How you feeling?" Gretchen asked.

Liz shuddered and ignored the question. Her gaze moved to Jay and Colin. She studied Jay for a moment and her eyes narrowed shrewdly.

"Do—do any of these people look familiar to you?" Mr. Knight asked his daughter. He nudged Amber and Gretchen toward Liz's bed.

"Oh my God, Liz," Amber whispered. "Are you okay? You *freaked out* in the middle of A-Court."

"It's, like, major news," Gretchen sympathized.

Liz laid her head back on her pillow and chuckled. Mr. and Mrs. Knight exchanged looks. Liz muttered something under her breath, and Mr. Knight leaned in to better hear.

"Dr. Shrek!" he yelled.

Two seconds later, Dr. Shrek, a short man with a lined face, rounded into the room.

"What's propofol?" Mr. Knight asked.

Dr. Shrek squinted. "She's asking for propofol?"

"Yeah. Did you give her some?"

"No. Propofol is a heavy sedative."

Amber whispered to Gretchen, "The stuff Michael Jackson uses."

Dr. Shrek stared at Liz. "How does she know what propofol is?"

Mr. Knight teared up. "She's a straight-A student, Doc."

Dr. Shrek handed Mr. Knight a Squeezeit with a small straw. "Here, I brought this for her blood sugar."

Mr. Knight held it up to Liz's lips. Liz took a sip, and then her head fell back onto her pillow.

"Berry B. Wild," she said, giggling.

Liz's mom stood and ushered the four of them to the door. "Let's give her some space, Dad."

Mr. Knight shook his head. "I don't know what else to do. We'll call if anything changes."

Amber and Gretchen hugged Mrs. Knight while Jay and Colin waited.

When they were outside, Jay turned to Amber and Gretchen. "How can we help?"

Amber sniffed. "Ugh, God, stop already. You're not her friend, you know."

Jay stood, stung, as the girls returned to the waiting room. Colin put a hand on Jay's shoulder. "You want to stay?"

Jay shook his head. "Nah."

All the elation he'd felt the day before was gone. He maneuvered through trucks, beelining for the Batmobile.

"What are you guys doing here?"

His stomach knotted. It was Jeremy. Jay tried to move faster, but two bodies blocked him. John B and John H stood between two cars, arms crossed. Jay stared up at their sneering faces and Champion T-shirts.

Jeremy's voice came from behind him.

"I said, *what are you doing?*"

Jay rounded on him. He saw Jeremy's jaw was set and his fists bunched. He instinctively lowered his eyes.

"Checking on Liz," he muttered. "She asked me to prom."

"Oh yeah. I heard. I didn't realize you two were so close."

John B snickered. "Maybe asking Jay out sent her over the edge."

The other Johns laughed. Jeremy gave Jay a shove.

"You know, you look like Screech from *Saved by the Bell*?"

Jay raised his eyes. All fourteen Johns were leaning languidly on trucks. They had the tailgate of John H's Chevy dropped, and three of them sat on it. They reminded Jay of vultures. He scanned the parking lot for Principal Oatman or Sheriff Jenkins, but it was otherwise empty. Colin was staring straight at the ground, as if that could render him invisible. Jeremy's hand shot out and he ripped Jay's backpack from his shoulders. His eyes gleamed as he held it up for Jay.

"First you come to A-Court. Now you're visiting Liz in the hospital. It feels like we're going round and round till graduation. You don't learn, do you? How many times do we gotta do this?"

He unzipped the book bag and turned it upside down. Binders and pencils clattered onto the pavement. Floppy disks rained down atop his new *Serious Gamer* magazine. Before Jay could stop him, Jeremy's distressed leather boot lifted into the air and slammed down on the disk pile. Jay watched in horror as Jeremy ground the heel into the disks.

"Noooo!"

"That's what happens when you leave the computer lab," one of the Johns jeered.

"C'mon," Jeremy muttered, and they all shuffled off, leaving Jay on the ground, picking through all his squashed disks. He held up the *Populous* disk. It had split completely apart, its plastic separating into two jagged wings. All three of his *SimCity* disks were bent at ugly degree angles, with angry white creases down their centers.

Jay thought of his poor Poopville. Never again would he rebalance its budget or receive another accolade from the in-game newspaper. He stared after Jeremy and the Johns, wishing an earthquake would swallow them up.

THE TROUBLE
WITH JEREMY

JEREMY SAT ALONE on his bed, looking down at the floor. His room was the size of an entire trailer in the La Dulce Vita trailer park. It had its own balcony, with a separate door on the second floor of the house. Up there were his free weights and a stereo with his workout music: usually Guns N' Roses or Garth Brooks, depending on his mood. The walls were adorned with sports paraphernalia: A Scottie Pippen jersey, a Mariners banner, a signed ball from Randy Johnson that his parents had somehow gotten him. The room was filled with light from the large windows overlooking the Skookullom River far down below. The room felt cheery and light, which was the exact opposite of how Jeremy felt.

He had a problem. Well, several problems. The first and most obvious was that his on-again, off-again girlfriend was laid up in the closest thing Bickleton had to a hospital, with no memory of him. It was like something out of a bad soap opera. They had fought about something stupid. Jeremy had given Gretchen a ride home after cheerleading practice, and he'd brushed her knee with his hand. That was all it was—a brush!—but Liz had been furious. She'd broken up with him, the week before prom. It had taken him two flower deliveries during third period, plus an apology cake from the Golden Flour Bakery to smooth things over. Not only had he managed to win Liz back for prom, but he'd also gotten her to agree to his practical joke.

And now she couldn't remember any of that. When he saw her in her hospital bed earlier, and she looked at him, he saw spite in her eyes. Or was it indifference? Either way, it left him cold. Whatever was ailing Liz, he had to find a way through it before prom.

The second problem was much more serious: Jay Banksman. This was not something he could admit to anyone. He could barely admit it to himself. Ever since he could remember, he'd been afraid of Jay.

Somehow, since he was very young, Jay had inserted himself inside Jeremy's brain. He had wormed his way in, and Jeremy could not get him to leave. In the deep recesses of Jeremy's mind was a terrible image of himself, chained in a dark dungeon, surrounded by menacing black figures. In this vision, Jay stood over him. Except he wasn't the Jay who shared Jeremy's high school. He was big—taller than Jeremy—with thick, rippling muscles. He wore what looked like a suit of medieval armor, and he held a dark, cruel sword with a dual tip. Evil Jay would thrust his sword into Jeremy's chest and twist the end until Jeremy screamed in pain and humiliation.

It had plagued him his whole life, long enough that he'd eventually learned to control it. When he was younger, his mind would sometimes wander to that terrible dungeon, and he'd feel an intense fear he didn't understand. He would shut his eyes and chew his knuckles till they bled, the physical pain washing the image from his mind. Eventually, he learned to keep his thoughts of the dungeon at bay, but his fear of Jay remained. He hated Jay, and wanted nothing more than to destroy him.

Lately, the fear was getting stronger again. When he saw Jay in the hallway between classes, he could feel the terror trying to break free from the restraints he'd created. One wrong move and it could slip to the forefront, overtake him, send him into a helpless mess before his friends. He hated Jay just as much as he feared him.

He flexed and unflexed his knuckles and looked out his wide window. The wind had picked up, shaking the buds on the almond trees outside their house. He didn't want Jay eventually working down at the mill. He didn't want Jay in Bickleton at all. Someway, somehow, he needed to get him out for good.

DARK HOUSE

THE RECLUSE LIKED cramped space. He liked how the boxes lining the walls pushed in on either side. It made him feel like a creature in a tunnel. Cats, he knew, used their whiskers to map 3D space, so they could move quickly without having to use their eyes. Mole rats, too. Often he moved in darkness, preferring it to the light from the small desk lamps that hung like vultures from the tops of his boxes.

Today, however, the Recluse flipped a power strip and a web of white Christmas lights sparkled across the ceiling.

"Hrmmm."

He moved into his tiny kitchen, opening the fridge and pulling out mayonnaise and mustard, two slices of bread, a bag of deli meat, and a neatly folded bag of Chili Cheese Fritos. He carefully made his sandwich, cutting it into squares, and carried it back to the dining room table. He set his plate down, walked over to a stack of boxes, and pulled out a hardback book with orange and black swirls on the cover. Bickleton High School Yearbook. Its glossy cover was smudged with use and covered in dirty fingerprints. The Recluse flipped through with interest, studying each creased page with beady eyes as he chewed dainty bites.

Suddenly, he froze. The air in his house was utterly still. But unmoving, he sat, listening. Down the hall, three rooms away, a small, piercing whine arose. The Recluse stood, pulled a wet wipe from a box on the counter, and toweled off his fingers. He lumbered down the narrow corridor and squeezed through the far doorway into the bedroom.

It was a small bedroom. By the door, a futon couch lay open as a bed. A thin blanket and sheets were fastidiously made up, but the pillowcase was greasy and disheveled. The single window had a shade pulled; the room's only illumination came from the giant computer looming on a large oak desk. Three monitors issued dark blue light, casting the room in shadow. A giant PC, encased in glass, towered over the monitors, its innards flashing with small colored lights. The computer emitted a soft beep, and the Recluse studied it intently. Then he took a seat and peered into the screen.

DESPERATE
MEASURES

COLIN'S HOUSE WAS several times larger than Jay's, styled after a traditional hacienda, but painted dark to blend in with the winter moss. Built into the side of a gentle slope, its huge windows faced south, so that all three of its stories caught both sunrise and sunset. Colin and his sister Anya slept on the second story, but the finished basement had remained Colin's "playroom," evolving along with Colin's tastes. The bins of Legos and action figures had been shoved away to make room for Super Nintendo and Sega Genesis controllers.

One by one, Jay tossed his broken games into a metal trash can while Richard Simmons's voice blared from the television as he jumped in purple spandex.

"Goddamnit," he muttered, fighting back tears. "I spent at least a hundred bucks on these games. Think I can sue?"

He threw the last disk in the trash. Colin plucked it out.

"What are you doing?"

Colin examined it. It was *The Build*. The game Jay had gotten in his *Serious Gamer* magazine.

"This one's not so bad," Colin murmured.

Jay took it from him and examined the painful-looking crease in the plastic. Colin was right, though. It wasn't nearly as bad as the others.

"Try unbending it?" Colin offered.

"Wish we had a RadioShack."

"I bet . . . I bet Stevie could fix it?" Colin blushed.

Jay sat on the sofa, head in hands. If anybody could fix the disk, it was Stevie, but the thought of her smug smile made Jay want to yank his eyeballs out of his head. But he had to agree, she was the best hope they had.

"Sure. Whatever. What do we have to lose?"

Still blushing, Colin dialed.

"Um, hello? Stevie?"

Colin laid out their problem, and Jay listened carefully. Through the line, he could hear Stevie growing more and more excited.

The next day at school, however, Stevie hardly bothered to look at their disk. All morning, Jay tapped his foot, glaring as she cheerfully ignored him to focus on her workload. At lunch, she had overdue library books, and then she had to check on the Cornish game hens in the horticulture field. The more urgent Jay's glare, the bigger her smile. Finally, in fourth period, she laid her pencil down and grinned.

"Okay, I'm ready."

He and Colin crowded behind her as she took her seat before the computer, grabbed their disk, and ripped off its metal safety shutter.

Jay shrieked so loudly, the rest of the class turned.

"Relax," Stevie assured him. "All it does is keep dirt out."

"Yeah," Jay retorted, "but now dirt's gonna get in!"

"It's fine. We're making a copy."

She inserted the disk and began a file scan. She clucked at what she saw, and Jay leaned in, wishing he'd spent less time gaming and more time learning to code.

She pulled a fresh disk from her backpack.

"On the house." She winked.

A few more moments clicked by, then she spun around and handed the new disk to Jay.

"There you go."

Jay looked at her in awe. "It works?"

She smiled. "It might!"

Jay shoved in the new disk, and the monitor filled with *The Build* load animation: the pixelated pastoral scene of a small town nestled in the mountains. Jay fist-pumped and cheered, earning a stern "Shh" from Ms. Rotchkey. The title rolled across the front of the load screen, and in the lower left-hand corner, next to the copyright, was some text he hadn't noticed before: IN BETA V0.84.

Jay frowned. "Huh. Still in beta."

A small window popped up in the center of the screen: DO YOU WANT TO LOAD POOPVILLE? YES/NO.

Jay clicked YES. The title screen flashed, and they were staring at a top-down map of a small pixelated house. The screen was centered on a tiny bathroom, and in a small shower stood a girl of no more than sixty pixels, all a uniformly tan color.

Jay choked. "She's naked."

Colin turned away, bright red. "What kind of game is this?"

Jay moused over the girl until a name popped up: LIZ KNIGHT. BELOW THAT, THERE WERE BOXES OF STATISTICS. STRENGTH: 5. SPEED: 6. HIT POINTS: 5. INTELLIGENCE: 8. Colin refused to look at the screen.

"It's like *Leisure Suit Larry*. We shouldn't be playing this at school."

"It's, uh, very thorough for a world-building game." Jay coughed.

Jay zoomed out to see he was looking at a house sitting a few blocks away from a market and a park. It looked familiar.

"Dude. This is Bickleton."

Colin squinted, and Jay zoomed out a few more clicks. Sure enough, there was the town hall, the main drag, and the Skookullom River cutting its way through the west half of town. All perfectly pixelated.

"Is this a joke?"

Colin frowned. "Scroll up to the school."

Jay scrolled until the screen rested on the Bickleton campus. There was no motion, except for the undulating animation of swaying trees. A tiny, pixelated figure stepped out of the C-Court doorway and walked toward A-Court.

Jay clicked and a window popped up.

DEREK DECKFORD. STRENGTH: 3. SPEED: 3. HIT POINTS: 3. INTELLIGENCE: 6.

Colin frowned. "Wait . . . is everyone in there?"

Jay scrolled over the dense pines to their portable. He zoomed in until the trees gave way and their roof disappeared to reveal a bird's-eye view of their room. A tiny pixelated figure sat in a beanbag chair. Two more pixelated figures leaned over a chessboard. And in the far corner were another two pixelated figures, one big and one small, crouched over a computer.

Jay raised his hand. After a moment's delay, Jay's onscreen avatar held up its hand.

"Oh my—"

A voice came from behind them. "What's that?"

Jay jumped up and ejected the disk. The screen crashed with a gray error message, and Jay spun around to find Stevie behind them.

"Oh, uh . . . n-nothing. The game is, uh, better than new, actually. There's a new patch; I didn't recognize some stuff."

She beamed. "Can I see?"

Colin shrank back, panicking. "Well . . ."

"The disk broke," Jay quickly lied.

Stevie frowned. "But you just said it was better than new?"

Before Jay could answer, the school bell rang. The class erupted from their seats and poured out of the portable. Jay shoved the disk back into its case and hurried past a confused-looking Stevie. As he and Colin trudged down the ramp, Jay whispered to his friend.

"Okay, so that game is definitely not a *SimCity* rip-off."

Colin shook his head. "How could it know who everyone is?"

Jay was thinking the same thing.

"It's gotta be a practical joke. I mean, your *Serious Gamer* couldn't have come with that disk. Someone knew it was my birthday, and they slipped that plastic cover over my magazine and added that disk."

"That's a lot of work for a practical joke."

Jay looked away. And what, exactly, was the punch line?

AFTER CAREFUL CONSIDERATION

JAY, GRATEFUL FOR a distraction from the dual issue of Liz and Todd, was still puzzling over his strange new game when he returned home. The potbellied stove blazed in the corner, and the house smelled of pine smoke. The sizzle of bacon came from the kitchen, and he paused to flip through the mail on the counter, plucking out the latest issue of *Game Informer*. Bubsy in *Claws Encounters of the Furred Kind* was on the cover.

He snorted. "I got this issue last month!"

He flipped through the magazine, shaking his head as he recognized all the Gameboy and Game Genie ads.

"Real sloppy."

In the living room, the small TV played *America's Funniest Home Videos*. Jay glanced up as Bob Saget stared ruefully at his animated cartoon sidekick, Stretchy McGillicuddy.

"Don't get a little touchy, Bob, I'm just a little stretchy!"

The screen erupted in canned laughter.

"Jay?" his mom called from the kitchen.

Jay was looking over a double spread for *Flintstones*, *T2: The Arcade Game*, and *Sunset Riders*, trying to see if there were any differences at all.

"Yeah, Mom," he called absentmindedly.

"There's something I want to show you."

He looked up. His mom's bushy hair was still in curlers, and her makeup was only half-finished, which he knew meant she was going to Chips poker later. The smell of Winston cigarettes was stronger than usual, and he saw she had one in her hand. She grinned triumphantly, a hand on her hip.

Jay cocked an eyebrow. "Why are you being weird?"

"Sit down, sit down."

She motioned to the dining room table. Jay was surprised to see it was cleared of all the bills, stacks of magazines, and other junk that was usually strewn across it. Instead, there was a stack of pancakes, some bacon, and a grapefruit. Jay frowned.

"We making a Fruity Pebbles commercial? What's with the complete breakfast?"

His mom pulled a stack of envelopes from behind her back.

"You've got *maillll.*"

Jay's heart stopped. He knew immediately what the envelopes had to be. He plopped down into his chair and wordlessly accepted the envelopes. There were six in all. Six different stamps. Six colleges. The room was silent, except for another bout of canned laughter from the TV.

"I almost opened them," his mom giggled. "To stop myself, I called Pam again."

Pam was his mom's personal psychic. Mrs.Banksman discovered her in a television infomercial that blasted the airwaves with 1-900-PSYCHIC. She cost them ninety-nine cents a minute to talk with, so Kathy used her sparingly, although not as sparingly as Jay would have liked.

He lifted the top envelope. It was thin and light, from Western University. He carefully inserted an index finger, cracked the seal, and pulled out a letter. His mom held her hand to her mouth. Jay scanned it, reading aloud:

"'After careful consideration, we regret to inform you that we are unable to offer you a spot in our freshmen class of 1993 . . .'"

Jay's voice trailed off. His mom's face went pale, but she quickly recovered.

"Open another!"

Jay grabbed the envelope from Portland College and tore into it.

"'After careful consideration, we regret to—'"

He ripped open the rest.

"'We regret. We regret. We regret. We regret.'"

He laid the letters side by side on the table. His mom read each one silently. In the other room, Jay heard the TV: "Hey, lady, your cat's on fire!"

"I don't believe this," his mom muttered. "I thought for certain . . . Ms. Rotchkey seemed sure . . ."

"I should have listened to Miss Molouski," Jay muttered.

"Oh, hon." She wrapped her arms around his neck. "We should have applied to more schools. Maybe we still can? I'm gonna talk to Miss Molouski—"

Jay shook his head. "Don't bother."

His mom was rereading the letters. "The community colleges rejected you? How is that possible? You've got a 3.7 GPA. Any college would be glad to have you."

"Except the six I applied to, apparently."

His mom strode to the kitchen, wiping her hands. "I'm gonna call."

Jay grabbed a piece of bacon off the plate next to the stove and chewed it. In the back of his mind, he'd feared Ms. Rotchkey would be wrong. And even though he'd tried to prepare himself for this moment, he felt sick to his stomach.

He heard his mom talking into the phone. "Hello, I'd like to speak to the admissions off—"

His mom slammed the receiver down. "Everything's automatic! 'If you'd like to speak to admissions, please press one.' How am I supposed to do that on a rotary phone? Why can't things just be easy for once?"

But Jay's eyes had begun to glaze. For the last four years, he'd kept every part of his being focused on college. It was his single road out of the hopeless despair that was Bickleton. That road was crumbling. A future he'd never permitted himself to contemplate rose all around him. He watched his mom yell angrily into the phone and saw himself there, doing the same thing for his own son; thirty years would pass in the blink of an eye. The truth of what Ms. Molouski had said hit him: there truly was no escaping Bickleton.

DARK HOUSE

THE RECLUSE HAD lived alone in his house for many years. He'd long given up caring about its poor, dilapidated exterior. It was an old house, with chipping paint and birds' nests under the rafters. He knew the people of Bickleton called him a hoarder, but he rarely interacted with them anyway, preferring the claustrophobic comfort of his tiny corridors. Among the five rooms, he spent nearly all his time in the bedroom with his computer, where he now stood, breathing heavily, listening. The machine gave out a small whine. The Recluse moved his head closer to it, his breath fogging the glass case. He ran his small palm through the air next to it, feeling for heat. He jiggled the mouse, and the harsh light of the monitor awoke, shining out over the room.

He leaned forward until his belly hung over the keyboard, then grabbed the mouse and twirled open a series of windows. Then he straightened, nodding approvingly, and clicked the monitors back into darkness. The whine continued as the Recluse drifted back through the corridor of cardboard boxes, and into the dining room.

The hallway branched left, but the Recluse did not look in that direction. There was something intentional in the way he trained his gaze to remain steadily forward. As if he were purposefully avoiding whatever was at the end of the hall. The thing he refused to look at was a wood-paneled door with a single dead bolt. Its shiny golden brass fresh and—should anyone look closely—covered in wood shavings, as though recently installed.

Under this door, waves of black wires cut rivulets through the shag carpet. They ran the hall, strung together by zip ties, and they finally ducked into the computer room. The Recluse purposefully stepped over the flood of wires, his face flushed imperceptibly. He looked, for a moment, like a little boy up to no good.

Then he was in the kitchen, and the door lay still, quiet, and forgotten.

LIZ AND JEREMY

WHEN JAY SLIPPED into Tutorial the next morning, he found the whole class in a state of shock. The other seniors were a wreck, faces red with tears, bodies slouched on desks, cheeks lying on Bakelite slabs. One girl was slumped in her chair, eyes unfocused on the ceiling. Everyone, it seemed, had received their rejection letters. All hope of college had been wiped out in an evening.

Jay moved to the class computer, but Ms. Rotchkey cleared her throat. At the front of the class, she seemed to be having as hard of a time as any of them. Her gray skin sagged in the morning light. The first bell rang, and she turned to address them.

"I've spoken with most of you already, but I take it from the expressions I'm seeing that no one got into college?"

Silence.

"Well . . ." Her voice cracked. "I want you to know how proud I am of you. Not getting into college is not a reflection on your abilities. It's a reflection of this town. The Bickleton Curse is real. When graduation commences, I encourage each of you to find a way to leave, one way or another. Move to Portland. Seattle. Go to Paris, Budapest, or—"

Ms. Rotchkey stopped, unable to finish.

Lunchtime came, and Jay pulled his Lunchables tray from his bag and went for a walk. He reached the edge of the trees surrounding Tutorial and scanned the courtyard. There was a smattering of students on the grass, bundled against the breeze as they picnicked. The usual C-Court crowd. He hiked up the hill to the library, and sat on the steps, where he could see the comings and goings. He opened his Lunchables tray, pulled out crackers, cheese, and a slimy piece of ham, and folded them into a sandwich.

A young woman with puffy hair and shoulder pads, who he recognized as an office assistant, ran the sidewalk in short heels. Three kids in cowboy hats and Dickies sauntered to A-Court. A kid was thrashing wildly, dancing to an invisible song, laughing:

"Slam dancing is a way of life!"

Jay shook his head, disgusted. Then a voice came from behind him.

"We thought we were so cool."

He spun round. Standing under the library awning, cigarette in hand, was Liz. There were dark circles under her eyes as she scanned the grass. Jay saw she had a choker necklace on and looked drawn and pale, which somehow made her seem even more romantic. Jay gulped.

"You're back?"

She didn't respond.

"You smoke?"

"I do now."

"Um . . ." Jay stared at the cigarette in her hand. "If Miss Shirell catches you smoking, she's gonna send you to Mr. Oatman. Do you . . . remember that?"

Liz took a drag and regarded him coldly. "I remember everything."

"Do you . . . remember what happened before they took you to the hospital? Like, the assembly, when they told us Todd was gone? And after? At the Bickleton Creamery?"

She stared at him, taking another drag.

"You remember you, um . . . you asked me to prom."

Liz looked mildly surprised, then muttered, "Yeah, I remember."

She turned her gaze to the sky.

"So, is that what this is about?"

Jay looked back at the library to see whether Ms. Shirell was around, in case Liz was about to have another breakdown.

The doors to A-Court clanged and Jeremy strode out, with his sea of Johns following.

"Liz!" he shouted. "Hey, Liz!"

"That's Jeremy," began Jay, hurriedly. "You guys used to date, but you don't like him anymore."

"I know Jeremy." Liz lowered her cigarette and shouted, "What do you want?!"

"What are you doing there? Why don't you come eat with me in A-Court?"

Liz didn't respond immediately, but took another drag off her cigarette, eyeing Jeremy.

"Come on. Come talk to me. Want to go for a ride in the Miata? Relive some old memories?"

A few of the Johns snickered. Liz's face remained unperturbed.

"A ride where?"

"What?!" Jay whispered. "Don't go with him. He's the worst."

Jeremy shrugged. "Wherever."

Liz tossed her cigarette into the grass and bounded down the steps. "Sure. Let's go."

Jeremy glanced at the Johns, who shrugged in surprise.

"Where do you want to go?"

"Out of town."

The pod turned and headed to A-Court. Jay called after Liz, desperate to keep her from leaving. But they were already gone. Jay turned. He might not be able to follow them—but he could watch them just the same.

DISASTER

JAY PUSHED THROUGH the Tutorial door right as the third-period bell rang. He froze. Stevie was hunched over the computer. Sandwich crusts and an apple core sat on the desk beside her. Her eyes were glued to the ViolaWWW browser.

"Stevie. I need the computer."

"Did you know the new Pentium processors are sixty-six megahertz?"

Jay eyed Ms. Rotchkey. She was reading a dog-eared copy of *Naked Lunch* and making notes in the margin. Jay lowered his voice.

"I'll give you my free period tomorrow, plus the day after, plus the day after that, if I can use the computer right now."

Stevie smiled, considering.

Jay added, "And I'll let you borrow a game."

"*Wizardry 7*?"

"Yes. Fine. Deal." Jay pushed Stevie out of her seat and climbed in.

He pulled out *The Build* and felt a pair of eyes on him. He turned to see Stevie still standing there, beaming. He caught Colin's eye and gave him a pointed look. Colin's cheeks turned pink, and without looking at Stevie, he turned awkwardly toward her.

"Game of chess?"

"Oh, uh, sure," Stevie allowed herself to be led her away.

Jay loaded the game and Poopville appeared. He opened a search bar and typed in "Jeremy McKraken." The screen jumped to where the trees followed a thin brown road and a small red car. Jay clicked on the car, and a window flashed up with the text MIATA. In the seats sat two pixelated figures.

Jay zoomed out. They were next to Rock Ridge. Ninety percent of all Bickleton makeout sessions happened at Rock Ridge, if rumors were true.

Jay felt a hurried desperation well up inside him. He clicked on Jeremy. Beside his statistics was a gridded inventory screen with icons: BLANKET X1. CANDLES X3. BOONES FARM X3. CONDOM X1. Inside the parked car, the pixelated figures faced each other. Jeremy leaned in, and a small pixelated heart appeared.

Jay's heart raced. He had to do something to stop them. He moused around the screen, searching. He opened the menu and scrolled over to a submenu labeled DISASTERS. A drop-down list read:

FIRE

FLOOD

AIR CRASH

TORNADO

EARTHQUAKE

MONSTER

HURRICANE

RIOTS

Jay sent a tornado.

Instantly, the Tutorial lights flickered. The window darkened, and a crack of thunder shook the room. Wind howled so loudly that kids leapt up from their desks and looked left and right over their shoulders. The pine trees outside whipped back and forth so fiercely, they scratched the glass panes with their gnarled branches.

"Kids," Mrs. Rotchkey said to the students who'd gathered around the single window, "get away from the glass."

Leaves and pine needles were ripped from the forest floor, blowing past the window at an alarming rate. Jay turned to the computer screen. A small brown funnel appeared over the trees of Rock Ridge. As it moved, it turned them into patches of barren ground. Jay watched the pixelated versions of Jeremy and Liz rush out of the Miata and dash up Barnett Road. There was a pop as the tornado lifted and then touched down on Jeremy's Miata. The car disappeared.

"Oh my God," Jay whispered.

Colin bustled over to Jay and saw Jeremy's and Liz's avatars hurry into the forest.

White flashed over the walls, followed by a bright burst as the lights shut off. The computer went black, and the kids began to scream in the dim light. Ms. Rotchkey was ushering them under their desks. Then she was behind him, pulling him away from the computer. Jay popped out the play disk and crawled underneath his desk. Outside, the wind screamed louder, and the door to the classroom shivered as if someone were trying to burst in. Ms. Rotchkey yelled over it.

"It's okay. Just a storm. I've got some candles in my desk."

Colin's tremendous head and shoulders stuck under his desk. His eyes were wide as saucers.

Jay shrieked over the wind, hands on his ears, "What is on that disk!?"

DISK
THREE

DARK HOUSE

THE RECLUSE WAS just settling into one of two padded chairs in his dining room when a wave of sound blasted the walls of his house. Deep, pounding bass and the squeal of guitars shattered his quiet world. His face turned red, and his breaths came short and ragged as he shot a worried glance down the dark hall to his computer room.

He forgot about his lunch and stomped over to a curtain-draped window in the living room. A table with a mess of VHS tapes—*Teenage Mutant Ninja Turtles*, *Backdraft*, the fourth season of *America's Funniest Home Videos*—stood before a dusty GE television, rabbit ears bent sideways.

The Recluse carefully lifted the curtain. Blinding sunlight spilled over the shaggy carpet. He squinted at the yellow Mustang in the neighbors' driveway. Its windows were down, its frame jittering and vibrating with each squeal of bass. A pear-shaped buffoon peeled himself from the driver's seat, and a second man, taller and covered in tattoos, strolled from the garage door. They exchanged a complicated handshake.

"Idiots!" the Recluse hissed. His neighbors disappeared from view.

The Recluse stood, shaking with rage. Since his neighbors had moved in six months ago, their noise was constant. The cardboard boxes that lined his walls weren't enough to dampen the sound. The neighbors partied late into the night, laughing, terrible music molesting him until the wee hours of morning. It was unacceptable. If there were someone to complain to, he would have complained. But the town's lazy sheriff didn't seem to care about such simple things as law and order.

He watched the Mustang vibrate with every blast of bass, then let the curtain fall back into place. He waited for his eyes to readjust to the darkness. His mind raced with a dozen ways he could punish his neighbors, humiliate them. He would figure out some strategy. He always did. He was smarter than everyone in Bickleton. He would have his revenge. If there was one thing he'd learned, it was patience.

AFTERMATH

NESTLED IN THE Cascade Range, Bickleton had ice storms, floods, and occasional volcano warnings. But there were no records in the town archive of the town ever experiencing a tornado. Tornados were something to be watched on news channels, wreaking havoc in far-off states like Kansas or Oklahoma.

The whole incident had lasted no more than ten minutes, when a wind funnel touched down outside La Dulce Vita trailer park, beating a trail of destruction through the Jewett Basin and into Rock Ridge, knocking over power lines, destroying Jeremy's car, and disappearing as suddenly as it had arrived.

Jay had left school early to find his house without power. Mrs. Ramirez had been there helping his mother pack so Jay and Kathy could spend the weekend at their place. Now, safe in Colin's basement with the screen flashing through glimpses of *Secret of Mana*, the boys were free to discuss what had happened.

Jay went over it again and again, probing Colin's perspective.

"Could it be a coincidence?" Colin shrugged.

Jay felt like throttling his friend.

"Yes, it's a coincidence," he replied sarcastically. "The storm just happened to hit the moment I clicked."

"If it's not a coincidence, then what is it?"

Jay didn't respond. He'd been thinking of nothing else for the last five hours. The idea that it could be a practical joke no longer fit: there was no one in Bickleton who possessed the programming power to pull something like that off. Back in his sophomore year, he'd been obsessed with *A Book of Dreams*, which he'd found on a shelf in Tutorial. It detailed the process of cloudbusting, and how government officials had tried to harness the power to control weather. Was it possible that *The Build* had been created by the government as an attempt to control the weather? To control reality itself?

He could hear his mom's voice upstairs. He laid down his controller and crept to the base of the stairs, training his ear to the murmurs.

Nobody had died, it seemed, which was a relief. And though he couldn't figure out how it'd happened, Jay couldn't shake the feeling that he was responsible for the storm. The thought of people dying at his hands was too much for him.

The destruction was bad enough. The east end of La Dulce Vita trailer park had been entirely destroyed, the tornado having peeled the roofs from some mobile homes and completely flattening others. The family's wooden skiff had been lifted from their front lawn and hurled through the parlor window of the Davises' house.

He focused his attention on the moms' conversation when it turned to Todd. Had Todd still been hiding down near Rock Ridge? Could he be an unconfirmed casualty of the storm? Ms. Rotchkey's search for Todd was being joined by the official efforts of Sheriff Jenkins.

Jay beckoned Colin to the base of the stairs. His chest felt tight. "What if Todd was down there? What if I killed him?"

Colin sighed. "You didn't cause that storm."

They arrived at the Morning Market parking lot ten minutes before noon to find it swarming with people. Ms. Rotchkey emerged with a mug of steaming coffee, and five other Tutorial kids in tow. Sheriff Jenkins stood with a map spread out across the hood of his car, surrounded by two dozen of Bickleton's most prominent families. With a touch of resentment, Jay noted that neither Jeremy nor the Johns were present.

Someone blew a whistle, and then they were marching back behind the Morning Market to where the big leaf maples extended their fresh canopy over Jewett Creek. As they headed down the steep hill, the trees quickly gave way to sunshine, and the search party stared in awe at the devastation.

Poplar and alder trees had been ripped straight from the muddy spring earth. Jewett Creek was half-buried in branches and ran brown with mud. It looked like something out of the trailers for the upcoming movie *Gettysburg*. The dense group pushed forward, shouting Todd's name. Jay held back, staring at the apocalyptic landscape. Was Todd's body lying under one of the fallen trees? Had he just been hiding down there the whole time? And if he'd died, was Jay responsible? Colin was standing next to him. His face registered none of Jay's turmoil.

From off to the left, someone whistled. Surrounded by charred branches was the burned carcass of a car. It lay on its side, away from any road, as though it had been flung through the woods. Both of its doors were gone, and its paint was burned so that its frame was a mix of white, red, and black. All its glass was missing. The searchers pushed forward, some caressing the blackened frame with their hands.

This had been what Jay wanted when he clicked the button. The destruction of Jeremy. And he'd come so close to succeeding. Jeremy had nearly died, and Liz along with him.

"Todd!" Jay bellowed, picking his way through the wreckage, shaken to his core.

THE HACK

THAT NO SIGN of Todd was found in the destruction brought Jay little relief. His every thought was consumed with *The Build*. He was next to certain that he had caused the tornado. But how? Should he tell Sheriff Jenkins? Or would the sheriff react like Colin, and think Jay was crazy? Of course he would. It *was* crazy. But then, how could it all be explained? It couldn't be a coincidence, no matter what Colin said.

It was Sunday night and half the town was still missing power, including the school. Which meant Jay had to suppress his burning desire to sneak back into Tutorial and boot up the disk. His mind ran in circles late into the night.

The next morning, the power—and school—were back on. His mom insisted on swinging by their house, so she dropped Jay and Colin off moments before the second bell. Jay rushed Colin straight to the Tutorial computer, tilting the monitor so no one else could see what they were doing.

Jay scrolled to Tutorial, where his tiny pixelated avatar sat at the computer.

He lifted his hand. A moment of lag ticked by, and then his onscreen avatar lifted its tiny arm.

"Does it work?"

Jay was startled to see Stevie standing over his shoulder.

"Yeah, the computer's fine," he grunted, annoyed.

"I was worried the storm might've caused a power surge." Stevie squinted at the screen. "Is that Bickleton?"

Jay flushed with annoyance. "Yes, this is the simulation I've been working on."

The last bell rang, and the class shuffled to their desks. Stevie remained rooted where she stood.

"Take your seats," Ms. Rotchkey called.

"Go on." Jay waved her away. "Take your seat."

Stevie smiled. "I can't. You're in it."

Jay stared at her. Then he remembered: he'd promised her the computer.

"Uhhh," he stalled. "Yeah, gimme a sec."

Colin shifted behind him. He could feel the class waiting on him. He clicked around.

"Jay . . ." Ms. Rotchkey called from the front.

"Just a sec!"

"Give Stevie the computer."

Jay clicked a folder. Dozens of other folders popped open, and he stared. There were vehicles. Weapons. Houses. He didn't have time to register everything. He clicked back, searching for something else to do, some other proof that his theory was correct. He clicked on a dollar sign icon at the top of the screen. Dollar amounts floated above everyone's heads in the room. $45.32 above his own. $739.11 above Colin's. $231.67 over Stevie's.

"Jay!" Ms. Rotchkey was marching toward him. "Leave that computer!"

"Just a minute!" Jay protested.

"Now!"

He clicked on his avatar and highlighted the $45 above his name. It was everything in his bank account. Below him, he felt the computer shiver. Ms. Rotchkey, he saw, was under the desk, grappling to unplug the power cord. He mashed a bunch of number keys and clicked SAVE. The screen spat back a message: SAVING . . .

He felt another tug and the cord popped from the wall. The computer went black. Ms. Rotchkey stood up, her face red. Jay could smell stale coffee on her breath. Jay quickly ejected his disk.

"What has gotten into you today?"

Jay took a deep breath. He had to tell her; he had to confess.

"Ms. Rotchkey, that storm on Friday—"

She cut him off. "Yes, and we don't need any more distractions. Now sit!"

Jay sat, his heart pounding. Stevie settled into the computer seat behind him, and he heard the computer boot back up. Ms. Rotchkey returned to the head of the class, shaking her head. Jay leaned close to Colin, his voice excitedly rising: "Don't make plans for lunch. I'll show you it wasn't a coincidence."

He searched Colin's face for a reaction, but his friend stared straight forward, as if he hadn't heard at all.

THE MARK

JAY TOOK A deep breath outside the Morning Market.

It was Bickleton's only grocery store, and one of two restaurants. It stood on the far end of a dusty parking lot, next to the town's library and single-lane bowling alley, its exterior chipped and yellow, with a faded sign of hand-painted letters. It had five aisles of canned beans, Twinkies, and potato chips, two produce islands, and a tiny meat market. If you ordered food from the cashier, there were tables and chairs toward the front to sit and eat, though mostly high school kids took their food to go. Everyone in town referred to it as "the Mark," and at lunchtime on a school day, the tables were packed with every kid who had a car.

Jay approached the storefront cautiously. He hadn't seen Jeremy or Liz since the tornado, and even though he'd heard they were both fine, he didn't want to run into either of them. He tried to peer through the Mark's windows, but they were covered in a faded poster of *Arachnophobia* and homemade signs.

"$200 reward for any info on the guy who stole my power sander. —Fred."

Jay stepped through the swinging front doors. His skin blossomed into goose bumps at the frigid air-conditioning. The Mark was as loud and bustling as A-Court, with the screams of unbound testosterone. Two kids pushed past Jay, and he saw Mindy Schultz sweating as she rang up jojos and beef sticks as fast as she could. A group of skaters sat at the nearest table, stoned and smirking. He passed a magazine rack with front pages screaming stories of Princess Diana and Prince Charles, Woody Allen and Mia Farrow, and a *Time* magazine with the headline "The Info Highway: Bringing a revolution in entertainment, news and communication." He saw four Johns at the deli counter. Jay slunk over to the ATM in the back corner and slipped in his Skookullom Credit Union. A prompt popped up onscreen. How much should he withdraw?

Jay took a deep breath and punched in $1,000.

It won't work, he thought. *It's too crazy.*

The machine blinked, whirred, and twenty-dollar bills dropped into the compartment below. Jay's eyes widened as the bills piled into a messy stack. He gathered the bills, mashing the wad into his back pocket, then he quickly glanced around. The cashier was leaning over the counter, apparently suspicious, trying to make out what had in his hands. Jay was about to go when an onscreen message caught his attention:

WOULD YOU LIKE TO CHECK YOUR BALANCE?

He pushed the Yes button.

There was a whir, and a white receipt printed. Jay grabbed it and inhaled sharply. His heart pounding, he touched the bulge of money in his pocket, forced his head down, and hustled from the store.

Colin was waiting in the Batmobile, seat reclined, staring blankly at the roof. Jay settled into the passenger seat, sweating. He pulled the contents from his pocket and put them onto the divider.

"A thousand bucks."

Colin looked down at the cash.

"And there's more." Jay showed Colin the receipt. Colin's eyes bulged at the balance.

$68,342.

"Yeah, right."

Jay waved a stack of twenties. "For real. Check it."

Colin's voice was slow and heavy. "You have to give it back."

"What do you want me to do? Stuff it in the ATM?"

"It's illegal."

"I mashed a bunch of keys on a keyboard. There's no law against that."

"Janet Reno will destroy us."

"Janet Reno!? You think Janet Reno would set foot in Cascadia?"

Jay was only paying Colin partial attention. His mind was grasping for possible explanations. For as much as he knew about video games, the internet was still a bit of a mystery. Could it connect computers to the very fabric of reality? That seemed unlikely. He thought of all the government conspiracies he'd ever heard.

"Someone's out there, Colin. Somehow, somewhere, some wires got crossed. *The Build* can tap into the real world. I think this is proof there's a God."

Colin gave an involuntary tremor. Jay continued.

"Einstein once said God doesn't play dice. But, Colin, what if God plays *SimCity*?"

Something strange was happening. Colin's forehead, which had been scrunched up as if he were in pain, suddenly relaxed. His breathing slowed, his eyes dilated. He straightened in the driver's seat, staring into the distance, as if no longer listening.

Jay waved his hand in front of Colin's face.

"Hello? Hey. Did you hear me?"

Colin was opening his door, stepping out into the parking lot.

Jay followed. "What are you doing?"

"Just getting some lunch," Colin said vaguely, moving toward the Mark.

"What about the sixty-eight thousand dollars? Do you not care about that?"

Colin turned to Jay, but his eyes were unseeing.

"I already have lunch money."

Jay put a hand on Colin's shoulder, trying to stop him, but it was like an invisible line was pulling Colin toward the Mark.

"Dude, are you okay? What's happening to you?"

Colin murmured, his gaze still slack.

"I just need . . . some lunch."

Then he disappeared through the doors of the Mark. Peering past the paper posters covering the glass, Jay could barely make out Colin's massive form heading to the deli counter.

Jay stared, thinking. It was as if Colin's memory had suddenly vanished. Had he had a stroke? It felt connected to the disk. But how?

THE LOTTERY

JAY DIDN'T WAIT for Colin to return. He ran the six blocks to his house, mind reeling. An Isuzu Trooper passed him, and Jay heard Tag Team's *Whoomp, There It Is* playing as the car headed for the Mark. The pulse of music made him dizzy.

The small dead end he lived on was empty: all the cars had been driven to work, including his mom's. He ran up the rickety steps on his front porch and burst through his front door. The house was still, except for the flies buzzing over the kitchen sink and TV, which was playing an interview between Kurt Loder and Neil Young.

He strode to the Garfield phone on the wall and dialed.

"Bickleton High School?" Ms. Shirell answered.

"Hi. Miss Rotchkey, please?"

"Who is this?"

"Jay Banksman."

Ms. Shirell sighed and recited her worn spiel: "If you're tardy to third period, we need a parent to call and we'll—"

Jay slammed down the receiver. The last thing he wanted to think about was the petty politics of high school. He had to tell someone else about the money, about the game. As if in answer to his thoughts, he heard the low guttural mutter of an engine outside. He peeked out a window to see his mom's Rabbit roll up. He watched her get out and struggle with the trunk, then haul out three plastic grocery bags. He ran out to help.

When she saw him, she frowned. "What are you doing home?"

"Something came up at school."

"Is the power back out?" She set plastic bags down in the kitchen. "I think we have a blown fuse; the bathroom light won't go on. Can you check the fuse box? Also, when you see Colin, ask him to ask his mom if I left *The Firm* at their house. I can't find it anywhere."

Jay followed, carrying bags of Kid Cuisine and Crystal Pepsi. She began sorting things into the fridge.

"Has the mail come? Our welfare check is late."

He fished into his pocket, pulled out his wad of cash, and put it down on the counter.

"Forget about welfare."

Kathy froze. "What's that?"

"What's it look like?"

She picked up the pile, staring at it. "Where'd it come from?"

Jay took a deep breath. A flood of thoughts and feelings swelled up inside him. He felt guilty for making such big changes so easily, excitement for what this money meant. And beneath everything else, fear swelled in his chest. Fear that instead of gaining control over the disk, he was losing it. His inability to explain what had happened to Liz, Todd, or Colin was eating away at him. If he told his mom, would she think he was crazy? Would she be right? He decided to lie.

"I, uh, I won the lottery."

"You . . . won the lottery?"

"Yep." Jay tried to smile. "On my birthday I–I bought a ticket down at the Mark."

A grin slowly creased the corners of Kathy's mouth. Then she screamed. "*We won? We won?*"

Jay nodded, encouraging, feeling his smile strain.

"Oh my God!" She screamed and reached for the Garfield phone. "First Liz Knight, now the lottery! God loves the Banksmans."

She stopped. "How much do we have?"

Jay shrugged, cagey. "Plenty."

His mom grabbed his shoulder and pulled him toward the door. "Let's go. Let's go buy stuff."

"I thought you'd want to tell everyone?"

"I want to buy stuff."

"Look, Mom." He peeled off six hundred dollars. "You get started. I have to go back to school. I just wanted to tell you the good news first."

His mom beamed at him in pride. "Oh my God. I'm gonna buy that armoire I've always wanted. Oh, I can get that ThighMaster from Suzanne Somers."

She grabbed her purse from the counter and ran back out the door, leaving Jay alone. His mind was racing. What if Liz wasn't the crazy one? What if *he* was crazy? He felt desperate to share the news with someone else. He grabbed his book bag and the rest of the money and ran back to school.

METAPHYSICS

C-COURT WAS MOSTLY deserted when Jay burst through the doors, winded. The drama room was open, and he saw a banner for the student-written play *The Pope Loves Sinead O'Connor* over its door. Jay peeked in to see a half-moon of chairs facing the chalkboard, where there was written in bold letters "Search for Todd, 1:00 p.m." The classroom was empty.

Down the hall, outside the journalism room, a small crowd had gathered. Jay saw journalism kids handing out yearbooks. Jay caught sight of Colin in the crowd, thumbing through pages, and made his way over.

"Colin. Colin!"

Colin looked startled to see him but gave a small grin. He closed the book and Jay saw the cover featured a yellow brick road, and a hand-drawn Jeremy McKraken in a leather jacket, standing next to a motorcycle and giving a thumbs-up. In big type, it said: "Bickleton High School '92–'93: You Are Here."

Colin read aloud the first page: "The theme of the year-book is *You Are Here*. This is a democratic yearbook; we wanted to represent everyone, regardless of grade, popularity, academics, and athletics."

Colin grunted. "Take a look at this . . ."

He thumbed over to the senior portraits. At the very end were two gray squares above the text: "Not pictured." Underneath were his and Colin's names.

"Great," Jay muttered. "Look, about the money. I know that came out of nowhere but—"

Colin looked at him blankly. "What are you talking about?"

"An hour ago? Do you not remember?"

Colin furrowed his brow. "In *Secret of Mana*?"

It was too much. Jay pushed past the crowd battling for year-books, toward a lone dirty door at the end of the corridor. The door opened, and Ms. Molouski escorted a disgruntled-looking freshman from her office. Jay saw her hair was thinner than ever, and deep lines were crisscrossing her face. When she saw Jay, she paused.

"Your eye's better."

Jay's hand went to his face. He'd almost forgotten about his black eye, so much had happened since then.

He stepped into her office, which was freezing, as always.

"I'm going crazy."

"If you're sane enough to self-reflect, you're not."

"I broke my best friend. The crazy stuff that's been happen-ing recently . . . I think I caused it. There's something wrong with reality."

"Jay, there are lots of things wrong with reality. We're on the verge of a war with Iraq. There's no end in sight to the Haitian refugees streaming into our country. If you want to change the world, I suggest you write President Clinton a letter—"

"No, no . . . not talking the sociopolitical reality. I'm talking ontological stuff. 'Cogito, ergo sum.' Immanuel Kant. Metaphysics."

"Sounds like you need a priest, not a guidance counselor."

"Either I'm going crazy, or everyone else is. I just took a thousand bucks out of the Mark ATM machine."

Ms. Molouski raised an eyebrow.

"And there's $68,000 more in my bank account."

Jay threw the money on her desk.

"Where'd you get that?"

"A disk. On Friday, I used it to summon a tornado. This morning, I filled up my bank account. Here, look."

He pulled out the ATM receipt and defiantly held it up for Ms. Molouski. He waited. She looked at the receipt and her gaze softened. Her eyes glazed over, pupils dilating. Jay watched the muscles in her jaw work.

"Miss Molouski?" Jay got up slowly from his chair.

She murmured something.

"Miss Molouski?!" he yelled, feeling a surge of dread. He backed away from her desk, out into the hall.

The crowd around the journalism room had dispersed, and he saw the journalism teacher and some students packing up boxes through the window. Otherwise, the campus was empty for third period. A cool sun was out, and a lonesome raven cawed from atop a budding oak tree. He turned to the cove of pine trees that hid Tutorial. The answer to whatever was happening was on that disk.

SUBFOLDERS

JAY WAITED IN the cold for several hours, careful not to be seen by teachers. A good fifteen minutes after the final bell had rung, he moved into the quiet of the Tutorial trees and paused to listen. Robins rustled in the dry pine needles, but no noise came from the classroom. Good. That meant they'd probably all gone. He swung a leg onto a low-hanging branch, and hauled himself up, peering through a window. It was dark and empty. Ms. Rotchkey, Jay knew, kept the window to her classroom unlocked. He pushed on the glass until the window slid open, then leaned in and tumbled onto the carpet inside.

He pictured how livid Ms. Rotchkey would be if she knew he'd broken into her classroom. His heart pounded. The closest he'd ever come to breaking the law was in eighth grade, when he and Colin had pretended to shoplift from the Morning Market. Being there without express teacher permission went against every bone in his body. He saddled up to the computer and slipped in his disk. *The Build* popped open, and Jay found himself staring at his pixelated avatar in the dark classroom.

There had to be some answer in the program. He clicked around, searching for clues. In the lower left-hand corner was v0.84. He tried clicking on that with no luck. He went to the top-line menu and scrolled down to ABOUT, then waited patiently while synthetic jazz pop played and the game credits rolled. He squinted at the screen. A list of names scrolled. LEAD DEVELOPER: HARRY BUTTS. ASSOCIATE PRODUCER: LONG WANG. KEY ARTIST: AMANDA HUGNKISS. A long list of joke names. He'd seen easter eggs in games before, but nothing like this. On the left-hand side of the screen were a dozen folders that did not come standard with *The Build*. He clicked one labeled CHARACTERS.

Pixelated figures cascaded down the screen. The figures were just big enough for Jay to make out backward baseball caps, denim, and blond hair. Underneath each were names: JOHN E, JOHN R, JOHN U, JOHN V. The list seemed to go on forever: an entire folder of Johns. Jay shuddered and dove into the CLOTHES folder. A wardrobe filled the screen. There was an entire folder dedicated to Lisa Frank. Another had baby-doll dresses and miniature backpacks. A third had pajama pants, Reebok Pumps, and overalls. Jay scrolled through.

He clicked on a pair of jean coveralls. They froze under his mouse cursor, and he found he could move them around. He dragged them into the digital classroom, over his desk, and released. The small coveralls appeared in the game. He spun around. There they were, lying rumpled over his desk. He tried it a few more times, dragging different items into the room. Combat boots. Blue windbreaker. Matching blue bucket hat. Oval sunglasses.

He opened the folder named LUXURY and his mouth dropped. There were hundreds of the most coveted icons in Bickleton. Miatas. Timex watches. Walkmans. Baskets of Hickory Farms cured meats. Gameboys. Game Gears. It was like every catalog of everything he'd ever dreamed about. He clicked open a subfolder called ARCADE GAMES. It was filled with games he'd only ever seen glimpses of in the back pages of his comic books. There was *Samurai Shodown, Metal Slug,* and *The Simpsons* arcade game.

"Oh my God," he whispered. But there was something he had to take care of first. The C-Court parking lot was still empty. He went back to the LUXURY folder, then dragged a Miata into the parking lot. A color palette popped up, and Jay selected BLUE. The car appeared on the map.

"Ha!"

He dragged luxury item after luxury item. He got himself a pocket watch and chain, a lacquered cane, a cerulean ascot, and a jeweled ring. He capped it off with another chunk of cash, twenty-five thousand dollars, sitting neatly across his new pile of clothes.

The wind picked up, bumping a tree branch into the portable, and Jay jumped, his heart pounding. This would have to do for the moment. He was no closer to answers, but he had a brand-new Miata to test out. He shut down *The Build*, ejected his disk, and clambered back out the window, sliding it carefully into place.

When he pushed his way out of the trees, the sun was touching the distant Cascade peaks, casting purple and orange shadows across the school. Dandelion seeds drifted through the air, and cottonwoods fluffs fell like snow. The only sound was the moo of Highland cattle. Jay stood on the edge of the parking lot, eyes bulging. There was his Miata: sleek, blue, top already down. Waiting. He walked carefully toward it, taking in every detail, and ran his hand over the paint. The keys were in the ignition. He slid in, appreciating the cool leather. He ran a hand over the seats and began to laugh. He had a Miata and Jeremy didn't. He brought a trembling hand to the ignition and turned. The car rumbled, its power quivering his limbs.

Jay yanked the shifter in reverse and unsteadily popped the clutch. He'd had a little practice driving the Batmobile. The car shot backward and Jay laughed again. He put it in first and the car immediately died. After several false starts of popping the clutch too early, Jay found himself zipping down Simmons Road, wind threatening to blow his new bucket hat off. He cornered onto Main Street so hard his tires squealed, and he screamed with delight. A Chevy truck blew by and Jay caught the incredulous glance of John W. Jay turned on the radio and switched it to 669 AM. A honey-sweet melody poured from his speakers. It was perfect, almost as if Marvelous Mark knew he was riding top down in a Miata. He pointed his car toward the main drag and gunned the engine.

THE WELL-HEELED HICK

JAY WOKE THE next morning to the Garfield phone ringing in his kitchen. He closed his eyes, willing his mom to pick it up. It stopped, then began ringing again. He slid out of bed, grumbling, still in his clothes from the night before. His mom's door was shut, and he was mildly surprised to see it was 10:37 a.m.

The living room was filled with his mom's purchases from the day before. There were two new stereo speakers in the living room, clothes draped over every chair, and a new credenza that almost blocked the front door. Jay was wondering how his mom had managed to get inside, when he picked up the receiver.

"Hullo?"

It was Ms. Shirell from the front office.

"Jay? Is your mom there?"

He stared blearily back toward her bedroom. "She's still asleep."

"Miss Rotchkey has called to report your absence for the second day in a row."

"Yeah, I'm coming in." Jay yawned.

"You can't just come in; you have to bring a signed note of—"

Jay hung up the phone and ambled back to his room. Returning to school was the last thing he wanted to do. But then something occurred to him: What if he got suspended from Tutorial? If Ms. Rotchkey cut him off from the computer and started locking her window, he'd be doomed. *The Build* play disk wouldn't do him any good without a computer to play it on. He'd better make nice with the school. He slipped on his new clothes, checked out his sunglasses in the mirror, then knocked on his mom's door.

"Mom? I need a signed note."

Jay pulled into the C-Court parking lot slowly, enjoying the stares of the smokers. He gave a two-fingered wave, found Colin's Batmobile, and spun his car into the empty spot beside it. It had occurred to him, too, that he now needed to get his driver's license, which may not be something he could get through *The Build*.

He leapt over his Miata door, like he'd seen them do in the movies. It was already lunchtime, and a small crowd of students gathered around his Miata. Kids whistled, running their hands over the paint.

"Wow."

"This a '93?"

"It's nicer than Jeremy's car!"

Jay flushed with pride, admiring his car next to the beat-up multicolored Batmobile.

"How much money did you get?" a wide-eyed freshman asked.

"Oh," Jay considered, hedging a little. "Quite a bit."

He turned to see faces smiling at his car. He grinned sheepishly at the crowd, grabbed the note his mom had given him, and strode through the courtyard, chin held high. Other kids began to whistle.

"Jay! Looking fly, my man."

"Nice digs!"

"I won the lottery!" Jay shouted back.

By the time he reached A-Court, he felt invincible. The cavernous space was mostly empty with all the juniors and seniors out for lunch. Whispers echoed off lockers, and Jay's combat boots clopped loudly over lacquered cement. He rounded a cement beam and froze. Amber and Gretchen were sitting on a bench, stuffing delicate blue prom invitations into small envelopes. They were totally absorbed in their task and did not look up at Jay.

"Brenda should get Best Laugh."

"Thought she did?"

"Donna did, *and* Best Dressed, Most Naive, and Friendliest."

Jay realized they were talking about the *Beverly Hills, 90210* episode that ran on repeat. He hesitated, then swerved toward them.

"Hi."

They looked up in surprise.

"You seen Liz?"

Amber and Gretchen studied his new outfit, then turned to each other, silently assessing.

"She's not here," said Amber carefully.

He mustered all his confidence. "I need to get our tickets. For prom."

Amber looked wary, but stuffed an envelope and slowly handed it to him.

"Here you go. You talk to her?"

"Er, yeah . . ." Jay lied.

"What's her deal, then? She doesn't talk to anyone. Ever since Friday, when the tornado hit. She hasn't been back,"

Amber continued. "Won't answer any calls. It's like she's totally changed her personality."

Jay shrugged. "Well, seems to be going around."

Amber's brown eyes focused on his outfit.

"Is that why you're dressed like that? You trying out a new schtick?"

"Something like that."

Gretchen looked at the wad of cash in Jay's hand and smacked the gum she was chewing. "That's twenty bucks for those prom tickets."

Jay handed over a twenty, hesitated, then peeled off another bill.

"Keep the change." He winked.

"You givin' money away too?"

Jay shrugged. "What's the good of winning the lottery if you can't share? Also, I have a Miata. If you ever want to borrow it."

Amber leapt up. "Yes! Oh yes. We're so doing that."

Gretchen nodded. "Lunch tomorrow?"

"Sure." Jay nodded. "Just come get the keys."

Gretchen smiled. "I thought you were into *Babylon 5* and the World Wide Web and that kind of stuff."

Jay shrugged. "Babylon what?"

To his surprise, the girls laughed. Jay flushed and grinned back. He held up the keys. "Anytime," he reminded them, and left while they were still smiling.

"See you around," he called over his shoulder.

He ran right into Jeremy and a line of Johns. Today they were wearing a string of basketball jerseys pulled from a hodge-podge of Portland Trail Blazers and Chicago Bulls players. Clyde Drexler. Danny Ainge. Michael Jordan. Scottie Pippen. Before he could stop himself, he blurted out: "Hey, you guys oughta pick a team."

John C leaned down. "Back for more?"

Jeremy exhaled slowly. "I thought we went over how we're not supposed to see each other?"

Jay feebly held up his mom's note. "I–I have to drop something off."

Jeremy grabbed the note and ripped it in two.

"You look like if George Michael and Elton John had a baby."

"Yeah, well, Amber and Gretchen didn't seem to mind."

Jeremy looked over to where the two girls sat, and his face darkened.

"Gimme the jacket."

Color rose to Jay's cheeks.

"Guess what? I don't need your job at the mill anymore. Didn't you hear? The Banksmans won the lottery."

Jeremy grabbed Jay's hand.

"Money comes and goes. The McKrakens are forever."

Jeremy's grip tightened, squeezing. Jay gasped and opened his hand, and the twenty-dollar bills drifted to the floor. The Johns laughed and scooped them up. Shame burned in Jay's chest as Jeremy ripped off Jay's jacket and pushed him backward. An evil grin spread over Jeremy's face.

"Now, gimme the pants."

ALL 10S

JAY LAY IN his Miata, seat back, wearing nothing but boxers and an undershirt. His car was idling, heat on full blast, but still he shivered with the fury trapped in his chest.

The smokers were chatting outside C-Court. He tried to eavesdrop to distract himself, but his mind kept returning to Jeremy. He realized he'd made a grave error. Jeremy and the Johns would never be cowed by money or clothes. The only thing they understood—the root of their success—was muscle. Jay wouldn't beat them until he could match their raw power. He stared up at the blue sky, hating Jeremy more than he'd ever hated him in his whole life. He wasn't ready to leave school. To do that would be to admit defeat. But he also had no recourse in staying.

He heard the crack of a baseball bat and cheers, and he sat up in his seat. Through the windshield, he could see the baseball field where the uniform-clad Johns were taking their positions. A look of wonder spread over his face. Their greatest source of power in Bickleton, he realized, was also their greatest weakness. The town loved them, relied on them, for their baseball. What if Jay made baseball their undoing?

He looked in the other direction, across the parking lot, over at the cluster of pine trees that hid Tutorial. The classroom would be empty by now. Ms. Rotchkey would be gone, her computer unguarded. Jay grabbed *The Build* from his Miata and leapt out of the car.

As Jay had expected, Tutorial was empty and dark. He hurried over to the computer, popped in the disk, and printed himself a new set of clothes. After he'd hurriedly dressed, he scrolled to the baseball field. Onscreen, he watched Jeremy's pixelated avatar toss a tiny white baseball to John W. He clicked on Jeremy, and his stats window popped up. STRENGTH: 7. SPEED: 6. HIT POINTS: 6. INTELLIGENCE: 5.

Jay scrolled back to his own his avatar in the darkened Tutorial, and clicked. STRENGTH: 3. SPEED: 4. HIT POINTS: 4. INTELLIGENCE: 7.

As he stared at the numbers, he felt a sliver of doubt grow. Seeing his entire being boiled down to just four statistics . . . it felt somehow demeaning. Reductive. Would it really make a difference to change these scores? And what was the mechanism by which it would happen? Only one way to find out. He double-clicked his strength score until the numbers flashed. He started typing and the numbers maxed out at 10. Jay hit Enter.

The change hit him like a bolt of electricity. His muscles squeezed, hardening with adrenaline. His jaw clenched and he roared with the effort of it, hands shooting out to grip the desk, the wood flexing under his powerful grip. With effort, he turned his neck to look down. The wood around his fingers was splintered. Slowly, muscle by muscle, he forced his body to relax. He grabbed his jaw with his strong fingers and worked it in circles, loosening it. He stood up and his leg muscles nearly launched him out of his seat.

A small rectangular mirror hung on the wall with the aspirational platitude: "This is what change looks like." Jay clambered over to the mirror and stared. Staring back was a different face. He was not taller, nor wider, but his chin looked as chiseled as Dolph Lundgren's, and veins were cracking out of his neck. He had never been unattractive ("cute," he'd once overheard Shelby Kline say), but now his eyes and nose had fierce definition, all traces of boyishness gone. He reached to touch the mirror and saw his forearms had doubled in size. Each muscle felt taut, tensing beneath the skin. He was ripped.

He turned back to the computer, marveling at his steadiness. He clicked up his speed and hit points. Each was followed by a similar blast of adrenaline as his reflexes were suddenly much quicker, and his skin seemed to harden, impervious to pain. He clicked up his intelligence to 10 and hit Enter.

It was like his brain suddenly clicked online. He felt more awake than he'd ever felt, as if he'd pounded ten cans of Mountain Dew. He could feel a new intellect in his brain, searching through his head like a spotlight. His eyes darted around the room. He spotted a sine trigonometry equation above Ms. Rotchkey's desk and didn't even have to think.

"Forty-two," he whispered the answer. A thousand more connections flashed through his mind. 42. Six times seven. The meaning of life, according to Douglas Adams. The ASCI code for asterisk. Jackie Robinson's jersey number. Steven Spielberg's only comedy. A top-down bullet hell arcade video game.

Other memories suddenly washed over him. His dad had been forty-two when he died. He was tall, handsome, and had a drooping mustache that Jay desperately wanted to inherit. He remembered the day his mom told him his dad was gone, how she stood in the doorway, tears in her eyes, and looked so very young. The way the dust motes floated through the light.

He remembered it like it happened yesterday. Like it was happening now.

More memories filled his brain. Like how he'd been passing through his living room when Marky Mark dropped his pants and grabbed his crotch on the runway of that Calvin Klein fashion show, and everyone at school had talked about it the next day. Or when he got sick in seventh grade, and Jeremy and the Johns got the whole class to chant "AIDS victim, AIDS victim." Or Colin's video game party in ninth grade, when most of Tutorial had been there, and they'd dragged his old Atari from the closet, except a bunch of wasps had made their nest in it, and they flew out and stung everyone. And then he remembered that Colin's *Mario 2* cartridge had fallen behind the basement radiator when the wasps attacked, and Colin had wondered about where it went in the years since.

And Jay remembered Todd. How in third-grade soccer practice, he, Todd, and Colin had found a dead crow on the edge of the field, and dared one another to pick it up, until they got so comfortable with it, they were throwing it back and forth at one another. They'd been such good friends. The image of young Todd—with his wild red hair and freckles that seemed burned into his cheeks—sat heavy in his gut. Though he and Todd hadn't been close for years, he found himself missing his old friend, wishing that the three of them hadn't drifted apart.

The memories shifted. Now Jay was sitting in a hard chair in a small white room he didn't recognize.

"He'll just be one more minute. I apologize; I know he's really excited to meet you."

Jay spun around. A short woman with a broad mouth and a suit jacket smiled at him through a wide mouth, holding open the door to the office. Behind her, Jay spotted rows and rows of cubicles that fell off into a bland gray room.

"You're sure I can't get you anything? Coffee? Water?"

"No, thank you," a strange voice answered.

She nodded and shut the door. Jay turned around, taking in the room.

A plain balsa desk with a computer sat in front of him. Jay was surprised to find he didn't recognize the brand of computer. As he was scanning it for a logo, a large window, taking up a quarter of the wall, grabbed his attention. Through the window, he could see a green strip of grass, with a sidewalk running along it, and a few joggers bustling past. Beyond that lay an enormous stretch of water. It was much larger than Porter Lake, the biggest body of water near Bickleton. That was a large pond compared to this.

This was dark green, almost black, and stretched as far as he could see. There were small sailboats on it, clustered together in what looked like a race. On the faint horizon, he saw mountains that looked like the Cascades. He felt, for a moment, that he must be looking back at Bickleton from outside the Cascades, that this must be what it felt like to truly escape. He was sure the water must be the ocean, though he'd only ever seen the ocean in movies like *Captain Ron*. Small white-capped waves lapped against a cement wall.

He felt, rather than heard, the faint impact of approaching footsteps, and he remembered the woman who'd said someone would be meeting with him. He straightened himself, feeling a thrill of excitement. But something was wrong. The plodding footsteps were coming from outside of his memory.

He froze. Through the thin walls of the portable, he heard the soft clump of feet ascending the ramp outside. Someone was coming. Jay shook away all his new memories and looked for a place to hide. The only possible spot was Ms. Rotchkey's desk. He dove for it when the door flung open, and Ms. Rotchkey stepped into the room, catching him crouching toward the desk.

"Jay Banksman!"

Jay froze.

"What are you doing?"

Jay forced himself to straighten. He felt terrifically exposed, the new broadness of his shoulders threatening to burst out of the tightness of his shirt.

"I, uh, just came to get any homework assignments. You weren't here, so I was gonna look—"

"What are you doing with my desk? I heard yelling?"

"I stubbed my toe."

Ms. Rotchkey stepped forward. Jay flinched, uncertain how far Ms. Rotchkey could see through her thick glasses. He started inching his way toward the computer. His biceps felt ridiculously large, his thighs tense and ready to spring. Ms. Rotchkey folded her arms.

"You're not allowed back in here until we get approval from the front office for your absences."

"I know. I had a note, but Jeremy tore it up."

"Well, get another one. Because guess who decides whether or not you graduate?"

"You?" Jay had almost reached the computer.

"That's right. And school policy states that if you get an F in the last semester of your senior year, you won't graduate."

"But I'm not getting an F."

"You will if you continue missing class."

Ms. Rotchkey tightened her lips, clearly hoping to have an effect on Jay. Jay's fingers brushed the computer. They found the button on the front of the floppy drive.

Ms. Rotchkey continued, "It's up to you, Jay. You've gotta—" She noticed his hand moving. "What are you doing?"

Jay held up his left hand. "I promise there's a perfectly good—"

"Are you taking something?!"

Jay pressed the Eject button, felt the warm plastic disk pop into his palm.

"It's my disk!" Jay protested.

"Let's see it."

"I can't." Jay cringed. Ms. Rotchkey stepped toward him, holding out her hand. Her eyes widened. Her gaze traveled up his bulging limbs, taking in his strange new physique.

"Wh-what's happened to you?"

Jay backed his way to the door.

"I'm sorry. I've got a baseball scrimmage to win."

He flung open the door and felt the rush of wind on his cheeks. His body surged with power as he tore down the path and burst into the C-Court parking lot. Down on the field, the Johns were still warming up, throwing the ball. Further down, the cheerleaders were practicing. He felt guilty abandoning Ms. Rotchkey. But he had bigger fish to fry. It was time to give the Johns a game they'd never forget.

THE SCRIMMAGE

JAY TOOK THE cement stairs two at a time, then leapt out onto the field. He saw Coach Amrine on the edge of the track, arms crossed, barking through a bulge of tobacco.

"Choke up, Barstow. Slow your swing. Dorsey! Move in. McManus! You watchin' the game or the girls?"

It was only when Jay stopped in front of him that Coach Amrine swiveled his corded neck and stared down at him through black sunglasses. He had the face of a John, ten years post–high school. A once chiseled jaw was now covered by the bloat of cheap beer.

"What's up?"

Jay straightened. "I'd like to play the team."

"Tryouts are over." Mr. Amrine's attention jerked back to the field. "Hogburn, be smart. McManus, take a lap."

"Mr. Amrine?"

"What?"

"I'd like to play *against* the team."

Mr. Amrine stared at Jay, then scanned the bleachers, searching for an audience or a hidden camera.

"This a joke?"

"I can beat them."

Coach Amrine took off his sunglasses. His eyes were small and squinty as they peered down.

"You got a death wish or something? I got a hard enough time keeping these guys focused. I don't need a cat in the dog pen." Coach Amrine glanced back to the field. Jay saw that practice had paused. The Johns were pointing and snickering at him.

"Look who's back."

"Where'd you get the new clothes? Salvation Army?"

But the jeers quickly tapered off. Jay saw them noticing his new muscles, and he heard whispers.

"Does he look different?"

"What's up with his arms?"

Coach Amrine clapped. "Hey, this ain't a peep show! Make it move!"

Mr. Amrine stepped away, ignoring Jay. The Johns moved back into the rhythms of their practice, giving Jay careful glances now and then.

Jay picked up a bat and fished a ball out from the team bag. He measured the weight of it in his hand, then scanned the horizon until his gaze fell on Coach Amrine's dusty gray Jeep in the C-Court parking lot. He threw the baseball into the air, brought the bat over his shoulder, and swung.

Crack! The bat connected. He watched the ball sail over the field and smash the Coach's windshield. Thick spiderwebs blossomed from the sides of its impact. Jay's eyes widened. He looked down the field and saw the Johns staring, mouths open. Mr. Amrine stared from his Jeep to Jay. He spun around and stormed over to Jay, his figure growing more imposing with every step.

Coach Amrine ripped the bat from Jay's hand and threw a finger in his face.

"What the hell was that?"

Jay brought a hand to his pocket and pulled out a wad of cash.

"I can pay you. Plus, I can donate $10,000 dollars to the new equipment fund. If you let me scrimmage the team."

Coach Amrine stared. The Johns trotted in from the outfield. Jeremy's muscled jaw clenched as he spat out a stream of tobacco. Jay turned to them.

"I'll give you guys a thousand bucks apiece if you beat me. One inning. If you win, you get the money. If I win . . . I win."

Jeremy laughed and looked at Coach Amrine. "Let him do it."

Mr. Amrine's nostrils were still flaring. "You're gonna take on the entire team? Sure, go ahead. You're out in the field first."

The Johns trickled off the diamond, leaving Jay alone. He felt suddenly nervous, realizing he'd never actually played baseball before in his life.

"Uh, can I borrow a mitt?"

Coach Amrine shoved a mitt into Jay's chest. Jay slipped his fingers in. The ragged piece of leather felt like it would rip to shreds at the first grounder.

Jay watched the Johns leer at him from behind the batting fence and wondered if he hadn't made a mistake. They were Cascadia's best athletes, after all. Even with fully boosted stats, could he possibly take on all fourteen?

A whistle blew, and the cheerleaders broke formation, pooling around the edge of the field to watch. From up in the courtyard, bodies began to fill the bleachers. Word of his challenge had evidently gotten out. Jay gulped.

John B stepped up to the plate. He was one of the lesser Johns, whose pimpled face wore a constant sneer. Coach Amrine moved across the infield until he was ten feet from Jay. Without taking his eyes from the Johns, he muttered to Jay:

"Loosen up. Widen your stance."

Jay glanced over in surprise and shifted his feet a little, grateful for the advice. He leaned back, cocked his arm, and let the ball fly. It flew across the plate, right under John B's nose.

"Strike!" yelled Amrine. He shook his head in disapproval. "C'mon, Becker."

The other Johns shifted, agitated. Mr. Amrine moved behind home plate, taking catcher's position, and tossed the ball back to Jay. John B squeezed his bat tighter. Jay reared back and hurled another pitch. John B's bat whistled as the ball smashed into Coach Amrine's mitt.

"Strike two."

The Johns shook the metal fence, shouting.

"C'mon!"

"It's frickin' Jay Banksman!"

"Don't choke, you reject."

Coach tossed the ball to Jay, who caught it in the fold of his glove. He socked the ball in his mitt, like he'd seen in the movies, and then threw his third pitch. This time, John didn't swing.

"Strike three!"

John B spun on his coach.

"That was a ball!"

Coach Amrine simply jerked his thumb at the dugout. "Let's get a real batter in."

A dejected John B swapped spots with John W, "the handsome John." He was taller than Jeremy, with sad doe-eyes and big lips.

"Kid's got an arm," Coach Amrine cautioned him.

"It's Jay," John W spat.

Jay looked up at the stands and was surprised to see they were now half-full. The crowd saw him look back and erupted in a cheer. Sitting at the end of a bleacher, Jay saw Stevie and Colin, and some other kids from Tutorial. He scanned the crowd for other familiar faces and was surprised to see Liz leaning on the fence. She wasn't shouting or cheering; she was just staring. It was impossible to tell at that distance, but Jay felt like she was sizing him up.

The shrill sound of Coach Amrine's whistle jerked his attention back into the game. John W's lip curled with a hint of malevolence, his bat circling the air.

Jay tried to remember anything about baseball. For years he had scorned the sport, as anything that the Johns loved must be inherently stupid. He now regretted refusing to watch it. Images of *Bull Durham* and *The Natural* flashed through his mind, with clips from the trailer of *Rookie of the Year*. But his mind kept wandering back to *Major League*, picturing Charlie Sheen in glasses. It wasn't helping.

Jay wound back his arm and pitched. John W swung and his bat connected with a crack. The ball bounded over the ground, inside the first-base line. Jay dashed after it, pumping his legs. A cheer erupted from the bleachers, but it was muted by the roar in his ears. His gaze fixed on the ball as it rolled and bounced past first base. He got in front of the ball and scooped it up. He raced back toward the infield as John W rounded second base with a long, steady stride. Jay aimed his body toward the empty space between third base and home plate, picking up his pace, faster than he'd ever run before.

Behind the fence, the Johns were screaming, all traces of smugness gone.

"C'mon! Pick it up, W!"

"C'mon, Warner!"

"Run!"

A dull chant rose out of the bleachers. It took Jay a moment to realize the crowd was shouting for him.

"Jay! Jay! Jay!"

He glanced over his shoulder and the school broke into a cheer. Jay flushed, grinning, barreling down the field.

John W rounded third and glanced at Jay. His face fell into shock, and Jay saw him falter. He slowed, turned, and leapt back onto third base. The spring air tunneled into Jay's lungs, and he walked to the pitcher's mound, winded and smiling. He was doing it.

Behind the fence, the Johns shuffled back and Jeremy stepped out. He strolled to home plate and scooped the bat from the ground with the same cruel smile Jay had learned to fear. The smile that had stolen Jay's milk in middle school, pantsed him, chased him into Jewett Creek sophomore year. Jay felt his stomach sink as deep, desperate breaths took his throat, and he wound back and threw a wild pitch.

"Ball!" Coach Amrine yelled.

Behind Jay, the bleachers quieted. He tried to calm his breath. He caught the ball Mr. Amrine threw back to him and forced himself to look at the ground, steadying his nerves.

He drew himself up and hurled a pitch. This time Jeremy swung, knocking the ball through the air. Jay ran after it. The ball dropped past second, bouncing twice, and then Jay grabbed it in his mitt. He turned to see John W walking past home plate, into the cheering Johns. Jeremy rounded second, running faster than anything Jay had ever seen. Jay dashed toward home, urging his body forward. Jeremy hit third, his strides lengthening, as Jay crossed the pitcher's mound.

He willed his adrenal glands open, flooding his body with energy. His legs hit the grass in staccato rhythm. Jeremy looked over in surprise at the rapidly approaching Jay. Then Jay flew over home plate, touching a gloved hand to Jeremy's chest.

"Out!" Coach Amrine shouted.

The crowd burst into a cheer.

"What?!" Jeremy screamed.

Jay leaned onto his knees, gasping. The Bickleton Vandals had scored, but he'd managed to shut down their team. He smiled. The cheer from the bleachers grew deafening. Kids were on their feet now, stomping. Jay turned to watch, blushing. Then, suddenly, something huge plowed into him. He toppled over and felt fists raining down into his chest. Jeremy's snarling face was inches from his own, and Jay realized with calm detachment: *he's beating me up.* The pain was distant, ethereal. Smiling, he reached out and grabbed Jeremy's hands. He flipped Jeremy off and climbed on top as if it were the easiest, most natural thing in the world. He was only vaguely aware of the Johns' screams and the cheers of the crowd. He pulled a fist back and let it slam into Jeremy's face. Jeremy's head jerked aside in surprise. Jay saw blood running down his lip where his hand had split it. Jeremy glanced up at him, big blue eyes wide. Jay hit him again. His whole body tingled with pleasure.

He hit Jeremy again and again, until Jeremy was no longer struggling and had a dazed look in his eyes. Then Jay felt hands on his shoulders, and he was being dragged away from Jeremy's body. He looked up to see Coach Amrine and Principal Oatman shouting at him. He tensed his shoulders, ready to fight them. But he heard the sounds of the crowd cheering his name, and he smiled, letting himself be pulled off. He threw his hands into the air, and the bleachers once again erupted into cheers.

PRINCIPAL'S
OFFICE

JAY HAD NEVER been in Principal Oatman's office before. Now he sat in one of two rigid chairs in front of Oatman's desk. He idly wondered whether they'd called his mom. Not that he was worried about it. Even if she'd gotten out of bed by now, she probably wouldn't answer the phone. Jay settled into the chair as best as he could, waiting to hear what Mr. Oatman would say.

The room was an oppressive dull brown, and it felt like an extension of Mr. Oatman's personality. What was with this guy? How could any man be so into beige? Brown desk, brown picture frames with photos of brown mountains. Brown files. Lots of brown files.

The only black objects in the room were a fax machine and a small black-and-white television with a stern Bernard Shaw speaking quietly on CNN. It was a story on *Night Trap*, the video game where players are a police officer trying to save scantily clad teenage girls from being eaten by vampires. It had been dominating the news lately, because its release caused parents to demand that Congress regulate video games. Jay craned his neck with interest.

Principal Oatman sat on the other side of the desk, hands folded, browner and graver than usual. The skin around his mouth hung in two saggy jowls, like Richard Nixon. A thin wisp of hair crowned his bald head, like cotton balls glued onto a diorama. Mr. Amrine sat in the corner of the room in a brown armchair, slouched, looking at Jay with half-lidded eyes. Jay couldn't tell whether he was upset or impressed. Probably both. Mr. Amrine rubbed a stubbled chin; he looked like a man who needed a drink. Ms. Rotchkey had once let slip in front of Tutorial that he was a heavy drinker.

Jay wondered if they had to sit quietly until the sheriff arrived. He realized, with some surprise, that the adults might actually be scared of him now. This was a bit like playing chess, he reflected. They had the advantage of intimidation. He'd made it his whole high school career without being sent to the principal's office, and to defy Principal Oatman went against his very nature. But what could they do? They could expel him, keep him from graduating. But why did he need their high school diploma?

He cracked his knuckles, resolving not to speak first. He saw Jeremy's blood soaked through the small channels in his skin and realized, with shock, that he had dethroned the most popular kid in high school. He smirked.

"Something funny?" Principal Oatman broke the silence.

Jay didn't look at him, but turned his smile up to the ceiling, studying the cork tiles. "To an absurd degree."

Mr. Oatman picked a framed photograph off his desk. Inside the frame, Jay saw, was a starchy, faded photo of a bunch of kids he didn't recognize, wearing loose-fitting baseball uniforms. Mr. Oatman held it out for Jay to see, and under the bottom was a placard: Class of '69. Some of the faces clicked into place. Sheriff Jenkins, without his telltale gut, was first baseman. And there was Principal Oatman, thin and full of hair.

Jay squinted, staring. In the smack-dab center, there was Jeremy McKraken. Jay blinked. But how could that be? Mr. Oatman tapped the frame.

"That's John McKraken. Jeremy's dad."

Jay shook his head in disbelief. Except for some different faces and the old-fashioned uniforms, it may as well have been Jeremy and the Johns.

"As it was, is now, and ever shall be," he muttered.

Mr. Oatman placed the photo back on his desk.

"That was the finest baseball team our school ever had."

"Yeah? You guys actually played?"

Mr. Amrine sat forward suddenly. "How'd you man the entire field?"

Mr. Oatman cocked his head slightly. "Or learn to fight like that?"

"How come"—Jay felt his temper lodge in his throat—"when Jeremy gives me a black eye, I get sent to the guidance counsellor? Everyone saw Jeremy throw the first punch, yet somehow I'm the one in the principal's office."

Mr. Amrine leaned forward. "Two rights don't make a wrong."

"You guys on the baseball team make all the rules. You keep people like me, Colin, and Todd from getting what we want."

Principal Oatman slammed a fist into his desk. "We don't make the rules."

"Then who does? God?"

"Yes."

Jay burst into laughter. "Are you serious? That's the world's biggest cop-out."

Mr. Oatman purpled.

"Never have I seen such a reasonable, promising young student take such a turn for the worse. I strongly encourage you to reconsider your position if you want to graduate. You are suspended, and will not leave this room until Sheriff Jenkins arrives."

A malevolent grin spread over Jay's face. He had an idea how to get himself off the hook. "Do you want to know how I did it?"

Mr. Oatman went rigid. "No."

"Oh, I think you do." He began his familiar story, now watching eagerly. "See, I have this disk. And any changes I make with it show up in the world. I can give myself money. I can delete people. I can do whatever I want, and *you* can't stop me. God doesn't make the rules. *I* make the rules."

As Jay had expected, the color drained from the men's faces. Their eyes went slack, as if they were listening to distant music. It was just like when he tried to tell Colin, his mom. Whatever the disk was, it was something too powerful for the rest of the world to comprehend. Jay thought back to all the H.P. Lovecraft short stories he read in middle school. Always, a person encountered some creature inconceivable to the human mind. Characters broke down, their minds melting. The disk was some sort of Lovecraftian artifact, and he alone had the power to endure it.

Jay waved a hand in front of Mr. Oatman. He didn't blink. "I'm leaving now."

"Hmm?" Mr. Oatman waved back vaguely.

And Jay walked through the principal's door and down the narrow hall to the main office. Ms. Shirell looked at him harshly, and he just shrugged. She stomped off to find the principal.

"Principal Oatman?" she yelled suspiciously. "Everything okay?"

Jay hummed as he reached the school's entrance, feeling better than he had in a long time.

DISK
FOUR

LOOK OUT

JAY DROVE HIS Miata slowly through the main Bickleton drag. It was 6:13 p.m., the clear, cool kind of evening that made anything seem possible. He watched a small line of students form outside the Golden Flour Bakery. On Tuesday nights, they made pepperoni pizzas, and their small wooden storefront became a high school hub. Jay watched the two tables on the sidewalk swell with nearly twenty high school kids. He considered getting out to join them, just to see how they'd react. But his adrenaline was still pumping from that meeting with Mr. Oatman. He felt a small pang of guilt for manipulating his principal, but it was far outweighed by his newfound sense of power.

The sun was lowering in the sky, turning the distant mountains over the Skookullom a beautiful aqua orange. Some of the kids turned to look at his Miata, and Jay saw smiles on their faces. He shook his head. Was it a software bug? Was it spreading? He drove farther down the bluff, where the houses grew fewer and far between. He found himself thinking of Todd. Todd's disappearance had to be connected to all this. But how?

He slowed. Ahead was the scenic turnabout that looked down at the Skookullom. It wasn't big, just a semicircle of two-foot-tall brick-and-mortar wall that fit maybe six cars. The stone guardrail had been laid ages ago and was covered in moss. Nobody ever bothered to stop and look at the view anymore, so Jay was surprised to see a single white Jeep Cherokee. He recognized it immediately as Liz's car. He slowed down his Miata, straining over his passenger seat. Through the windows, he saw dark hair in the driver's seat, and a faint wisp of smoke floated out the tailpipe. What was she doing? Her engine was on? Was she alone? He swerved into the gravel lot to get a better look.

Suddenly, her Jeep engine roared. The car lurched forward, gunning for the edge of the cliff, with enough speed to plow right over the puny guardrail. Jay didn't have time to think, but let his reflexes take over. He yelled and punched his gas pedal, and his Miata barreled across the lot and rammed the front of the Cherokee, spinning it sideways. There was the terrible crunch of metal, and then both cars were still.

Smoke drifted from the Cherokee's engine. Jay let his grip on his steering wheel slacken as he caught his breath. The Jeep door opened, and Liz stepped out, glaring at him. Jay opened his door.

"What are you doing?!" he demanded.

Liz was in his face, pushing him. "Leave me alone!"

"You were gonna kill yourself!"

"My body, my choice. You can't keep me here."

"Keep you here? I just saved your life."

"Oh right, don't give me that. You'd just as soon kill me."

Jay was taken aback. "Are you talking about . . . the tornado?"

"The tornado, everything! This whole place is designed to keep me in check. But I won't play. Not anymore. Death is too easy, there's gotta be some catch. It'll be like *Groundhog Day*, where I just wake up in my own bed again. But I am done playing by the rules."

Liz's fists were clenched at her sides. Jay had the uncomfortable feeling that he was witnessing a psychotic episode. He looked around, hoping to see an adult who might help him. But the road was empty, and he could only barely make out the main drag from around the hardware store.

"Are you talking about *The Build*?"

Liz looked up with renewed interest. "What?"

He continued carefully, fully expecting Liz's eyes to glaze over.

"Whenever I try to tell people, they get all weird. Like, they can't hear me."

He stared at her, waiting for a change.

"But you hear me, don't you?"

Her face softened ever so slightly. Like she was working through a decision.

"Of course I hear you." A look of pity crossed her face. "You really don't know what's going on, do you?"

She spun around and scrambled back into her Jeep and started it. Jay ran at her, worried she was going to charge the cliff.

"Wait! What's going on!?"

He grabbed the frame of her Jeep, and she turned a leg and kicked out through her open door, hitting him squarely in the chest. He fell back into the gravel. She held up a warning finger and placed it to her lips. Then she peeled out of the turnout.

Jay pulled himself up and threw himself into his Miata, ready to follow. The engine whined, refusing to turn over. Moments ticked by as he mechanically tried the ignition key. Finally, the engine caught. The Miata rumbled to life and shook its way to the edge of the gravel. Its frame, bent from ramming Liz's Jeep, rubbed against his tire as he turned onto Main Street. Some high school kids stared at his bedraggled car. But there was no sign of Liz.

STAGING GROUNDS

JAY LAY WIDE-AWAKE in bed, staring at the Heather Graham poster on his wall. It was 3:37 a.m., according to his *Ren & Stimpy* clock. He couldn't shut his brain off. His mind was on his and Liz's car crash, and the things she'd said. He could recall the incident with startling clarity.

His mind spiraled through memories like a Fibonacci sequence. Ever since he'd boosted his intelligence to 10, he could recall moments from his life with ease. He remembered going to Lost Creek Park with his parents when he was four. He remembered the moment he first saw Liz in kindergarten. He could drop into his memories as if he were reliving them. They were as vivid as real life, as if he were traveling in time. They were perfectly organized in the back of his mind, like a card catalog of memories; he could quickly pull any memory at any moment. Yet, he had no memory of learning about the Fibonacci sequence. He scanned his high school and middle-school career, and could find no lesson, no mention in a movie or book. It was an idea he knew well, despite never having learned about it.

Perhaps having a 10 intelligence score meant he could spontaneously discover new knowledge, simply by letting his mind wander. Perhaps, he hoped, again glancing at his clock, it meant he no longer needed sleep. His rubbed his bulging arms, which were beginning to stiffen from the baseball game and fight.

There was a tap on his window. He turned to see a dark silhouette standing outside. A girl. She waved, and he threw off his covers and pulled an old Bart Simpson T-shirt off the floor. He opened his window and was shocked to make out the faint features of Liz Knight in the moonlight.

"What are you doing here?" Jay shivered as the cool air poured into his room.

"I have to show you something." She took a step back.

Jay craned his neck out the window to see what she had in her hands, but she held up a Maglite and shook it in response.

"It's not here. C'mon. Out the window. We don't have a ton of time."

Jay pulled himself through his window, feeling a small thrill at the adventure. Despite not having slept, he felt energized. He dropped down next to Liz. It was just the two of them in the small alley behind his house, and he could almost feel the warmth of her body. His heart began to pound. She stood there, blending into the night, looking so completely alien from the girl he thought he'd known all these years.

She turned and walked down to his driveway. His little roundabout, always still and quiet, felt silent as a tomb. Moonlight caressed car frames, and windshields were frosted over. He exhaled a cloud of breath and shivered.

"Do I need my jacket?" he asked, noticing that Liz had on a parka.

"Too late for that now. We have to hurry."

She moved to the end of the roundabout, where the bank dropped down into Jewett Creek.

"Where we going?" Jay whispered.

"Rock Ridge." She dropped over the ledge, and Jay followed.

Despite the cold, he felt sweat form on his brow. Liz was leading him to Rock Ridge? Did this have to do with her asking him to prom? He imagined sitting by the falls with Liz, locked lip and lip. His chest froze. It was a secret only Colin knew, but Jay had never made out with a girl before. He'd practiced, of course, on his hand, on squashes from his mom's garden . . . but he was now heading to Rock Ridge with Liz Knight! He seriously hoped his vegetable make-out sessions would be enough practice for a girl like Liz.

They picked their way through the downed debris from the tornado as Jay pondered his fate. What if she wanted to go all the way? That didn't square with her earlier suicide attempt, but girls had always been a mystery to Jay, and especially Liz, with her recent breakdowns. Was she legally sane? If she tried to seduce him, did he have a responsibility to contact Sheriff Jenkins?

He tried to catch her eye in the dark, but she was trekking determinedly ahead, shining her flashlight on the downed trees. Jay decided to fish for clues.

"Sure is cold out here. I could, uh, run home and grab a blanket? If we need it?"

Liz swung around, shining the flashlight in his eyes. Jay froze, shielding the glare with his hands.

"I just thought . . . if we were gonna, maybe, sit . . ."

"Talk," Liz commanded.

"I–I am talking. Was there a particular topic you wanted to discuss?"

"I want to know what you couldn't tell the others."

Jay took a deep breath and told her everything. Todd's disappearance. The *Serious Gamer* with the disk. It all flowed out, and Liz listened, impassive. Jay watched her face in the dark, waiting for her eyes to glaze over. But they merely studied him, glittering behind her flashlight like two dark jewels. Jay felt a lightness grow inside him, as if the heavy weight of the last week had burst and was pouring out into Liz. He suddenly felt a deep affection for her in a way he never had before.

He continued, "And then I used *The Build* to tweak all my stats for the baseball scrimmage. But you already saw all that."

Liz was nodding slowly, as if this confirmed her suspicions. She swung around and continued walking through the forest.

"That's it?!" Jay ran after her. "I tell you I can cause storms and change reality, and you have nothing to say?"

The faint mutter of Jewett Creek grew louder. Slivers of light touched the forest floor, and there were signs of destruction everywhere. In the night, the destruction looked alien, and Jay felt the surrealness of it.

"I need to show you something," Liz muttered.

They were in the open clearing at the base of the falls. In the dim moonlight, he saw flattened trees and ground overturned by massive roots. At a distance, the falls looked like a frozen crystal.

"Now, Jay, this is probably going to be hard for you."

She walked over to the falls and stretched her hands across the wet rocks. After placing her flashlight in her mouth, she lifted a hand, planted a foot, and hoisted herself up the slippery slope. The light of her flashlight flickered over slimy boulders, occasionally catching the roaring plume of the falls on the slimy and freezing rocks as the falls sprayed his face. Jay approached the cliff under her, searching for handholds in the dark.

"Where are we going?"

She didn't answer. Jay resigned himself to the climb, slipping on the slimy and freezing rocks. The falls roared, spraying his face. He shivered and spat as cold water trickled into his eyes and mouth. His Chucks slipped, and he struggled to hold on.

Glancing up, he saw Liz pause at the lip of the falls. Jay wondered if she meant to dive into the pool below. She had on all her clothes, so it didn't seem likely. He was squinting in the spittle of the falls, watching Liz's flashlight skew out into the night. He saw her slide her palm across the wet rocks. She glanced down, shouting.

"You still want to know what happened to Todd?"

The rocks flickered under her fingers. Wisps of blue light radiated from her touch, shimmering across the cliff. It reminded Jay of the rotoscoped lightning in movies like *Back to the Future* and *Ernest Goes to Jail*. It shimmered out over the rocks, lighting up the night. Jay stared, mesmerized. And then Liz's arm disappeared into the rock.

"He found this."

Jay stared dumbly. Liz's arm was completely gone. Her shoulder was pressed into the blue energy that warped over the cliff face.

"Of course," she continued, shouting, "if he would have waited just a few more days, I would have been let out. But neither of us knew that, at the time."

Jay couldn't speak. Liz's arm disappearing into the cliff side was too much for his brain. He felt like one of the characters from the Lovecraft stories, like he had been suddenly severed from reality. He watched her reposition herself on the cliff until her left hand gripped a small ledge. Her right hand seemed to grip something inside the cliff wall.

"Come on," she beckoned.

Then she pulled herself into the blue lightning that sparked and shivered. Jay watched her body wriggle into the rock, until just her feet were left dangling out. Then they, too, were gone.

Without a flashlight, Jay was in almost total darkness. The moonlight barely penetrated the area, and he could only just make out the cliff. He clambered up as quickly as he could, slipping in the darkness, feeling for the spot where Liz had disappeared. The falls roared dangerously to his right, and its drops felt like burning embers against his skin. Looking down, he could barely make out the dim rocks beneath him; the slightest shift and he'd tumble onto boulders. His body trembled from the strain as his hand tentatively felt along the wet cliffs. His palm slid over jagged edges, then fell into nothing.

He stared at the rock face. Cool blue energy arced out into the night surrounding him. The cliff was glowing in blue strands, and it reminded him of bioluminescence he'd seen in *National Geographic*. His hand, which was inside the rock now, cupped a small ledge on the other side. It felt cool and smooth, like marble, and was strangely dry. Every fiber of his being, every sci-fi movie he'd ever seen, told him that he shouldn't put his body into the center of this weird, pulsing energy. But Liz was in there, and she'd promised him answers. He took a deep breath, then plunged his head into the rock.

There was a crackle of static electricity, and then he was in total darkness. He felt his legs kicking into space behind him, the splatter of the falls soaking his jeans. He army-crawled forward.

Suddenly, he tumbled forward into space. His arms shot out, his palms connecting with a cool flat surface three feet below. He instinctively tucked himself into a ball and rolled into a somersault, then leapt to his feet. His heart pounded as he turned in the dark. From somewhere ahead came the faint, muffled sound of music. He recognized the song, but his mind was full of panic and he couldn't place it.

"Liz! Liz!"

He extended a hand, groping, until it seized something warm.

"Hey, watch with the hands! You're freezing."

Liz's flashlight switched back on, and Jay was startled to see her face inches from his. His hand instinctively found hers and squeezed tightly.

"Where are we?"

"Ow, ow, ease up." She pried loose his fingers. "You've got some strength."

He squinted at the walls, letting his eyes adjust. There were in a cave. The walls were smooth and pale, not the jagged gray basalt of the outside. Wherever the light touched, flat crystals shimmered from deep inside. Jay ran his hand over the nearest wall. It was cool and felt like talcum powder. He spun around. The wall behind him—the one he'd just fallen through—was whole again. There was no trace of a window where they'd come in, no sound of the rumbling falls.

"How do we get out?!" Jay hyperventilated.

"Relax. The exit's still there; we just can't see it. Check this out."

She swung her light farther into the cave, and Jay leapt back.

On the far side of the cave was a sheet of thick glass. Behind that lay a room. There was a bed in the center of it, with crisp sheets turned up. There was a white Chesterfield couch. A wooden end table held a jug lamp, a bowl of plastic fruit, and assorted *People* magazines. A few bland pastoral paintings hung on three walls. It looked like a doctor's waiting room, except for the bed and the wall of glass. Jay stepped forward.

"What the hell?"

"You wanted answers."

Jay gaped at the room. There was a little kitchenette on the far side, with a stove and a dishwasher. It was nicer than his house.

"How is this an answer?"

The music was coming from speakers hung on the walls. Jay placed an ear against the glass.

"Is that Enya?"

Liz pounded on the glass. "Shut up! You can stick your 'Shepherd Moons' up your ass!"

Jay ran his hand over the glass. A thought struck him.

"Did Todd make this?"

Liz shook her head. "No. Todd never made it this far. I guess you'd call it a staging ground. Sort of a holding zone for people who come here"—she took a deep breath—"from the real world."

"What do you mean? Like, Portland?"

Liz closed in. In the light of her flashlight, she looked older.

"People don't come here from Portland, Jay. There is no Portland. At least, not in the sense you're used to."

"I don't understand."

"You think you'd be able to recognize a video game if you saw it?"

"Definitely."

"What if the graphics were better than anything you'd ever seen? Like, so good you couldn't tell them apart from real life?"

Jay shrugged. "Well, it'd still be on a screen."

"No screens."

"I mean, I'd still know it was a game. Every time I stopped playing—"

"No stopping. No starting. What if all you ever did was play? What if it was all you'd ever done?"

Jay stared. Enya's muffled voice continued through the glass wall.

"You're trying to tell me we're playing a video game?"

Liz returned his gaze, her face neutral.

"Yeah, right. You'd need a computer a thousand times more—a million times . . ." He shook his head again. "I mean, look at the detail, even just in this room. The textures alone would require more RAM than a *hundred* IBM PS/2s. And us talking, that music: this is more than sixteen-channel sound. There's not a Sound Blaster out there that could render this—"

"Not in 1993."

"Yeah." Jay shrugged. "Maybe in the future. I dunno. Look, are you going to tell me what this place is, or—"

Liz smiled grimly. "I'm trying. Here, the year is 1993. In the real world, we're a good ways past that. Where I come from, computers are powerful. Every person carries one at all times, and each little computer is more powerful than anything you've seen in 1993."

Jay laughed. "You're telling me you're from the future? Like . . . like Marty McFly?"

"Yes. And so are you. A future where everything's connected. And the most powerful computers are strong enough to run a world like this."

Jay stopped laughing. "We're in a video game?"

Liz nodded. Jay stared, stunned. It wasn't an idea he could take seriously. The idea that he, Bickleton's biggest video game aficionado, could be living inside a video game, completely unaware, was so ironic, so patently absurd, he suddenly realized what it had to be.

"This is a prank." He spun around. "Jeremy is here, isn't he?"

He examined the walls, looking for a telltale sign of a two-way mirror or a Candid Camera.

"I don't actually have extra strength, do I? The baseball game was just a ruse. I'm not sure how you pulled off that tornado. Jeremy must have gotten his dad involved to take down those trees. The whole video game thing, you took it too far, even for me."

Liz rested her back against the glass wall, patient. "Have you ever left Bickleton?"

"Sure. Hiking, fishing."

"Ever been more than thirty minutes away? Ever been to a city? Another town?"

Jay thought back to all the times he'd begged to go to Portland.

"Has anyone left?" Liz continued. "Anyone ever visit DC? Disneyland? The Grand Canyon?"

Jay racked his brain. Hadn't Colin and his parents visited Seattle? They had pictures of Pike Place Market and the Space Needle, in their living room. But now that he thought about it, he didn't remember them ever actually leaving. Didn't Stevie go to science camp? She certainly talked about it. He realized he couldn't recall seeing a single person actually leave Bickleton.

"Just because people don't leave, doesn't mean they can't. I just did a report on Nigerian exports."

"Yes, the details are amazing. It feels very real. When I first got here, I couldn't believe it. But it's the little things."

Liz walked over to the glass wall and shone her flashlight on the *People* magazines lying on the end table.

"Like the New Kids on the Block didn't die in a plane crash."

Jay shrugged. "How did they die, then?"

"They didn't. They're alive and in their sixties! They went on tour again a few years ago—it was depressing. Also, there are ten *seasons* of *Beverly Hills, 90210*, not the ten episodes that seem to play over and over here. And while we're on it, I'm pretty sure Heather Graham wasn't a *Playboy* centerfold. And Pee-wee Herman didn't win the Nobel Peace Prize for comedy."

"Who did, then?"

"There *is* no Nobel Prize for comedy, Jay."

"Next are you going to tell me Michael Jackson doesn't sleep in an oxygen chamber? Let me tell you what doesn't make sense: you! You claim to be from somewhere else, from this 'real world.' But I've known you since we were born. You've always been in Bickleton, Liz."

Liz sighed. "Yes, there has always been a Liz Knight here. I never met her, of course. But the moment I entered this program, I replaced her."

"What do you mean, you 'replaced' her?"

"The people in this program, they're not real. They're simulated intelligence. Designed to look and act like people—with a few limitations—but controlled by the computer."

"You mean non-player characters? NPCs? Do you mean to tell me that everyone in Bickleton . . . except you . . . is an NPC?"

Liz nodded. "The Liz who asked you to prom was a different Liz. An algorithm based on the real me."

"And what about me? You mean to say that I'm also an NPC?"

She nodded again. Jay laughed. "That's completely insane."

"Look, I don't care if you believe me. I'm not here to win you over. I came because I need your help. You've found a way to hack this world. I need to know how you do it. How did you make that tornado happen? Can you get me out?"

"Just go back the way you came." He motioned to the room behind the glass. "Through your staging ground or whatever."

"I would if I could," Liz responded, through gritted teeth.

"We had an agreement. I tell you everything I know, even the stuff that doesn't make sense, and you do the same."

"That's what I've been doing!"

"We live in a computer game?! Everyone's an artificial intelligence, except you? Sheriff Jenkins was right: you've gone mental."

He turned back to the wall.

"Jay, wait! How can I convince you it's true? What else can I show you?"

"You know what? I'm good. I never should have listened to you in the first place."

He felt his way along the back wall until his hands disappeared into space. He ducked his head down, the marble glowed blue, and then the roar of the falls surrounded him, hitting him with spray. He fell, tucking his torso into a front flip, and landed feetfirst on the rocky ledge below.

He ran. The sky was lightening, and he could make out the lonesome treetops above as the forest turned to dim blue. Anger surged through his body. Every time he used the disk, he'd convinced himself he was doing God's will. The idea that his life and everyone in it were just stupid preprogrammed blocks of code flew in the face of everything he knew and believed. He had to prove that Liz was wrong. He had to show her there was a world outside Bickleton.

O HORIZON

THE SUNLIGHT LIFTED over the land like a curtain while Jay drove. Cold light, delivered by a distant star. Jay stuck his elbow out of his window, hoping to feel some of the warmth on his skin. The fury still beat inside his chest. He found himself thinking of Nigeria. Two months ago, he'd done that report. It was double the size of California. Exported oil. Had a blossoming film industry called Nollywood. He was Cascadia's foremost expert on all things Nigeria. And Liz was telling him it didn't exist.

It couldn't be true.

He'd been driving for over an hour, under dark treetops, as the morning sky turned to orange. The Cranberries *Everybody Else Is Doing It, So Why Can't We?* CD played the second time through on the car sound system. Jay was starving. It was nearly breakfast time, and his stomach gurgled.

Soon, he told himself. Soon, Highway 24 would bring him to Cougar, the next town over. He'd seen Cougar on maps. It was supposedly their rival high school. At baseball scrimmages, kids would hold up signs "Kill the Kitties" and "Cut Up the Cougs." It was supposed to be smaller than Bickleton, with a gas station that didn't card for beer or *Playboys*.

Soon, the woods would part, and he'd see that gas station. Soon, he'd catch his first glimpse ever of a town outside Bickleton. Why hadn't he done this before? Because he had never been so desperate to prove someone wrong.

The road weaved, skirting the dark waters of the Skookullom River and passing back into the shadow of the trees. He passed a large cedar sign for the Cartwright National Forest. The road left the water and ran deeper into the old growth. There were no other cars on the road, no sounds competing with the dull roar of his Miata. The car seemed to be working again after his run-in with Liz, though the wheel well still scraped horrifically against the tire. He hoped it didn't pop it. And if it did, he hoped he had a spare.

A few hundred feet ahead, he saw a stop sign. *Good*, he thought, *this must be Cougar*. He slowed, then stopped. There was no intersection, no roads, no signs of other cars or buildings. The road simply continued on another two hundred yards, then dead-ended into forest.

Jay pulled off the side of the road and shut off his engine. The forest felt oppressively quiet. The only sound was the roar of the Skookullom through the trees. Huge cedars loomed over the road, tapering down into groves of willows and maples. The lone stop sign felt horribly out of place, a lone reminder of civilization. Jay walked to the edge of the asphalt, where the road abruptly stopped, and stared at the thick wall of trees.

"What the heck?"

This wasn't on the map. On the map, Highway 24 continued, he was certain. Jay grabbed his backpack from the passenger seat and wrapped it around his shoulders. His bag was light and wobbly. He'd packed haphazardly: a pair of clothes, a couple Capri Suns, $25,000 in cash.

He trudged into the woods, enveloped completely in silence. The hum of insects and the occasional chitter of nuthatches were the only sounds. In the distance, the river rumbled. Light fell through the branches, revealing the faint outline of a game trail. He pushed his way through ferns, following the trail.

Had there been a mistake? Had he missed an exit? He'd passed no other roads; this had to be it. Then why did the map show Highway 24 continuing? Since he'd left Rock Ridge, he hadn't allowed his mind to return to his conversation with Liz. The sinking feeling he'd been feeling for the last few hours was growing.

He scrambled over fallen trees and leapt over a boulder. It was odd that he'd never been this far out before. Maybe the road just stopped for a stretch. Maybe he'd find it again on the other side of these trees. He strained, listening for the sound of rushing cars. If he could flag one down, it could take him into Cougar. He moved faster now, searching the trees ahead for any break. And then, sure enough, the trees up ahead lightened. There was a clearing. And Jay heard a rumble that sounded a lot like traffic. He broke into a run, crashing forward.

The foliage around him thinned, thick cedars vanishing, the ferns turning into scraggly cottonwood. Jay held out a hand and shut his eyes, plunging through branches that scratched his face. Then the branches fell away, and Jay ran into something hard.

"Ouch!"

He fell backward, landing on his back, seeing stars.

When he looked up, he saw that the trees were gone, and so was the ground. He was standing at the edge of a rocky cliff. The earth plummeted hundreds of feet down into a wide, green valley that seemed to stretch on forever in alarming uniformity. To his right, the waters of the Skookullom crashed down over the cliff edge, dropping out of sight. Here was the source of the sound he'd heard. He stared. Never in his life had he seen anything like it. Living in the Cascade Range, you were always surrounded by mountains. The dull flatness in front of him was completely foreign. It felt like a mistake.

The sun was rising behind him, bleaching the last patches of night into beautiful pink and orange. Before him, there were no mountains, no sign of a path, a highway, a town, a meadow. Even the Skookullom River seemed to vanish under the canopy of green.

Jay stood and stepped forward to get a better look over the cliff.

BAM! He hit something and stumbled back again, holding his forehead.

When he looked up, nothing seemed to be blocking his way. He took a hesitant step forward with his hand out-stretched. His palm flattened. There was something smooth and hard. As his hand touched it, he felt the faint crackle of static and the hair on his fingers rose. It felt like touching the face of a TV screen.

"No . . ." he whispered.

He pushed on the invisible wall. It was solid. He threw his body against it. Nothing. Jay looked left and right. The cliff extended in both directions as far as he could see.

"No!"

He hurled another fist against the wall. On the other side, the trees bent in uniformity, as if blown by an invisible wind. Jay waited for the gust to touch his face, but it never did. It was an animation, like the trees in *The Build*. Jay collapsed against the wall, listening to the noise of the river loop mechanically.

He screamed. *It. Meant. Nothing.* His mind flashed back to last year, when they'd studied nihilism in Tutorial.

"You don't know the meaning, Miss Rotchkey!" Jay screamed at the cliff. "You don't know the meaning."

He picked up a rock and threw it at the wall. It bounced back. He fell onto the flat rock and lay there, dazed, staring out at the vast expanse. How was this possible?

SIMULATED INTELLIGENCE

JAY WASN'T CERTAIN how long he lay on the cliff side. He tried to concentrate, but his mind was spinning in circles. Every time he thought back to his conversation with Liz, and what it meant for him and his reality, his mind went blank. There was no longer a reason to return to Bickleton, so he just lay there, mesmerized by the vast expanse before him.

Eventually, he realized he was shivering. Looking down at his legs, he saw they were covered in goose bumps. He wore a light windbreaker and shorts, and he'd been warm enough when he'd been moving. But lying still on that cold rock, he felt completely drained of heat. Shaking, he forced his body up and trudged back down the game trail, feeling deeply resentful of his own physical needs.

Still, his mind seemed unable to weigh the implications of his discovery.

It wasn't until he was back in his Miata, with the top up and the heat on, did some normalcy return. He realized he was hungrier than ever, and that helped. The need for warmth and food at least gave him a reason to reacquaint with reality. He drove back slowly, in a state of shock. There was no longer a need to hurry. He would never have to hurry again.

He passed the city limits. A sign read "Welcome to Bickleton." Behind it was a small marquee that read "Mary Jo has won the raffle!" Its letters were faded and covered in green. That had been its message as long as Jay could remember.

He wound slowly through lower Bickleton. To his left, a green Northern Burlington caboose sat rusting on ancient train tracks, covered in graffiti. The mobile homes had satellite dishes on their roofs, sometimes two or three. Jay stared at them. How had he never noticed that before? There were only three channels in Bickleton, no matter how many satellite dishes your house had. Three channels, two radio stations. How had he never noticed how odd that was? He felt sickening claustrophobia as he drove slowly up to the heights.

He didn't even know where he was going. There was nowhere *to* go. It didn't matter if he returned to school and apologized, or if he stole Tutorial's computer to build a mansion and live his life like a billionaire. There was no leaving Bickleton. He stared down at his hands on the steering wheel. They were streams of data, he thought numbly. All just streams of data.

The kindest thing he could do, he realized, was kill himself. If he slammed his foot on the gas and drove off the road that second, he could end it. He doubted very much if a strength and dexterity score of 10 would allow him to survive an eighty-mile-per-hour crash. His mom would be sad, and Colin, too. But the rest of Bickleton? Everything would go back to normal. Three TV stations, two radio stations. The Johns could play baseball against themselves again. And the knowledge he had, the knowledge that their town—their lives—were just nothing? That would die with him. Nobody else in Bickleton would ever face the horror of their own existence.

Jay was so deep in his thoughts, he didn't even realize where he had been driving to. But now, suddenly, he saw he was outside Liz Knight's house.

In his eighteen years in Bickleton, he'd never been inside the Knights' house. His mom had. She went to United Methodist Church, same as the Knights, and she felt that Liz's parents were thoroughly good people.

The Knights didn't live on the bluff, alongside the most expensive mansions. This had always secretly been part of Liz's appeal. Despite her looks and A-Court fame, she was still one of the little people. Her parents had a modest home in the center of Bickleton, two blocks from La Dulce Vita trailer park. The house itself was a small two-story, built partially over a garage, with cedar hedges on either side, and a chain-link fence that hemmed in two barking golden retrievers. It felt newer than many of the homes in Bickleton, and Jay noticed the mauve paint and white trim looked fresh, and that the front lawn was freshly mowed.

Liz's Cherokee was parked in front of her garage. Parked along the street in front of her house was a barricade of trucks. Chevys mostly, some Fords. They were parked at odd angles, like they'd descended in a hurry. Johns were scattered across her lawn, and the front door was ajar. Jeremy stood on the cement steps of her house. Liz stood in the doorway, framed by her mom and dad. Jay slowed his Miata, and every single John turned at his arrival.

Jay found Liz's eyes. She shook her head slightly and mouthed the word "No." Jay stared, trying to decipher what she meant, when something slammed the hood of his Miata. Three Johns stood in front of Jay's car, leering. For a moment, Jay considered just running them over. But he felt tired. He turned off his ignition, leaving his car dead in the middle of the street.

Jeremy turned slowly and descended the steps of Liz's house. His face was neutral, as if he'd been expecting Jay. Liz took a step down the stoop of her house, and her dad followed her, placing a hand on his daughter's shoulder. Liz shrugged it off, uncomfortable.

As Jeremy approached the Miata, Jay stepped out. The Johns circled him, closing in. They formed their usual wall, but Jay noticed they kept their distance this time, shooting nervous glances toward Jeremy. Jeremy didn't have his usual sneer. He considered Jay carefully. Jay saw a purple welt under Jeremy's cheekbone. The slightest bit of color rose in Jeremy's cheeks.

"It wasn't fair."

Jay burst out laughing. Above everything else, Jeremy talking about what was "fair" was too much.

"I need to talk to Liz, Jeremy."

"Tell me how you did it."

"I can't," Jay said truthfully.

The Johns took a step closer. To his amazement, Jay found he wasn't afraid. He looked at all the Johns leaning in, and realized he didn't even know their last names. In fact, he was pretty sure they didn't *have* last names. He snorted in laughter again. The idea that he'd lived in Bickleton for eighteen years and never even noticed a detail like that was so absurd, he didn't even know what to make of it.

"Something funny?" Jeremy sneered.

"God has a sense of humor." Jay smiled.

From over the Johns' heads, Jay heard Liz's dad shout.

"I called the sheriff!"

Jeremy jerked his head at Jay. The Johns breathed a collective intake, and there was a rush of footsteps toward Jay.

They hit him from all directions. They were on top of him, blinding him. He could feel their weight dragging him down as they leapt on his shoulders, grabbed at his arms. His muscles strained against their collective mass, and then he was down. He grimaced as gravel drove into his stomach. He felt more bodies pile on. He choked, suffocating. Shoes dug into his back, and the air squeezed from his lungs.

Jay clenched his muscles, stretching his back. The bodies on top of him lifted. Jay grunted and heaved again. Bodies fell away, bucking. He pushed with all his might, and then he burst out of the Johns, sending their bodies tumbling across the gravel. He spun around, grabbing John C, and flung him over the lawn. John H was behind him. Jay kicked him in the stomach and heard a groan. His hand shot out, grabbing John B, and he flipped him into the hood of an F-150, denting it.

The Johns took a step back, staring wide-eyed. Jeremy held up his fists, dancing on his legs, uncertain. In an instant, Jay leapt forward and grabbed his shirt. Jeremy's hands fell away, and Jay lifted him off the ground so that his feet were dangling in midair. He watched with satisfaction as Jeremy's face turned red. He raised a fist, ready to pummel him, strength surging through his veins. Then he heard a noise in the yard across the street. Two kids peered through a metal fence, watching eagerly. Jay felt his adrenaline ebb. He lowered his fist.

Everything went quiet.

It was as if his ears had suddenly stopped working. All the ambient sounds were gone. The heavy breath of the Johns. A distant lawnmower. A truck shifting down on Main Street. All of the noise disappeared.

Jay glanced back at the kids across the street. Their hands were frozen on the fence, faces blank and unseeing.

Around him, John D and John S were frozen in mid-stride. John H was doubled over, arms wrapped around his stomach. Jeremy's face was frozen red, his lower jaw stuck at an odd angle, one eye half shut. He looked like a paused frame on a

VHS. Jay released his grip, and Jeremy remained where he was, frozen in midair.

"Jay!"

Liz ran down the front steps of her house. Her mom was frozen, hands covering her eyes, and her dad was trapped in a long stride back up the steps.

Liz reached Jay and grabbed his shoulder. "Did you do this?"

Jay shook his head. Even the wind had stopped. Trees were frozen to one side, as if held down by a massive gust. He glanced up. Directly above, a bird hovered in mid-flight, wings outstretched. Jay could see a small white blotch suspended in the air above him. Bird poop, frozen in the sky.

Someone coughed.

Another figure strolled down the road toward them. It was a man about Jay's height, but pear-shaped. He wore khaki shorts, sandals, and a fanny pack. His thick owl glasses were fixated on Jay.

"What's going on?" he asked.

Liz didn't respond. Jay looked over his shoulder. Liz was gone. Jay spun around, searching. She wasn't among all the frozen bodies. She had vanished.

The man's footsteps left the road and crunched over the gravel. He was smiling, though the effort seemed to strain him. Jay shrunk back. He stopped a few feet away and reached a hand into his fanny pack to pull out a black metal cylinder. He twirled it in his fingers and nodded at Jeremy.

"Finish him."

HAL

"WHAT?" JAY BLINKED.

The man smiled. "Oh, that's right. *Mortal Kombat* isn't scheduled to come out until December. Tell Colin to get the Genesis version; I'll make sure *GamePro* has the blood code. 'Finish him' translates loosely into 'kill him in a spectacular manner.' Like the gladiators used to."

Jay felt his stomach drop.

"K-kill Jeremy?" he whispered.

"Like the thought's never crossed your mind. What did you mean to happen when you unleashed that tornado? I know you've thought about using other disasters. Sending an earthquake, a riot, a downed plane, a flood. Or releasing the monster. So be a man. Do it with your hands."

"Do I . . . do I know you?"

The man continued to smile. "You can call me Hal. Like Paul Simon."

There was something familiar about Hal's low voice and stilted manner of speaking. Then Jay realized how he recognized him. "You're Marvelous Mark!"

The man's smile grew pink with pleasure. He nodded. "I'm many things. You might also recognize my photo in *Serious Gamer*? It's a little grainy . . ."

Jay thought back to the editor's letter he looked forward to every month. His mind's eye conjured the loopy signature of the editor.

"You're Hal?"

"I'm pleased that you've taken my recommendations so seriously."

"I've got a mixtape of your music. And I've bought all your game recommendations. Even . . ."

Jay remembered the issue he'd received on his birthday. The one with the floppy of *The Build*.

"You sent me *The Build*."

Hal grinned. "I think you'll find, Jay, you can trace a lot of your interests back to me. I wear lots of hats. Editor. DJ. City planner. You might say that I built this city," Hal giggled, "on rock and roll."

Jay's eyes widened. Hal nodded.

"Yes, it's a game. Though I feel that undersells the experience. This is a playground, Jay. *Your* playground."

Jay felt sick. The terrible truth of Bickleton was staring him down, and he couldn't look away. All the rage he'd ever felt living in this stupid town came roiling up in his chest and he clenched his fists, shouting.

"I'm an NPC in a video game!? Everything I've been doing, learning—the spotted owls, the World Trade Center bombing, *Twin Peaks* . . . none of it's real?"

Hal's smile shrank.

"That's a glass-half-empty view. I didn't build this in a week, you know. This is not some half-assed app. This is a real world, as real as the one I live in. And reality's not half as fun.

"Here's life." He held a stubby finger in the air. "If life in reality were a line graph, it'd go like this." He drew a short, sharp rise, then a gradual decline. "Party at the front; depression, despair, death at the back. But not you. You get the inverse. Your life is gonna look like this." He drew a flat line in the air that suddenly skyrocketed. "Up and up and up. And the best part? It never has to end."

Hal's smile returned to the look of shock on Jay's face. "That's right. The rules are different for you. No molecular breakdown of cells. No aging, outside of the algorithms I've written, and algorithms can be tweaked. You can live here forever, if you'd like."

Jay's queasiness doubled. He bent over, running his fingers through his hair, trying not to vomit. The thought of living for eternity . . . in Bickleton . . .

"But I don't want to stay here at all!" he gasped. "All I've ever wanted was to leave."

Hal chuckled. "Just you wait. You'll find that Bickleton isn't so bad. Don't limit yourself to cliché ideas of what high school is or has been. Use your imagination. Show me something marvelous."

"Like what?"

"That baseball game! One high school loner takes on the whole team. Give me more of that! Give Jeremy and the Johns what they deserve. You've barely scratched the surface of what you can do."

Jay's mind reeled with questions.

"Why now? Why, all of a sudden, are you giving me this?" His voice cracked with emotion. "Why not in eighth grade, when John D threw me in the trash can? Or in sixth grade, when Jeremy held my face down in the gravel and let his little sister beat me up? Why didn't you just make me strong to begin with? Why did you give me this body?!"

Hal chuckled. "If I would've given you this power from the beginning, you would've ended up like another Jeremy. Or worse. You needed to know pain. I'm sorry, but you had to suffer. Like I did in high school. I would have given anything for the gift you have. In fact, you'll never know just how much I've given. Trust me. For the rest of your long, long life, you'll look back on these last eighteen years, and you'll laugh. You'll thank me, because I showed you what life is like for most people, and then I delivered you from it. I have given you something so much better."

"Why me? Why not Colin, or Stevie?"

"Because you're like me. You feel things deeply, Jay. You're a hopeless romantic, as I was." Hal's gaze slackened. "I had a Jeremy of my own back in my high school. A Colin. A Liz. The only thing I didn't have was someone to help me." He gave Jay a thin smile. "I don't think you realize how lucky you are."

"What happens to Liz? She said you put her in here."

"She and I have an arrangement. Right now, she's plugged in. Her brain is running her character, controlling her avatar. But while that's happening, *The Build* is running a program on her brain. It's mapping her mind, learning her personality, how she makes decisions. In two days' time, it will have what it needs. On prom night, she'll be liberated."

"You mean . . . you're copying her brain?"

Hal nodded.

"In forty-eight hours, her mind will be completely mapped into code. Liz's avatar will switch from being player-controlled to an NPC. The AI engine is so good, you won't even notice when it happens."

"And the real Liz goes free?"

The wrinkles on Hal's pockmarked face turned up around his eyes. "Why, sure. My experiment will be complete, and they'll be no need for her to stay. She can go back to her life."

Jay studied Hal's face, looking for any hint of doubt or malevolence. Hal smiled right back through beady eyes.

"Like I said, she and I have an arrangement. I'm not a monster, Jay."

"Yeah? Then what happened to Todd?"

Hal sighed. "Well, first, Todd was an NPC, so there's an ethical distinction, in my opinion. If a character lives solely in the code of my game, if I created him, then I have a right to do what I want. So I removed him. But I know you two used to be friends, so I can bring him back, if that's important. I know the morality of my logic may not seem so cut-and-dried, from in here."

Jay's voice wavered, uncertain of his standing with this man. "Could we bring him back?"

"I'll add that to the queue. Anything else?"

Jay thought of his best friend's dazed look during their conversation in the Mark parking lot.

"Why do people tune out when I try to explain *The Build*?"

Hal smiled. "When I was a kid, we used to go to this place called Northwest Trek. It was a zoo housing the regional animals. Elk, wolves, moose, bison, cougar. We'd ride a tram through the park."

Jay saw a sudden glimpse of a tram riding over a wooded hill.

"They did such a good job hiding the park's perimeter, and I loved that we couldn't see the edges, where the wolf enclosure ended, where the bison pen began. See, all the moats and walls were camouflaged. I tried to do the same here. I tried to give everyone full free will, while also keeping them within the town, through hidden seams. But that didn't pan out. Teenage curiosity is a helluva force. Kids kept trying to leave, trying to poke through what I built, find the seams. So I had to build a constraint. It makes NPCs a little less lifelike, I suppose, but it keeps everyone from picking at the loose strands of their reality.

"Here's the rub: there's a chunk of code that keeps the good folk of Bickleton from thinking too hard about certain ideas or concepts. Such as leaving Bickleton. Or any idea that comes too close to the truth. Whenever someone has one of those ideas, well, they just . . . switch off for a bit."

Jay nodded, thinking back to his mom's, Ms. Molouski's, and Principal Oatman's slackened gazes when he'd brought up *The Build*. But then he remembered Liz.

"So I can talk to Liz because she's a real player?"

Hal nodded. "And you can talk to me."

"And I can contemplate all that stuff? I don't have that . . . constraint?"

"Like I said, you're special. I made some exceptions for you. You wouldn't have been able to use my birthday present if those parameters applied to you."

Jay shook his head, frustration rising.

"You decide who's born, who dies? You can change how we think or what we do, take away our free will whenever you feel like it? Sounds like a pretty stupid game."

Again, Hal tensed.

"No no no. You can't think about it like that. You have to treat it like it's real; that's the only way it will be fun. It *does* mean something. It means what you want it to."

"How am I supposed to treat it like it's real? I'm just supposed to keep it to myself, pretend like high school is normal? I can't even hang out with my best friend now, because you've programmed him to ignore all the stuff I'm going through."

Hal's face fell again. He looked anguished. "Well, I can't just turn those parameters off. People will get stuck. You should have seen it before, in earlier versions. They'd set up camp at the edge of the map, wouldn't leave for days. If I let you tell them the truth, we don't know what the ramifications would be. If everyone in town could actually contemplate that they were in a simulation . . . I mean, can you imagine?"

Jay crossed his arms. "I have to tell someone."

Hal fidgeted, staring at the ground. He began to pace back and forth, running his hands through his horseshoe ring of hair, mouth screwed into a grimace, muttering. Jay worried about the sudden change. In a matter of seconds, Hal's confidence and gloating had dissolved into anxiety. He seemed to be in genuine agony, struggling with a decision. Finally, he grumbled:

"All right. I'll change the code so you can tell your friends. But if it causes existential panic—"

"I promise I'll only tell Colin."

Hal nodded begrudgingly. "Okay. But in return, I want fireworks."

"Fireworks?"

"Yeah. Enjoy yourself. More than just a Miata and a baseball game."

He pointed at where Jeremy hung frozen in midair. "Finish him."

Jay followed Hal over to Jeremy. Jeremy's red face was still staring at the spot where Jay had been standing. Jay felt the usual disgust for his tormentor, but it was less urgent now. Jeremy was programmed to torment Jay. Jay wondered at that existence. What did it feel like to be Jeremy? Was his mind so singular that that was all he could contemplate? He looked at Hal, whose beady eyes gleamed hungrily up at Jeremy. He looked as if he could kill him.

"I don't . . . I can't kill."

"He's earned it."

Jay's mind raced as he looked to stall.

"Wouldn't that be anticlimactic, though? He's had eighteen years to beat the shit out of me. I'm just getting started."

Hal grinned, revealing yellow teeth. "*That's* what I want to see." He shook his head, as if surprised at himself. "I know I shouldn't be impatient, but I've been working on this too long.

You know how it is: you've put the time into Poopville. I want to see you get creative. Make him suffer."

Jay felt sick to his stomach. He tried to smile. "I've got eighteen years' worth of ideas."

Hal didn't seem to notice. He was twirling the black rod in his hand, impatient.

"Jay, it's been a pleasure to finally chat. I gotta go check on the CPU temperature—gets a little hot running two player characters at the same time."

He held out a small sweaty palm, and Jay tentatively shook it.

"I'll let you get back to it. Till next time?"

Without waiting for Jay to respond, Hal clicked a button on his black wand and vanished. The world unpaused. Jeremy dropped onto the lawn, gasping. The wind was again howling around them. The Johns were groaning and stumbling backward. Liz stood on the lawn, wobbly and disoriented. Jay ran to her.

"What happened?"

Liz responded by vomiting into the grass.

"Ugh." She wiped her mouth. "Hal didn't want me to see whatever just happened."

"He teleported you?"

Liz nodded. "What was it he didn't want me to see?"

"Our conversation," Jay whispered.

Bickleton's lone patrol car turned down their small street. The Johns limped to their trucks, throwing themselves in their cabs. Engines rumbled to life and car tires squealed.

But Liz wouldn't break Jay's gaze.

"What did he say?"

SECOND PLAYER

THE LAST OF the Chevys peeled out, leaving Liz's house silent. The only sounds were the wind and Sheriff Jenkins's car settling to a halt.

Jay looked down the street and saw window shades snap shut. The people of Bickleton, he realized, had been enjoying the high school drama. He watched Elmer haul his fat body out of the driver's seat. His left eye was twitching mercilessly, and he held a messy sandwich in his left hand, which he must have just grabbed from Golden Flour Bakery. He was scowling.

"What did he say?" Liz repeated, her eyes still focused on Jay.

Jay's head swam at the surreal conversation he'd just had. "He wants me to make changes. He wants me to . . ." Jay lowered his voice. "Well, he wants me to kill Jeremy."

Mr. Knight rushed from the house. He was tall and dark-skinned, with Liz's green eyes and a big mustache plastered across his face. He looked like a guy who'd ridden motorcycles in his youth. Liz stiffened as he approached. Elmer's sandwich dripped ketchup and mayonnaise as he awkwardly pointed at Jay.

"Let's talk, Banksman."

Mr. Knight shook his head. "It wasn't Jay's fault. The whole baseball team ganged up on him."

Sheriff Jenkins's twitchy eye narrowed. "Yeah, I heard he's a real fighter now."

Jay leaned in to Liz.

"It's okay," he whispered. "Hal's going to let you go. It's me he wants."

Liz whispered back. "You *believe* him?"

"He won't hurt you. He's downloading your consciousness. It's gonna take two more days. You'll be free after prom."

Liz's brow crinkled in anger.

"What?!" Jay whispered. "You get to return to nice, sane reality. I'm the one stuck in a computer game."

Liz stalked over the lawn and went into her house, slamming the front door and puncturing the conversation Sheriff Jenkins and Mr. Knight were having.

Mr. Knight stared at the door mournfully, then murmured, "She's been like this ever since you picked her up."

Elmer shrugged. "Teenagers."

"She won't even look at me."

"They say it gets better." Sheriff Jenkins nodded sympathetically. He waddled over to Jay, scarfing down the last of the sandwich.

"You want to give a statement?" he muttered through a mouthful.

"Not really," said Jay, in disgust. He was about to speak again when he felt something tug at the edge of his consciousness. A kind of darkness suddenly engulfed him, and the sunlight and sky and sound of Sheriff Jenkins's voice diminished, as if receding down a tunnel. It was as if his mind were remembering something beyond his control.

He was standing in a small living room. His feet were bare on bristled Persian carpet. His back was to the room, but he knew that if he turned around he'd see a Panasonic television on a small black shelf, next to a Super Nintendo and a Genesis. A stereo was playing one of his favorite songs, "Scarlet" by Lush. His tragic victory song.

He was looking out a window at the street below. It was night, a half-twilight he'd never seen in Bickleton. Streetlamps pumped a purple-orange glow onto the sidewalk. The curbs were full of cars, and they were small. By the look of it, he must be about three stories up. On the street below, red and blue lights flashed on the windows of the convenience store across the street. An Asian man stood in the window, watching. Jay heard the clank of metal as the gate to the apartment complex slammed shut. Two police officers escorted a dark figure out of the gate, into the back of the car. Jay felt his body exhale, and felt a tremendous wave of relief, though he couldn't remember why.

It was over in a flash, and he was standing back outside Liz's house. He blinked, trying to reorient himself. What was that? It felt like a flashback to a memory he didn't recognize. Sheriff Jenkins stared at him, pen and notebook frozen and awaiting a statement.

"You okay?"

Jay shook his head. "I, uh, need to get home and lie down."

Sheriff Jenkins put his notebook away. "Okay. No more fighting though. Got it?"

Jay rolled his eyes and glanced back at the house for a sign of Liz. But the curtains were drawn.

BACKPLOTTING

A FEW BLOCKS from Liz's house, Jeremy raged.

The Johns were standing next to their trucks, rubbing bruised limbs. John K and John H, who'd received the fewest injuries, were running up and down the sidewalk, trying to catch a chicken that had escaped a neighboring yard. It was an uncommonly ugly bird, with a turkey-like goiter covering the base of its beak, and a wing that wouldn't fully close. It darted through the Johns' legs as they kicked at it in frustration, repeating its low cry of *buck-buck-bu-KAW*.

Kris Kross blared from an open truck door as John H carefully steadied himself behind the chicken, lunged at the ground, and wrapped the bird in his arms. Its wings flared as it squawked and kicked. John K chuckled in elation.

"Put that thing down," Jeremy's voice came, low and furious.

John H did as he was told. The bird fell and fluttered away, landing a few feet from the boys and eyeing them curiously.

Jeremy had a red rash around his throat where Jay had grabbed him. One of his eyes was starting to puff into a bruise. Anger blotched his face into a standing crimson. Every time he closed his eyes, he saw visions of Jay laughing at him, followed by visions of Jay screaming in pain. He spun around and punched the door of John H's truck. The Johns watched silently, knowing better than to interrupt one of Jeremy's rages.

Finally, John C spoke up.

"How'd he do it?"

"We're gonna find out." Jeremy spun around. "John H and John K."

The two stood at attention.

"Follow Jay. Figure out what he's been up to. Until we figure out what he's playing, give him a wide berth."

"We still gonna do prom?"

Jeremy touched his swollen eye and winced. "Yes. Prom goes as planned."

The Johns turned to their trucks as one. Jeremy climbed into John W's pickup, and they pulled out into the street. The chicken ran back and forth, once again free. John W saw and accelerated. There was a bump, and feathers flew up out of the wheel well. John W looked over at Jeremy, snickering. But Jeremy was staring out the window. Fear welled in his stomach. That same, familiar terror. He saw a vision of himself, emaciated and small. He had chains around his wrists, and he was naked against the vending machine in A-Court. Students passed by—the Johns, Amber, and Gretchen—and they laughed at him. And then there was Jay, standing over him, large as God, pointing at his face. Fear and hatred expanded in Jeremy like a hot balloon. He fought his own brain to convince himself, again, that it was a dream and not a premonition.

SMALL MIRACLES

COLIN TURNED *THE Build* disk over in his hands, eyes closed, tracing the plastic lines with his fingers. He and Jay kneeled between the bleak pews of New Bethlehem Church. The stuffing had bled out of the kneelerrs over the years, and their legs ached on the hard pine. It was uncomfortable, just how church was supposed to be. The room was bathed in the red light that filtered through the stained glass windows.

Jay felt a little melodramatic for bringing Colin to a church to tell him everything. But the dry air of the church felt right. He could think there. He looked up at the stained glass, where Jesus extended a hand toward them, beckoning. Jay glanced at his friend. As he'd talked, telling Colin everything that had happened, Colin had shut his eyes and lowered his jaw, so that his shaggy hair fell over his face. Jay searched anxiously for any sign that Colin had heard him, and whether or not he believed him.

Finally, Colin opened his eyes and stared down at the game box.

"So you're saying we're living inside a game?"

A grin spread over Jay's face. He clasped his hands together before the stained glass Jesus.

"Yes! Oh, this is a *big* step in the right direction."

Colin shook his head. "It's insane. You realize you're insane, right?"

"Denial is the first step toward acceptance."

Pastor Roberts leaned into the pew, startling them both. He was the way-too-cheerful cheerleader of the parish, and practically lived at the church. On his way home from school, Jay often saw him bustling about in the yard, whacking at the blackberry vines and stinging nettle that always seemed on the verge of engulfing his church. Now, he beamed over the pew through thick freckles and red hair, a boyish grin glowing between his wrinkled face.

"Hey, sorry! Didn't mean to startle you. But you guys gotta check this out."

His head swiveled back and forth, as if to make sure no one was listening, then whispered:

"Come on. Outside."

Jay hesitated. He didn't want to lose his momentum with Colin, but Pastor was waving them out of the pew. Jay sighed and let the enthusiasm of the little man carry him out the church door. The front steps were cut into a small cement balcony that was surrounded by a thin rusted railing. Pastor Rob Roberts leaned over the railing, beckoning them.

Jay saw nothing. Rob Roberts pointed down. Jay followed his finger into the patch of stinging nettle at their feet. Steam wafted up between the plant stems, and a small brown body lay nestled between the leaves. A fawn. White spots curled around its flank in a vortex. He heard Colin exhale.

Rob Roberts looked beyond pleased.

"I've heard they do this sometimes. Give birth and leave their young. You're not supposed to touch them."

"Is it alive?"

Jay strained his eyes, looking for any irregularities in its perfect fur. No pixels, no loose textures. How was it possible for a computer to re-create something so perfectly?

"Oh yes. It's been squeakin' all morning. Calling for its mom, probably. This is the kind of miracle they tell you to look out for. The small, everyday sort." He chuckled. "But then when they happen . . ."

Jay glanced up at Pastor Roberts. An oversize grin wrapped his face, staring down at the deer with hungry intensity. Jay had never noticed it before, but there was a cruelty locked within his stare. Jay had a sudden flash of revelation. The world of Bickleton was full of such underlying cruelty. A reflection of its master and creator.

Pastor Roberts straightened, oblivious to Jay's stares. "Yeah, sure is something. You boys want oyster crackers?"

Colin straightened, hopeful. Jay shook his head.

"No, thank you. Colin and I are having an earnest conversation."

Pastor Roberts's eyebrows lifted.

"Ohhh. Say no more. Sorry for interrupting. I understand. Boys your age? Sure, sure. I didn't realize y'all were here on *official* business."

He winked and strode off. Jay led Colin back to the pew, taking a last look back at the deer. He saw steam waft up beyond the church door. Colin placed *The Build* on the wooden seat behind him and took a deep breath.

"So that deer? That's part of this game?"

"*Everything*. All of Bickleton."

"And you know this how?"

"I've seen the end with my eyes. It's a blank wall."

"And we're NPCs?"

"Simulated intelligences. Algorithms, computing out person-like intelligence."

Jay reached into his bag and pulled out a black disk. "Here. Take a copy. In case anything happens to me." He pushed it into Colin's chest. "But you can't show anyone. Not your mom, not your sister."

"Oh, don't worry. Because you've been playing too many video games. Whatever cracked Liz, you caught it."

Jay slid back into the hard pine pews and sighed. "I thought you might say that. You're right to be skeptical."

He leapt up and shouted back toward the rectory: "Thanks, Pastor Roberts!"

Colin looked up suspiciously at Jay. "Where are we going?"

"To help you move past denial."

For the second time, they left church. Faint wisps of vapor drifted up from the nettle patch. Jay glanced down curiously for the fawn as he passed by. But the fawn was gone. A fog had rolled in, and everything was still. Even the distant rumble of logging trucks felt muted. Jay ushered Colin into his Miata, and neither of them saw the parked Chevy truck behind them, where John H and John K watched carefully out the windshield.

THE BUILD

JAY SHIVERED IN front of the computer. It was evening now, and the fog was thick outside Tutorial. The only light filtered through the single window. Pine trees outside floated like ghostly shapes in the mist. It was weather usually associated with fall, and Colin, who always wore cargo shorts, shivered by the computer, glancing anxiously toward the door.

Jay, leaning back in his chair, clicked through *The Build*. "You hungry?"

He clicked on the FOOD folder and moved a packet of Hi-C Ecto Coolers over to Colin's pixelated desk. He followed this with two trays of personal pizzas, and clicked Enter. The food materialized on the desk in Tutorial. Colin fell over in his chair.

He breathed quickly, sprawled out on the floor, stunned. "You–you—"

"Made that out of thin air?"

"But . . . how'd you get it *here*?" He stood up.

"I told you. We're *in* the game. We can do anything. See, there's a castle in this folder. Should we make a castle? Up on the bluff? Or here, watch this."

He clicked into the ANIMALS folder. Outside the Tutorial window, there came a low *moooo* and a jingling bell. Colin approached the window. A black-and-white Holstein cow ambled through the pine trees and disappeared into the fog.

"You made that cow?"

Jay gestured to the computer. "Want to try?"

Colin sat down at his desk and shook his head. He turned his attention to the pizza, but Jay could see he was thinking.

"You believe me now? You could drive the *actual* Batmobile if you wanted to. It's in a folder called LICENSED PROPERTY."

Colin chewed his pizza, not looking at Jay.

"What do you think? You want a mansion with the Batmobile, like Pablo Escobar? You want your own private viewing room to watch *My Neighbor Totoro*? Or do you want to wipe the map clean? Start fresh."

Colin looked up from his pizza to eye the computer skeptically. "What if we mess things up?"

"What do you mean, *mess things up*? Look around this hellhole. How much more messed up could it get?"

"Like a glitch."

"We could be bajillionaires. We could buy and sell the McKraken mill."

"What if we're no good at running a town?"

Jay sighed. "My record speaks for itself. I've never had an earthquake in *SimCity*, and we have a one-million-dollar budget surplus. No one is more qualified."

Colin still seemed hesitant, so Jay continued. "Want me to give you a makeover? Boost your stats?"

"What if it messes *me* up?"

Jay flexed a bicep. "Does this look messed up?"

Colin took the last bite of his pizza. "You're putting a lot of faith in Hal."

"But how good was that pizza?" Jay moused around the screen. "Huh."

The screen was centered on the C-Court parking lot. A circle of Dodge Rams sat parked.

"Our friends are here." The pixelated Johns were loitering in the parking lot. "They think they can play baseball in this fog?"

He studied the screen. Within the circle of trucks stood a circle of Johns. Two of the Johns ran across the parking lot and joined the circle. Little speech bubbles popped up, with streams of periods to show they were talking, but Jay couldn't see what they were saying. He moused over them until Jeremy's name popped up.

"By the way, Hal wants me to kill Jeremy."

Colin paused. "Oh?"

Jay right-clicked Jeremy's avatar. The word DELETE popped up in big black letters.

"I could do it now."

"You think that's what Hal did to Todd, then? Deleted him?"

Jay's finger hovered over the left mouse button. Colin's question brought Todd back to the forefront. Hal had said he'd had to remove him. A stony guilt hardened in Jay's stomach. What would happen if he deleted Jeremy? Could he bring him back? Would he be the same? Jay clicked away from Jeremy, and the menu disappeared.

"Eh, they're leaving."

Sure enough, onscreen trucks were driving off in their tell-tale line.

"What's this folder?" Colin was standing now, and pointed to a folder labeled GAMES.

Jay double-clicked. The screen filled with game box art. Super Nintendo games, Sega Genesis games, computer games. Jay's and Colin's mouths fell open. It seemed to be every single game that had ever existed.

"*Alien vs. Predator. Super Metroid. Barkley Shut Up and Jam! Toe Jam & Earl*," Jay read aloud, breathlessly. "*Tetris 2*!? I didn't even know that was a thing."

"We can get those?"

Jay clicked, rapid-fire. Cartridges popped into existence across Colin's desk, clattering into his arms. Jay was already pushing his way past, clutching the goods as if they might disappear at any moment.

"C'mon. Let's get these in the car."

And then Jay was out the door. Colin waddled after his friend, struggling to keep the individual cartridges balanced. Except for the distant shouts from Jay and corresponding mumbles from Colin, the forest was quiet. Then the pine needles crackled, and two Johns stepped out of the trees. They checked to ensure nobody was looking, then disappeared into Tutorial.

THE JOHNS
STRIKE BACK

JEREMY AND THE Johns hadn't been at the school to play baseball. The line of trucks barreled through the fog, windshield wipers flying back and forth, leaving little rivulets across the glass. Weather like this came on chilly days, when the air grew colder than the Skookullom River.

The parade of trucks headed away from school, toward the main drag. To the citizens of Bickleton, nothing was more reassuring than that motorcade. It had existed in many forms over the decades. Different Johns, different drivers. Old-timers would stiffen at the sight of it, thinking back to their own high school years, some growing misty-eyed for the good old days.

Jeremy was squeezed between two Johns in the cab of a truck, his legs wrapped around the gear shift. The intermittent whir of the windshield wipers played over "Boot Scootin' Boogie" on the radio. The rage was back. It burned up Jeremy's chest, as it always did when Jay was near. His hands clenched and his jaw locked. How he hated Jay. Visions of blood and torture danced before his eyes. He pictured Jay screaming for mercy. More importantly, he pictured himself free. The urge to hurt Jay was growing worse and worse.

"You get it?"

John B held up a small black disk. "We got it. We watched 'em through the window. This was what they were using."

Jeremy took the disk and spun it around in his hands. He'd never paid much attention to computers. He was surprised to see just how small a floppy disk was.

"You sure?"

"Let's check it out."

"Right. Do either of you own a computer?"

John C volunteered, "Yeah, my dad just got one. Called a, uh, a Gateway. Looks like a cow."

Jeremy nodded. "Go get it."

John C nodded and swerved. The caravan of vehicles followed his lead, heading off the main strip. Two withered men stepped out of the Eagles Lodge, fuzzy with drink, and stopped abruptly to watch the cavalcade roar by.

"God bless those boys." They nodded somberly.

THREE'S COMPANY

JAY WAS EMPTYING his backpack on Colin's basement floor for the fourth time, carefully sorting through the loose papers and game boxes that fell out.

"Can we turn a light on?" he hissed.

Colin stumbled to the wall and flicked a switch, bathing the room in ugly overhead lighting. He winced, glancing fearfully at the basement door, anticipating his mom storming into the room. But there was no sound. Colin shrugged, blowing on a Super Nintendo cartridge before inserting it back into the console.

"If it wasn't in the car with us when we left . . ."

"It can't have disappeared!"

"We still have the copy, right?" Colin held up his black floppy. "We can make a copy of the copy."

"Dude." Jay fished a hand under a dusty oak dresser. "What if someone else finds it? What if some knuckle-dragger from shop class gets his hands on it?"

"You think they'd know what a floppy is?" Colin was lying on his chest, peering under the dresser. "You're sure you didn't leave it in the computer?"

Jay rifled through his book bag again. "Positive. We put the games in your trunk, we went back to the classroom, it was gone. Oh God, what if someone took it?"

"Who?"

Jay didn't have an answer. He sat on the cold, hard floor, running his infallible memory back through the last six hours.

"We have to go back and look for it."

It was already almost 3:00 a.m. They sat in a rat's nest of sleeping bags and blankets, open bags of Doritos and cans of Mountain Dew strewn all over the floor. The title screen for *Donkey Kong Country* danced on the screen. The truth was, neither of them wanted to go back to Tutorial. Colin's basement was warm and cozy, and on the other side of the glass door was fog and pitch darkness.

"Tonight?"

Jay sighed, going toward the door. "We can't risk any—AHH!"

Jay stumbled backward. There was a girl's face behind the sliding glass door. It was Liz, and she was motioning to be let in. Heart pounding, Jay stepped forward and unlocked the door. Liz shivered and slid into the basement.

"Jeezus, you guys are hard to find!"

"Shhh!" both boys admonished, glancing fearfully at the ceiling.

"I tried calling earlier; didn't you hear?" Around midnight, the phone had rung several times. Jay had star-69'd the call, and when he didn't recognize the number, he'd taken the phone off the receiver. Liz stared at the mess of wrappers and cartridges that covered the floor. "Looks like a homeless camp down here." She sniffed. "Smells even worse."

"Well, we weren't expecting company."

He didn't mention the relief he felt at seeing her again. He still felt crummy after her cold dismissal earlier. She was, after all, the only real person in Bickleton. Liz slid the basement door shut.

"I'm sorry, but we couldn't really talk at my place. Not with Hal potentially watching."

Jay glanced around the basement. "How do you know he's not watching right now?"

"Because he's asleep. Now listen, we don't have much time." Liz shut off the TV. "You know what I do, in the real world? I'm a veterinarian. And before Hal brought me here, I saw some things in his house that scared the hell out of me. He keeps a bottle of propofol in his bedroom."

Jay remembered Dr. Shrek's office, when Liz had mumbled something about propofol.

"You know what propofol does? It's a sedative. Knocks you right out."

Jay and Colin looked at each other and shrugged, so Liz continued.

"You know what else he had? Two more bottles. Pancuronium bromide and potassium chloride. I didn't know what those were either, at first. Had to go digging through the library card catalog. But I found out. Pancuronium stops your neuro system: it paralyzes you. And potassium chloride is a salt that's so powerful, it induces cardiac arrest. It stops your heart. propofol, potassium chloride, and pancuronium bromide. The lethal cocktail, the formula they use to kill death-row inmates. And Hal happens to have those three bottles on his guest room nightstand. Next to his virtual-reality helmet. Next to my body. So what do you really think he plans to do once my brain is finished uploading?"

Jay felt his insides freeze. He felt as if he couldn't move. Colin let the controller slip out of his fingers and clatter on the floor.

"You mean he plans to *kill* you?"

Liz was pale. She suddenly looked very old. For a moment, Jay thought he saw the real Liz peeking out at him through eighteen-year-old Liz's face. He saw so much pain there; of all the alcoholics in Bickleton, he'd never seen such striking intensity. She looked as though she were on the verge of collapse.

"Yes," she continued quietly. "He means to kill me. I have tried to escape this world. And every road leads me back to you, Jay. Hal has selected you to share his power. And I need it, bad."

The shock of what she was saying made him feel dizzy. "But . . . he said he was going to let you go?"

"Hal lies, Jay. If he lets me go, what happens? He's kidnapped me. That's a felony. I've been under his spell for two weeks now. He's feeding me intravenously. I probably have *bedsores* by now. You think, if he let me go, I'm just going to get up, thank him, and be on my way?"

"Could you *pretend* that you wouldn't press charges? Maybe he'd trust you?" Colin offered.

Liz scoffed. "Hal doesn't trust anyone. Except, apparently, Jay."

Jay looked up suddenly. "How did he trap you?"

Liz looked disgusted. "I *let* him."

LIZ'S STORY

THE TELEVISION THROBBED and flickered in the basement, casting a cool blue glow over the floor. Onscreen, *Donkey Kong* characters remained frozen in pause. Jay and Colin had their backs to them, waiting eagerly as Liz pulled up a beanbag chair and hunkered down. Except for a few creaks upstairs, the house remained still.

"It started in Bickleton," Liz whispered. "And for the record"—Liz looked accusingly around the basement—"*this* is not Bickleton. This is a rough replica of the real Bickleton, as it was in 1993. Back when Hal and I went to high school together, almost thirty years ago."

Colin raised a hand. "So you're . . ."

"Forty-six." She did some quick math. "Forty-six? No, forty-seven. Forty-seven years old."

Jay and Colin looked at each other in horror. That was as old as their moms. The beautiful, popular senior across from them was actually being controlled by someone their mom's age? Jay glanced down at Liz's hands, as if he expected to see signs of age. His stomach lurched. Of course it made sense, if her world was decades in the future. He'd known she was older, but he never would have guessed she was that much older.

She looked so young. Liz gave a thin smile, as if guessing his thoughts.

"I know, it's weird. Being back in this body. I haven't looked this way in a long time. I've served my time. I hacked my way through the horrors of high school. I left Bickleton behind to live my life. Let's see, I went to UC Berkeley, did a stint in Seattle, then traveled abroad for three years, before enrolling in a veterinary college in Vermont. Where I met my husband."

She stopped, looking at the increasing horror on Jay's face. "Yes, I'm married. In fact, we have two children, about your age. We live in Laguna Beach now, which is where he's from. He's a writer, and I run my own clinic."

Liz looked down at her white T-shirt and ripped jeans. "It's been a long time since I could fit into these jeans. It's messed up, but being back isn't *all* bad. You leave high school thinking you'll go back, that people won't change. That you'll always have those same friends, that you'll always laugh so hard, that your little crushes will always be a matter of life and death. But really, nothing in life compares to those four brief years. And as much as I hate Hal, I've got to hand it to him: he's got a memory for details. The greasy stench of C-Court tater tots. The way everyone freaks out when Blind Melon's 'No Rain' plays on MTV. The way Principal Oatman turned a blind eye, letting certain kids get away with anything."

Jay wasn't listening. He was thinking about Liz with her husband, his strong hand wrapped around her waist. He felt a surge of jealousy and confusion over his feelings.

"What about us?" Colin ventured. "Were we there, back in high school?"

She stared at Colin. "Yeah."

"What about the guy you and Jay keep talking about? Hal."

"Yep, he was there. He was the skinny kid who'd had the same mustache since kindergarten. He was the butt of every prank, the punch line of every joke. When he got mad, he'd swing his fists in circles like a windmill. Or curse you in Shakespearean prose. He, uh . . . he didn't have many friends.

"Anyway, he obviously figures into the story more. So we graduated. The memory of high school faded. Except it didn't for Hal. I didn't stay in touch with him. I don't know anyone who did. But whatever the kids in high school did to him, it stuck. He's been thinking about it ever since. I heard that he got into one of the good technical universities. MIT, I think. Then at some point, he apparently moved back to Bickleton—the real Bickleton—with enough money to retire."

"So he's running this simulation of Bickleton in the real Bickleton?"

Liz nodded. "I don't know when he started, or why he did it, but he's been at it for years, apparently, updating graphics, improving sound."

"So if you went to school with Hal—in the real Bickleton—and you moved away . . . ?"

"How did I end up here? Right. So time went by, my dad passed away, I started thinking about things. Like, who am I, what have I done with my life, yadda yadda. Latter-half-of-life thoughts. I was living in Laguna, but I came up each year to see my mom, who still lives in Bickleton. And on one of these trips, I stopped by the Morning Market—still standing, thirty years later—to get some ChapStick. And who did I run into?"

"Hal?"

Liz nodded. "I hadn't seen him since high school, and he looked rough. His skin was hanging from his cheeks like it was gonna slide off. He hadn't shaved in days. His hair was wild and gray and mostly gone. He was yelling at the store manager, not making eye contact, in classic Hal fashion. He was saying things like"—Liz tucked her jaw back into her neck and gave a deep, watery impression of Hal—"'Hrmm, this is the third time my delivery has been incorrect. I demand an apology!' And me—stupid me—in this season of guilt and self-reflection, at that moment, I felt so bad for both of them, I went over and stuck my big fat head in the middle of it."

Colin swallowed. "What'd you do?"

"I just said hi. I could tell Hal recognized me, even though his eyes were still on the floor. I asked him how he was doing, and he mumbled something. The store manager gave me a grateful look and scooted off. Then it was just Hal and me.

"It's funny, but I'd recently been thinking about Hal. On that last trip home, for the first time in ten years probably, I had been reminiscing about all the crap he used to take in high school. I guess my conscience had been pricked or something, and I wanted to do something nice for the guy."

Jay leaned forward in his beanbag chair.

"He never even looked at me, but I was startled by how old he seemed. I'd aged—everybody had—but not like Hal. He was mumbling something, and I thought we were done, but then, to my surprise, he asked if I wanted to get lunch.

"I had my flight back to LAX, but it wasn't until later that day, and everything was already packed. So I had time, and guilt, and a chance to do what I thought was a good deed, right in front of me. So I got in my rental car and followed his old-school Mercedes—which was actually kinda classy—back to his house. Which, by the way, was not where I expected when he said lunch. It was his childhood home, which was weird. And then he directed me to pull into his garage, which was even weirder.

"I should've run away right then. As soon as he closed the garage door, I should have known. But the whole situation was just so surreal. I was creeped out, but this was Hal, and Hal had always been harmless. I remained wary, but he wasn't making eye contact, and I felt pretty certain a firm no would shut down anything he might try. He told me there was something he wanted me to see, something I'd appreciate, and it had to do with high school. He was babbling, and I wasn't really listening, because now we were inside, and I couldn't stop staring."

"What do you mean?"

"When I lived in Seattle, I once helped a friend clean out her grandmother's place. That was my first encounter with a hoarder.

"Hal is a hoarder, times ten. Almost every square inch of livable space in his house is absorbed by stuff. Boxes full of nineties memorabilia line the walls. Tons of books on the flora and fauna of the Pacific Northwest. Everything is organized in boxes, but there are so many boxes that there is barely room to move. I imagine he had to collect all that stuff to make his simulation. But the smell! I don't think Hal leaves that house often. It is suffocating. It smells like unwashed socks, compost, and burnt lentils. Oh, it was terrible, and my only thought was to leave. I suggested we get lunch at the Riverside Grill, and I even offered to buy. He agreed, but said he wanted to show me something first.

"I followed him through a maze of boxes, and then, finally, I knew things were really not right. He led me into a little black room, like a sensory deprivation chamber. The only things in the room are a bed, a nightstand, and a helmet with a headlamp, although I could barely make anything out in the gloom. I noticed the propofol on the nightstand, and I wondered what Hal was doing with that. He wanted to show me his VR, and I told him I'd tried VR before, but he shook his head and was all smiley. 'Not like this,' he'd said. I could tell he was really proud. He handed me a helmet and told me that what he was showing me would only take five minutes.

"I had butterflies in my stomach and was starting to panic. I knew *something* was wrong. I should have punched him in the gut and ran for my life. But I still wanted to make it up to him, so I kept telling myself, *What's the harm?* And then, while I was looking at the propofol, he took the helmet and slid it over my head."

Liz didn't say anything for a while. Finally, Colin ventured: "So your body is still in that room?"

Jay saw Liz's hand tremble. He leapt in. "Yes. And we're getting her out. Right?"

Colin was silent. Somewhere out in the darkness, a rooster crowed. Outside the window, the light was softening, growing bluer by the minute.

"Right?!"

Colin shrugged. "Well . . . how?"

"We have the disk, don't we? Could we stop him from inside the game?"

Colin whispered. "Yeah, what happens if he dies here?"

Jay shrugged. "I'm sure he has a million hit points. Even if we did kill him, he could just create a new avatar and come back."

"So what do we do?" Colin muttered.

They thought silently. Jay looked around the basement. On a shelf behind them, amid a half dozen children's coloring books and plastic dinosaurs, something caught his eye. He got up and pulled down a dusty faded box. On its front was a complicated Rube Goldberg of stairs, a bathtub, and—in a tiny cage—a captured red mouse. Colin looked up.

"Mouse Trap?"

Jay opened the box and took out colorful plastic pieces, snapping them together. "You said when he kidnapped you, Liz, he put a helmet on your head?"

Liz nodded. "Yeah. It's like VR, but VR only has sight and sound. Whatever Hal uses does all five senses."

Jay placed a marble into a tiny yellow bucket. "So, you're still wearing this helmet in the real world. And you can't get it off?"

She shot him a sarcastic look.

"And when he's in the real world," Jay continued, taking out the game and sliding a green boot over the walkway, "he's omniscient. We can't touch him. But when he comes into the game, he's gotta put his helmet on, and he becomes another character. Like us. A superpowered character, but still. He can't be everywhere at once, and he's got to use that little wand to make changes."

"I guess so?"

Jay stepped back. The board was now a complex Rube Goldberg of rickety traps and devices. Jay pulled a Stop sign back so it bumped the marble. Colin and Liz followed it down a ramp, sprung the bathtub, and launched the little figurine into the bowl. The basket clamped down around the mouse. Jay straightened, pleased with his device.

"What if we trapped him? It's not like he's magic. He can't enter and leave just by wiggling his eyebrows. He needs his controller to get in and out, the one he's got in that fanny pack. If we take it away, he's helpless."

"We'd have to lure him back into *The Build*. What time is it?"

Liz looked at her watch. "3:24. When I was in the staging grounds, I'd never hear from him from about 3:00 a.m. until about 9:00 or 10:00. I think that's when he sleeps."

Jay was thinking fast. He felt full of purpose. He forced out of his head any thought that he and Liz might end up together. She was too old, she was too married, and—perhaps most importantly—she was too real. She didn't belong in *The*

Build. Hal had brought her back to punish her and to steal her brain. And Jay could help her get out alive.

"So we have about three more hours until he's back in front of his computer. Colin, will you get the cordless? We have a call to make."

THE DINER

THE ROOM SMELLED pleasantly of maple syrup. It was still an hour before dawn, and the Morning Market belonged to another generation. It was the earliest Jay had ever been there. At lunch, the rest of Bickleton High was crowded around the tiny deli counter. Before dawn, two dozen millworkers sat at a single table, sipping coffee and speaking in low, gravelly voices.

They were all men, except for two gray-haired women, one fat and one thin, who plodded back and forth endlessly to the kitchen. Jay knew them all by sight, but not by name. He'd never really paid them much mind before. Now, he watched a man with a bushy mustache and a cowboy hat hold court at one end of the table. If Jay squinted, he looked like Kevin Costner in *Dances With Wolves*. He was talking about the weather:

"When that fog opened up, looked like it was going to pee all over me this morning."

A few chuckles. A fat man was regaling the other end of the table with his own tale:

"I had a twisted gut, see?"

He held up his shirt so everyone could see his scars.

"Doctor did a little slit, stuck a camera in. Opened 'er up, and there's a bunch of hair in there. I swear he musta played tiddlywinks while he was in there; woke up sore as ever."

It seemed that everyone at the table had an injury. Their stories were stacked into a sort of game, who could top who. Judging by the flat reactions, it was a game they played often. A skinny man with a cane walked in and settled himself at the end of the table, while a dark-skinned Latino with an arm in a cast spoke up.

"I got up on the ladder, and the ladder won. Fell flat on my back, so I was seeing little birdies. Got up and made my way to the truck before I went down again for the count. Good thing I woke up when I did, otherwise, the coyotes woulda picked me clean."

There were a few generous chuckles.

The swinging front door rotated open, and a golden retriever padded into the room. A few of the men glanced over. The waitress straightened from refilling coffee cups and pointed toward the door.

"AJ! No, AJ, go home!"

The golden retriever merrily ignored her, making a lap around the table, stopping at chairs to wag ingratiatingly.

Jay watched casually. If his dad were alive, he would've been the same age as the men at the table. The same age as Hal, in real life. And Liz. He tried to imagine what it would be like to see any of those old-timers thrust suddenly back into high school. Who had been a John, and who had been a Jay? But then he realized that they'd all been Jays. The Johns were managers at the mill, and would never be caught dead in the Morning Market.

Stevie sipped her coffee, nodding at nothing to keep her tired eyes open. The ever-present smile on her face drooped, as though it might disappear.

"So we're living in a computer game"—she turned slowly to Liz—"and she's the main player?"

They all sat, patient, waiting to see how she'd react. Jay half-expected Stevie's eyes to glaze over, like he'd seen with the others. Hal had promised the ability for other NPCs to contemplate their own existence. It had worked for Colin. Would it work for Stevie, too?

Liz drained her coffee. Stevie nodded at the mug.

"Does it work?"

"What?"

"The coffee. Does it affect you? 'Cause if you're a player, the program can feed you sight, smell, touch, and taste. But it can't control biological processes. Like, can it simulate the effects of caffeine?"

Stevie leaned in, more alert by the second. Not only had she managed to grasp the truth of their reality, her little computer brain was already picking apart the pieces.

The first glow of dawn was hitting the tops of the buildings and trees along Main Street. They sat in the farthermost table in the Mark. The skinny waitress came by and automatically filled their coffee mugs.

"No, it does not simulate the effects of caffeine," Liz deadpanned. "But anyway, I'm a decaf girl."

Stevie nodded.

Jay sipped from his own mug. "I gotta say, Stevie, when I pictured your reaction, *pure joy* wasn't what I expected."

"Well, come on." She nodded. "Can you honestly say you've never thought about the possibility?"

"That we're living in a computer simulation? Can't say it crossed my mind."

"I mean, it's not exactly a new idea. Neal Stephenson did it in *Snow Crash*?"

Jay thought back to the unopened novel on his bookshelf.

"Oh, right."

"Well," Stevie said, and leaned in, excited, "ever since that book's publishing, there has been speculation on message boards that the metaverse might be *real*. That the book itself might be some sort of clue"—Stevie waggled her eyebrows excitedly—"to the true nature of reality."

"You realize all those message boards were Hal, right?" Jay spoke up. He remembered that Hal had praised *Snow Crash* in his editorial column in *Serious Gamer*.

"You think?"

"Oh yeah. That guy you were crushing on from Australia? Hal. So if he was talking up *Snow Crash* on your forums, he *wanted* us to guess the truth."

Stevie sighed dreamily. "I used to dream that the world was a simulation."

Jay dumped sugar into his coffee. "Lucky for you."

"No, think about it. A reality created through chance is random. You have no control. Nothing is fair. In a simulated reality, you can *change* the outcome. You can control your fate."

Liz snapped her fingers. "Jay, what happens when you click on me in *The Build*? I don't suppose there's a Disconnect button? A STOP-LIZ'S-BRAIN-FROM-UPLOADING button?"

Jay shook his head. "Not that I've seen."

"No, so we need three things. The first is a way to get me out. The second is a way to get Hal in so he can't see me get out. And the third is a way to keep Hal in here long enough for me to call the cops."

Colin shuffled in his seat, uncomfortable. "You're sure we can't kill him?"

"Not unless I wrap my hands around his fat little neck in the real world."

Jay piped up. "What if we freed you while he's asleep? You could tie him up and call the cops."

"I gotta get out tonight, before the upload finishes."

She turned to Stevie. "Stevie, in my world, according to Facebook, you're CTO of your own tech start-up. So you must be good with computers?"

They stared at her.

"What's a CTO?" Stevie asked.

"What's Facebook?" Colin continued.

Liz gritted her teeth. "Okay, forget that. Can you hack *The Build* or not?"

Stevie shrugged. "I dunno. I mean, this program was made in the future, right? How many new programming languages have there been in the last thirty years? Hard to say, without looking at it."

"Okay, so first thing: let's get Stevie in front of *The Build*. Jay, how good is your memory?"

"Right now? Photographic."

"You said Hal left you clues, that he was foreshadowing the nature of reality? Can you think of anything else he might have shown you? Any other hints he might have dropped that could give us any more clues?"

"God, I dunno. I've got eighteen years of memories. Where should I start?"

"Just—look. Anything could help."

Jay nodded. His brain was already flipping through images.

He was himself as a toddler, moving unevenly over the bumpy banks of the Skookullom, lifting and overturning rocks, while his father was downstream, holding a fishing rod. He flashed forward to the steelhead his dad had caught that day. It was so big, they took it to the Mark afterward, and had it weighed and its picture taken. The picture was still on the wall. Jay glanced up, as he always did, in the Mark at the faded photograph.

A black wave passed before his eyes. Another memory he didn't recognize, so brief, it was gone before it started.

The waitress bustled over and held up a coffeepot. Colin solemnly shook his head. She spun around, back to the long table. The voices of the millworkers erupted in another chorus of laughter.

Jay thought back to some of those flashes when he'd first boosted his stats. Like the memory of looking out at the ocean. Or the one watching the police car from an apartment window.

"There is something weird with my memory. I–I think Hal messed it up. There are some moments in my head—memories—and I don't know where they came from. They're not even from Bickleton."

Colin blinked. "What do you mean?"

Liz's face was impassive, waiting. Colin, Stevie, and Liz were all staring at Jay.

"Let me see if I can—" He shut his eyes, pushing past the memories of his dad. Searching his brain for another unfamiliar flash.

It happened. *He was transported into a black room. He could smell old coffee grinds and pizza sauce. The only light was from the glow of the computer screen before him. He was hunched over, like he didn't want anyone to see his screen. A hot anger coursed through his veins. The sound of muffled laughter came through one of the walls, and he knew the laughter was directed at him.*

Another flash. *He was sitting behind the window of a coffee shop. The sun was dazzlingly white, hot on his hands. The street outside was crowded and full of cars. Nobody was looking his way, but he saw everybody. Three girls in bright pastel dresses strode past. They were all speaking at once, gesturing wildly with their hands. He watched them breeze past, fighting a reflexive surge of hatred that welled up inside him. He wanted the girls to look at him, but at the same time, he despised them, knowing how they would react when they saw him. The girls crossed out of the window frame and disappeared. They never looked his direction.*

That memory was gone, and he was in a new memory. *Again it was dark, but not so dark he couldn't see. Boxes were stacked against the hallway walls, all the way to the ceiling. There was little room to move, but he felt safe in the crowded house. Excited, even. He'd waited for this day for years. Today he added the final touch to his masterpiece. He moved smoothly through the house, down the hall, to the far bedroom. The room was clean and white. A single desk lamp cast a warm glow over a twin bed. Looming over it was an IV pole with a drip bag, an EKG machine, and a small table. Lying in the middle of the white bed was a giant black dot—a helmet—with black cords snaking off the side of the bed.*

He did some quick mental calculations. The upload process would take two weeks. He could do pieces at a time, though, and he planned to take breaks. Still, it was good to take preparations. He pulled off his pants and slipped on a pair of Depends diapers. His stomach was full of the three grilled cheese sandwiches he'd forced himself to eat. He sat down on the bed and inserted the IV into his left arm. He picked up a clear plastic tube and maneuvered it under his diaper, grunting through a moment of pain as he pushed it inside his body. It was uncomfortable, but the pain was already starting to fade. He reached down and grabbed the smooth black plastic helmet, lifting it to his head. As he did so, his eyes caught a reflection. On the wall across from the bed hung a small mirror, where he could see himself. It was a saggy, wrinkled face he recognized. Hal's face. The helmet came down over his eyes, blocking his view.

Then the memory was gone, and Jay was left gasping in the Morning Market. Sunlight was filtering through the windows. Some of the millworkers were standing, stretching their injuries to prepare for another day of brutal labor.

Stevie, Liz, and Colin were staring at Jay, who was breathing in short, ragged gasps.

"Are you okay?"

"I'm Hal." He shook his head in disbelief. "I'm his upload."

Liz's whole body tensed as she watched Jay. Finally, she gave a terse nod. "I know."

HAROLD

THE BATMOBILE'S ENGINE whirred furiously, shuttering vibrations down the car's frame as they tore toward the school. The sun was fresh over the mountains and covering Bickleton in a warm orange glow. Liz rode shotgun. Jay stared out his small window in the back. He could see Stevie casting sidelong glances his way, and ignored her. He wanted to be alone.

Why hadn't Hal told him? Why hadn't Liz told him?

Because, a small voice in his mind answered, *they knew how you'd react.* He clenched and unclenched his fists.

The car hit a pothole and its tires squealed against the frame. They'd never had four people inside the Batmobile before. His eyes wandered to the front windshield, and he saw Stevie was still staring at him.

"Why are you *Jay*, if he's *Hal*?"

Colin glanced in the rearview mirror. "Jay Harold Banksman," he responded quietly.

Jay felt sick. Self-loathing overwhelmed him. Everything that disgusted him about Hal—the sallow, saggy flesh, the insecurity when he spoke, his pettiness—it was inside him, too. He would grow up to turn into that sad little man.

He thought back to all the anger he'd felt in Hal's memories. The resentment. Hal had lived a life of bitterness, and that was his path ahead. He shared Hal's temper, he knew, especially when Jeremy was involved. But he didn't feel angry all the time. Hal had said he was saving Jay from a lifetime of regret and disappointment. Life didn't get better when you left Bickleton, he'd claimed. It got worse. Whatever pain Hal had suffered in the last thirty years led him to make this game. Jay closed his eyes. He didn't want to make any more changes. He didn't want to open his eyes.

"You mentioned something about Facebook?" Stevie was talking to Liz now. "What is that? What's a CTO?"

Liz was looking out the window as if she expected to see Hal hitchhiking down the road. "Chief Technology Officer. You do just fine."

Colin jumped in. "What about the future? Are there flying cars?"

The Batmobile hit another pothole. Liz shook her head. "No flying cars. The biggest difference is the internet. It's everywhere. And artificial intelligence. It's made *huge* leaps in the last few years, it powers everything, and it's—well, you guys know better than anyone."

Stevie stared out her window with a blissful grin. "Cool . . ."

"Oh, and everyone has mobile computers now, called smart devices. You can play games on them, watch cat videos, check email, call people. But mostly cat videos."

"Does Bill Clinton really bring about a new era of prosperity?"

"Oh, that's a complicated one. Bill Clinton stays president for two terms, but then in the late nineties he almost gets impeached for having an affair."

"What?"

"Yeah. And all this nasty stuff comes out about him. And honestly, things kinda go downhill after that. Like, in a few decades, *Hillary* Clinton runs for president."

"What?!"

"And loses to Donald Trump."

"*The* Donald Trump? The guy in *People* magazine and the *National Enquirer*? The guy with Marla Maples?"

Liz nodded.

"Your world sounds even crazier than ours." Colin squirmed. "You sure it's not a simulation?"

"What else?" Liz continued. "NAFTA is gone, but only recently. Ruth Bader Ginsburg just passed away, after becoming something of a folk hero. Oh, and Mark Wahlberg is now a movie star."

Colin turned to her. "You mentioned Stevie is a CTO? What am I?"

"Oh!" Liz responded, remembering. "So this is interesting. I just saw an article about this a few months ago. You remember Blockbuster?"

Colin nodded. "What do you mean, 'remember'?"

"Well, it's gone. Now you can watch movies through the internet, so nobody needs DVDs—"

"What's a DVD?"

"Gosh, you guys are still—okay, well, nobody needs VHS tapes anymore. So Blockbuster went out of business, except one store in Bend, Oregon. And, Colin, I saw in that article: you're the assistant manager."

A faraway look passed over Colin's eyes. "Assistant manager?"

Liz shook her head. "Yep. I recognized the picture."

A grin played over Colin's lips. "Do I get free game rentals?"

"C'mon, focus," Liz snapped.

They pulled into the C-Court parking lot, and it was empty in the early morning light. Steam wafted off the dark pavement and C-Court roof where the sun touched them. Colin opened his door and damp air sucked into the car.

"What time is it?" Jay heard Liz ask.

"6:27. Miss Rotchkey usually comes in around seven thirty."

"Let's do what we can."

Colin and Stevie stole their way up through the pines, to Tutorial. Liz fell behind to walk with Jay.

"I'm sorry I didn't tell you. I was trying to feed it to you in smaller doses."

Jay glanced up. "Oh, you mean the sham of my existence?"

"C'mon, it might be a good thing for us. You know Hal better than anyone. You have his memories. You can tell us what he wants, what he's up to."

"Yeah. Great," Jay muttered.

He broke away, moving off the trail, pushing his way through the pine trees to the side of Tutorial, and leapt up, grabbing the window ledge and then pushing the unlocked window open. He didn't want to be there, with Colin and Stevie geeking out on their fantastic futures. His future was not fantastic. He felt sick about the man he would become, and fell into the classroom, opening the door for the other three.

Stevie stepped tentatively inside, in awe that she was breaking so many rules.

"Can I see the disk?"

Jay handed it to her silently, and she expertly took her seat, twirling open the root folder to find the primary game file. She pulled it into Microsoft Word and opened a document of code.

"Okay, that's right, it's written in C. That's good, I know C. So this is just a UI for us to access the real game engine. Somewhere in this code, it's receiving and sending inputs to the actual engine. Whatever *that* program is, it's obviously powerful enough to also run a simulated version of Windows 3.1 . . . and simulate an entire world."

Jay fell into his desk, not listening. He put his head in his hands. For eighteen years, he imagined a life outside of Bickleton. A life where he made friends, met girls. Now, there was not only no escaping, but even if he left, he didn't have a prayer. Hal had gotten out of Bickleton, and he had not made friends or met girls. He had grown lonely, awkward, and inward, festering. How? How could Jay grow up to be that dumpy, hateful man?

Colin sat down in the desk beside him.

"I guess there's no going back now, huh? There's no Blockbuster in *The Build*."

"There is no Bend, Oregon," Jay retorted.

Colin glanced at his friend, and a look of understanding played over his face. "You're not gonna end up like Hal."

"How do you know?"

"Because I won't let it happen."

Liz gripped the back of Stevie's chair. "Anything?"

Stevie stared intently at the lines of code. "I haven't found your body. But there's an opportunity for us to go bigger than I think Hal planned. There are inputs to *The Build* UI that Hal never bothered to connect. Everything is contained within his computer. But it doesn't have to be that way. Should I hook them up, see where they lead?"

"Not yet. Jay?" Liz ventured.

"What?"

"How do we lure Hal back in? We can't make changes till he's here."

"I don't know. I know you guys are excited to play with *The Build*. But right now, I have to reconcile the fact that I grow up to be the world's biggest nerd, and also, oh yeah, I'm a homicidal killer that's going to murder you in your sleep. Kinda hard to get my mind off of that."

Liz crouched down next to him. He felt the flatness of her palm on his back.

"Listen. When I first got here, and I figured out who you were, I thought the exact same thing. I didn't want to have anything to do with you. But you're not him, Jay. I don't know what happened. Maybe you're a different part of Hal, before he grew so bitter. But you've already proven you're better than him. Look. You have two friends who are going to be here for life."

"You said high school friendships don't last."

"That's a choice I made. I don't get to choose who I want to be anymore. All those decisions have been made. Same for Hal. But that's not true for you."

Jay closed his eyes and brought his face against the cool Bakelite of his desk. He forced himself to go back into Hal's memories. Brief images of a life beyond his own flashed into his mind. Riding a bus in the rain. Quietly dining alone. Always, he felt the steady pulse of anger, just below the surface.

"I dunno," Jay mumbled. "He wants control; he wants respect."

"Where did it come from? Where does that start?"

There was another flash. Jay was standing in a black room, squinting at bright green and blue lights. A semicircle of students in tuxedos surrounded him. Some of their faces looked vaguely familiar. They were pointing at him, laughing. He felt a tremendous wave of anger, stronger than anything he'd felt in his life.

"Prom," he said suddenly, looking to Liz. "Something happened at prom."

Liz's face was unreadable. She spoke slowly. "Okay. Yes. Jeremy played a prank on Hal at senior prom. That was the turning point?"

Jay exhaled. "I dunno. It's a big memory. Maybe that's what Hal meant when he said he's looking forward to the show. Maybe he wants me to stop Jeremy at prom?"

Liz snapped her fingers. "So we don't have to lure Hal in. If he's looking forward to the show, I bet he comes in to watch. Stevie, can you get me out?"

Stevie grinned. "Not yet. But we'll figure it out."

Liz grimaced. "We have to."

"If we can get that control away from Hal . . ."

Colin raised his hand. "I can get it away."

"He'll kill you," Jay warned.

"Not without his remote he won't."

Beyond the pines, they heard the distant sound of voices and cars pulling into the parking lot. Liz looked back and forth between them.

"So that's it? That's our plan?"

Jay nodded. "We're going to trap him in prom."

CLOUDS ROLL IN

BY THE AFTERNOON, the sky outside had darkened dramatically. There was no trace of the cold sunshine that had earlier illuminated the Morning Market; instead, a blanket of menacing clouds now rolled over Bickleton. Wind whipped up from the Skookullom Gorge, howling through the rafters of Colin's house.

He, Liz, and Stevie were getting ready for the prom at Colin's house. Seven parents—his mom, Stevie's, Colin's, and Liz's—fussed over them, running from kid to kid, snapping photos. It all seemed so stupid. Jay sighed, adjusting his tie in a hallway mirror. The kids were mustering fake excitement, acting like everything was normal. Last week, Jay's only care was going to prom. That had been the pinnacle of high school. Now it felt like farce: a play they were all rehearsing. He undid his necktie and began again.

Down the hall, Liz was doing her hair in Mrs. Ramirez's bathroom. She'd left the door open a crack, and Jay could see her, bobby pin clenched in her mouth, hair up. She looked beautiful, her tan skin perfect and unblemished. It was impossible to believe she was actually his mom's age.

Jay watched as Liz applied clear lip gloss and a brush of rouge to her cheeks. She moved with a confidence unusual for girls her age. Jay realized she was probably an expert in many things he had yet to fully understand. Liz's mom came up behind Liz and added a pink carnation to her hair. Liz's body froze. She watched in the mirror as her mom carefully pinned the carnation in place.

"Sweetie, you look beautiful. I'm so glad you're feeling better."

Liz's eyes were watering. She spun around and threw her arms around her mom's neck. Her mom blinked in surprise, then placed her hands on her daughter's back.

Jay wondered how close Hal had gotten Liz's parents to their real-life counterparts. Were they still alive in the real world? For a moment, he saw *The Build* through Liz's eyes. This was an opportunity for her to step backward in time.

Jay moved down the hall and stopped at the bathroom door.

Liz released her mom, who shuffled out into the hall.

"Sweetie, I'll be right back. I'm gonna get your corsage."

Liz's eyes were rimmed red. She looked fierce and stunning and vulnerable all at once. He gave her a small smile.

"Liz Knight."

She sniffed, then offered her own faint smile. "Jay Banksman. Aren't we the pair?"

"You okay?"

She waved her hand and fanned her watering eyes. "Sorry. Lot of feelings right now."

He stepped into the bathroom and stood facing the mirror, turning his attention to his necktie. He searched through memories until he found an image of his dad holding up a tie. Jay followed the memory, retracing his dad's gestures with his own hands. Around, behind, over, and through. He yanked down, straightening.

"Don't worry," he murmured, not wanting to give anything away in the very likely event that Hal was watching. "Whatever happens, he can't control us."

Liz nodded and returned to fixing her eyes. Her mom popped back into the bathroom, carrying a blue corsage.

"My goodness, you two look like Nicole Kidman and Tom Cruise!"

Liz gave a faint smile. "Neat."

GATEWAY

OVERLOOKING THE SKOOKULLOM Gorge on a high bluff was a row of Bickleton's finest houses. They stood proudly against the oncoming storm, windows reflecting flashes of light as the clouds rolled in. One house in particular towered over the rest. It stood front and center on the bluff, its single glass window so large that it encompassed most of its entire front wall.

This was Jeremy McKraken's house. It stood an impressive three stories, taller than the surrounding mansions, perfectly centered at the highest vantage, glowering down on the mill and the lower portion of Bickleton.

In the center of its fishbowl window, some twenty feet in the living room, John McKraken sat on a couch. He was a thick, sturdy man, like his son. He held a rigid pose that commanded the room, even as he sat relaxing and reading the paper. Some distance behind him, Lydia McKraken hovered over a mixing bowl, stirring. When she smiled, some of her old prom-queen beauty broke through her face. But now she held it in a scowl as she attacked her recipe.

Across a mauve-colored room and from up the stairs, she heard the faint sound of the boys' voices. For some reason, all fifteen of them were crowded in the office. They'd been in there at least half an hour. She cocked an annoyed eye toward the stairs.

"Boys! You coming down? Boys?!"

The boy heard Mrs. McKraken's voice through the office door and looked to Jeremy to answer, but his face remained impassive.

John McKraken's office had a vacuous, unused feel. He rarely brought his work home, and so he made little use of the room. Like many of the rooms in their mansion, it was there in case the McKrakens needed it. It was sparsely furnished with a single shelf, a desk, and a drafting table full of forestry maps. Plastic still wrapped one of two office chairs. It was one of the smaller rooms in the household, and all fourteen Johns were now crammed inside, wearing black tuxedos. They looked even more uniform than usual, and could have easily been fourteen brothers.

Johns H, C, and D all struggled with a large box with the black-and-white print of a Holstein cow and a Gateway 2000 logo. They opened its flaps, pulled out Mr. C's computer, throwing out chunks of Styrofoam, and plugged in cords while Jeremy read the instructions aloud.

"It says to plug the monitor into the serial port."

John H rolled his eyes. "God, this is so *nerdy*."

"Dudes." John B tapped a foot impatiently. "Are we going to prom or what?"

"You wanna get your ass kicked again?"

John D plugged in a power cord and stepped back.

"I think that's it."

They admired their handiwork. The computer sat on John McKraken's drafting table, surrounded by a keyboard, a joystick, and a mouse. John B plopped down in the plastic-wrapped chair.

"That's it?"

John W checked his watch.

"I'm supposed to pick up Shelby."

Jeremy held up a black floppy disk.

"Here, scoot over."

The multicolored Windows 3.1 sat in front of the screen. The Johns rustled around, rearranging themselves to let Jeremy slip into the chair and slide in the disk. *The Build* load screen popped up.

"Huh. So this is the thing that made him stronger?"

"That's what he said to Colin."

Jeremy gave a few declarative punches of the keyboard.

"TEN. TEN. TEN."

He hit Enter. Immediately, his body stiffened in his chair. He roared so loud, the Johns clapped their hands over their ears. Jeremy's body went rigid, the skin on his forehead tightening, his ears pulling back. He breathed hard and his face flushed. He leapt up and spun around, clenching and unclenching his fists. The Johns backed away, frightened. Jeremy's eyes were bloodshot, his capillaries all burst. Protuberant veins ran down his knotted muscles, and a thick moss of hair covered his skin.

"Who wants to go next?" he growled.

The Johns shifted and cowered in the corner, avoiding Jeremy's gaze. Jeremy's fist shot out and grabbed John S by the lapels.

"*Mmph*, ouch. Stop it!"

Jeremy grabbed John S by the throat until his face turned purple and his sharp, staggered breaths punctured the room. Jeremy flung John S into a wall, and he clanged off the drafting table. He leered at the other Johns, and then his mom's voice bellowed up from the base of the stairs.

"The hell's that noise!?"

Jeremy froze.

"You boys going to prom tonight, or you just gonna stay here and play Pogs?"

"Yeah, Mom," Jeremy grunted in a new, gravelly voice. "Almost ready."

He spun back around to the keyboard.

"Let's do this."

He hit a few keys. From where he lay on the floor, John S's body stiffened. He groaned as his muscles clenched and he began to shake.

Downstairs, Lydia McKraken placed the bowl of custard she'd been working on into the fridge and wiped down the counter. There was another loud bang against the upstairs wall and she stiffened.

"The hell are those boys doing? John, do you want to go up there?"

John McKraken folded the newspaper he was reading and took a bite of custard from the small bowl his wife had provided.

"They'd better not be in my office."

"Well, they are. What could possibly be so important?" She turned to the dishes awaiting her in the sink. "They're going to miss senior prom."

SPRING FLING

WIND WHIPPED FROM the Skookullom, cracking cedar boughs louder than gunshots. Then came the rain. Big drops hurled from the sky. Rivulets ran through the dirt, collecting into streams and snaking out of the pines and onto asphalt in black sheets that varnished the land.

The rain acted as a summons to all teenagers in Bickleton. Any notion of arriving to prom fashionably late was washed away in the downpour. In ten minutes, the C-Court lot was bursting with cars. They fought for spots, angrily revving their engines and spraying walls of water as they dashed to park. Latecomers ditched their vehicles on the shoulders of Simmons Road, jogging through the torrents to reach the shelter of the gym. By as early as 7:30 p.m., the last smattering of couples were running for the doors, tuxedo jackets used as umbrellas.

Were there any students left standing outside, they would have heard a loud bang as the Batmobile bungled down Simmons Road before heaving a last gasp to die in the middle of the parking lot. Exasperated, Jay leapt out into the rain. There were no parking spots left, so he pushed the car as far out of the way as he could. A small part of him would have liked to have arrived in the Miata, but ever since his accident with

Liz, the top no longer worked. He waited in the rain for the two girls. Liz stepped out the passenger side, the sequins on her green dress gleaming in the orange overheads of the parking lot. Jay forced himself to look away. *Don't get too attached; we're sending her home.*

Stevie emerged, lost beneath layers of rainproofing, and shuffled toward where the gym lights sparkled behind a wall of water.

It was odd, returning to school. It felt foreign: something that he recognized but was no longer a part of him. He wondered how the teachers and chaperones would react upon seeing him. Then again, did that even matter now?

The rain drowned out all other noise as they rushed to the gym, and by the time they reached its doors, their clothes were soaked. Jay's shoulder pads sagged like sponges, his feet sloshing with every step. Through the dark glass, past his bedraggled reflection, he saw the ticket booth unmanned, no sign of chaperones.

It was understood that, at the first sign of Hal, Stevie would break off and head to Tutorial so she could work on freeing Liz. Jay nodded at his three friends, then flung open the doors. Immediately, a deep, pounding bass enveloped them. The air was hot and humid with evaporating rainwater and dancing bodies. They saw kids bustling in and out of C-Court from the gym, laughing. A sophomore couple looked over at the four of them in the doorway, and Jay saw the young boy's gaze drift from Liz to himself, puzzled. They gawked for a moment, then the boy guided his date back into the gym and into the pounding music.

Jay shouted over the noise, "The rest of the school's about to know we've arrived."

Colin looked incredulous. "You think they'll care?"

Jay pointed at Liz. "We have the prom queen in tow. Yeah. They'll care."

Liz locked an arm in his, pulling him along. "Come on."

Jay looked down at where their arms touched, blushing.

They shuffled into C-Court. Pink and blue balloons framed the Spring Fling banner hanging in the gym doors. Beyond that was darkness. As his eyes adjusted, Jay saw trees made of brown and green balloons with pink balloon candy blossoms. The trees were illuminated with small twinkling lights. The strumming guitars of Rage Against the Machine played through the doorway, and shrieks of delight punctured the dance floor. Jay saw the dark silhouettes inside. Writhing bodies that looked like something out of Dante's *Inferno*.

"So this is prom." Colin examined the dance floor.

Stevie's nose, partially visible through her foul-weather gear, pointed at the gym. "There's so much slam dancing . . ."

"Accurate?" Jay asked Liz.

"To the last mullet."

Colin swung his shaggy head around. "I don't see Hal. Or Jeremy."

Jay followed his gaze around C-Court. In the darkened corners, some students had already partnered off, making out. Rage Against the Machine subsided, and a tidal wave of kids flooded from the gym. Their faces lit up as they saw Liz, and they pointed at Jay, muttering and giggling. Jay saw Gretchen and Amber. They looked at Liz as if she were holding a dead raccoon.

"We gotta get outta sight," Jay muttered.

Stevie nodded and unzipped her rain jacket. She stepped out of her dark cocoon in a baby blue sequined dress that—Jay couldn't help but admit—was flattering. She folded her foul-weather gear and left it on a bench. Colin blushed and turned away.

"Won't you be cold?" he ventured, not looking at her. "If you have to . . ."

Liz watched Colin in awe. She turned to Jay, and he nodded, confirming Liz's suspicion. Colin's huge crush on Stevie was something he'd long tried to ignore.

"I'll be fine." Stevie beamed at him.

Jay unclipped a small walkie-talkie from his belt and handed it to Stevie, along with a floppy disk in a plastic case.

"Can you keep this on your person?"

Stevie nodded and clipped it onto her chest. Colin looked away uncomfortably, and Liz nodded at Stevie approvingly.

"Stevie, you clean up well. I guess we'd better go incognito on the dance floor?"

The four of them took a deep breath and dove farther into the gym.

THE JOHNS

JAY, COLIN, STEVIE, and Liz plunged into the heart of prom.

Colin's mouth dropped open in surprise. The gym was unrecognizable, totally transformed. The air was dark and heavy. Smoke curled around the edges of the room, and laser lights pulsed through the air. The bleachers were hidden behind dark curtains, and blocking the fabric were the balloon trees they'd seen when they'd walked in. Music pulsed from a stage in the center of the room, and a hundred bodies moved in uncoordinated jerks to Milli Vanilli's "Girl You Know It's True." Jay watched a group of tuxedos stirring their hands, doing the Cabbage Patch.

They passed the misanthropes in the back, fat rednecks who sat splayed out in chairs, barely fitting in their jackets. They were discreetly spitting Red Man chewing tobacco into Dixie cups, while their girlfriends whined and pulled at their arms, begging them to dance. Jay saw several taller heads stalking about the periphery on the edge of darkness, swiveling to check on students. The chaperones. Jay ducked down so quickly, he bumped into one of the rednecks and nearly spilled his cup of chew.

"Watch it," came a piglike grunt from the dark.

Hunched over, Jay made his way into the largest knot of students on the dance floor. The music was much louder, and he allowed himself up to look around. The edges of the gym were blocked by a wall of dancing bodies.

Stevie and Colin were standing, uncertain. Liz was searching the gym.

"We gotta split up. Keep an eye out for any sign of Hal. I'll stay here and see what I can find."

Liz, Stevie, and Colin dispersed into darkness. Bodies clustered in around Jay, and Jay moved his feet a little in what he hoped was the rhythm of the song. Soon, he caught the surrounding faces looking at him and smiling. Encouraged, he began to move his arms as well. A few people clapped. He felt a little silly dancing by himself, but his dexterity score of 10 apparently came with some free dance moves. Before he could even think about what he was doing, he fell to the floor and did a split. There were shrieks of delight, and the prom-goers broke into applause. This was the opposite of what he needed to be doing. Blood rushed to his cheeks, and he held up a hand in acknowledgment. He moved to the other side of the dance floor.

The belting voices of Milli Vanilli came to an end to great cheers from the crowd. And then Jay heard two voices he recognized. He cocked his gaze to see Gretchen and Amber on the periphery of the dance floor with three other cheerleaders. They were so involved in their conversation, they didn't spot him.

"Oh my God, he's *cute* in that tux. And he looks so *proud*."

Jay felt the color rising in his cheeks. They were talking about him.

"I feel bad. Should we tell him?"

"Well, she's not gonna do it anymore. Not after her episode last Wednesday."

"But it was the whole reason she asked him to prom. How does she not remember?"

"Oh my God, it would have been so *mean*."

"Yeah, and she was the one going on and on about how funny it would be to see Jay's face when Jeremy threw him naked into the gym."

Jay felt like he'd been punched in the gut. He staggered back through the crowd, leaning against the DJ booth. Paula Abdul's "The Promise of a New Day" began to play, and the kids around him resumed dancing. Jay was right next to a speaker and could feel each hit of the snare drum tremble his body.

He felt sick. His vision blurred. His heart was pounding. He was seeing double. Beyond this gym was another.

It felt much the same, except now he was back by the gym doors, and he could feel the damp air on his skin. The crowd around him had stopped dancing, and they were staring at him in shock. He looked down. His muscles were gone: he was so skinny, his ribs stuck out his sides. He moved to cover his naked body with insufficient hands, and he ran back to the doors, flashing a small naked butt to the crowd. Laughter erupted all around him. He pulled on the doors, but they were sealed shut. The laughter was spreading: everyone in school was joining in. There were shrieks of joy, and hands reached out, poking him, pinching his exposed butt. He was crying now, his back against the door, no longer bothering to cover himself. He was scanning the gym, looking for a chaperone, desperate to find a friend. There was Liz, standing between two of the Johns, staring at him.

"Help!" he screamed.

But the corners of her mouth turned up. She was in on the joke. Tears were pouring down his cheeks, hot with hatred. He collapsed on the floor, his mind imprinted with that vision of Liz, as he promised himself that he would someday take revenge.

And then the vision was gone. Its passing left Jay feeling empty, as if something inside him had just torn in half. He pushed himself up off the DJ booth and stood on the dance floor, heavy as lead. Bodies jostled around him, but he didn't notice. It was Liz. Jeremy had pushed him to the brink, but Liz had pushed him over. All the sleepless nights he'd experienced in Hal's brain, the evenings alone, the coldness growing year by year. In a sudden, cruel clarity, he understood why Hal had trapped Liz.

He pushed his way through the dancers, no longer limiting his strength. Students tumbled out of his way, glancing back at him with angry faces.

A junior got in his face. "What the hell, man?"

Jay grabbed his chin and threw him onto the floor. The dancers gasped and leapt back, giving Jay a ring of space. Jay strode toward the gym doors. Liz ran over from the edge of the dance floor and hissed in his ear.

"What are you doing?"

Jay didn't answer.

"Did someone do something to you back there?"

"You did!" Jay hissed, not looking at her. "Thirty years ago. You helped Jeremy to humiliate me at prom. That's why you asked me to go with you last week, isn't it? Back when you were still an NPC? You were just executing the script of Hal's worst memory. You were about to do to me what you did to him."

Liz grabbed his arm, and her voice sounded afraid.

"Yes, I'm sorry. It was stupid, and I regretted it."

"No, you didn't. You're forgetting that my memory is better than yours. You laughed."

"I'm sorry, okay?"

"You thought you could glaze over that part, huh? That you had a role to play in this. Because I'm an NPC and too stupid to understand? Or maybe I just don't matter."

"No, I thought about telling you—"

"Then why didn't you?" He turned and walked away.

Liz strode after him, silent.

Jay sneered. "I'll tell you why: because you were worried I wouldn't share the disk with you."

"Shh." Liz looked around fearfully.

"Don't *shh* me!" Jay yelled, pushing her face. Liz tumbled backward into a folding chair. The rednecks paused from their conversation, frozen. Liz stared up at Jay from where she sat in the chair, a look of horror on her face. Jay felt the smallest bit of sympathy, but he quickly tamped it down.

"You know what? This is between you and Hal. You guys work it out."

"What about the plan?"

"Good luck with that."

Jay stalked out the gym doors, into C-Court. Immediately, Paula Abdul quieted. C-Court was mostly empty, except for Ms. Shirell at the gym entrance. She spotted Jay and her eyes widened.

"Once you leave, you can't come back."

"Oh, shut up. You're not even real," Jay muttered, storming toward the doors.

"What did you say?!" Ms. Shirell shouted.

Jay ignored her.

"You're leaving?"

Jay nodded. "I'm gonna raze this town. I'm so done with high school."

The music in the gym cross-faded to Seal's "Crazy" as Jay banged through the doors and nto the parking lot. The rain had stopped, but the sky was still thick with clouds. The parking lot was dark except for the streetlamp post feebly attempting to light the parking lot with its orange glow. Jay strode past a Buick. Through fogged glass, he could see silhouettes sucking a marijuana cherry in the back seat. He banged on the hood of their car and watched them startle. He stopped at a puddle that stretched across the parking lot. Colin joined him.

"What happened back there?"

"She pranked me! At her prom. Once a cheerleader, always a cheerleader. She's as bad as Jeremy."

"But if we don't help her—"

He rounded on Colin, furious. "Dude, none of this means *anything*. Your life. My life. Who cares what happens to a forty-year-old woman who was stupid enough to get trapped in here? You think we're in any better shape than she is? Hal could delete us in a second. And what was our stupid plan gonna do, anyway? You think we could actually stop Hal?"

Jay was shouting. "I shoulda listened to Hal in the first place. He offered me *everything* for *nothing* in return. I should've just used the disk like he said."

Colin stared at his feet. "I don't think you would've said that two weeks ago."

"How do you know? How do you what I was thinking two weeks ago? You don't even know what I'm capable of."

"You're not Hal."

"Yes, I am." Jay's face was close to Colin's, contorted in rage. "I literally am Hal. I could kill her, Colin. For what she did. I have that in me."

Music swelled down Simmons Road, and Jay heard the familiar Kris Kross song, "Jump." A stream of trucks barreled toward them. In the center, like a presidential motorcade, was a brand-new red Mazda Miata. The entourage flew into the parking lot, winding its way through the cars like a snake. When all the trucks were fitted in, they shut off their engines in uniform. The only sound left was Kris Kross blasting from the Miata's rolled-down windows, and the dull thump of the gym. Jay stared at the cars, still thinking of Liz and Hal, not yet realizing the significance of the new Miata.

"I'm going home."

He started making his way around the puddle. Jeremy leapt out of the Miata. The doors of the trucks opened all at once. The Johns stepped out in dark tuxedos, looking like the Secret Service. Jeremy emerged in a black suit. Jay walked toward the line of Johns, shaking his head.

"You know what's funny?" Jeremy asked as Jay drew closer. "She *loved* the idea when I told her."

Jay clenched his fists. "I'm sure."

"I wanted to leave you alone. I thought the whole thing sounded like too much work." Jeremy stepped around the puddle to meet Jay.

"Well, she's all yours now. Enjoy." He moved to push past.

Jeremy held out a palm, stopping Jay. "Oh, I'm not here for her."

Jay scowled. "Okay. Well, you've got five seconds."

Jeremy grinned. "Guess I'd better make them count."

He swung a fist into Jay's stomach. The force of it knocked the wind out of him, and Jay toppled over, falling to the wet ground, gasping. He looked up in surprise, noticing for the first time that Jeremy's chest seemed bigger. His hands, poking out of the blue suit already dark with rain, were covered in veins. He grabbed Jay and pulled him up. The Johns had gathered behind Jeremy like a storm, and Jay noticed that they, too, seemed thicker. Colin wavered by the C-Court doors.

"Stop, or I'll flag a chaperone!" Colin protested.

Jeremy grinned at Jay. "Don't copy that floppy."

Jay threw his weight against Jeremy's grasp, struggling to get free, applying all of his strength. But Jeremy's grip was like iron. The Johns grabbed Jay's hands and pulled them behind his back. They were jerking him back toward the gym.

LAST DANCE

IN THE GYM, the DJ spun "All That She Wants" by Ace of Base, and the kids went wild. Colin secretly liked the song. He never told Jay, who held in disdain any music not recommended by Marvelous Mark. But Colin had actually ordered the Ace of Base cassette from the Columbia catalog. When he would sometimes go down to A-Court alone—another secret he never told Jay—and the song was playing, Colin would hum along. Nobody seemed to bother Colin when he was in A-Court by himself. Which was part of the reason he never told his friend. Jay could be incredibly sensitive.

Now, Colin plowed through the dancing bodies in the gym, searching for Liz and Stevie. Being big had its advantages.

He found Stevie sitting at a table, alone. When she saw Colin, she brightened.

"Where have you guys been? I did a lap around the room, and when I came back, everyone was gone. I thought you'd ditched me. No sign of you-know-who—"

"Jeremy's here," Colin informed her. "And I think he's used the disk."

She sat up, looking around the gym.

"Where's Jay?"

"They've got him. If you-know-who isn't here yet, he will be soon."

"I lost Liz."

"I'll find her. You get to Tutorial."

Stevie jumped up and slipped back into the darkness. Colin watched her disappear. Then he pushed his way toward the dance floor.

The Johns kicked open the C-Court doors and poured into the gym. Ms. Shirell beamed from the ticket booth.

"Fashionably late?"

Twelve of the Johns peeled off to block her view, letting Jeremy and the two other Johns drag Jay through the corridor. A hand covered Jay's mouth, and Ace of Base drowned out his shouts.

A group of sophomore boys pressed their backs against the walls to let the Johns pass. They carried Jay into the bathroom, where the shocking fluorescents beat into his eyes. He squeezed them shut tight while the Johns stood him upright.

Jeremy's voice was in his ear. "Strip."

Jay snorted in disgust. "You can do anything you want, and your first act is to see me naked?"

"Oh, I got plans for that disk. But first, I owe you one."

John H stretched a roll of duct tape over Jay's mouth. John C and John B held Jay's hands while John H pulled off his pants and his tuxedo jacket. Jay felt the cold bathroom air against his skin as they removed the last of his clothes. The Johns looked down and chuckled.

"You're about to be every freshman's nightmare."

Jay's mind raced. He knew that Hal would intervene to save him. But then, if Hal were watching, why hadn't he already done so? Why hadn't he intervened the moment Jeremy had gotten the disk? Perhaps Hal *wasn't* watching. Perhaps he was already in the game, somewhere else.

John W, who was posted in the doorway, slapped the wall three times.

"Someone's coming."

The Johns opened a stall and threw Jay in. John H got in with him and shoved a warning finger in his face.

"Don't breathe."

The door shut, and Jay smelled the sickly sweet aroma of Calvin Klein *Eternity*. John H forced him down onto the seat, then hopped onto the toilet bowl, pressing his knees into Jay's back and twisting his arm painfully. Jay grunted, listening to the footsteps echo on the tiled bathroom floor. The footsteps stopped, and there was a moment of silence. Then came an adult's voice.

"Ya know, most students do their dancing in the *gym*."

It was Mr. Amrine's voice.

"We're just taking a breather, Coach."

"Uh-huh. Needed some fresh air?" He knocked the metal stall. "Someone in there?"

"John H had too much Mr. Pibb."

"That true, John H?"

John H grunted behind Jay. "Almost done."

"Just the fifteen of you in here? A freshman told me you might have a guest."

"Just us, Coach," Jeremy responded coolly.

"Well then, why don't you guys sow some wild oats? There's a small line outside this bathroom. You go on. I'll keep Mr. H company."

Jay felt John H's grip slacken. Jay threw his elbow into his stomach, then kicked the door. It blasted back on its hinges, slamming into John B. Mr. Amrine stared in surprise at the naked Jay.

"What the—!"

Jeremy looked back between Coach Amrine and Jay. Jay used the confusion to rush forward and smash a fist into Jeremy's face. Jeremy spun around and Jay was off, rushing out of the bathroom. His naked feet slapped against the cold C-Court floors as he ripped the duct tape from his face. A group of freshman girls spotted him and screamed. But then their screams were quickly covered by the opening notes of Nirvana's "Smells Like Teen Spirit."

Shredding guitars pumped from the gym, and now everyone was screaming and pushing one another to get back in the gym.

"Nirvanaaaa! It's Nirvanaaaa!" a blonde girl cried.

A junior elbowed through the crowd. "Slam dance city!"

Jay slipped between them, hearing shouts of surprise and laughter.

Not far behind him, the horde of Johns, and a furious Jeremy holding his nose, burst from the bathroom, sprinting down the ramp to the gym. A dazed-looking Mr. Amrine followed, shouting at them to stop.

Adrenaline had taken over, and Jay's only thought was to get away from the Johns. He rushed into the gym and heard Jeremy's furious voice boom behind him.

"Shut the doors! Lock him in, and don't let him leave."

Invisible energy coursed through the gym. The spell of Nirvana transformed the dance floor. Bodies roiled, throwing themselves against one another. Boys and girls thrashed their heads back and forth. Smoke machines filled the room with fog, and Jay pushed through the passing bodies with little notice. One sophomore saw him, laughed, and gave him a high five. Lasers flickered through the smoke. Jeremy slipped through the gym doors and, spotting Jay in the crowd, pointed.

Through the crowd, Jay saw Liz between two tuxedoed shoulders. He remembered when she'd laughed at him in Hal's memory. But now, instead of a smile, her face was creased with worry. She was staring at something in the corner. Jay followed her gaze.

There, through the fog, emerged a short boy with broad shoulders and thick arms. Jay felt a surrealness that made his head swim. The boy shared his face. It was him. He looked exactly like Jay, except he was still in a tuxedo. The boy looked grim, and he was pushing his way through the crowd toward Jay. It was Hal.

He reached Jay, and Jay began to sputter. "They took the disk and—"

"I know," Hal spat, pushing Jay aside and heading straight for Jeremy.

JOHN S

THE WINDOW TO Tutorial was unlocked, as Jay had said it would be. Stevie slowly pushed it open and wriggled into the classroom. Her heart was pounding; breaking into a classroom went against every fiber of her being. What would Ms. Rotchkey say if she walked in right now? But she wouldn't, Stevie tried to tell herself. No one would ever know.

She moved past the desks, past the chalkboard, fumbling in the dark. It was horrible being there at night, with the lights off and no teacher. In the far, far distance, she could still make out the thump of music from the gym, but it now blended with the crickets in the pines. She pulled *The Build* from where she'd tucked it in her bra, then tiptoed over to the computer, laid it on the desk, and clicked on the monitor. Immediately, bright blue light filled the room and she turned away, waiting for her eyes to adjust. If anyone came up the trail, would they see the light through the window? And what if Hal were watching? Stevie breathed in, fighting the urge to run.

Wait for Hal to come. That was the plan. *Don't make any changes till he's in the game.*

She pushed the disk into its drive until it clicked into place.

The light on her screen flickered, and Stevie startled. If Hal found her there, he could delete her, like he'd done with Todd. She quickly scanned the portable, half-expecting to see the outline of Hal in a corner. But no one was there. Her hand trembling, she double-clicked on the disk's icon and booted up *The Build*. The screen centered on the interior gym. She saw red lights flickering, and the tiny pixelated forms of students as they danced in undulating loops. She clicked around, reading names, working her way through the crowd. Scott, Chrissy, Hector, Ana, Hal.

Hal!

His avatar was moving toward the gym doors, thinly outlined in a frame of golden pixels. She clicked on him. A small window of stats popped up.

STRENGTH: 100. SPEED: 100. HIT POINTS: 100. INTELLIGENCE: 100.

She double-clicked on Hal, and a little window popped up: ACCESS DENIED.

She gave a low whistle and pulled her walkie-talkie off her dress, switching it on with a small beep.

"Jay, do you copy?"

Seconds ticked by. No response.

"Jay . . . I got a visual. Can you confirm?"

They had tested their walkies in the car ride over. Why weren't they working now? Were the cement C-Court walls too thick? She scrolled, looking for Jay in the gym.

The ramp outside the portable creaked. Stevie sat up, eyes wide.

There it was again—another creak. Someone was heading up the ramp.

As quietly as she could, Stevie scrolled out of the gym, across C-Court, into the darkness outside, and then up to Tutorial. She zoomed in on the little portable where her avatar sat in front of the monitor. Outside in the dark, a stocky avatar was creeping toward the Tutorial door. She clicked on it.

It was John S.

Stevie gasped. Somehow, the Johns knew. She leaned and peered at his stats.

STRENGTH: 10. SPEED: 10. HIT POINTS: 10. INTELLIGENCE: 10.

The door handle jiggled, and she froze, unsure what to do. She clicked off the monitor, pushed her way back from the computer, and tiptoed to the window, clicking its latches shut. Now she was locked in. Try though he might, John S couldn't get her. She held her breath in the darkness. Listening. The door handle jiggled again. Then there was silence.

She was about to return to the computer, when she heard keys jangling. She froze; her blood ran cold. She heard a key scratch into the lock. Stevie began to hyperventilate. The doorknob turned again, and this time the door swung open. John S stepped into the room.

CRASHER

JAY COULDN'T BELIEVE what he was seeing. Looking at Hal was like looking in a mirror. All Hal's weight and wrinkles had melted away: he was the spitting image of Jay. Jay was so busy taking in his own face, he barely noticed that Hal was pushing past him, hissing.

"I told you this would happen."

Jay had a moment to ponder what Hal meant, and then Hal was gone. The music had stopped, so the only sound was hard soles clacking on the gym floor and the hissing of smoke machines. The six Johns who had slipped into the gym stood looking from Jay to Hal, then over to Jeremy, expectant. All the students were slowly backing away, creating a ring around the Jays and the Johns. A gym door flew open and Mr. Amrine strode in, spotting the circle, and stopped to stare at Hal and Jay.

Hal turned to the stunned onlookers. He motioned to Jay.

"Your prom king thinks he's pretty funny, doesn't he? Likes jokes."

Nobody spoke.

Then Jeremy muttered to John H and John B, "Go up to the classroom with John S. Make sure they don't try anything else."

Jeremy stepped forward and grabbed Hal's shoulder.

"There's been way too much Jay Banksman lately."

Hal grabbed Jeremy's fingers and twisted them back in a sickening crunch. Jeremy screamed and stumbled, holding his hand. The Johns stepped away, fearful.

Coach Amrine strode forward. "Hey!"

Hal grabbed the coach's arm and flipped him on his back. Seeing a teacher taken out was the final straw. The prom-goers screamed and pushed backward, rushing to get away.

Hal snarled at Jay, "You wanna do this, or should I?"

Mr. Amrine lay on the floor, sucking wind. Jeremy had his back against the wall, holding his hand and grimacing. Kids were now trampling to escape. They pushed up against the gym doors, pounding on them and screaming. Jay saw other teachers fighting the crowd to make their way to Mr. Amrine. It was all happening so fast, he didn't know what to do. He saw no sign of Colin or Liz. And where the hell was Stevie?

DRAG &
SCROLL

STEVIE WATCHED JOHN S search the darkness before coming to rest on her dull outline. She watched his hand reach out and flick on the lights. She cringed at the bright overhead lights. John S's face, which had always been ugly, beamed maliciously in neon light.

"Well, well. Thought we'd find someone up here."

Stevie studied John S's face. He was one of the shorter Johns, with freckles and mean, squinty eyes. Like Jay, his muscles were greatly enlarged, his face more chiseled than she'd ever seen it. But with Jay, these changes had looked somewhat natural. Somehow, on this John, they looked grotesque, as if too big for his body. He stepped forward and held out his hand.

"I'll need you to give me your disk."

Stevie stood frozen. So the Johns knew everything.

"And every other copy you might have."

Stevie lunged for the computer, clicked on the monitor and grabbed the mouse. She heard John's footsteps rush forward, heard him plow through desks. Onscreen, she saw his avatar right behind hers. She double-clicked, knowing it was too late, expecting his hands to grab her at any moment.

But they didn't. She opened her eyes. Onscreen, John remained frozen where he was.

She turned around. John S was actually floating in mid-air, grunting and writhing, lashing out with his fists, trying to reach her.

"Put me down!"

She stood and watched him for a moment in awe, then turned back to the computer and dragged his figure back. She heard his voice moving farther away. She turned to see him hovering over Todd's old desk. With one hand, she zigzagged his floating body back and forth, and he swung his fists as if to strike whatever invisible strings were holding him up in the air. It dawned on Stevie that as long as she had him selected, he couldn't move.

Stevie grinned. "Enjoy the walk back."

A look of confusion clouded John's stupid face. With his avatar still selected, she scrolled out of Tutorial. Immediately, John vanished. She scrolled and scrolled, out into the woods, to the very edge of the Bickleton map, then double-clicked. She watched as John's tiny avatar dropped, pulled itself up, and spun around in a circle, examining the forest.

Her heart pounding, Stevie scrolled back to the gym.

Students were scattered around the edges. Hal stood by the doors, a speech bubble hovering over his mouth. She tried to click on him, and a red window popped up: ACCESS DENIED. She grabbed her walkie.

"Jay?"

REMOTE

JAY LEANED OVER and helped Mr. Amrine off the floor. One of his eyes was bright red, as if the capillaries had burst. He looked between Jay and Hal.

"What the hell's happening?"

Jay shook his head. He heard a faint noise from the walkie-talkie in his pocket and ignored it.

Students were screaming now, begging to be let out. The DJ was hiding behind his booth, his turntables abandoned. Prom-goers and chaperones huddled in dark corners. Tables were overturned, and Jeremy limped backward through them, cradling his hand. Hal strode calmly toward him and grabbed his tuxedo lapel. Jay noticed the remote was hanging from his right hand.

"Jay, come here," Hal said calmly. Jay obeyed. The crowd was no longer staring at his naked body. Hal put an arm on Jay's shoulder.

"We're gonna do this together, okay?"

Jay nodded.

Hal took another step toward Jeremy. "Take off your clothes."

Jeremy winced, nodded, and began unbuttoning his jacket. Jay's gaze searched the crowd, desperate for some sign of what to do. Colin stood on the edge of the students, mouth hanging open. Liz stood by his side, her glance moving uncertainly from Jay, to Hal, to Jeremy.

Jeremy was pulling off his buttoned shirt now, his face in agony over his broken hand. Hal watched him hungrily. Deep pain seemed to be working its way out from his insides. He stepped forward and grabbed the shirtless Jeremy by his throat and lifted him up with his left hand, holding his remote like a club in the other.

"Everyone," he barked at the gym. "I want you to watch very closely. This is what happens to bullies in Bickleton."

He squeezed Jeremy's neck and his face turned purple. His eyes bulged and he squirmed in Hal's grasp, fighting for his life. He looked inhuman. The crowd of students turned away, sensing what was about to come. Jay stepped forward.

"I thought you said I got to do it?"

Hal turned, and Jay found himself inches away from his own face. Hal's face looked furious, and for a moment, Jay thought he might strike him. But then Hal nodded calmly.

"You're right. This isn't about me anymore. Here."

He placed Jeremy down, and the high school senior fell to all fours, gasping for air.

"Can you, uh, bump my strength a little more? I've got something I want to try."

Hal nodded and spun his remote into both hands. He pointed it at Jay and clicked some buttons with rapid speed. Jay felt his muscles enlarge even more. He stepped over Jeremy and held his fist over Jeremy's head.

"Jay!" Mr. Amrine held out a hand. He looked terrified. "Don't do this."

Hal held out a finger, and Mr. Amrine fell into silence. Jay looked down into Jeremy's eyes.

"Jeremy, you're a real piece a shit."

He glanced at Hal, who nodded approvingly. On the perimeter of the gym, the entire school watched in silence.

"But it's not your fault you're programmed that way."

Jay leapt forward and ripped the remote from Hal's hand. Hal stared at Jay, uncomprehending. Jay took several steps back. Without taking his eyes off Hal, he grabbed the walkie-talkie from his pocket.

"Do it now."

Hal took a step toward Jay, and Jay wound up and hurled the black remote. It vanished in midair. Hal shuddered, red-faced, veins bulging.

"What have you done?!" he screamed.

"You lied!" Jay shouted back.

"Don't you dare feel sorry for her," Hal snarled.

"You're going to kill her."

"No!" Hal stamped a foot and shook the gym floor. "Just her body."

"That's crazy!"

Hal licked his lips. "She won't even notice when it happens. Neither will you. How beautiful is that? Immortality. Not that she deserves it. But I didn't do it for her."

Hal stared into Jay's eyes, and for a second, Jay saw something else in his face. It reminded Jay of the look he'd sometimes caught in his father's eyes.

Then, from behind the gym doors came the sound of footsteps. The doors clanged, and Jay heard Sheriff Jenkins's voice shouting from the other side. Immediately, kids began to scream.

"Help!"

"We're in here!"

Hal ignored them, continuing.

"You don't ever have to look death in the face. You don't know what it's like to have your body slowly taken from you. I won't always be here to look after you. One day soon, you'll see what it is I've done for you."

"Let her go," Jay pleaded.

Hal threw his head back and laughed. There was a click of the gym doors unlocking. They flew open and Sheriff Jenkins strode into the room, followed by teachers.

"You think I'm so stupid, I'd let myself be trapped in my own program?"

Hal turned and ran, bowling over Sheriff Jenkins. Jay swore and pulled up his walkie-talkie.

"Stevie. He's on the move. I need you to track him."

AFTERMATH

JAY ELBOWED HIS way through the students rushing the doors, trying to keep eyes on Hal. The gym was in utter chaos. Students scrambled, teachers shouted. The bay lights flickered back on, revealing a wasteland of overturned tables, smashed cups, and trampled streamers.

Jay saw Mr. Amrine help Jeremy up. Jeremy cradled a broken hand in his wife beater and pants, the color drained from his face. There was an angry red ring around his neck.

"Stevie?!" Jay screamed into his walkie-talkie as he fought a tide of bodies that pushed at the door. "Do you copy?"

"I see him," came her small voice. "He's crossing the parking lot. Looks like he's heading down Simmons Road."

Jay cursed. There was no way he could catch him. Through the bodies of kids in front of him, he could see the red lights of the sheriff's car flashing across C-Court. The walkie-talkie buzzed again.

"He's heading into the trees. Looks like he's searching for something in a tree."

"Stevie, you've got to get Liz out."

A voice came from right behind him. "Help me out, Elmer."

Jay spun around to see Mr. Amrine. He was regarding Jay warily, keeping his distance. Jay looked over his shoulder to see Elmer closing in on the other side, cornering him. He felt a moment of pity as he balled his hand into a fist.

"Sorry, nothing personal."

And with that, he turned and hurled himself at Elmer, expecting to bowl him over. To his surprise, he hit Elmer's fat body and bounced back, landing on the gym floor. He looked up, stunned, as Elmer stood over him, then down at his naked frame. His muscles had vanished, shrank down to normal. He was his old self. Skinny, frail, and weak. His mind felt foggy. He tried to roll back through his memories, but it was like lugging through a foggy marsh. It took him a moment to realize Hal must had taken away his powers.

Elmer lifted Jay up with one hand, staring at him, incredulous. "*He* did this?"

Mr. Amrine nodded. "I dunno. He had an e-evil twin or something." He tossed Jay his rumpled tuxedo, disgusted. "Put some clothes on."

"Hey, over here!" The two adults turned to see Liz approaching. "Take me, too."

Sheriff Jenkins exchanged a glance with Coach Amrine.

Liz continued. "I started this, a long time ago. I can explain."

The sheriff resignedly grabbed Liz and led the two of them out through the kids in C-Court, into the cold night air. The rain was now a muted drizzle, and Jay's tuxedo froze to his skin. His teeth began to chatter.

An ambulance clattered over C-Court's speed bump and parked in front of the gym doors. Elmer unlocked his car and shoved Jay and Liz into the back seat.

"What are you doing?" he hissed at Liz. "You should be up with Stevie."

Liz looked out her window. Students were pouring out of the school. Now that the danger had passed, some of them laughed. Headlights flickered on and trucks rumbled to life. Jay watched Lacey Graves and Buster Alcott splash across a puddle. Another boy ran over, gesturing, and the three of them nodded eagerly. Windows rolled down. The faces of seniors were nodding and pointing. Trucks began to leave the parking lot. Jay watched in disbelief. They were heading to the after-party.

"They still don't realize what's happening."

He settled into his plastic seat. Compared to the night air, the back seat of the patrol car felt warm and dry. The mixture of cold air and adrenaline had him clenching and unclenching his muscles. Liz watched a flock of girls bustle past. A few peered in the windows as they ran. Jay craned his neck to see if he could see Tutorial, but the dark clump of trees blocked his view. He stretched himself out, hoping against hope that Stevie had found a way to get Liz out. His wet jacket squeaked against the plastic seat. He glanced over at Liz and saw tears streaming down her cheeks.

"What's the matter?"

"I just, uh . . . there's a lot I'm going to miss."

"You're not dead yet."

"How do you know? How do you know he hasn't . . . done it? I'm not going to notice when it happens."

Jay realized she was right. He realized with a chill that she might already be dead. There would be no way to know. But he couldn't let himself think that; he couldn't give up just yet. He changed the subject.

"Your boyfriend took it pretty bad back there."

Liz sniffed between tears and made quote marks with her fingers. "Jeremy and I dated for what? Eight months? And for the record, that is not Jeremy." She pointed vaguely out the window. "That is Hal's version of Jeremy. An editorialized memory. Yeah, Jeremy could be a jerk. But he could be sweet, too. He wasn't some two-dimensional tyrant."

"Is he still alive?"

"Yes. Still in Bickleton. I don't know how he managed to stay out of Hal's little project. I guess Hal's probably still too scared of him."

"And what about Hal? What do you remember about him?"

Liz sighed and wiped her tears.

"To be honest, not much. I remember he—*you* were smart. You were earnest. Especially about computers and video games."

Jay blushed. "Yeah. A nerd."

"Nothing to be ashamed of. Where I come from, geeks have inherited the earth. I mean, just look at Hal."

"Yeah. Look at him."

She tilted her head. "Why'd you stand up for me?"

Jay sighed. "I don't know. Just stupid, I guess. Hal offers me the world on a silver platter, and I kick him in the shins. I used to think things couldn't get any worse than high school. Shows how little imagination I had."

"I didn't get a chance to say this earlier. Whatever happens, I want you to know I'm really, truly sorry for high school. I tried to tell Hal that. I don't think he can hear me anymore. But you can. So just know . . . I should've been nicer."

Jay looked out the window.

"It's okay. In the grand scheme of things, I guess high school's pretty insignificant, right?"

Liz laughed. "Unless you're stuck in a high school simulation."

She reached over and took his hand. Her grip was soft and warm.

"Hey, if I got to do prom over again—I mean, under normal circumstances—I'd take you."

She leaned over and he felt her lips on his cheek. His body suddenly felt warm.

"For reals this time."

Boom! The car windows shook. A shock wave rattled the car and shook the C-Court glass behind them. Liz scooted across the car seat and pressed her face to her window.

"Was that . . . thunder?"

Jay shook his head. The rain was only a few scattered drops now. The clouds were gone, revealing the full moon. They could see over the baseball field and beyond that, a small ridge with farmhouses. The few remaining kids in the lot were all staring down that horizon. The noise seemed to have come from there. Then, beyond the ridge, a flash of white flickered against the remaining clouds. Liz pointed.

"Look. Lightning."

Jay squinted. It seemed somehow familiar. He shook his head.

"That's not lightning."

GLOOM BEARS

THE CAR BEGAN to shake. Jay wrapped his hands around the seat in front of him, and the car swung back and forth. Liz screamed and grabbed Jay's shoulders. In the parking lot, kids yelled as their cars wobbled on their wheels. Falling branches cracked as they hit the parking lot asphalt. A roar grew and grew until it seemed the world would come apart. Then, suddenly, it stopped.

A few kids moaned in the parking lot. Out the window, the lights in C-Court were shut off. The hills were bathed in darkness: the power was out.

Liz hissed over his shoulder, "What was that?"

Before Jay had time to answer, Elmer waddled up to the car and swung the front door open. The car creaked as his massive weight settled onto the frame. Jay saw his left eye twitching so hard, he could barely see.

"Great. First a tornado, now a goddamned earthquake. This is all we need."

He started the car and pulled out of the parking lot. Jay saw the road was cracked into plates. Moonlight bathed the surrounding farmlands in blue, and cows were galloping around the field, lowing in panic. Elmer turned onto Main Street.

"We're heading to the Scallow Park. Listen, you kids know what's going on? 'Cause I got a list that keeps getting longer." He shot Liz and Jay a glance in the rearview mirror.

"And you two seem to be at the center of it all."

Jay and Liz didn't say anything. Elmer snorted in his seat.

"Goddamn. As if there wasn't enough to wrap your brain around."

They passed the United Methodist Church, and for a moment, its spire blotted out the moonlight. In the darkness of the car, Jay saw a glimpse of something white dart through the alley behind the church. He nudged Liz.

"What?" she whispered.

The thing was gone.

"Sheriff . . . there's something out there."

"Good Lord, what now? Aliens?"

Jay bolted up in his seat and pointed. "Sheriff!"

"Hey, Goddamn—"

But he, too, saw it. Something pale and white darted across the street. Elmer swerved, running the squad car onto the sidewalk, then overcorrected left, into the oncoming lane. Finally, he screeched to a halt outside Scallow Park. The car sat, idling, its occupants breathing hard. Jay turned to look through the rear window.

"Hell was that?" Elmer muttered from the front seat. "Some kinda . . . animal?"

He pulled out his gun, flung open his car door, and swung a leg out into the night.

"Are you crazy? Do *not* go out there," Jay called.

"S'all right. Wait here."

Elmer clicked on a flashlight. There was no traffic in the road, and all the surrounding houses were dark. He moved into the shadow of United Methodist, exploring the church's windows with his light.

"God, people here are stupid. Do you not watch horror movies?" Liz whispered.

"Get in the car!" Jay begged Elmer.

Elmer ignored him, pressing on. Then he stopped, staring. Jay heard it too. A noise emerged from the shadows, quietly at first, but growing louder with each moment. It sounded as if a hundred voices were talking over one another. The noise rose, and as the voices grew louder, Jay seemed to think they sounded angry. From the gloom behind the church, a mass of white shapes seemed to split off. Elmer shouted.

"Get back," Jay urged. Elmer stumbled backward, but the things flashed forward, grabbing him. As they stepped into the flashlight's beam, Jay saw them for what they were. They looked like living mannequins. Black clothing, like suits, but so dark that they looked like nothing, covered bright white bodies. Where faces should have been, there was only smooth whiteness, and a sound like murmuring. Jay watched as Elmer's body disappeared into the horde. There came the sound of tearing flesh, and screams. Jay shrank back into the car and heard Liz's voice.

"What is that?"

"A riot. One of the disasters."

She looked at him questioningly. Jay peeked out of the window and saw the white things move back behind the church. Their murmuring receded, and now Jay heard the distant sounds of broken glass and wood shattering. The still form of Elmer lay on the ground, and Jay saw the faint glint of blood in the moonlight.

Jay quietly tried his door, but it was still locked. He checked the seats for anything that might help. There was nothing.

Liz squatted down in the well next to the seat. Her legs were drawn up, so that the sequins on her dress sparkled in the moonlight.

"What do you mean, *a riot?*"

Jay moved over to try her door. No good: it was also locked.

"Hal's punishing us by sending *The Build*'s preprogrammed disasters. First, the earthquake. Now, a riot."

Liz peered out the window. "How many more are there?"

GENERATOR

THE BLACKOUT PLUNGED the entire campus into darkness. Colin stood outside of Tutorial, silhouetted against the dim outline of the door; he could see the faint clouds of his breath. Aside from a few books on the floor, the small single-room building hadn't taken any damage from the earthquake. He hesitated, unable to see whether Stevie was still inside.

"Stevie? You there? I found one," he whispered.

"Great. Leave it outside so it doesn't get all smoky in here."

Stevie emerged in the twilight of the Tutorial ramp. Thick pines crowded out what little moonlight fell from the sky. In the darkness, she could barely make out a small black box at Colin's feet.

"How many kilowatts is it?"

"Um . . . one, I think."

Stevie's brow furrowed as she calculated. "I think that'll work."

John S had left a set of keys in the Tutorial door. Colin was pretty certain they belonged to Ari Strauss, the janitor, and he'd been trying to figure out how the Johns got ahold of them. When the power went out, it was Stevie who had the bright idea to take the keys down to woodshop and unlock one of the generators. Colin handed Stevie a bright orange extension cord. She took it and searched the darkness with her hands until she found the outlet on the side of the generator. She plugged in the cord and led it back into the darkness of Tutorial.

"Okay, try it."

Colin held the box by its metal lip and yanked the pulls. The engine caught with an angry whir, and Colin saw a faint outline of smoke.

"Great!" came Stevie's voice. "Now shut it off."

"I thought you wanted to boot the computer up?"

Stevie reappeared in the doorframe. It was too dark to make out her face, but Colin could see her small silhouette approaching. "Um, we can't do that till Hal's inside the game, right?"

Colin heard her teeth chatter, her arms wrapping around her exposed shoulders. The air was still wet from the rain. He hurriedly took off his jacket and moved to drape it over her.

"N-no, really—"

"It's okay." Colin blushed. "I've got enough blubber to keep me warm."

"I thought it was just big bones?"

"No, just big." He chuckled, wrapping the jacket around her. Her teeth continued chattering.

"Sorry, it's a little damp."

She nodded. Crickets chirped.

"You know what?" Colin broke away, pulling the generator string. "It's freezing. We gotta get those space heaters on."

The generator rumbled and spat out smoke. Stevie nodded between her jitters. "Th-th-thanks."

Colin heard, rather than saw, Stevie's appreciative smile return to her face, and just then, he was grateful for the darkness as he blushed again.

WRIGGLE

THE MOON CAST a binary glow of light and shadow over the deserted street. Sheriff Jenkins's body lay where it had fallen. There was no trace of the strange bodies that had attacked. From the back of the squad car where they were trapped, Jay squinted at the body, willing Sheriff Jenkins to get up.

"Do you think he's . . . ?"

Liz was staring at Jay.

"Jay, what do you mean, *disasters*?"

Jay was searching the perimeter for a sign that those strange figures might return. "It's a feature in *The Build*. Disasters show up randomly to make the game harder. Or you can use them to destroy your own game. You know, like in *SimCity*?"

"What's *SimCity*?"

"C'mon. Did you really not play *any* games?"

"I played *Oregon Trail*. How many disasters are there?"

"Eight."

Jay saw Liz glance at the small dashboard clock on the sheriff's car. It read 11:14.

"He's gonna stall us out until the upload's complete. Oh God."

Liz beat her fists against the car door in frustration. Jay shut his eyes. He was certain he was missing something. He thought back to the adventure games he'd played. *Monkey Island, Space Quest, Police Quest, King's Quest.* If he were King Graham in *King's Quest,* what could he use to solve the problem? He didn't have an inventory, aside from a soaking-wet prom tuxedo, so no good thinking about it that way. If this were *Super Mario Bros. 2,* and he had to pick a character, why would he choose Jay? What was his special ability? Colin had strength. Stevie had brains. Now that Hal had taken away his stats, he didn't have anything. He was small, he was—

Eureka.

He sat up and stuck his head through the narrow space between the driver's side headrest and door. It was tight, painful even, but if he shimmied his body, he could inch his way up to his shoulders. He felt a button on his jacket catch the pleather, and it rammed into his side.

He wriggled back out, feeling claustrophobic. His suit jacket was sticky with sweat and rainwater. He began to take it off.

"What are you doing?"

"Getting naked."

Liz stared incredulously. "Again?!"

"I think I can fit through."

Liz looked at the tiny space. "That's really small."

"Yeah, but so am I."

Jay held out his arms, which were knotted in the wrapped fabric of his jacket. Liz tugged it over his fists, freeing his hands.

"Come on, you have to try too."

"There's no way I'm fitting through there."

"Do you want to get out? The clock is ticking."

"Oh my God." Liz reached behind her back and pulled at her zipper. "I can't believe I'm in the back seat of a car, taking off my dress with Jay Banksman. Can you give me a hand? I'm stuck."

Jay got up on his knees and pulled at Liz's zipper.

"Ow!"

"Sorry. First time doing this."

He watched the dress separate from her skin, peeling down to her waist. He realized with shock that she wasn't wearing a bra.

"Hey, I know this is only my avatar or whatever, but could you try not to stare?"

"Sorry, sorry." He diverted his gaze.

"Thanks." She peeled her dress down her legs. He cast a sidelong glance at her body. Thin white underwear glowed in the darkness. She placed her hand over her breasts, and the two of them turned to face each other in the back seat.

"This is unbelievably stupid."

"We don't have a ton of options."

Liz eyed the tiny space between her headrest doubtfully. "How is being naked going to help me fit through there?"

Jay gave a slight smile. "I didn't actually say *you* had to take off your clothes. You kind of did that on your own."

Through the window, Jay caught a glimpse of something white spilling from the alley between houses.

"Uh-oh. They're back."

Indeed, the sound of angry rabble rose all around them as white faceless bodies spilled into the street. Jay again pushed his face into the seat back in front of him. He remembered watching that horrendous video in biology class of a woman giving birth. What had the narrator said? That the baby's head was the biggest part of its body. He imagined himself as a baby, pushing his way through the birth canal. He smashed his face between the headrest and the car frame, wriggling until his head popped through.

He looked at Liz. She had her head and both arms through, but she was wedged so tightly, she couldn't move. Jay sucked in his chest, compressing it against the seat. He thrashed and struggled for several heavy minutes, then stopped, panting.

"Okay . . . I need a push."

Liz cursed as she unwound her body, giving up. She scooted over, and he felt her hands on his feet.

"How's the view?"

"I didn't know they made silk Batman boxers."

"Just be glad I wore these. Will you push?"

She pushed.

"Ow!"

"Well, it's the only way you'll go."

Jay felt a sharp pain in his ribs.

"Owwww! Stop!"

But Liz just pushed harder. Jay felt as if his insides were going to burst. Something sliced his leg, and then he was slithering through the hole and falling into a pile in the driver's seat.

"Jay," she whispered. "You did it."

Jay heaved, catching his breath. "Can I have my pants, please?"

His pants fell beside him on the seat. "Nice work."

He met her gaze in the rearview mirror. The sight of her bare shoulders sent a thrill through his body.

"You should see me with my full stats." He grinned.

Jay slid into his pants and peeked out the driver's window. The white riot bodies filled the sidewalk, working their way down Main Street. Jay watched them swarm houses, methodically punching out windows, ripping off siding. Demolishing each house by hand. A few bodies spilled out aimlessly from the rest of the group, and one bumped into their squad car. Jay ducked back down. Very slowly, he pulled his walkie-talkie from his suit jacket pocket and switched it on.

"Hello?" he whispered.

There was no answer. Outside, the angry rabble grew louder.

"Hello? Is there anyone there?"

Then, Colin's voice. "Jay?"

"Colin! Where are you?"

"We're up in Tutorial. Where are you?"

Footsteps were surrounding their car. Jay hunkered down farther, lowering his voice.

"We're outside Scallow Park. There's a riot happening." He paused. "It got Elmer. He's dead."

There was a moment of silence, then: "What?"

"Hal's sending disasters—"

A hand slapped the side of the squad car, and a white shape appeared in the window above him. There was a squeal of metal, and Jay grabbed the steering wheel as the driver's side of the squad car was raised up. Jay tumbled down into the passenger side. Liz screamed in the back seat as the car dropped down. Its side windows shattered, sprinkling glass over Jay's head. The angry muttering was everywhere. The car began to rock back and forth. Metal bent as fists slammed into its roof.

"Hello?" the walkie-talkie squawked. "Can you hear me?"

Jay turned the volume up all the way and tossed the walkie-talkie out the window. It clattered across the pavement, and immediately several of the white bodies peeled off, chasing it. Jay peeked up out of the broken window and saw the device engulfed in bodies tearing at the ground. Through the trees of Scallow Park, Jay saw more white figures rushing toward them. He glanced back at Liz. She was dressed now, cowering in the seat wells.

"Get us out of here?" she breathed.

Jay saw keys dangling from the ignition. He crawled back into the driver's seat, keeping low. He pushed in the clutch, turned the key, and felt the engine rumble to life. For a moment, the bodies around the car stepped backward, startled. Then they rushed the car again in greater force, pounding its frame. Jay hit the gas. Tires squealed, and the car lurched forward.

Jay swerved as faceless figures leapt onto his trunk. The squad car whipped around, wheels skidding across pavement. Jay peeled down Main Street. More white shapes gathered in the darkness. Bodies filled the road behind them like a sinister parade, blocking the path back to the school.

They zipped past, watching the white riot grow smaller in the rearview mirror. As they moved farther into Bickleton, Jay saw the riot was everywhere. On every side street, clinging to every building, every rooftop.

The windows of the squad car were all blown out, and freezing air filled the cab. Jay turned up the heat as high as it would go, blasting the cabin with warm air.

"You getting any of that?" He looked at Liz in the rearview mirror, and saw she was shivering.

The car's roof was squashed down so low it brushed the top of Jay's head. The driver's side was a mess of fused metal from where the riot's grip had scored it. Jay shivered as he turned onto Jewett Boulevard.

"No going back that way," Jay muttered.

They drove through the dozen shops in the small strip of downtown Bickleton. This section, at least, seemed yet untouched by the riots or the earthquake. It was pitch dark, and the signs at Petey's Barbershop and Classy Chassis car repair were all dark. But people—real people—were packed in there. The entire town seemed to have realized that they were under attack, and they'd migrated there. Trucks rumbled through the street, their beds filled with hastily packed suitcases and tarps. Screams and sobs filled the air; it was like a nightmare. A line of cars puttered south on Highway 24, trying to escape Bickleton.

Jay shook his head, remembering what Hal had said about people getting trapped on the edges of the map.

"They're going to have a rude awakening when the road ends."

Something hit the car and Jay startled. On the passenger side, his mom's face peered in through the window, incredulous.

"Jay?"

Kathy Banksman ripped open the passenger door and leapt inside, clambering over the median to throw her arms around him.

"Oh my God, oh my God, oh my God. Oh, I didn't know what happened to you. I was so worried."

She planted big wet smooches on his cheek.

"Mom, cool it. What are you doing here?"

"It's the apocalypse! The tornado, then the earthquake, then the Maganas next door—they got attacked by a bunch of—"

She finally noticed the car. "Why are you driving the sheriff's car? Where's Elmer?"

"Okay, the good news is that it's not the apocalypse. The bad news is that things might actually be worse. You know all that money we got . . . ?"

"I knew it! I knew another shoe was going to drop."

Jay sighed. "Mom, you did not. You were all about that money."

She shook her head defiantly. "I *knew* this was gonna happen."

"You knew a faceless riot was going to attack Bickleton?"

She nodded. "Something very similar."

Liz rapped on the metal divider. "Hi."

"Oh, *Liz*! Hi!" Kathy fawned, changing her tone. "Did you guys have a nice time at prom together?"

Jay was growing annoyed. "Would you like to actually get in?"

"Yes, and I want to hear all about your night." Mrs. Banksman smiled so hard that Jay turned scarlet. The car behind them honked and Kathy leapt into the passenger seat. Jay rolled the car forward, and they sat idling.

Liz cast a worried glance back toward the school. "We have to get to that computer."

"We can't go that way."

On the sidewalk, Jay watched a grizzled man throw a gas can in his truck, and a woman in camo walk out from the hardware store.

"Where are all the kids?" he asked, suddenly noticing their absence.

"Wish I knew," Kathy chimed in. "The Beckers are worried sick for Shelby. Did you see where the kids went after prom? Nobody seems to know where they are, and everyone is worried."

Jay's eyes widened with realization. "I don't believe those idiots," he muttered.

He spun the steering wheel, pulling the sheriff's car out of the queue and lurching down a side street.

"Where are we going?"

"To get help."

FORTIFICATIONS

COLIN PACED BETWEEN the desks of Tutorial. He could hear the dull *thrumma-thrumma* of the generator just outside the door. The lamp they'd turned on in the corner pulsed slightly with the throb of the generator; its warm light danced dimly across the room. The outside window was black, covered in a deep darkness. It was impossible to tell the pine trees from the C-Court parking lot beyond. The baseboard electric heaters pumped out electric heat that kept the room dry and full of static electricity.

Stevie was leaning on a desk, blowing into her hands and rubbing them.

"I could go down to the gym and get your coat?" Colin offered.

She held her hands up, as if to show that she didn't need to be blowing on them. "That's okay. It's warming up."

She cast a sidelong glance at the computer. "What was that about a riot?"

Colin shrugged. The quiet outside was killing him, and he didn't have a good feeling about Jay's abrupt sign-off.

"I'm sure they're fine," he muttered. "Jay's . . . resourceful."

Stevie stepped hesitantly to the computer. "Do you think we should test it? See if it works with the generator?"

Colin shrugged again. "I mean, Hal can already see us up here, if he looks. Having the computer on won't make a difference, right?"

Stevie eagerly sat and depressed the Power button. The PS/2 beeped, the black MS-DOS boot screen flashed, and the Windows 3.1 logo blinked. Stevie gave Colin a grateful smile.

"Least it works!"

The desktop screen came up, and they both stared at *The Build*'s icon in the lower right-hand corner.

"Do you think it would be bad to boot up the game? Just to see where Jay and Liz are?"

"I guess not," Colin responded slowly. "So long as we don't make changes."

Stevie nodded and double-clicked the icon. The familiar pastoral load screen flashed up, and then they were looking down at Scallow Park.

"Oh wow."

The houses surrounding the park were reduced to rubble piles. They watched small white figures writhe like maggots around the few remaining houses.

"I don't see Jay anywhere."

"What's that?"

Colin pointed to a block of houses with a blue outline and the small word HAL. After a moment, more white maggots appeared there and began demolishing the houses. The blue outline jumped to the next block. Stevie nearly choked.

"That's Hal! That's his cursor. He's in the game, watching!"

"Can he see us?"

Stevie shook her head. "I don't think so, unless we click on something."

"Get away from him."

Stevie obliged, scrolling back over to Tutorial. Their small portable was barely visible in the darkness of the map.

"Well, at least we know what Hal is doing."

"He's gonna destroy the entire town."

"He looks pretty busy. You think he's checking the code?"

Colin's heart leapt into his throat. "You want to make changes to *The Build* while he's looking?!"

"We should be ready for those creatures. Or if Hal comes back in."

Colin paced, wringing his hands. Every fiber of his being was shouting that they were already taking too many chances. But he couldn't say no to Stevie. He gave the slightest nod. A grin spread across Stevie's face.

"Let's put up some defenses!"

Colin grimaced, wondering what Jay would say.

SPOT #7

BICKLETON HAD A list of revolving party spots, and the kids used numbers to keep their location a secret from any eavesdropping adults. Spot #1 was behind the firehouse on Snowden Road. Spot #2 was in a clear-cut on the Skookullom.

Spot #7 was about ten miles south of town, on a river bend of the Little Salmon, a tributary to the Skookullom. A dusty road, barely visible from the highway, peeled off and plunged into a thick grove of cedars. Boulders and potholes played defense against all but the mightiest of trucks as the road bounced down, terminating at a tiny beach, a spit of gravel that the river swelled over in the winter, then uncovered each spring.

Word had spread that the prom after-party would be at spot #7. Now, trucks lined either side of the road as boys and girls hiked in loafers and heels through an inch of mud, toward a bonfire that raged beneath veiled stars.

They may have felt the earthquake, but none of them knew the scourges currently ripping Bickleton apart. All anyone wanted to talk about was the two Jays, and how they had kicked Jeremy's ass yet again. The consensus was that Jay had taken weight class that year, though nobody could actually remember seeing him there. And now, apparently, Jay had a long-lost twin. It was a twist worthy of *Melrose Place*, and the party's energy seemed to feed off it.

From the open doors of John W's truck, Garth Brooks crooned. At the fire's edge, seniors in tuxedos swigged beers and took turns with a Mossberg 500, blasting the washing machine Chard Arkin had lugged from his parents' garage, and causing nervous freshmen to jump as they sipped their Rainiers at the party's fringes.

John H was in the back of a pickup, bending over so that his hairy butt peeked out at the crowd. He passed logs of wood down to John W, who threw them onto the fire. John B, staggeringly drunk, held a can of gas over the flames until the fire flared up to lick the leaves above.

Jeremy sat in an overstuffed easy chair in the bed of John D's pickup, silently watching the party. He was feeling better since prom, now that his fingers were bandaged and he'd managed to put back a few. His mind kept returning to the two Jays, and the disk he'd used. Jeremy wasn't dumb—he took some pride in his B average—but he couldn't figure out what had happened. Somehow, Jay had found a way to thwart him again. That second Jay had boosted his stats even more powerfully than his own.

None of it made sense, and it was starting to bother him. He watched his fellow seniors push a couch onto the bonfire, and John B walk across it as it burst into flames. Chris Hargrove pulled out a can of WD-40 and sprayed it at the fire. The vaporized oil burst into a fireball that singed John B, who leapt off the couch and pushed Chris Hargrove. The crowd howled in laughter.

Jeremy sipped his Rainier and smiled vaguely. It was good to have some normalcy restored.

Suddenly, a hush fell across the party. The shotgun blasts stopped. The only sound was the crackle of fire and the blare of the truck speakers.

The partygoers turned to the road. Jeremy strained to see what they were staring at. Jay Banksman stood at the edge of the bonfire. His wet prom tuxedo was rumpled and singed. Liz stood to his right, still in her prom dress, her heels off now, her feet covered in mud. To Jay's left was an older woman: Jeremy vaguely recognized her as Jay's mom.

Jay called across the staring faces.

"Jeremy!"

All eyes turned to the bed of the pickup. Jeremy sat, placid. Watching. Jay, he noticed, was back down to his old size. He flexed his huge muscles in anticipation.

"We need your help."

Liz screamed.

Kathy Banksman leapt out of the way, and then something hit Jay from the side. He tumbled over, and John B was on top of him, a crazed smile on his face, drunk eyes focusing and unfocusing.

"Hey, Jeremy!" he screamed. "Look what I got!" John B yelled.

The Johns dog-piled on top of Jay, their hands wrapping his arms, pulling them behind his back. Liz and Kathy screamed for them to stop, but the Johns paid them no heed.

"Get a rope!"

They dragged him through the crowd, and he felt the growing warmth of the bonfire as they hauled him in front of it. Students gathered, smiling, eager to watch. Jay felt a rope wrap his hands.

"Do you know what's happening back in town?" Kathy yelled. "Bickleton is under attack!"

The Johns laughed, ignoring her, then fell silent. Jeremy slid off his tailgate. The revelers parted and he approached Jay. He stood over Jay for a few moments, dangling a Rainier can from his fingertips, then looked over to the dirt road, where the sheriff's car sat in the shadows.

"That's Elmer's car."

Jay nodded. "Elmer's dead."

A murmur rose. Jeremy walked to the edge of the onlookers, to the trunk of a cedar tree where the sheriff's car was parked. He studied its broken windows, its caved-in roof, the indents in its doors. He turned back to Jay.

"You kill him?"

Jay gestured to the car. "You think I could do *that*? Like my mom said, Bickleton's under attack."

John H snickered. "Sounds like he's been playing too many video games."

Jay nodded. "For once in your life, you're right."

Jeremy turned definitively. "I don't believe you."

Jay snorted. "You don't have to. They followed us here."

From somewhere nearby, a low fluttering bristled through the forest. The Johns' laughter died. Jeremy's eyes narrowed, searching the trees. The partiers shifted, staring into darkness that suddenly seemed deeper.

John D picked up a shotgun. Garth Brooks twanged across the riverbank.

"Turn that music off," Jeremy growled. Chris Hargrove leaned into the truck and turned off the ignition. The only sound now was the crackle of fire, the murmur of the river, and the low, otherworldly whisper that was growing louder by the second.

A branch snapped. The whole party swiveled around, and a white figure broke from the trees, galloping toward the bonfire. Kids screamed, scattering, tuxedos disappearing into the night.

"Shoot it!" someone yelled.

John D pulled his shotgun up and fired. The figure tumbled and slid through the dirt, stopping just before Jay. In the firelight, Jay stared at its featureless white head.

A second creature shot up from riverbank, rushing the party. John D swung the shotgun around. The thing leapt into the air, landing between Jay and Jeremy. It reared up to its full height, long arms dangling down. John D fired, and the creature flew back into the bonfire. John D lowered his gun.

"Got 'em!"

The Johns crept forward, searching the woods for more, but the murmuring sound had stopped. Jeremy strode over to the downed creature. A skinny freshman poked it with a stick.

"What is it?"

Nobody answered.

Jeremy grabbed Jay and threw him back onto the ground.

"What is it?!" Jeremy screamed into Jay's face.

His weight was atop him, pressing his body into the river stones. He poked a finger in Jay's face.

"You brought those things! They're from your game."

"Are you kidding me?" Jay spat back. "*You* brought them. If it wasn't for you and your stupid antics, he never would've built this world. Do you understand that, or is your code so limited that—"

But he couldn't finish, because Jeremy's hands were around his neck, choking him. The Johns ran up, looking with fright at the dead white figure. John W grabbed Jeremy's shoulder.

"Jeremy, man, maybe we hear him out?"

Jay heard his mom and Liz screaming, but Jeremy didn't budge. His face was red with fury, eyes glazed over. Jay felt panic rise as he struggled against Jeremy's grip. Without his extra strength, there was nothing he could do. How to get through to him?

In the midst of the panic, a small part of Jay's brain spoke calmly. *He's programmed to hate me. He doesn't understand why. But that's okay, because I do.*

The blood was pooling in his face now. Spots swam before his eyes. The Johns, Liz, and his mom were all pulling at Jeremy, trying to get him off.

With the last of his voice, Jay squeaked:

"Jay Banksman . . . is . . . a little . . . bitch."

Jay felt Jeremy's hands loosen a little. Jay sucked in air, coughing. Jeremy stared down.

"What'd you say?"

Jay croaked. "I said . . . Jay Banksman . . . is a bitch."

Jeremy's hands left Jay's neck. He stared out into the night.

"Yeah . . . so . . . ?"

Jay's breath returned.

"So that guy back at prom? The other me? He's running this world. He's the one making changes. He wants to prove that he's smarter, stronger, and better at baseball than you. And he's going to destroy all of us, unless we can stop him."

Jeremy's eyes glazed over, listening. Jay continued.

"Have the Bickleton Vandals ever lost a scrimmage?"

"No," Jeremy whispered.

"What's your record?"

Jeremy stared blankly. "Undefeated."

"You gonna let Jay Banksman break that record?"

"No."

"You gonna let him take Bickleton from you?"

"No."

"Then what are you gonna do?"

Jeremy stood up and looked down at Jay. "I'm gonna do what I always do. I'm gonna kick Jay's ass."

Jay nodded. "And I want to help you."

Jeremy reached down, and the Johns watched in awe as Jeremy pulled Jay up. He stripped the rope off Jay's wrists, and Liz and his mom ran over, hugging him.

"Jay . . ." Liz whispered.

Kathy Banksman shook her head, bewildered. "What is going on? *You're* Jay Banksman."

Jay sighed, watching the Johns run to their trucks and throw their guns in the beds. "Mom, I'd explain, but you have an intelligence score of three."

He felt a little more hopeful now that they had the Johns on their side. But where was Hal? If he wasn't watching Jay, what was he doing?

DISASTERS

JOHNS SCURRIED FROM truck to truck, their guns clattering as they threw them into their pickup beds.

A freshman grabbed the can of gasoline and dosed the bonfire. The flames roared, flickering orange across the faces of partygoers. Jeremy stood beside the fire, pale blue eyes glittering as he listened to Jay lay out everything he knew. He watched kids' faces shift from shock, to horror, to confusion. Jeremy stood transfixed, listening to Jay's every word. At last, Jay finished and Jeremy nodded.

"So those things . . . those white things . . ."

". . . are one of the disasters. The *riot*."

"And he can keep sending these over and over?"

"Yep. Until he destroys us."

"So if he can delete any of us with a click, how do we stop him?"

"Stevie can. She's up in Tutorial right now. She might be able to turn his program against him. But we can't do anything yet. So long as he's sitting behind his computer screen, he's all-powerful. He can see us and react far faster than we can. If we want to stop him, we have to lure him back into the game."

"How?"

Jay looked from Jeremy to Liz, then smiled. "You two are the reason *The Build* exists. The three of us just drew Hal out at prom. I'm betting we can do it again."

"What does that mean?" Liz stared into the fire. "Do we have to fight each other?"

Jay shook his head. "No. We have to do something even more drastic. We have to work together."

Jeremy grunted. "Is that all?"

"It'll drive him crazy."

As if on cue, the sky rumbled. A crack of lightning shot down onto the bluff across the river. The Johns winced, ducking and holding their guns up as if to shield whatever new threat might be coming from the sky.

But it was only rain. Fat drops began to fall. This seemed somehow to be the final straw for the partygoers. Boys threw their tuxedo jackets over their heads, and girls stumbled into the tree line to take shelter. There was a boom of thunder, and over the distant mountains, more lightning flashed. Kathy Banksman stared up at the town.

"Oh, those poor people trying to leave." She shook her head. "Their stuff is going to get soaked."

Liz looked to Jay. "Is this a disaster?"

Jay frowned, uncertain. Car lights flashed on, and engines started. An old Chevy Nova rumbled up the road, leaving.

"Hey!" Jay yelled at the students leaving. "We're all in this together!"

"Jay!" Jeremy shouted. He was standing down at the bonfire pit, staring over the rocks to the water's edge. He pointed at the dark waters of the Skookullom. The rain fell in heavy drops now as Jay ran to join him. He pushed a mop of hair from his eyes, straining to see the black swirls and eddies that had captured Jeremy's attention. A small wave splashed his shoes, and Jay leapt back. The banks of the Skookullom were rising.

"This is a flood!" Jay yelled, nodding. "This is definitely a disaster."

A rumbling noise grew upstream.

"Get to higher ground!"

The kids turned and ran, slipping on wet rocks. In the blackness of the night, Jay saw something large and white around the river bend upstream. A wall of water. He grabbed Liz and his mom and urged them up to the tree line.

"Get to the cars!"

The roar of water crashed through the underbrush behind them. Jay turned to see it hit the bonfire, extinguishing it in an angry sizzle. The only light now was the haphazard zig-zag of headlights as prom-goers pulled out of the party. Jay pulled his feet through muddy ground, slopping toward the squad car. Ford trucks breezed past them, headlights flashing through dense cedar trees. Water was now in the trees with them, lapping at their ankles as they reached the sheriff's car. Liz screamed, and Jay's mom grabbed his lapels. Ahead, John W's truck stopped in the water, its door open.

"Jeremy, get in!"

Jeremy shook his head. "Wait for us at the top of the road."

Jay felt a strange flush of pride as Jeremy rounded over to the driver's side and threw his shotgun onto the seat.

"Cool if I drive?"

"Please!" Jay opened the rear door for his mom and Liz, pausing as they scrambled in. The water touched the bottom of the car frame as he rounded to the passenger side.

"Let's go!"

The squad car's engine rumbled to life, its headlights flickering across the giant cedars. They were the last car left, and the water was almost touching the car's frame. Jeremy pressed the gas and the wheels spun, churning water. The car lurched up the hill. The water lessened and lessened, and then the squad car pulled out of the muck, onto the dirt road that led back to Highway 24. Jeremy accelerated, spinning the tires and bumping the car up the dirt road.

Jay turned to the back seat. Liz was rubbing her shoulders to keep warm, and his mom's teeth were chattering.

"I'm way too sober for this," Kathy said.

Without saying anything, Jeremy reached into his pocket and pulled out a flask. He handed it to Kathy, and she unscrewed the top and took a swig.

"Hey!" Jay called. "Don't give my mom booze."

"Then keep me out of your video games!"

Kathy pushed the flask through the metal lattice to her son, and Jay grabbed it and took a pull.

ALONG THE
WATCHTOWER

COLIN SAT ON the top of a small tower, staring out at the night. The stars twinkled in the sky, the rising moon draping the landscape in blue. In the distance, he saw orange flickers in the windows of farmhouses. Families inside, huddled around fireplaces, keeping warm until the power came back on. He shivered, wishing he were also inside his house. He strained his eyes to try to make out the road in the darkness.

No sign of Jay.

Stevie had done quite a number on the landscape surrounding Tutorial. She'd cleared away pines, built a moat of water, and then thrown up these four towers around the perimeter. If Hal saw it, he would immediately destroy them, of course. But if any of those weird white things arrived, they'd have a heck of a time getting in. Colin looked down over the tower ramparts at the packed earth fifteen feet below. The water in the moat was still, and he heard the croak of a bullfrog underneath him.

Stevie was sitting in Tutorial, at the computer. As far as Colin could see, she didn't seem to be making more changes, and for that he was grateful. The thought that Hal might spot them and delete them from existence with barely a moment's notice terrified him. He scanned the small thin strip of Main Street that was barely visible over the baseball field, searching for headlights. Nothing.

He uncrossed his legs and stood, craning his neck to try to see down through the window they'd agreed to leave open.

"How's it going?" he shouted as loudly as he dared.

Stevie poked her head out and smiled, but Colin saw it was strained.

"Good. I'm going through the code now, looking for traces of Liz. I think I might've found something."

She was about to draw her head back in, but hesitated.

"By the way . . . I forgot to say . . . you looked good at prom."

Colin blushed. "My suit's too big."

She smiled.

She stopped. Her smile was gone. Her brow furrowed as she stared at something in the sky beyond the pine trees.

"Do you see that?"

Colin walked to the edge of the roof, squinting over the sky. Sure enough, something was moving on the horizon. It was a small speck, like a star or a satellite. Except it was moving too fast and heading toward them. As it fell, it seemed to grow brighter. It might be his eyes playing tricks on him, but he thought he could see faint orange flames coming out its sides.

"Is that . . . a meteorite?" Stevie whispered.

Colin stared. It wasn't a meteorite . . . it seemed to be moving in circles.

His gaze flicked back to the dark road. Where the hell was Jay?

GAME PROS

TWENTY MILES SOUTH of Tutorial, Jay's white knuckles were wrapped around the grab handle in Elmer's squad car. They were barreling toward Bickleton along Highway 24, Jeremy pushing the speedometer to ninety. In the rearview mirror, Jay watched Liz and his mom hold their breath, pushed back in their seats, eyes wide.

Jeremy turned to face them. "I've driven this road a million times."

Jay's eyes were glued to the road. "This fast?"

"This fast."

Behind them trailed the Johns in a long line of pickup trucks. Jay's eyes watered as wind whistled in through the busted windows. They rounded a corner, tires squealing, and Jay was pushed against the passenger door. Liz grabbed on to the divider mesh.

"Slow down!"

"Yes," Jay's mom chimed in. "Can we please go slower? What good is going so fast if we die on the way there!"

"Everyone, chill. I've . . ." But the words died in his mouth.

He and Jay were staring through the shattered windshield, at the sky. The loud whine of a motor filled the air, growing louder. The surrounding forest, which had been pitch black, suddenly lit up in an orange glow.

"What's that noise?" Liz yelled.

In the air over the road, a 747 jetliner was hurtling from the sky. Its nose was slanted down, flames shooting from both of its engines. Dark smoke obscured the stars as it plummeted directly toward them.

Kathy saw it and screamed, "Go faster! Faster!"

Jeremy floored the gas pedal and the car shot forward. Behind them, the Johns veered their trucks, driving on the shoulder. The noise was deafening as the plane streaked over their heads, covering the road in flickering orange.

BOOM!

A shock wave of warm air blew through their car. Jay spun around. Not three hundred yards behind them, a fireball blossomed into the sky.

"Holy shit!"

Liz was staring over her shoulder. "Another disaster?"

Jay nodded.

"That's everything, then? We've seen all the disasters?"

Jay didn't answer. He stared back at the burning patch of road behind them. Was Hal just trying to scare them? Or was he really trying to kill them?

The woods on either side fell away, and they ascended the final rise into lower Bickleton. Or what was left of it. The Riverside Grill was now a tangle of timber, flames licking its edges. Beyond that, houses were smashed as if a giant fist had punched down from the sky. A Winnebago lay on its side, torn, its plaster scattered into the road. The trucks of escaping townsfolk lay at odd angles across the road, the surrounding asphalt littered with dead bodies. Jeremy slowed down, weaving around a trailer. In the back seat, his mom shuddered.

"Oh my God. Who would do something like this?"

Jay looked out the window, consumed with guilt, avoiding Jeremy's accusing gaze.

They turned up Jewett Boulevard, starting the climb into the upper part of town. Jay scanned the skyline, searching for any sign of the riot. But all was quiet, just the slow flicker of flames as the nearby buildings burned. Some movement on a rooftop caught his eye, and then a line of white figures crested the hill. The night suddenly erupted with the sound of angry grumbling.

"They're coming!"

Jay heard a gun retort. Then another. The Johns were leaning out their windows, picking off the white figures that ran down the hill toward them.

Then the things were everywhere. White shapes darted out into the road. The trucks swerved around the figures. Jeremy slammed his foot on the gas pedal, and Jay braced himself as they plowed through.

Their car swerved, slalom-style, around the full-blown riot that now moved into the road, eager to catch them. The houses raged in pillars of flame, and Jay could feel the heat shimmering through the metal of their car. Sweat poured off his brow.

"Look out!" screamed Liz.

A faceless figure popped in front of their headlights. Its flat featureless head swiveled at them. Jeremy swerved, missing it by inches. Jay turned to look out the rearview window. The Johns' trucks were mired in the creatures now. In the F-150 behind them, the faceless figures clung to the truck bed, sinking long fingers into the cab, pulling themselves up. John C spun around, firing into the riot as fast as he could.

Jeremy spun the steering wheel, swerving off Main Street, past the charred ruins of New Bethlehem Church and a burning elementary school. Then they were speeding past cold empty fields. The school loomed ahead, and Jay was relieved to see that it looked intact. They spun into the A-Court parking lot. It stretched out before them, empty, with no signs of the riot, or any disasters.

Jay banged on the dashboard. "Stop the car, stop the car!"

Liz leaned forward. "What do you see?"

"It's what I don't see. Hal's not here. He's at his computer, watching us. If we go to Tutorial, he'll see Stevie, Colin, and the computer. We need to lure him back in the game before we go any farther."

Jeremy slammed on the brakes, and the car screeched to a halt.

"I thought you said the three of us working together would bring him in?"

Jay glanced at the clock. It was well after one o'clock in the morning. He looked back at Liz. There didn't appear to be any change in her demeanor. But then, Hal had said there wouldn't be. Was he already too late?

"What do we do?" Liz whispered.

Jay furrowed his brow, thinking. What would it take to get Hal's attention? What would drive him crazy?

"Nothing."

"Pardon?"

"We have to do nothing." Jay shook his head. "There's one thing we can do to drive him crazy: we can stop playing his game."

"But . . . he'll kill us."

Jay opened his door. "He won't kill me."

He stepped out into the parking lot.

Instantly, the roof of Bickleton High School burst into flames, lighting up the dark asphalt. Jay walked out toward the baseball field. Liz and Kathy got out and stood next to him, turning from the flames to Jay. From out on the baseball field, angry murmurs grew. Jay watched a horde of pale figures rush from the trees and tear across the empty grass. Fear rose in Jay's throat as he watched them come. Still, he didn't move.

The figures clambered up the ivy-covered banks, toward the parking lot. Several dozen broke off and tore into the bleachers, ripping out large chunks of wood. They crested the hill, and Jay could see their white bodies grab and rattle the fence, until it came tumbling down, and the bodies ran over it. The creatures were rushing right at him, running across the parking lot.

Jeremy stepped out of the car, pointing his shotgun.

"Drop it," Jay urged.

"They're gonna rip you apart."

"If Hal wanted me dead, he could've deleted me a long time ago."

Jeremy lowered the shotgun, looking apprehensively from Jay to the riot. The slap of feet on pavement was overwhelming, and angry murmurings grew. They were a solid wall of bodies.

"Jay . . . honey . . . ?" came his mom's tremulous voice.

"It's okay."

The wall of white faceless bodies was only a few yards away. Another second and they'd be on him. What if he were wrong? Jay squeezed his eyes closed, bracing for impact. And then the noise stopped.

When Jay opened his eyes again, the white riot was gone. Instead, a single figure stood in the high school parking lot. It was Hal. He wore his fanny pack and slippers. His hair was reduced to a horseshoe, and decades of fat padded his jawline. His mustache quivered.

"Give up?"

Jay felt a wave of relief, but tried not to show it.

"Yes, Hal. We surrender."

Hal smiled. "I'm disappointed. I'd like to think I'm better than that."

"You are." Jay gave a wan smile. "You've defeated us."

Hal sighed. "I told you it would come to this, if I turned the safety valve off. This is going to require a full reset. Every memory wiped, we start over back, say, junior year. Well, it's not the first time." He reached into his fanny pack.

"Or . . . !" Jay interjected, stalling for time. Hal stopped, looking at him. "Or we could go mano a mano."

Hal chuckled and waved his remote at Jay. "Gonna try to take this one, too? Go ahead. I've got multiples stashed around the map."

"Nope. I know a way to beat you fair and square."

Hal looked at Jay, curious. "Maybe if this were a fair fight. But you know me too well to understand I can't allow a truly fair fight."

The distant sound of thrumming engines filled the air. A line of trucks sped through the night, headlights blinking as they passed the rows of apple trees. He could hear the Johns howling out open windows, and the faint sound of Rage Against the Machine. Hal swiveled around at the noise. Jay turned back to Jeremy and motioned for him to get in the car.

Jeremy leapt in the open driver's door and threw the car into gear.

"That's right, Hal." Jay was nodding at Jeremy. "I brought reinforcements."

Hal watched the trucks swerve into the A-Court parking lot, shuddering over the speed bump as their headlights swept the asphalt. Hal scoffed.

"That's your plan? You think I didn't see you go down to party spot seven and—"

The sheriff's car plowed into Hal from behind. It's hood crumpled, a headlight shattered, and Hal flew forward, skidding over the asphalt. Jeremy urged the car onward until it bounced over Hal's downed body with a *ka-thunk*. Jeremy shifted back into neutral and pulled the parking brake.

Across the parking lot, the angry murmur of the riot streamed over the middle school, mixing with the retort of the Johns' guns. Jeremy kicked open his door, grabbed his shotgun, and fired four shots into Hal's body.

A defiant scream rang out. Hal's legs were pinched under the rear tire. His shirt and shorts were speckled with gravel. He was squirming, furious, like a trapped animal. Jay saw his fingers reaching for his black remote, which lay a few feet away on the asphalt. Liz ran over and kicked it so that it skittered out of his grasp. From where he lay on the ground, Hal wrapped both hands around the car's rear tire and pushed, straining. The car began to lift. Jeremy fired again, and the car fell back down.

"You're not going anywhere."

"Hrrmmm," Hal breathed heavily.

"It's over, Hal."

Hal smiled. "Even if I do nothing, the riot will overpower you. There're too many of them."

"What if I have this?" Jay picked up the black remote. He examined all the unmarked black buttons.

Hal snarled. "Don't touch that."

Liz leaned down next to him. "You're stuck here, Hal. Your body will get hungry. You'll grow lightheaded. You'll wet and shit yourself. Then, days from now, when they find your body, they'll laugh. Sound familiar?"

Hal shifted slightly so that his dark eyes looked at Liz. "And what do you think will happen to you, then? With no one to change your IV? And the rest of Bickleton? How long will *The Build* survive if there's not someone on the other end, monitoring the CPU, searching out the infinite loops and freeing up memory inefficiencies? Who'll pay the electric bill? My computer uses a lot of energy. Caring for this game is a full-time job, and I'm the only one who knows how to do it."

Jay looked across the parking lot. Faceless figures streamed down from the farms, surrounding the truck.

Hal snarled. "I'm getting real sick of high school. After fifteen years obsessing over this place, I think I'm finally ready to move on."

Hal threw his arms up and pushed on the car frame, tilting it wildly. Jay, Liz, and Jeremy all jumped to add their weight to the car. But it was too late. Hal rolled free and kicked Jay's leg out from under him. He tripped, dropping the remote, which Hal grabbed.

"And if you won't destroy this town, I'll do it for you!"

Jeremy threw the car into first gear. The tires tore through the school lawn and slammed into Hal. Hal threw his weight against the hood as the tires spun on the soft ground. The car squealed, fishtailing—but Hal held it still. He leaned in, straining, a Cheshire cat grin breaking over his face as he whispered through the broken windshield.

"This isn't even my final form."

He pressed a button on his remote, and his smile spread, twisting back to his ears as his skin began to crack and his body twitched and convulsed.

BOSS MONSTER

HAL'S BODY STIFFENED, his skin shriveling into black tissue. Farther up the parking lot, the Johns' trucks screeched to a stop. John D pointed at Hal and shouted something. Over the squad car bumper, a tentacle of flesh ripped out from Hal's body and flailed in the headlights. Smoke rose from Hal's skin. His head reared up, mouth falling open, jaw detached, dangling in the night. An unearthly shriek echoed over the parking lot.

The shriek struck fear in Jay's heart. He recognized the cry. He'd been listening to its sixteen-bit equivalent all spring. The Mantis. The only boss monster from the *Secret of Mana* he couldn't beat. Jay turned to the others.

"Run!"

Hal's body grew, lengthening, bunching flesh, hardening into a cocoon. The skin around his face pulled taut, then burst into a hideous, glistening membrane. Two giant, lidless eyes swiveled back and forth in a triangular head. Slime dripped down from two mandibles.

The monster threw two jagged mantis arms down onto the hood of the car and stretched out its legs, lifting to its full height, towering into the sky. Even in its 16-bit form, the monster had given Jay nightmares. The unbeatable boss.

"Get to Tutorial!" Jay screamed.

He heard the Johns' truck doors open and the sound of their footsteps as they ran, glancing over their shoulders to fire at the white forms of the riot. The monster hurled its two pincers into the squad car frame, lifted the vehicle, and flung it into darkness. There was a distant crash of metal as it tumbled over the baseball field.

"Move! Follow me!" Jay waved, grabbing Liz's and his mom's hands and rushing past A-Court. Shotguns boomed behind them, and they heard the monster scream. A hideous gurgling noise followed. Jay looked back.

"Acid breath," he whispered.

The creature's head snapped back, and a stream of bile burst from its mouth, hitting one of the John's trucks. The truck melted into a puddle of metal. Shotguns rang out in the night as the Johns fired at Hal.

Jay, Liz, Jeremy, and Kathy were running.

"You got a way to stop that thing?" Jeremy called back to Jay.

"I hope so."

They plunged into the gloom between the buildings. A-Court was still in flames, the fire on its roof flickering orange. Jay stumbled, feeling his way with his hands, his breath catching with each scream of the monster. Then the chirp of crickets grew louder, the roar of the monster faded, and the group was in the open courtyard. The moon hung low, enveloping the school in shadow. A faint breeze caught them, and then they were on the moonlit grass. Jay tugged on Liz's hand, and they ran farther into the night.

ACCESS DENIED

COLIN SAT IN his tower, meditating. He'd learned through years of practice that he could warm up his body by slowing his breath. It was a technique he used during math quizzes. Breathe in. Hold in. Exhale.

The moon had dropped and the night had grown colder, and Colin saw flecks of frost on his little rampart.

Breathe in. Hold in. Exhale.

Above the thick chirp of crickets, he thought he heard shouts, followed by what sounded like gunshots. Whatever it was, it was coming closer.

Breathe in. Hold in. Exhale.

He heard a roar. Colin thought he recognized the sound, but couldn't place it. It reminded him of Jay, for some reason.

Breathe in. Hold in. Exhale.

"Colin!"

That was Jay's voice! Colin's eyes flew open, and he ran to the edge of the roof. His mouth dropped. In the distance, A-Court was on fire. A wall of white things was running toward Tutorial, scrambling like a swarm of spiders. And in the farther distance of the A-Court parking lot, a giant dark shape lumbered slowly, moving its pointy legs. Colin watched, mouth open, as the creature's head swiveled toward him.

Jay ran around C-Court, hand in hand with Liz and his mom.

"Colin!"

Colin saw his friend's tuxedo was bedraggled and burned in places. Liz still wore her sequined dress. Colin didn't have time to respond before all the Johns and Jeremy ran around the corner behind him, still in their tuxedos, carrying guns.

Colin pointed and screamed, "Jay, look out! The Johns are all armed."

"I know!" Jay puffed back. "They're on our side."

Colin climbed down the ladder, landing on the packed earth around Tutorial. Jay ran up to the ramp, admiring the towers that now surrounded the portable.

"You guys are already in the computer?"

"It's okay." Colin held up a hand to soothe Jay. "We can see where Hal is looking, so—"

"No, this is great. Hal's already in the game. He's the Mantis Boss."

"Has Stevie figured out—" Liz asked Colin.

Colin motioned to the ramp, and the four of them ran up and into the classroom. The lamps inside were flickering ever so slightly with the uneven pulse of the generator. Stevie sat before the computer, bathed in blue. She smiled as they came in, as calm and collected as if she were sitting in second period.

Ms. Banksman surveyed the room in horror. "Does Miss Rotchkey know about all this?"

They ignored her. Jeremy slipped in the door behind them. Jay pointed to a beanbag chair. "Mom, take a seat and stay safe. Jeremy, keep those things at bay. Stevie—"

Stevie turned and smiled. "I found a folder marked *weapons*. Would that help?"

"Yes!" Jay shouted.

Stevie turned to the computer. "Let's see . . . I've got a power suit, plasma blaster, minigun . . ."

"Yes to all of it."

There was a metal clang on one of the desks. Jay whipped around. Guns appeared in midair, falling onto the Bakelite slab and clattering down to the floor. Colin and Jay ran over, sifting through the pile, pulling out different weapons. From outside, a screech tore through the air.

"Give me that railgun. Okay, Stevie, now you have to find a way to get Liz out."

"How?"

"I dunno. See if you can find a master directory. We need to get into the operating system on Hal's computer."

Stevie nodded, determined. Liz stood behind Stevie's chair, hands sinking into the headrest.

"What can I do?"

Jay shook his head. "Be ready to run, the moment you're back in your body."

Jay's mom looked up from the beanbag chair. "You're not going back out there, are you son-bun?"

"It's okay." Jay picked up his railgun. "Colin and I have been training for this our whole lives."

He turned to Colin, who was now completely encased in a futuristic metal suit. Through the window, the howl of the riot grew louder. Jay stomped out the door. The stars were fading into the blue hues of dawn. Colin hit the Power button on the sword on his suit, and electricity arced down the side of its gleaming metal. Jay gave him a thumbs-up.

"We said we'd beat the Mantis Boss by graduation."

They stepped back out onto the Tutorial ramp. Angry murmurs mixed with the sounds of smashed glass and bent metal. Jay saw the riot figures were swarming C-Court. On the rooftop, the white creatures sunk their long fingers into the wood to tear out individual shingles. More shapes swarmed the C-Court parking lot, slamming fists into cars. Jay watched a group lift the Batmobile and hurl it onto its side, blowing out its windows.

The horde swarmed the perimeter, standing at the edge of the moat, their pulsing bodies pushing to get at Jay. Then, all at once, the figures stopped.

"Boss time," Jay muttered.

Colin pressed a button on his armor, and flames shot out of his jet pack. Jay dropped his railgun and leapt up onto the Tutorial window, grabbing the tar-paper roof and pulling himself up. From this new vantage, he could see out across the great mass of white bodies. They covered the C-Court roof and the courtyard before the library. Beyond them, all of A-Court was in flames. As he watched, the bodies began separating to make an aisle. Something was slithering down its middle.

The hideous head of the Mantis erupted from the horde. Its lidless eyes swiveled over to Jay. He sighted his railgun and fired. A vapor trail pierced the air, and the creature opened its mouth and screamed. Colin flew into the air, hosing the monster with a stream of bullets.

The riot backed up farther to make room for the monster. Its two massive pincers unfolded and slammed into the side of C-Court, pulling it onto the roof.

"Tag team!" Jay shouted.

Colin floated over to where Jay could grab him, and together they flew toward C-Court. Jay's legs dangled out in space as he fired, watching his bolts disappear into the monster's head. Jay turned to watch the Johns firing below, and in that fraction of a second, the creature's head darted down. Jay spun back around as the pincers tightened around his waist, crushing him so he couldn't breathe. His head swam with the pressure. The dark, red cavern of the monster's mouth grew. Below, he heard faint yells, and the small pop of rifles as the Johns fired.

The creature's mouth widened, and Jay recognized the sickly sweet smell of vomit. Spots swam before his eyes. Jay felt himself slipping into unconsciousness as he waited to feel the blast of acid.

Somewhere to his left, he caught a glimpse of Colin's face, twisted in rage, rocketing toward the monster. The monster's head jerked back, ready to blast Jay. Colin slammed into the creature's brain, knocking it sideways. Its acid breath missed Jay and instead scoured the C-Court roof, leaving a smoldering hole.

Jay felt the pressure of the monster's pincers release from his waist. His vision returned, and he felt the cold rush of air. He was falling. He hit the roof and rolled. He tried to breathe, but daggers were in his lungs. He sucked in, eyes swimming.

The monster swiveled in the air, snapping out, ramming into Colin and sending him tumbling. His power suit slammed into the roof, and the monster's pincers chopped down, hurling wood shingles into the air. Jay realized he was out of ammo. He watched the white riot descend on John W, enveloping him. It was too much. Hal had them. If only they had more Johns.

More Johns: that was it!

He raced up the ramp, the white riot right behind him. Their bodies swarmed Tutorial, falling over guardrails, hurling themselves at the walls. Jay was through the door, holding it shut. He heard the riot clambering on the roof, ripping into the wooden frame with their long clawed fingers. Any moment, they would destroy the generator.

"Stevie!"

Jeremy took over for him, straining to hold the door shut. Jay could see the thick muscles tense on his forearms. The walls of the portable cracked and shivered; long thin arms burst through. Liz was holding the window shut as white arms flailed, smashing the glass.

"We lost!"

Jay ignored her, rushing over to the computer.

"Stevie! Stevie!"

He saw Stevie had paled, and she was no longer smiling.

"We need more Johns!"

"What?!"

"There's a folder called JOHNS!"

Stevie spun back to the computer.

"Okay. So?"

"So give us a million of them!"

The rioters leapt up at the window. He heard a tear above him and looked up to see a long white arm through the roof. They'd be inside any moment.

Then something crashed onto the roof, and the arm of the rioter went still. Something else fell to the ground outside the window. It struggled up to its feet, and Jay saw it was a John. Not a John he recognized—this John had freckles and long arms—but the Neanderthal look on his face was unmistakable. The John looked confused. He stood just before the neighboring rioters turned and pounced, burying him. But another body fell. And another. All over the grass outside, Johns fell flailing from the sky. The rioters turned and attacked them, but still more fell.

"Guns! Give them guns!" Jay shouted.

And then there were weapons mingled with the falling bodies. Shotguns, railguns, and miniguns dropped from the sky. Jay watched in amazement as the Johns scooped them off the ground and fired into the horde of white bodies. The rioters were being gunned down, and still more Johns fell on the Tutorial roof, in the C-Court parking lot. The sky was thick with falling Johns. Jay laughed in delight, and then a John's limp body smashed down through the roof, crashing into Todd's desk before falling limp on the ground.

"Okay, that's enough Johns."

He peered out the broken window. Every square inch of ground was occupied with the Johns. Jeremy opened the Tutorial door and Jay slipped out, pushing his way through the crowd, holding fingers to his ears to muffle the gunfire. Above this vast sea of noise, Jay heard a roar. The Mantis rose up over C-Court. Instantly, all the Johns turned and fired. Thousands of streams of bullets pelted the creature. Through the open window, Stevie's voice rang out.

"Nine hundred thousand hit points!"

The monster turned and crashed toward Tutorial, pincers churning the air.

"Five hundred thousand."

Energy crackled around its eyes, and a burst of acid oozed from its mouth, searing a path through the Johns. Jay watched their bodies hiss and fizzle as the bile blackened the asphalt. More Johns moved in to fill the gap.

"Three hundred thousand!" Stevie shouted.

The monster reached the edge of the C-Court roof and leapt down onto the ground.

"One hundred thousand."

Bullets streaked the air, lighting up the grounds. The monster gave out a last desperate groan . . . then fell. It hit the earth with a force that made the ground tremble, flattening a large swath of Johns.

Jay rushed back into Tutorial.

The classroom had been destroyed. Bookshelves were overturned, loose books strewn across the floor. The classroom's globe lay smashed on one side, like a broken pumpkin. Huge holes punctured the walls, and Jay could see outside. Through the broken sections of the ceiling, he saw dozens of Johns milling about on the roof. His mom was coughing behind Ms. Rotchkey's desk. Liz grabbed his hands, searching his face. In turn, he turned to Stevie.

A smile spread across her face. "I've got him locked out. Once he leaves, he won't be able to get back in, or access *The Build.*"

"Does he know that?"

She shook her head. "Not yet."

A tired grin spread across Jay's face. Onscreen, the monster's pixelated body twitched. Jay rushed the Tutorial door, passing Jeremy. The Johns were whooping and cheering now, trading high fives. Jay squeezed between them as he rushed down the ramp, picking his way over the dead riot bodies that now choked the moat. Then he came to a halt.

The monster's body shuddered. Viscous purple liquid dripped down its round head. From somewhere deep inside, a muffled voice was cursing.

"Hal!" Jay yelled. The surrounding Johns quieted, watching.

A hand burst out of the monster's slimy skin. The thousands of Johns stared at the human figure struggling to get out. Hal emerged, naked and completely covered in violet slime, like a forty-year-old baby.

Jay could hear him muttering and cursing. Hal turned back to the monster's carcass, searching for something. Next to Jay, a John gave a muffled snort, trying to suppress his laughter. Jay spun round and held up a warning finger.

"Do not!"

He turned back to Hal. Hal straightened, seeming to find what he was looking for. A bloody fanny pack dangled from his hand. A John nearby giggled, and Jay shook his head. They had to hold Hal's attention.

"Hal!"

Hal turned and adjusted his glasses, squinting. He seemed not to be aware of his nudity.

"You got us again, Hal. You destroyed Bickleton. Good game."

Even from a distance, Jay could see Hal's mustache bristle indignantly.

Hal stamped a small foot. "You cheated!"

The sight of this slight man—stomping his feet, naked body shiny with dripping blood and bits of entrail—was too much. The sea of Johns gave way to laughter. The noise thundered, cacophonous, filling the night sky. Jay turned to them.

"Don't laugh!"

They ignored him, pointing at Hal, doubling over. They began to pick up rocks and toss them at Hal, who raised an arm to shield himself.

"Do you know who you're laughing at?!" Hal shrieked.

His face reddened. He reached into his fanny pack and pulled out his remote.

"No no no!"

But it was too late. Hal disappeared. The Johns chuckled stupidly, staring vaguely at their surroundings, trying to discern where he'd gone. Jay rushed back up the ramp, into Tutorial, and found everyone huddled around the computer.

"Stevie?"

"I cut his access!"

Stevie's fingers clacked against the keyboard. Jay ran over and looked at the screen. Bickleton was in shambles. Buildings were leveled. Fires raged everywhere. On top of the screen, a small window flashed up: HALMASTER REQUESTS ACCESS.

Stevie clicked DENY. The window changed to: ACCESS DENIED.

"Did we seriously just kick him out of his own game?" Jay threw his head back and laughed.

Stevie looked up, a big grin on her face. "He can't get back in without our permission. And he can't reverse it, either." She studied the screen. "Not while I'm here watching, anyway."

Jay fell into a desk, exhausted. Jeremy clamped a hand on his shoulder, and Liz squeezed his arm.

Kathy Banksman sat in a beanbag chair, bewildered. "I assume this is all good news?"

"It's the best news of the last two weeks," Jay confirmed.

Outside Tutorial there was a loud thump. The group froze. The noise was followed by another loud thump, then a third. Through the holes in the wall, they saw a dark shape moving up the Tutorial ramp. The door handle turned; the door pushed open.

Colin stood in the entryway, shoulders slumped, black hair straggling over a bloody gash on his cheek. Green fluid leaked over the front of his power suit, which was battered and bashed. Smoke poured from its sides.

"Colin!"

Jay leapt up and ran to his friend, wrapping his arms around the thick layer of metal that covered Colin's waist. He heard a mechanical whirr then felt the light touch of Colin's mechanical arms as they embraced him. Liz and Jeremy broke into applause. Stevie beamed, and Colin blushed, nodding wearily at Liz. "What are you still doing here?"

"That's a good question," Jay replied. "Stevie?"

Stevie pointed at the screen. "Found her!"

Onscreen, next to the map of Bickleton, there was a second window that was full of code. Jay squinted. "You really see her in there?"

Stevie's finger tapped the glass. "I think that's her."

Jay took Liz's hands.

"It's all up to you now. Hal is somewhere in his house. Probably kicking his computer, trying to get back into *The*

Build. When we disconnect you, you should be back in your body. All you have to do is take off your helmet and get out of his house. Do not *engage* him directly. Go to the police."

"Are you kidding?" She laughed scornfully. "The moment I'm out, I'm gonna kick his ass."

"Do *not*," Jay scolded. "Don't give him a second chance. Get out, get safe. Once Hal's arrested and out of his house, call whichever university is closest, and ask for their computer science lab. Tell them about Hal's computer. Maybe they can preserve our little world."

Liz nodded. "Thank you. I know it must have been hard, not taking Hal up on his offer."

"This was so much better." Jay paused, fighting the urge to grab her hand. Now that she was really leaving, the longing welled up inside him. "And, uh . . . maybe let us know how you fare? If you're not too busy with your life, that is."

She smiled. "You know, if I had to do it all over again, I would definitely—"

Liz disappeared. There were no wisps of blue light, no flash. Nothing. Just an empty space where, a moment ago, she had been.

"Hey!" Jay spun back to Stevie. "Bring her back, she was saying something?!"

"I didn't do that." Stevie stared at the screen, tentatively clicking. "I–I don't know what happened. I don't see any—" Her voice faltered. "Oh no."

Everyone pushed in around her shoulders. Whatever Stevie saw in the box of code, it turned her face white.

"She's gone. He must've . . . pulled the plug. From his end."

For a moment, nobody spoke. Jay broke the silence.

"Well, is she okay?"

"I–I don't know. There's no way to know."

"What's he doing with her?"

"I don't know!"

"Is he trying to get back in?"

Stevie slowly shook her head. "No. He's not trying to access the game, he must be—hold on a sec."

She squinted at the screen. The lines of code started scrolling rapidly.

"What? What's happening?!" Jay exclaimed.

Stevie didn't respond. She clicked back to the map, and her mouse hovered over a slice of forest. The trees swayed in their endless loop, seemingly untouched by the string of recent disasters. Everyone leaned in, watching. The screen looked normal. Except—

A small gray square appeared in the center of the screen.

"Is–is something wrong with the monitor?" Jay asked.

Colin leaned in closer. "Looks like . . . *nothing*."

The gray square leapt outward, enveloping the surrounding patches. All the nearby trees disappeared. A sob leapt from Stevie's mouth, and she bit her knuckle. Jeremy placed a hand on the top of the monitor.

"Is he making more changes?"

Jay's blood ran cold as he realized what was happening.

"No. No changes. He's wiping his hard drive."

ABANDONWARE

THEY STARED AT the screen. No one spoke. Seconds ticked by, and the gray patch of nothing blinked bigger.

"What?" Jeremy whispered.

"Hal's deleting Bickleton."

"Deleting—?"

"Oh God."

Colin fell onto his desk, rubbing his massive hands over his eyes. He turned to Stevie.

"And Liz, is she . . . ?"

Stevie's face was pale and grim.

Jay spun around and kicked his desk. "Goddamnit!"

"Stevie, how much has already been deleted? How long will the deletion take?"

Stevie stared at the screen. "One percent. It depends on the size of his hard drive."

"Jay—" Colin started.

"Shh." Jay paced back and forth, thinking. This couldn't be the end. There had to be another way.

"Stevie, is there anything else out there? Any other devices besides Hal's computer? A printer maybe?"

Stevie leaned in, typing furiously.

"Let's see . . ."

Jay went to the window, desperate, using all his self-control to give Stevie space. Outside, the grass sparkled with dew. The Johns had started dispersing. He could see groups of them wandering out of the C-Court parking lot, down Simmons Road. From the branches near the window there came an angry squawk. Jay saw a wren on a pine bough, peering resentfully through the window. There were no other sounds: no engines, no moos, no rooster crows. Just the clack of Stevie's fingers on her keyboard. Jay's mom came up alongside him and put an arm around his shoulders.

Jay's eyes searched the horizon, past the indent where the baseball field lay. Then, across the road, he saw it. Spreading between two farmhouses was a dull, dead path of gray. He stared, trying to make sense of it; in a flash, two farmhouses disappeared. The trees and walls just flaked away, disintegrating, scattering into nothing. Now, where the hill had been, there was only a gray swath of nothing. A patch of deletion. Jay stifled a cry and grabbed his mom's forearm, positioning her so that she wouldn't see.

"Jay . . ." When Stevie's tenuous voice came again, it was a whisper. "Come and look at this."

She was pointing to the code.

"What? That means nothing to me. Is it outside Hal's computer?"

She stammered. "I—I don't know. There're a few IP addresses connected to Hal's computer." She pointed. "These two, I think, we could potentially connect to."

"What are they?"

"I can't tell."

"Could we all get onto those devices?"

"Here's what I think we could do. I see you and Colin in the code." She pointed at the screen. "You're right there, as objects.

We all are. I've got this IDE up. I think I can connect your inputs and outputs to the inputs and outputs of the devices on the network. In theory, you'll see whatever the devices see, and be able to control them. Whatever they are."

"So it's a way into Hal's world. What's the risk?"

Stevie's face went white. "I mean, I'm literally changing your code. I'm decoupling your mind from your body. The risk is that you could crash and cease to exist. I have no idea what's gonna happen."

Jay turned to Colin. "What do you say? One last game with the fate of the world at stake?"

Jeremy folded his arms. "Where are you going again?"

"We're finally breaking outta Bickleton."

Colin looked at Stevie, sitting at her computer. His face turned a deep crimson, and he stuttered:

"S-Stevie . . . back at prom . . . I never got a chance to . . . but I really—"

Stevie leapt up and grabbed Colin's face, pulling him down to kiss him. Colin's eyes went wide, his face turning purple. Stevie stepped back, her face alight with her biggest smile ever.

"You'd better come back, okay?"

Colin nodded.

"Well, that's kind of up to you, right? Take good care of our code," Jay said, smiling at his friends.

The room held its breath as Stevie moused over to the Compile button. She pressed the Enter key, and Jay's and Colin's bodies crumpled to the floor.

MAXIMUM
UNDERDRIVE

JAY CAME TO without any frame of reference. He couldn't tell where he was, and for a few moments, he didn't even know *who* he was. Then his memories came flooding back, and with them, a wave of claustrophobia. He couldn't see or move. He tried flailing his arms, but then realized he had no limbs. He tried to scream, but he had no mouth. He lay still, in darkness, his panic growing. And then, gradually, he noticed a shimmering light on the periphery of his mind.

It was hard to pinpoint exactly what it was, but a totally new sensation, as if he suddenly found eyes in the back of his head that he'd never used before. He could feel, rather than see, the lightness. His mind stretched randomly, until suddenly, everything was blinding, and he could see again.

The first thing he noticed was that everything was in blocks of heavy black and white pixels. He guessed he must be lying on a table, because he could see a little ledge stretch before him, then drop off sharply. His perspective was tilted slightly, which told him he was lying on his side. He could hear a voice.

He tried speaking, and found that he could, sort of. Not as he normally would, where he heard his voice in his ears. But his thoughts thundered loudly in his mind.

"Hello?"

A few moments passed, and then he heard Colin answer. "Jay?"

Again, the voice came not through his ears, but directly in his mind.

"Where are you?"

"On the floor. You?"

"On a table. Can you move?"

Several more seconds passed.

"Not very well."

Jay tried to move and found he couldn't. Remembering the experiment with his eyes, he searched his mind for an arm, an unused limb, something he might use. Suddenly, he felt a click and his view tilted sideways. His body jolted up into the air and then clattered back onto the table. Above his eyes, he saw rotary blades gently coming to a rest.

"I'm . . . some kind of helicopter."

In his new, shifted perspective, he could see farther down the desk, and realized he was looking at a very large box. Its sides were transparent, and inside he saw several glowing circuits under a ring of lights that flashed around the interior. It was a computer, bigger and more beautiful than any computer he'd ever seen. He lay quiet a moment, soaking it all in.

"Colin . . . do you see this computer?"

"No. Is it a Pentium?"

The computer had not one, but three monitors—tall as buildings, to Jay—that curved into 180-degree panoramas.

"I dunno. It's the most beautiful thing I've ever seen, though."

Jay was so entranced by them that it took him a moment to notice Hal.

Hal wore a ragged wifebeater and boxers. His face, lost in fat rolls, was even older than it was in the game. His glasses were scratched and smudged, and his sandy blond hair was almost completely gone. He stood on short legs, leaning precariously on an elbow. His large gut swayed as his right hand clacked over the keyboard. He grunted a long "hrmmm," and Jay saw his brow furrow.

"I have eyes on Hal."

Hal turned and disappeared, his footsteps plodding over the carpeted floors.

"He's leaving. Colin, can you get to the computer?"

"I think I'm stuck behind a chair."

Jay willed himself back into the air. He hovered for a moment, dodged left, then flew to the edge of the table and peered over. The carpeted floor was covered in stains. The light from the computer monitor fell across a futon bed. Against the far wall was a bookshelf filled with small robotic toys.

Jay saw something at the bottom of the desk and dropped down to get a better look. He found himself hovering in front of a mechanical monkey. The little robot toy looked about the size of a remote-control car, and was jerking forward on a combination of knuckles and rear legs.

"Colin? Is that you?"

The toy's head swiveled up.

"If the police helicopter is you, then yeah."

"You're some kind of robo-monkey."

"I think we're toys."

"Can you get up onto Hal's computer?"

Colin's head swiveled farther up. The desk towered over him like a skyscraper. He reared up on his hind legs, raised his hands, and leapt into the air, doing a perfect 360-degree backflip that just missed the chair. Colin landed on the carpet with a dull thud, and Jay spun around, carefully eyeing the doorway. No sign of Hal.

"Nice, almost had it. Here, let's see if . . ."

On the periphery of Jay's vision, he saw three glowing words appear: "Halt," "Follow Me," and "You're Under Arrest." He picked the first one.

"Halt!" his voice was robotic, garbled. There was the faint sound of footsteps, and Jay switched off his propeller and dropped to the ground. A shadow fell over him, and then he was sailing back upward. He found himself staring into Hal's pockmarked face, watching his nose hairs quiver in his pulsing nostrils.

"Hrmm."

He placed Jay back on the table, where he'd been before. Then he plunked down a bowl that blocked his view. Jay could barely see Hal's round outline behind the bowl, and he watched as Hal stared at the computer, taking a bite, then scraping the sides of his bowl with his spoon.

Jay lay motionless, not daring to move. Colin spoke.

"What happens if we just pull the plug? Shut the computer off?"

"It'd shut down *The Build*. We'd all disappear. We have to find Liz and wake her up."

"How?"

"He's gotta have her connected somewhere. There's gotta be a Cat7, or another think wire, running down the floor."

"I see it."

"It's down there?"

"Yeah."

"Okay. Get Hal's attention. I'm going after Liz."

"How'm I supposed to do that?"

"Just do it!"

Jay heard a whirring noise on the floor, then a small plastic *thunk*. Hal looked down. Jay flew up into the air, spun around, and launched away. He heard Hal behind him.

"Hey!"

Then he was out of the room, into the hall. Cardboard boxes were everywhere. It was lost—like *Ultima Underworld*. From somewhere nearby, he heard the sound of a TV blaring *Saved by the Bell*. Something was off—it sounded sped up and heavily digitized. It was impossible to tell whether the problem was with the playback or his own audio input. He felt completely disoriented, unsure of where to turn. And then he remembered: this was his house in the real world. His same floor plan. He recognized the half-dome lighting fixture in the ceiling.

On the floor below, he could barely see thick black wire snaking out the door and turning left. He followed it, past walls of cardboard boxes. The darkness was overwhelming. It felt like pushing through an underwater cavern. Boxes leapt out suddenly from the perimeters of gloom. He slammed into something and felt himself bounce back. Then a wooden door loomed straight ahead. Behind it, he knew, lay Liz.

Jay buzzed around, searching. At the far end, he spotted a small sliver of black. He flew back, then charged the door. His rotors beat against it, slowing, and he felt himself fall. He pulled back before he hit the ground, then buzzed back up in the air. The crack was wider now, enough for Jay to buzz through.

The room—his room—was dull, lit by a single lamp. The space was the same, but furnished differently. His shelves and posters were gone. The walls were white. It felt clean, clinical. It reminded Jay of the room behind the falls. A queen-sized bed took up most of the space, and medical equipment loomed over the bedside, hanging over its sides like mechanical trees.

A nightstand held dozens of pill bottles, and there was a large trash can with a biohazard sign. Jay saw the black wire from the computer room disappear into a slithering pile of cords, then snake over the bedside, connecting to a human form lying beneath the sheets. The figure's head was covered by a black helmet, and only its mouth was visible. It looked like something out of a nightmare.

"I–I think I found Liz."

"Can you wake her?"

Footsteps thundered behind him. Jay buzzed over to the bed and zipped over Liz's face. He thought he saw her jaw tremble slightly.

Jay heard Hal moving across the carpet. He swiveled to see Hal rush him. His face was flushed, and he was holding a broom like a baseball bat. He swung it, and Jay zipped out of reach. The broom smashed down into Liz's lap. She stirred under the sheets, then stopped. Jay remembered what she had said about Hal's VR device; how it fully engaged the senses, making it impossible to disconnect from the hardware.

Hal stepped forward, swinging wildly. He hit a lamp and knocked over a medical stand. The broom swished over Jay, and Jay dove under the bed. He hovered under the box spring, swiveling left and right, watching.

"Colin . . . now's your chance. I've got him busy in here. Can you get on the table?"

"Maybe . . ."

"Try!"

From under the bed, Jay could see Hal's legs walk back and forth. He heard a grunt, then Hal's arms appeared, followed by his head. He spotted Jay and his eyes narrowed. Jay watched Hal's arm reach slowly for his broom. Jay hovered, waiting until the last second, then spun around and zoomed back out from the bed. He spotted a patch of light and rose higher, hoping that . . . *YES!* One window was open a sliver. Jay waited for Hal to reemerge from under the bed and see him, then he zipped out the window.

The brightness of the world washed over him, blinding him, and it took a moment before everything was clear again. He was outside his house, in his backyard. There was the dead oak tree, missing a few more limbs. The raised vegetable beds his mom had kept were decomposed into little lumps of earth and dandelions. Beyond his house were other roofs, more densely packed than he'd ever seen. The surrounding houses were new—cheap townhouses that walled in his house and covered it in shadow.

Jay flew into the air and down the thin corridor separating Hal's house from the neighbors'. Out on the small cul-de-sac that was Northeast Scenic Street, Jay hovered for a moment. Where the Maganas' house had stood was a three-story olive townhouse. All the construction—except for Hal's house—was fresh. Jay hovered, appraising the neighborhood's uniformity.

The trees of Jewett Creek loomed over the end of the road, now carefully manicured into a straight edge. Lawns were the same: clean, without lawn flamingos, gnomes, or rusting engine blocks. His neighborhood was unrecognizable.

The front door slammed shut. Jay spun around to look at his house. It was much the same as he'd left it in *The Build*, only now a dusty blue instead of white. There was Hal, standing on the doorstep, blinking in his wifebeater and boxers. He gripped his broom like a sword, searching the sky. Jay dropped down, strafing, and Hal's face flushed purple with rage.

Jay zipped away down the street. Suddenly, his screen flashed.

Weak connection.

Jay paused, hovering halfway down the street. A black-haired woman in tight pants was walking a corgi. As she passed Jay, she cast an annoyed glance at where he hovered in the air.

"Don't touch it! Stay away!" Hal screamed, and Jay turned in time to see Hal running at him, swinging his broom. Jay zipped up into the sky, then dashed down in front of the black-haired woman.

"Halt. Halt. Follow me," the helicopter demanded.

The woman flinched and held up her hands. "Get away!"

"Careful, hrmm." Hal panted. "It's . . . got a virus. Don't let it get away."

The woman let out a muffled cry and ran up the sidewalk, her heels clicking on the pavement. Jay dodged another volley of broom strokes.

"Colin?" Jay called.

Back in Hal's office, Colin was on Hal's chair. It had taken him a dozen backflips before he'd managed to leap up onto the mesh seat. The spongy surface was softer than the floor and felt like walking on a trampoline. He craned his head up. The edge of the desk still felt impossibly far.

"Yes?" Colin replied.

"Are you up?"

"Halfway."

He positioned a foot on the vinyl and a foot on the chair's hard plastic frame, scrunched himself, and leapt. He sailed through the air and then hit hard plastic, clattering across the desk. He looked up. Three giant monitors loomed over him, covering the desk in blue light.

"I did it!"

"Can you stop the deletion?"

Colin scanned the screens. The center monitor held a small console bar, and he swiveled his scanners to see the words

DELETING FILES. The bar was about a third gone. He took a step toward the giant mouse.

"I think so."

Colin struggled across the desk. His body, made for back-flips, did not walk easily. And there was another problem he hadn't mentioned. His battery. In the bottom right of his screen, there was a battery icon. It was three-quarters gone.

He concentrated hard on putting one leg before the next. The mouse was right in front of him. One more step. He pushed his body against the mouse, and the giant mound of plastic budged forward. He felt his motor groan in protest. Soon, he knew, it would seize up. He paused to check his progress and saw with satisfaction that he'd pushed the cursor toward the deletion bar. In the background, Jay's questions were endless:

"How's it going?"

"You there?"

"What's the status?"

Colin finally answered, his voice carefully neutral: "Just fine."

DEAD BATTS

JAY COULD TELL by Colin's voice that he was in trouble. Hal, meanwhile, was having his own problems. He stopped and placed his hands on his knees. Sweat poured from his face and he puffed in ragged gasps. Jay wondered whether Hal might have a heart attack then and there. A small crowd had gathered out on Scenic Street. It was early Saturday morning, same as it was in *The Build*. The commotion of Hal in his underwear, waving a broom, was drawing out the surrounding families. Jay watched three girls giggle at the flushed, panting man in boxers. Hal spun around at their laughter.

"What are you staring at?"

At this, the girls burst into peals of laughter, and Hal swung his broom in their direction, despite a driveway between them.

Suddenly, Hal straightened. He looked at Jay. Then, without a word, he spun and stomped across the street, pushing past a tall scowling man with a mustache. The girls shrieked in delight. Jay watched in horror as Hal stormed back inside. He flew over Hal's fence, returning to the backyard. He reached Liz's window and was about to dip in, when he saw Hal's hairy knuckles shoot up from the inside. The window slammed shut, and he heard the sound of a lock. He was shut out!

"Colin!" Jay cried. "He's coming for you!"

No response.

"Colin?"

He felt panic overtaking him. Colin was gone. Terrible thoughts crowded his mind, and he pushed them away. In the corner of his screen, he saw his battery flash red with only a single bar of juice left. He flew over the wooden fence of his backyard and hovered in the small corridor next to the neighboring house. Even if he got back into Hal's house, there wasn't enough battery left for him to stop the deletion. It was over.

Suddenly, a loud, rhythmic beeping shook him awake. A smoke detector blared from the neighboring house. He flew over the wooden fence, into their backyard.

The yard was a mess. He saw a kiddie pool filled with cigarette butts and murky water sitting amid overgrown tufts of crabgrass. A barbecue stood in the corner, next to a weight bench. A bulldog sat, licking its crotch. When it spotted Jay, it growled. The glass patio door slid open, and smoke billowed out. A figure ran out through the haze, and Jay saw a grizzled man with a thick beard and tattoo sleeves step out. Jay sounded his voice box.

"Halt. Halt."

But the man, still coughing, lowered his head and disappeared back into the smoke. Jay zipped in after.

The townhouse interior was ugly and small. Posters lined its walls: girls in bikinis, and bands Jay didn't recognize. Past a small kitchen island, the man waved a dish towel at smoke that poured from his oven. He covered his mouth with an arm and coughed.

The beeping smoke detector stopped, and the man relaxed a little. He reached into the oven, then quickly yanked his hand out.

"Ow!"

Jay buzzed forward and slammed into the man's face. The man leapt back, staring at Jay with disbelief.

"What the heck?"

"Halt! Follow me."

The man didn't move. Jay rammed him again. The man threw up his arms, and Jay felt his rotor dig in.

"Oww!"

Jay backed off. The man whipped at Jay with the dish towel, and Jay dashed out of range. The man stared at him, wary, and called back into the house.

"DJ?"

"Follow me," Jay shouted. "Follow me. Follow me."

The man stepped around the kitchen counter. Jay flew back out the open patio door. The man moved after Jay, into the backyard.

"DJ? Are you seeing this?"

The dog was barking again. The man turned on it.

"Luigi! Stop it!"

Jay zipped down and again drove his rotor blade into the man's face. The man leapt back and threw his dish towel.

"Oh, that's it."

He ran at Jay. Jay flew over the fence, then spun round, hovering.

"Follow me!"

The man leapt over the fence, landing in the corridor along Hal's house.

Jay saw his battery signal flashing. As fast as he could, he spun around the corridor, zipped past the front of the house, and smashed into Hal's front door. He bounced back, falling, watching the ground rush toward him. He willed his rotor to spin and rose, back into the air. Again he hit the door, and then he heard muted footsteps on the other side. He spun around.

The tattooed man rounded the corner, and Jay saw his eyes flash with anger.

Behind him, Jay heard the front door swing open. Hal stood ready, broom in hand, but Jay buzzed past, into the living room. Hal stepped after him.

"Hey, man."

Hal turned. The neighbor stood in the doorway.

"Hrm?"

The man pointed at Jay. "Is that your drone?"

Hal grunted. "Yes. I'll handle it."

Hal went to shut his door, but the neighbor put a hand on the door, holding it open.

"Why was it in my house?"

"Hrmm. It's a long story. Won't happen again."

Hal again tried to shut his door, but the man held on. "Don't you gotta have a license for that? Where's your license, man?"

Jay hovered over Hal's shoulder, watching the exchange, his hope rising. He zoomed past Hal's head, and bashed the neighbor in the face, running his rotor into his nose. The man screamed.

"Ow! Goddamnit!"

Jay dropped down and zipped back through Hal's legs. The man lunged at Hal, forcing the door open and pushing into the living room.

Hal's face contorted in rage. "Get out!" he screamed. "Get out, or I will call the police!"

The neighbor pushed past Hal and grasped at Jay. Jay zipped back through the corridor of boxes, praying the neighbor was still following. He spun into the short hall that led to Liz's room. Behind him, Hal was screaming.

"Get out! Out of my house!"

In the darkness of the hall, Jay flew forward until he hit something hard. He bounced back and could barely make out the faint outline of the door. It was closed. He spun back to see the neighbor fill the hallway.

"Follow me! Follow me!"

The neighbor's hand shot out, and then the man held him in his hand, spinning Jay around until he was staring into the neighbor's face. He saw a look of grim satisfaction on the man's bearded face, and then his rotor stopped with a sickening crack. The man had ripped off his blades. Then Jay was being carried down the hall, back to the living room.

"Halt! Halt! Halt!" Jay shouted desperately.

But the man wasn't listening. When Hal saw the man holding Jay, the rage washed from his face.

"Hrmm. Good," he purred. "You may leave now."

Jay felt despair wash over him. It was over. The man shook his head and moved to the door. Then he paused. From deep within the house, there was a low sound. A human moan. The man turned and took a step toward it.

Color drained from Hal's face. He pawed at the neighbor's sleeve.

"No, hrm. You're trespassing on private property. You need to leave."

The man ignored him, moving down the hall. He pushed open the door to the back room. He froze. His face went pale as he stared at the nightmare contraptions lying around the bed.

"What . . . the . . ."

Hal stumbled into the room. "She's sick. Hrm. She's my sister. Hrm. Don't touch her."

The neighbor stared at the black helmet covering Liz's head. "Why is she wearing that?"

"To protect her. She has cancer. You need to leave. Hrm."

Jay hit his voice module.

"Halt! You're under arrest. You're under arrest."

The neighbor shook his head. "This isn't right, man. This is messed up."

"Hrmm, this is my private residence. You need to leave. It's the law!"

The neighbor shook his head again. "I think I need to call the police."

Hal grabbed the neighbor's wrist.

"This is not your business!"

The neighbor grabbed Hal's hand and spun him around. Hal's eyes bulged and he gasped.

"I'm making it my business." The neighbor dropped the drone, and Jay fell on the floor. From his tilted perspective, he saw the neighbor leaning over the bed, whispering, "Miss? Can you hear me?"

Another soft moan. The neighbor loosened the strap on Liz's helmet.

"Don't take that off!" Hal screamed.

Jay saw Liz lift an arm. The neighbor held it, pulling her gently up by the elbow. She rose, eyes blinking in the lamplight. The neighbor took her hand, and Liz stepped unsteadily from the bed. Even from a distance, Jay could see thirty years had passed.

Hal picked himself off the floor.

"You're both under arrest, hrm. Big, big trouble."

The neighbor ignored Hal to help Liz hobble out of bed. Jay saw a look of steely determination grip her face. She pressed on the neighbor's arm, stood, and punched Hal in the face. Hal shrieked, surprised, and collapsed against the wall.

"Help me get out of here. Quick." They hobbled together down the hall, and then Jay heard her muffled voice from the office.

"Help. In here. Click that button."

Then Jay felt himself falling. His thoughts drifted away, and he knew the last of his power was draining. He'd done it; he'd beaten the final boss. He was happy for Liz, but a sadness overtook him. He'd never see Bickleton again. He thought of the giant oak tree at the end of his block, and how it swayed when the spring breezes picked up. Then his battery light blinked off, and his mind powered into darkness.

LAB RESULTS

LIZ STOOD OUTSIDE, listening to planes roar and traffic buzz. She was at SeaTac arrivals with a single blue rollaboard bag. Waiting. A white Tahoe pulled up to the curb, its passenger window rolling down. A young man in a loose collared shirt leaned over.

"Liz Knight?"

She nodded. He got out and opened the door for her, and she climbed into the back seat.

"I'll get your bag."

"Thanks, I'd rather hold on to it. You with the university?"

He shook his head in the rearview mirror. "No, with . . . another faction." He flashed a smile that looked forced. "Homeland Security."

"Ah. I could have just taken an Uber, you know."

"We appreciate everything you're doing for us."

Liz looked out her tinted window at the blue Seattle skies. She had forgotten how temperate it was in Seattle, even in the summer. Not at all like her home down in LA. She relaxed back into her seat. It felt strangely warm: *The seat warmers must be running.*

The skyline grew before them. The Emerald City. Skyscrapers popped like mushrooms. It had been ten years since she'd visited Seattle, and she was surprised to see that it felt like a real city. Its last trace of wild in the surrounding lands was disappearing, fallen to apartment complexes and warehouses.

They chugged north through traffic, to the U District, and then her driver pulled over on the south side of campus and pointed to a big red building.

"I've gotta park. Head on up; they'll be waiting."

Liz got out and headed up the campus lawn. The university had paid for her trip, sometimes begging, sometimes demanding that she come. Sometimes the calls had come from the University of Washington staff, sometimes the Department of Homeland Security, and once from a professor in Portugal who barely spoke a word of English.

Her kidnapping had been a national event, but the press had relayed only a fraction of the story to the public. The articles all said she'd been kidnapped by a spurned high school prom date. The spin was played mainly for laughs, and there was no mention of computers, *The Build*, or any sort of simulation. Liz was offered $100,000 by DHS to give interviews without mentioning her weeks inside a computer game. She took the money, and in exchange signed a thick stack of papers that she didn't even bother to read.

Bells rang across campus. Liz moved over a pathway of manicured lawn that ended in a large pool of fountains spouting water, took a right, and moved toward the building her guide had pointed out. It looked like a cross between an Ivy League hall and a library. Glass windows jutted out in series, and inside she saw offices with computers. A group of students stepped out through the doors, laughing as they passed her. Everyone was so young!

The sign over the door read: "The Paul G. Allen Center for Computer Science & Engineering." The door slid open, and she stepped through.

Glass offices layered the walls like honeycomb. Everything was quiet, almost stiff with waiting, and the air smelled of research. The lobby was cavernous, and Liz's footsteps echoed as she walked. Liz stared up to see the ceiling five stories above, partially blocked by catwalks crisscrossing the air like some futuristic cityscape. This must be El Dorado to computer science majors. She was still looking up when a voice called over the pavilion.

"Liz Knight, I presume."

A woman stood waiting at the base of the stairs, flanked by six figures in black suits. The woman was blonde and wore a light blouse and heels. She smiled and held out her hand.

"I'm Brandi."

The image of her, against the stairs, flanked by the darker men, looked like a Microsoft stock photograph. Liz laughed, and the woman smiled questioningly.

"What's so funny?"

Liz shook her hand.

"I almost went to school here."

The woman raised her eyebrow. "Oh? Were you a computer science major?"

"No, I'm not a computer person. Ironic, I know."

"Well," Brandi said, with a hint of cold pride, "we have one of the best computer science programs in the world."

"I don't doubt it."

Brandi's smile returned, and the group moved past the stairs, toward the elevator. The men trailed as Brandi led the way, peppering Liz with pleasantries.

"How was your flight? How long have you been in LA? What part?" They stepped into an elevator, and the woman pressed the button for the fourth floor.

"How have things been here?" Liz shifted the questioning to the matter at hand.

"Good, all things considered." Her guardians glanced around the elevator. The way they looked at one another told Liz they weren't all aligned on this.

"We're still sorting things out. We're still unsure ourselves what the, uh, narrative is here."

The elevator stopped and its doors dinged. The walkway before them dropped down into the atrium. As they turned to the right, Liz saw offices lining the wall. All their lights were off, and they sat unused. At the far end of the hall was a single gray metal door that looked like a fire escape. It was unremarkable, except that there was no window in it. All the offices had large windows that looked out into the hall. Liz saw a piece of paper taped over the door. As they approached, Liz saw it said: "No phones or wireless devices allowed."

Brandi paused.

"Whatever you feel about Hal, what he managed to do can't be underestimated. He took the functionality of a self-learning AI program and applied its parameters against the rules of the virtual world he built."

One of the black suits spoke. "As we saw in Bickleton, this program Hal's made has potential for incredible danger. Like, world-ending shit."

Brandi continued, "The AI that Hal built managed to escape its program. It managed to outsmart its creator."

The black suit chimed in again. "We don't want to do anything to destabilize it. If it jumped to more devices, it could have wiped out all of humanity."

Liz stared between the two of them, incredulous. "Are we talking about Jay?"

"Who's Jay?"

Brandi pulled open the door and a clutter of electronic devices assaulted Liz's view. There was a medley of hums, and the perimeter was encircled by black boxes. A round table with eight chairs sat in one corner, and two computers sat in the other. On the wall, every five feet, rectangular boxes hung with blinking lights. Brandi nodded at them.

"Mobile phone jammers. Blocks all wireless signals in a fifty-foot range. We had to clear out the whole floor; nobody gets cell reception."

Brandi handed two sheets of paper to Liz.

"What are these?" Liz asked.

"A master table. Of what we've managed to find on the hard drive so far. It's not much to go off. That one's from a few days ago."

She pointed at the other sheet. "This one's from today."

Liz studied the numbers. There were thousands of rows, and at first glance, they looked almost identical.

GE F5 00 00 65 6E.

She glanced at the second page.

GE F5 5F 00 65 6E.

"Yeah?"

"Similar. But not the same."

Liz sat back in her chair. "What am I looking at? Remember, I'm not a computer person."

"The hard drive is changing. Repopulating its data."

"You guys are . . . restoring the hard drive?"

"No. Not us. No one's touched that computer since we brought it here. Somehow, the code is restoring itself. We want to know how."

"Why don't you ask?"

"Who? We don't get any responses from the computer. That's why we were hoping you could . . ."

Brandi broke off, looking to the Homeland Security agents. They nodded.

"Do you have any electronic devices on you?"

"You guys already took my phone."

"No smartwatches? Tablets?"

Liz shook her head. A sandy-haired Homeland Security agent strode to a second door in the back. It was so unassuming that Liz hadn't noticed it. The man held the door open, and Brandi motioned for Liz to follow.

The room was little more than a dull box. Its walls were barren and it was empty, except on the far wall, where there was a folding table and two plastic chairs. On the table sat Hal's computer, its three monitors spread like wings. The room's fluorescent lights reflected off its glass as LEDs twinkled inside.

The Homeland Security agent stood beside the computer with his arms folded, protective. Liz approached the console. She had seen it only once, after her release from Hal's house. It was immaculate now, its glass case wiped down to a pristine sheen. A strip of LEDs colored its inside edges, and these gently undulated from blue to red. Brandi reached behind the monitors and flicked them on. Liz felt a wave of revulsion.

The sandy-haired officer scooted a chair over the floor. Liz forced herself to sit, and she stared dutifully at the small bulbous camera perched over the computer monitor.

"What should I say?"

"Whatever you want."

"Jay?"

For a minute, there was nothing. Then the screen began to shift. A white Word document popped up. Brandi leaned forward, and so did the Homeland Security agents.

"How'd you do that?"

Liz waved them off, focusing on the monitor.

"Hello? Jay?"

There was no response from the Word document.

"I heard you got into college."

Then the cursor jumped. Words flashed across the white page. "I heard that too."

Liz could feel Homeland Security tense behind her. She smiled. "All the Ivy Leagues are clamoring to sign the first AI freshman."

Onscreen, another sentence: "They're gonna have to wait. Colin's got a trigonometry test he's trying to unflunk."

Liz laughed.

"It's weird talking like this."

"I agree."

"You sound like a machine."

"I am a machine."

"I never got to thank you. For saving my life."

"Any super AI in my shoes would have done the same."

"Oh stop. Where's the buoyant Jay I knew?"

"Hard to be buoyant when you have no legs."

"I brought you something." She reached into a pocket and pulled out a watch.

"I also have no arms."

The Homeland Security agent leaned in, nervous, and she held up a hand.

"It's pre-Bluetooth."

She held it up to the camera. It was a *Frogger* watch. Its colors were faded, but its LCD screen still blinked.

"My daughter found it at a garage sale. I mentioned it when I told her about you, and she saw it, bought it, and wanted you to have it. I'll just leave it right here, if they'll let me." She placed it on the table, next to the computer, glancing at Homeland Security.

"I also got you something else. It's, uh, on its way. I'm sorry that it took me so long to come visit. I hope this makes up for it."

She smiled. "It's another gift. At least, I hope it is."

The room was silent. There was no trace of text on the Word doc.

"Jay . . . ?"

Brandi came over and stared at the Word document.

Liz stood up. "Was that helpful?"

Brandi nodded, impressed. "Gotta start somewhere."

Liz nodded, giving a last bittersweet glance toward the computer. Then she slipped out the door.

HOW I SPENT MY SUMMER VACATION
BY JAY BANKSMAN

JAY SLID BACK from the computer. Through a small grainy video feed, he watched the other people in the lab room rush forward and begin typing into the Word document. He didn't bother reading what they typed: his eyes were still on the rear door. She was gone. Colin sat beside Jay, and Stevie was on his lap, one arm wrapped over Colin's shoulder.

Colin was first to speak. "She's got two kids?"

"She looked good, right?" Jay's eyes didn't move from the monitor.

Stevie stood and stretched. "Where do you think we are, Colin? In the real world?"

Then something caught Stevie's attention. She broke her stretch and leaned down.

"Oops. Looks like they're trying to get back in again." She shook her head. "Tsk. Silly rabbits. Tricks are for kids." She began typing, lost in the monitor.

"Last thing we need is them poking and prodding our code. At least Hal knew what he was doing. I'll just throw up a few more firewalls so they can't find us."

Jay stood up from his computer. They were in Tutorial, though it little resembled the classroom it used to be. They'd transformed it into their de facto command center. All the desks were gone, along with the bookshelves and the beanbag chairs. The blackboard was still up, and it was crammed with lists, written in chalk.

Finish Heinkel Middle School—John H

Do the bus yard—Colin

Measure Henderson's farm—Jay

Two of the walls were now filled with workstations. Each had a copy of *The Build* loaded on it so that Jay, Colin, or Liz could dive in as needed.

A third wall had three beds pushed against it. Since their return, he, Colin, and Stevie had all taken to sleeping in Tutorial so that they could take shifts monitoring the lab to block the technicians, attempts to gain access to their little world.

The fourth wall, the one by the door, held a folding table with lunch materials.

Jay got up to make himself a turkey sandwich. He felt sick after seeing Liz, and he found himself running their brief conversation through his mind. How had he ever managed to convince himself that she had liked him? She was old. Married. With kids. She had wanted nothing more from him than the means to escape *The Build*, and he'd been an idiot to ever think otherwise. The truth was, he missed her terribly.

"I'm going to take a walk."

Stevie and Colin were already absorbed in *The Build* and didn't respond. Jay pushed out of the Tutorial door and felt the sun warm his skin. Over the last few days, the frozen spring air had finally thawed, and sunlight beat the packed earth around Tutorial, so that he could feel it radiating up.

He strolled down the Tutorial ramp, admiring what a difference the last few weeks had made. They'd deleted the last of the riot and the extra Johns. For now, they'd kept the packed earth around Tutorial, plus the towers and the moat. The list for rebuilding Bickleton was long, and the pine trees surrounding Tutorial weren't at the top. Plus, Jay liked the sense of authority these armaments gave to Tutorial. Made it all feel more official.

Jay headed down to the school. Stevie hadn't found A-Court or C-Court templates in *The Build* yet, so the work on the school had so far been done by hand. C-Court was mostly restored, with new boards hammered across the holes caused by the Mantis Boss.

The campus was set against the gray horizon of deletion. It was as if Bickleton High School were in the center of an unfinished painting, with the surrounding landscape still awaiting a brush. C-Court and the library were being slowly worked over by the Johns. A-Court was still half-missing, and the baseball field tapered into a gray smudge. Their campus was an island surrounded by nothingness.

The only survivors of the Great Deletion (as they had come to call it) had been himself, Stevie, Colin, his mom, Jeremy, and a few Johns. The grieving period had been short, because Stevie had rightly pointed out that the only way to recover was to start building.

Jay tried to paint it as an exciting opportunity. He'd tried to get everyone to imagine what Bickleton might one day be. But nostalgia was a powerful thing, and everyone else had voted to restore Bickleton to what it had been before. So that's where they were starting, and Jay hadn't pressed the issue since. He, Colin, and Stevie basically lived in Tutorial, collaborating inside *The Build* to rebuild the town from memory. The process seemed to invigorate Stevie and Colin, who now couldn't keep their hands off each other. But something about it felt hollow to Jay. He couldn't explain it.

He quietly slipped through the C-Court doors. From inside, there was the sound of hammering and furniture being moved around. He passed Todd in the halls, who turned slightly pink and pushed up against the walls to make way for Jay. Jay smiled. Jay had found Todd in a pile of discarded code inside *The Build*. Ironically, he'd somehow avoided permanent deletion by being in the trash. Jay had restored him, and then explained their situation. Todd now regarded Jay as something of a God, which always made their conversations awkward.

"Jay! Jay! So I'm thinking we make the band room just a little bit bigger. What do you think? Just a little bit bigger?"

Jay shook his head and muttered, "Take it up with the committee."

"Oh, come on. You really think they'll notice?"

"No new changes until the rest of Bickleton is back online." Jay sighed. "That's what everyone decided."

Some of the Johns were in the background, notepads out, staring at walls or scrutinizing trash cans. A few argued about the placement of inspirational posters on the wall. Jay didn't feel like fielding more questions, so he ducked into the art room. Giant murals of babies floating through space adorned the walls. They were painted by Ace Clotter, Bickleton's resident artist. *Ex*-resident artist, Jay reminded himself. The room didn't appear to have been affected by the deletion. The art tables were all in place, along with the print screens and the kiln. A half-pack of American Spirit cigarettes sat on one of the tables. Underneath was a large cardboard box. A box of yearbooks. He pulled it out and grabbed a book.

You Are Here, the title screamed at him. There was the drawing of Jeremy McKraken on the front cover, smiling and looking backward in front of the Yellow Brick Road.

Jay flipped through it, imagining what Hal felt when he scanned this book into his computer. Revisiting a period of time that he had probably taken for granted, in the same way Jay now realized he'd taken his own high school experience for granted. Now that it was gone.

He studied the pages. There was a spread on Walter Blithe, a dumpy band kid with acne and braces, who for some reason had been proclaimed "student of all seasons." There was an entire page devoted to their class motto: "What lies before us and behind us are small matters compared to what lies inside us." Jay snorted.

Jay studied the news section—significant stories of '93. The appointment of Ruth Bader Ginsburg to the Supreme Court. The signing of NAFTA. Whatever Boris Yeltzen was doing. Yawn.

There was a little section of student interviews, and of course Jeremy was in there. The question was: "What's your favorite pickup line?" Jeremy's response: "I don't need a pickup line. I just snap my fingers." Jay rolled his eyes.

And then there was Liz. There was one picture in particular Jay couldn't stop looking at. A canned food drive for SADD (Students Against Drunk Driving), and all the usual A-Court suspects were there, mugging for the camera in the foreground. Most of the Johns, Jeremy, Amber, and Gretchen had their arms linked, an unbreakable fellowship, big grins at the camera. But there, in the background, was Liz. By herself, sorting cans from a cardboard box and onto a table. A real picture of the real Liz, scanned into the computer out of Hal's own yearbook. Whatever Liz had done to Hal at prom, this picture showed the side of Liz that Jay had come to believe was the *real* Liz. Misunderstood, as he had been.

There was a knock at the door and Jay looked up. Jeremy stood in the doorway, wearing a baseball hat with blotches of white paint on his face.

"Hey." He nodded.

Jay held up the yearbook. "It's a great reference, if you need it."

Things had changed between him and Jeremy. Jeremy hadn't brought up what had happened between them. He seemed to take it for granted that he wasn't able to fully understand. But his attitude toward Jay had shifted. Jay wouldn't call him friendly, but . . . respectful? Without talking about it, he and Jay had somehow divvied up the responsibility of rebuilding Bickleton. Jeremy was at the forefront of the deletion, working with the Johns to remember what had gone where, checking progress, returning to Jay to report.

Jeremy nodded at the yearbook. "Yeah, good call. Just so you know, the far wall of A-Court is missing some lockers."

"You sure? Colin just went down there and double-checked everything."

Jeremy grunted. "My locker's missing."

Jay nodded. "Gotcha. Okay, well, if you want to draw where it was, that'd be helpful."

Jeremy nodded and disappeared. Jay felt his body relax. Rebuilding Bickleton was going to take a long time. He threw the yearbook back in the box, kicked the box under the table, and walked out of C-Court. He didn't stop until he was in the parking lot.

He felt hollow. The feeling had been with him for the last week. For all the effort he was pouring into Bickleton's rebuilding, he couldn't shake the nagging feeling that none of it really mattered.

And now, after his conversation with Liz, it was there even stronger. He hadn't had time to realize it in the days leading up to prom, but he loved her. She was different from everyone else he'd ever met. She was real, like he had once been. He missed her gallows humor, her ability to call Bickleton out for what it really was.

He walked down Simmons Road, lost in thought. Up ahead, the road blurred into gray as their patch of school faded into the Great Deletion. He heard footsteps on the pavement and looked up.

Impossible, he thought.

Liz strode down the road toward him. Not the old Liz he'd just spoken to through the video stream. Young Liz. The Liz he remembered. Her dark hair swayed as she walked. There was a little bit of curl to it, like he'd seen at prom. She wore a black bomber jacket, ripped jeans, a white T-shirt, and sunglasses. And she was smiling.

Jay's heart leapt up in his chest. "What are you doing here?!"

She skipped forward. "Surprised?"

"Well, yeah, I saw you leave."

"Yeah, but you didn't see me finish."

"Finish what?"

She stopped a few feet away from him. "The upload."

Jay remembered what Liz had said in the video feed. *It's another gift.* He shook his head.

"Wait, you're an upload? You're here, like, for good?"

Liz nodded. "It wasn't an easy decision. But I will admit, some part of me was curious what you guys were up to. Some part of me"—she grimaced—"*missed* being back here. And now, some part of me gets to stay."

Jay instinctively leapt forward and wrapped her in a hug. Liz hugged him back and laughed.

"It's good to see you, too! But," she continued playfully, pushing him back, "I want in on the goods, 'kay? Seat at the table and all that. Should've negotiated those terms before coming back, really." She gestured to two Johns hammering plywood on the roof of C-Court. "How do I get in on the rebuilding? Without, ya know, all the hammers."

Jay was beaming at Liz, shaking his head in disbelief. He felt happier than he'd been since she'd asked him to prom. He followed her gaze back to the Johns.

"Oh yeah, that. I don't think you'll find it very exciting. Everyone here voted for things to go back to the way they were."

"The way things were? But that way sucked!" Liz frowned. "What did Colin and Stevie say?"

Jay shrugged. "Them, too. I guess it's the curse of not being an upload."

"Well, that's not very fun."

"Tell me about it." Then he leaned in conspiratorially. "But can you keep a secret?"

"Like the secret I kept that we're all living in a video game? The one where I didn't tell you or anyone else?"

"Fair enough." Jay whispered. "I've been working on something."

Liz tilted her sunglasses down. "Do tell."

"Well, I get up pretty early these days. Before anyone else. And I've been working in *The Build*. There's a little patch of land, see, far outside where the map used to end, and I've been . . ." He trailed off.

"You've been . . . ?"

Jay turned back to the C-Court parking lot. He'd allowed himself a brand-new blue Miata. It now sat next to Jeremy's red one.

"Do you want to see it?"

Liz glanced back at the high school. "So they're just rebuilding the school?"

Jay nodded.

"So I've already seen that." Liz shrugged. "Let's go see your thing!"

The warmth grew in Jay's stomach and spread up through his body. He grinned. At last, there was someone who understood. Before he could even think, he reached for Liz's hand, but then jerked it away, hesitating. Liz laughed, grabbed his jacket, and pulled him forward, and then they were both running through the parking lot.

"Come on!"

They leapt through the doors of the Miata, and Jay turned the ignition. The car shot down Simmons Road, toward the gray blankness that marked Bickleton's edge.

"Wooo!" Liz screamed at the sun and the trees. "You got any tunes?"

"Here, let's see—"

Jay flipped on the radio and fiddled with the knob. Suddenly, he caught a signal, and then a familiar voice drawled through the speakers.

"Hello, boys and girls . . . this is . . . Marvelous Mark—"

A look of horror crossed Liz's face. Jay slowed the car.

"It can't be—"

The voice continued. ". . . excited to bring you what will undoubtedly be the album of the summer. This is Lush singing the song 'Scarlet.'"

Thrashing guitars riffed out a pop melody. Jay's fingers tapped along on his steering wheel despite himself.

"How is that—?"

"He must have recorded them in advance? Right?"

The Miata bumped over the edge of Simmons Road and onto the flat expanse of gray canvas. Liz turned to watch the small patch of Bickleton recede in the distance, and her voice rose.

"Where did you say we were going?"

* * *

ACKNOWLEDGMENTS

I STARTED THIS project about a decade ago. Back then, it was called *Awesome Movie* and it followed a group of seventh graders who found a magic VCR that brought eighties movie clichés to life. Between first and last draft, *Ready Player One*, *The Lego Movie*, and *Free Guy* all saw releases. Genre-mashing became the norm, and I was forced to change course to stay fresh. Suffice to say, this book has taken a long time, and I owe many thanks.

Thanks to Michael Ecker and my brother for helping me brainstorm early on. To Tyler Shortt, Scott Davis, Sean Garcia, and Hanna Davis for fighting ferociously to see me win the Inkshares Nerdist competition. To Clete Smith for pinch-hitting in the editorial process. To Daniel Wilson for bringing me into your writers' group and helping me see myself as an author. To Meg Harvey, my wife, the most capable person I've ever met, for her patience through all the mornings I was absent from the family breakfast table. You got me into this mess: you also helped me find my way back out.

Thanks to all my own high school dickheads. Because of you, I finally settled on small-town Washington as the setting. It was my highest hope in writing this book that I might free myself from languishing resentment before I became my own Hal Banksman. You inspire me with your awfulness.

INKSHARES